THE SEA-CROSSED FISHERMAN

Yashar Kemal was born in 1923 in the small village Hemite, which lies in the cotton-growing plains of Chukurova. Later, in Istanbul, he became a reporter on the newspaper *Cumhuriyet* and in 1952 he published a book of short stories, *Yellow Heat*. In 1955 came his first novel *Ince Memed*, published in English under the title *Memed, My Hawk*. This won the Varlik Prize for the best novel of the year. His novels include *Beyond the Mountain* (3 volumes), *The Legend of Ararat*, *The Drumming-Out*, *The Legend of the Thousand Bulls*, *Murder in the Ironsmiths Market* (3 volumes), *To Crush the Serpent*, *The Saga of the Seagull*, *The Birds Have Also Gone*, *Little Nobody* and *The Pomegranate Tree on the Knoll*. Other published works include a volume of *Collected Short Stories*, *Essays and Political Articles*, *God's Soldiers* (Reports on Delinquent Children), and a novel for the young, *The Sultan of the Elephants and the Red-Bearded Lame Ant*.

Yashar Kemal is married and has one son. His wife, Thilda Kemal, translates his books into English.

T0315613

By the same author

Memed, My Hawk
The Wind from the Plain
Anatolian Tales
They Burn the Thistles
Iron Earth, Copper Sky
The Legend of Ararat
The Legend of the Thousand Bulls
The Undying Grass
The Lords of Akchasaz
The Saga of a Seagull
The Birds Have Also Gone*

Available in Minerva

YASHAR KEMAL

THE
SEA-CROSSED
FISHERMAN

A novel translated from the Turkish by
Thilda Kemal

Minerva

A Minerva Paperback

THE SEA-CROSSED FISHERMAN

Originally published in Turkey as *Deniz Küstü*
by Milliyet Yayinlari, Istanbul, 1978
First published in Great Britain in English translation 1985
by Collins Harvill
First paperback edition published 1986
by Methuen London
This Minerva edition published 1990
by Mandarin Paperbacks
Michelin House, 81 Fulham Road, London SW3 6RB

Minerva is an imprint of the Octopus Publishing Group

Copyright © Yashar Kemal 1978
English translation copyright © Thilda Kemal 1985

A CIP catalogue record for this book
is available from the British Library

ISBN 0 7493 9057 3

The Random House Group Limited supports The Forest Stewardship
Council® (FSC®), the leading international forest-certification organisation.
Our books carrying the FSC label are printed on FSC®-certified paper.
FSC is the only forest-certification scheme supported by the leading
environmental organisations, including Greenpeace. Our
paper procurement policy can be found at
www.randomhouse.co.uk/environment

MIX
Paper | Supporting
responsible forestry
FSC® C018179

Printed and bound in Great Britain by Clays Ltd, St Ives plc

PRONUNCIATION GUIDE

Letter	Approximate pronunciation
a	as in French *avoir*, English *man*
c	j as in *jam*
ç	ch as in *church*
e	as in *bed* or the French *e*
g	as in *goat*
ğ	a soft g that lengthens the preceding vowel and never occurs at the beginning of a word
h	as in *house*
o	like French *eau*
ö	as in German *König*, French eu in *deux*
s	as in *sing*
ş	sh as in *shall*
u	as in *push*
ü	as in German *führer*, French u in *tu*
y	as in *yet*

A glossary of Turkish words that appear in the text may be found at the end of the book.

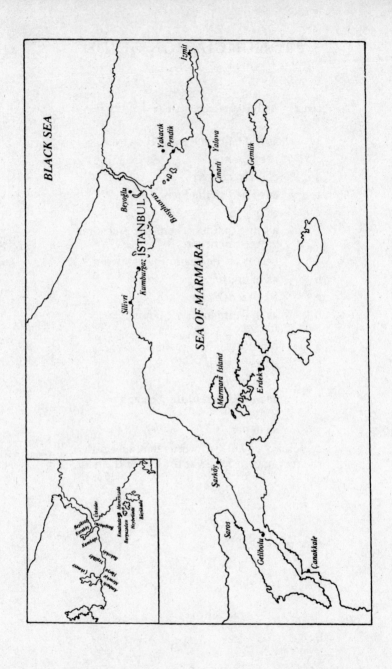

I

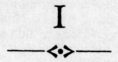

The rough-hewn door was kicked wide open, letting in a dusty blast from the mad south wind that was churning up the sea that day, and Zeynel appeared on the threshold, a gun in his hand. He hesitated, but only for a moment. Then, with slow deliberate aim, he pointed the gun at Ihsan and fired shot after shot. The men in the coffee-house froze in their seats.

Ihsan uttered a piercing scream. Blood gushed from his neck and he slipped from his chair to the floor.

Almost in the same instant, Fisher Selim sprang up and seized Zeynel's wrist. He wrenched the gun from his hand, then looked in amazement from the smoking muzzle to the young man who made no attempt to get away. Suddenly, a resounding slap startled us all. Selim's left hand was at Zeynel's collar, while his right pounded away like a sledge-hammer. The gun, no longer smoking now, had rolled under the coffee-range.

At last Selim let go, breathing hard, while Zeynel still cowered there, seemingly quite at a loss. The dead man lay on his side, hands clenched, legs drawn up to his belly, steeped in the blood that had trickled all the way to the door, his long yellow moustache stained with blood, his eyes bulging in a stare of horror and disbelief.

Selim looked at Zeynel wonderingly, as though he were seeing him for the first time, then bent down over the corpse, touched a finger to it and quickly snatched it away, as from a flame. He straightened up and came nose to nose with Zeynel. 'Take this,' he hissed, and spat in his face. Again and again the spittle struck Zeynel, whiplike. Then Selim staggered drunkenly out of the coffee-house, past the Seagull Casino, and on towards the Florya beaches, oblivious of the waves that crashed like thunder over the asphalt road.

Only then did Zeynel lift his head, as though waking from a dream. He stepped over Ihsan's body, retrieved the gun from under the coffee-range and walked to the door. There he stopped, leaning on the jamb, and gazed at each one of us in turn until his eyes rested on Ihsan. A tinge of astonishment flitted across his face. 'Son-of-a-bitch,' he muttered, 'I'm done for now because of you.' He glared at us all. 'Tell me,' he said, 'you've witnessed everything. What harm did I ever do to that bastard Selim that he should treat me like that?'

No one answered him.

'Speak, damn you! You saw how he shamed me in front of you all. Shouldn't I now do something to him, too? Tell me . . . Why don't you speak out? Are you all tombstones?'

He started pacing up and down the coffee-house, taking care not to step in the pools of blood.

'Speak, damn you! Cowards! Just because I'm holding a gun and this wretch is lying there in his blood, you're all tongue-tied, aren't you? Scared spitless! Why don't you answer me, you tombstones? You, Süleyman, look at you, you lumbering lout, you great clumsy bear! Where's all that swagger of yours gone to? You'll be grovelling under the table next and wetting your pants too . . .' He gave a mad shout of laughter. 'Who knows, maybe you've done so already and that's why you won't budge.'

He aimed the gun at Süleyman. 'Get up, blunderbuss! Just look at that bulk! You could hack three men out of him.'

Süleyman put his hands on the table and tried to rise, only to fall back helplessly. His face was white as parchment.

'You, Laz Erkan, see if Süleyman's mucked up his pants.'

Laz Erkan seized Süleyman by the arm and hauled him up. He looked at the chair, then dutifully inspected the seat of his pants. 'Unh-unh,' he shook his head. 'He hasn't.

Zeynel laughed. 'He was so frightened, the old gasbag, he couldn't even move his bowels.'

Süleyman muttered something under his breath and, at that, Zeynel stepped up to him. 'What did you say, what?' He thrust the gun at Süleyman's face. 'Say it again or I'll pump some lead into you too.'

'Don't, Zeynel, my child,' Süleyman breathed as if in a prayer. 'Don't . . . There's a God above . . .'

Zeynel ground his teeth. 'What? Why, you bastard whose mother I . . . So it's a God above when it comes to me, eh? What about you?' And he swung the gun at Süleyman's head as hard as he could. The blood began to stream down Süleyman's face and shirt and gathered in a pool on the table.

8

'Laz Erkan, wipe that bastard's blood off. He won't croak, never fear. This'll just keep him from the sea for a month so he won't be after catching all the fish of the Marmara in one night.'

Erkan promptly grabbed the napkin from the coffee-house keeper's shoulder and mopped up the blood.

'Wretch!' Zeynel snarled at Süleyman. 'D'you remember how – was it five years ago – once when we were taking fish from the trawl, you stepped on my hand with your hobnailed boot? How the flesh peeled off and the white bone was laid bare? How you laughed, you godless scoundrel . . . ?'

He went to the door, looked out into the road and swerved back, tackling now another man, then another and another. It was as though he was bent on settling a lifetime's accounts. When he came to me, he smiled bitterly and his eyes filled with tears. 'You've heard it all, brother,' he said mournfully. 'Aren't I human too? Didn't a woman give birth to me like all of you?'

I was silent.

'At least say something, brother. You've been around. You know the ways of the world.'

'What can I say, Zeynel?' His revolver was trained right on my heart.

'Look,' he continued. 'This one's dead, that one's wounded. As for the others, I've got them where they're worse than dead. And now the police will come. But I won't give myself up. See!' He indicated his pockets. They were bulging with bullets. 'I came prepared. I'm not one to let my skin be punctured easily! D'you think Selim's gone to the police?'

'I don't think so,' I replied calmly.

'Now tell me, I haven't done such a bad job, have I?'

'I don't know, Zeynel.'

'He deserved it, the bastard. So did he,' he added, pointing to Süleyman. 'And the others too.' He glanced outside. 'The street lamps are on. Good . . . In a little while I may be killed. Who knows how it feels to die . . . ? That bastard's dead all right, but look at his eyes . . .'

Nobody uttered a word. Zeynel switched on the light. Under the naked glare of the huge hundred-and-fifty-watt bulb the men's long yellow faces seemed even longer. Only Laz Erkan was smiling.

'Tell me, brother – you know about such things – would they hang me if I gave myself up? Just because I've killed this son-of-

9

a-bitch and wounded a miserable gasbag? They wouldn't, would they?'

'Who knows . . . ? Maybe . . .'

'Who knows! Maybe!' he mocked me. 'Your kind can be such diplomats!'

At this moment Selim appeared on the threshold and at the sight of him Zeynel was thrown into a panic. He rushed to the door, pushed Selim aside and fled into the night.

'What happened?' Selim asked. 'Haven't the police come yet?'

'Did you call them?' I asked.

'No, I didn't,' he said gruffly.

'Then whatever have you been doing all this time?' old Father Hakki enquired.

Selim ran his hand through his hair. 'Why, Hakki, this gun . . . I put out to sea in my boat and fired a hundred shots maybe . . . Just to see . . . What a gun! Like the Angel of Death . . . And then I realized I'd run out of ammunition . . . So . . . Ah, if I'd had just one bullet left, he'd never have been able to get out of here . . .'

The police finally turned up late in the night. I was woken up at home and detained for questioning, together with the whole of Menekşe village. Fisher Selim was there too and I heard him muttering to himself several times: 'Aaah, if only I'd had just one bullet left . . .'

2

------ <•> ------

Ihsan's funeral took place on the following day and all of
Menekşe flocked into the new mosque of Cennetmahalle.
Ihsan's virtues, his courage, his good looks, his generosity were
extolled, while his dubious activities as pimp and bodyguard'to
Meliha's notorious bawdy house were passed over in silence.

After the funeral we all went down to the coffee-house.
Remzi, the only one not to have attended, was outside selling
fish, which he had displayed on a large tin sheet. 'I wouldn't go
to the funeral of that pimp, that cuckold!' he shouted to the
world at large, exhaling a devastating stench of wine. 'Who
would attend such a low-down creature's funeral? Only low-
down creatures like him . . .'

Şaban, the coffee-house keeper, had brewed the tea. It was
ready for us, steaming in the slim-waisted gilt-rimmed glasses.
Everyone was tired. We sipped our tea in silence. Then some
men sat down to play gin rummy, while others paired off at the
backgammon boards. Outside, a bright sun flooded the sea,
which today was not like water at all, but a rippling expanse of
blinding blue sparks that filled you with joy and made you long
to sail away to its very limits.

Ibo Efendi leaned on his cane, his chubby face with its grizzled
week-old beard rapt in thought. Laz Erkan was scrawling little
drawings on a large sheet of paper. He had enormous hands and
eyes that squinted slightly. Now and then, laying his ballpoint
aside, he looked around expectantly, as if to say: Well, come on,
what are you waiting for . . . ?

There was something heavy in the air, a frustrated, seething
impatience. The men seemed to be bursting to talk. It wanted
but a little prod to get them going. Remzi's voice could be heard
outside against the rat-a-tat of a motorboat. A cock crowed from
over Yeşilköy way. The tension was too much for me and I was
about to make my escape when Fisher Selim stood up, his tall
broad frame reaching almost to the ceiling. The tips of his

greying ruddy moustache were twisted to a fine point. His wide brow was deeply furrowed like that of a man who has gone through much in life. A strong chin lent character to the full lips and sunken cheeks, and the large blue eyes shone all the more brightly for the web of wrinkles about them. They were usually narrowed, though, peering steadfastly as if at something which he could never have enough of looking at. He took some coins out of his pocket, put them on the table and buttoned up his brown serge parka. His brown trousers hugged his strong thighs and he was wearing yellow rubber boots. A red sash bound his waist. He strode out with long steps, then, for some reason, poked his head in again. His eyes swept over the men a little haughtily, then met mine, and the semblance of a smile flitted over his face. It seems to me it was at this moment our friendship and his trust really began, the upshot of many years' unspoken sympathy. He turned away and made for the little bridge that leads to one of the public beaches.

An aeroplane roared past, very low above us, followed by the helicopter which flew over the coffee-house every day at this hour, making for Thrace.

'Bastard! Murderer!' Süleyman snarled. 'He's the one who killed Ihsan. He could have snatched that revolver from Zeynel before it went off.'

'Of course he could!' Ibo Efendi concurred, lifting his bearded chin from the cane. 'It was all a put-up job.'

'It was indeed!' Şaban, the coffee-house keeper, agreed. 'I had a good view from here. Selim never moved until Zeynel had fired. And three times too . . .'

Süleyman turned to me. 'Tell me, wasn't it a put-up job? They must have plotted it together.'

'Plotted it together!' old Father Hakki mocked, ignoring Süleyman's black look. 'Why, you heathen, when did you ever see Fisher Selim so much as speak one word to Zeynel?'

'It's Selim who killed Ihsan, not Zeynel,' Süleyman insisted.

Remzi, who had been listening through the door, now strode in angrily, filling the whole room with his sour, wine-laden breath. 'Have you no fear of God, you bastards?' he shouted. 'How dare you slander a man so?'

Atom Salih darted forward. 'Dog!' he hissed. 'Fisher Selim's dog, that's what you are!'

'Dog yourself!' Remzi retorted. They fell on each other with fists and blows. No one attempted to stop them and after a while they left off by themselves and drifted out of the coffee-house.

Ibo Efendi struck his cane on the floor. 'If Fisher Selim had been a better man,' he said, 'Ihsan would have been with us now and not in his grave.'

Şaban brought us all fresh glasses of tea.

'That skinflint Selim killed Ihsan as sure as if he'd fired the shot,' Circassian Yusuf chimed in.

'Of course!' Süleyman said, puffing hard at his cigarette. 'It was all on purpose. Catching Zeynel by the wrist and all that . . . Why didn't he tie him up and hand him over to the police?'

'Why did he spit on him?'

'Because it disgusted him even to touch him,' Laz Erkan laughed.

'He was afraid.' Mahmut, who had been sitting in a corner, spoke out for the first time. All eyes turned to him. 'You shouldn't be deceived by his high and mighty airs. He's something of a coward really. Not that he's a bad man, but he's afraid of things, of the dark and the graveyard. Even of fish and cats and dogs . . . Even of himself . . .'

'Oh, come on, Mahmut!' I protested. 'That's a bit thick . . .'

'But it's true, brother. I swear it. He's not one for talking and I know why. It's fear ties his tongue and makes him stutter. He'll kill himself one day because of that fear.'

'You're making it up!'

'Cross my heart, brother, that man might go crazy with fear.'

Atom Salih burst into the room. 'The mean wretch!' he cried. 'To think we were almost killing each other, Remzi and I, because of him!'

'Have you made it up, then?' Kurdish Hasan asked.

'Of course,' Atom Salih grinned. 'He kissed my hand, so why shouldn't we?'

Remzi's short rattleboned body leaned through the doorway. 'It was him kissed my hand,' he shouted.

'What!'

Salih was about to pounce on him again when Remzi retracted. 'All right, brother, all right, I kissed your hand first.'

'So you did,' Atom Salih said proudly. He took Remzi's arm and, with weaving steps, the two of them made for the tavern across the road.

Tongues were loosened after that. The men began picking

Fisher Selim to pieces.

'Does anyone even know where he comes from?'

'Remember when he was sick and I nursed him? Three whole months I cooked soup for him and bought him medicines. And all the while I begged and pleaded with him . . . "Look, Selim," I said, "you're in a bad way. Tell me where you've hidden your money . . . Isn't it a shame to let all that money rot away uselessly? Look, Fisher Selim, I've been taking care of you all this time, washing you and all . . . Even shaving you with my own hand! You're dying anyway . . . I'm not asking you for anything. Only show me where the money is. It's not right that this country's money should go to waste . . ." He was at his last gasp, yet still he waved me away. So I picked him up and carried him out to his boat. "You can croak in your own boat," I said, "no need to soil my house!" '

'You're lying, Osman! I remember very well, you never took him out to his boat.'

'I certainly did! But he was back by my hearth the very next morning, moribund as he was. So I fed him for another month . . .'

'Well, he paid you quite a tidy sum for it!'

'What? With all those soups I cooked?'

'If he'd died, his boat and everything would have been yours.'

'As though you looked after him for love! How much money did he give you?'

'A mere ten lira! The miser! There never was such a stingy fellow.'

'He'll soak week-old crusts in water and gulp down the mush!'

'He eats only bread and the small fry of his catch . . .'

'Gobbling them down all raw, like a seagull!'

'Has anyone seen him eat anything else?'

'Someone gave him an orange once – was it ten years ago or fifteen? He kept it for a whole week, only smelling it. Then at last he peeled it and sliced it very thin and spent all day eating it!'

'A man who's got heaps of money!'

'He doesn't put it in a bank either.'

'Where can he be hiding it?'

'Who knows? Under the sea probably.'

'With seamarks only he knows about.'

'After he got over that illness, it was as if I never existed!'

'Yes, he never even said hello to Osman . . .'

'And he took care not to be sick again!'

'Out of pure stinginess!'

'He'd realized illness is a costly business.'

'And death too . . .'

'So he'll never die!'

'That old handwoven parka of his, he had it on his back when he first came here years ago.'

'One shirt has to last him seven years at least.'

'He won't even wash his underpants for fear they'll wear out!'

'Oh, he killed Ihsan all right!'

'Did you notice how he snatched the revolver from Zeynel's hand and threw it down? And then ran away?'

'Just so we shouldn't do anything ourselves.'

'The double-crosser!'

'As tight-lipped as he's tight-fisted . . .'

'Measuring his words out of a dropper . . .'

'Who's ever seen the inside of his house, eh?'

'He won't let a soul step over the threshold . . .'

Süleyman rose, flinging his arms out wide. 'You all witnessed it. Selim helped Zeynel escape. If the police . . .'

'He actually whisked him out of our hands.'

'Any one of us could have caught him.'

'Easily . . .'

'It's because we all took it for granted that Selim . . .'

'It's because we were all frozen with fright,' Laz Erkan broke in. 'That's the truth of the matter. Wetting our pants, we were, with that revolver pointed at us!'

'And Zeynel heaping insults on us all the while . . .'

'The miserable wretch . . .'

'But it was Selim made him do it, that's certain.'

Süleyman's head was swathed in a white cloth, like a turban. 'I was so shocked, it was like an invisible hand was pinning me down.'

'Of course,' Ibo Efendi said. 'If not, you would have done something.'

Süleyman's hand went to his head. 'Yes, I would . . .' He thought better of it. 'Anyway, Selim's at the bottom of it all. Are you game? When the police come back . . .'

'Yes, yes . . .'

'I'm not!' Laz Erkan said.

'Count me out too,' Mahmut said.

'Well, we don't need dogs like you,' Süleyman retorted. 'We've got plenty of witnesses.'

'A murderer!'

'And that business at the beaches?'

'Tell them, Yusuf!'

'What can I say? We used to go pimping together . . .'

'Why, the bastard . . .'

'The things we did to make money! I squandered mine in the bars of Beyoğlu, but he saved his.'

'Rubbish,' Father Hakki growled, shaking his mane of white hair. 'He never went pimping with you or anyone else. He may be a miser, a coward, a little mad, but he wouldn't sell women or steal or anything like that. I've known him for years. And he wouldn't lie either.'

'No, he wouldn't lie,' Ibo Efendi admitted.

'And don't forget he's been very useful to the village,' Şaban said. 'It was he who thought of hiring out rowing-boats to the young people who come over from Istanbul.'

'Hah, that was just so they should fuck in his boat!' Süleyman scoffed. 'As though he did it in a good cause, the pimp!'

'Be quiet, Süleyman,' Mahmut snapped. 'That's going too far.'

'Well, anyway,' Ibo Efendi said, 'we all saw how he let Zeynel escape. We can tell the police.'

Just then Fisher Selim's tall frame loomed in the doorway.

'Come in, come in, Fisher Selim,' some of the men called, rising in a flurry to greet him.

Selim sat down at an empty table near the door. 'Only think!' he said. 'If I'd had just one bullet left, I'd never have let him escape. Just one . . .' He fell silent.

No one spoke. Şaban brought him some tea, steaming in its glass. Fisher Selim drank it down in three gulps, placed some money on the table and rose to go.

As soon as he was out of the coffee-house, the men were at him worse than ever.

'Mark my words, that Zeynel won't let him get away with it!'

'He'll kill him sooner or later, just as he killed Ihsan.'

'Skin him alive, Zeynel will!'

'You can't treat a man like that.'

'Snatch his revolver away from him and spit in his face!'

'Would Zeynel ever swallow that?'

'He'll take his revenge.'

'Selim's taken fright already. All in a flutter he is, can't keep still for a minute.'

'Like a bitch with a burnt paw!'

'Oh, yes, Zeynel will skin him alive . . .'

'After killing Ihsan . . .'

'And perhaps he was right to do it.'

'Maybe there was something between him and Ihsan.'

'It's not good to meddle with a man who's just killed.'

'Our Prophet has prescribed that you touch not the snake that is drinking water . . .'

'Ah, he'll get his deserts, that Selim, sure as fate!'

'Sooner or later . . .'

3

When such things are going on, I stay away from Menekşe for weeks, even months on end. Of course I long to go there. Of course I miss my friends, Skipper Nuri, old Kazim Agha, Ilya, Master Leon, Tartar Ali. Yet I cannot bring myself to sit in that coffee-house. I cannot look anyone in the face, just as though I were the guilty one. The world is like that, I know. People are like that. There is nothing I can do about it. That's what I try to tell myself, but it's no use. I cannot bear it. I feel as though something dirty, something evil, something hostile has rubbed itself against me. How could they do this to a man like Fisher Selim and still sit and drink tea with him, talk to him, play backgammon with him? I simply cannot understand it.

I wish I had a tiny island here, near Menekşe, and on that island a small house, just two rooms, and a garden where I would plant olive saplings which I would coax into growth by caressing them with my eyes every day . . . The olive grows so quietly . . . It is the most humble of trees. Who knows, perhaps it puts out only one or two leaves each year . . . ? So it would be the grandchildren of the people living on my island who would eat the first fruit of these olive trees, never knowing who had planted them . . . How silvery their pointed leaves would be in the sunlight! I would also like to have a greyhound. And a foal too, a thoroughbred that I would raise myself. The other houses on my island would always be open to me, as familiar as my own, the people living in them closer than brothers. We would run to each other's aid, sharing everything, joys and sorrows alike.

How often have I not dreamed of such an island! Dreamed that the people on it multiplied, that they never hurt each other, that the fishermen did not take little children out to sea in wintry weather, making them pick the fish out of the freezing nets, without even paying them their due afterwards . . . Dreamed that children were not beaten or abused, that they did

18

not line up like birds on the shore in the cruel northwester, eyes large with anxiety, waiting to unload the incoming fishing boats, so as to earn a little money, barely enough to buy a handful of dried sunflower seeds, a *simit*, a ticket to the movies. . . . Dreamed that Laz Mustafa never again has to go hoeing day after day in the parsley, radish, cabbage and lettuce plots out by the city walls, his hands hard as rubber wheels, so as to feed his nine children with a bare crust of bread. Yes, even Laz Mustafa is happy on my island. Every evening he dresses up his nine children in neat clothes and takes them for a stroll on the wharf. Young girls and lads in couples row out across the deep blue sea. They fish, they make love in the sun. Nobody disturbs them, nobody even looks at them . . . Tartar Ali's son would never have set fire to his boat and perished in the flames. And Bekaroğlu, that best of men, would find happiness by marrying the widow Hatçe, who had been left with eleven children to raise. I can see those children running out joyfully when they spy his skin-and-bones figure trudging up the slope, and helping him carry the heavy fishing nets still wet from the sea . . . All kinds of pleasant things happen on my island. People give free rein to their dreams. They are not ashamed, not afraid that these dreams may never come true, not laden with the curse of having to bury their hopes deep inside them . . .

And my island in Menekşe will always be there as long as I live, and I and Mahmut and Ilya and Master Leon the mason will never grow tired of weaving dreams about it. One day we'll find a way of luring Ahmet from his wicked life and make him settle there. Another day, we'll throw out drunken Haydar who bothers and abuses that poor old whore, Zeliha, banging on her door in the middle of the night . . . We would have greyhounds on our island, with long slim legs, narrow arched bodies, lovely to behold, but we would not take them out rabbit-hunting. We would all be friends on my island, men and greyhounds and rabbits, too. Yes, we would dream dreams on my island and believe with all our hearts that they could come true.

Could there ever be any such place in Menekşe? Have we not let our dreams get the better of hard reality? Is not Istanbul city close by, noisy, dirty, swarming, laying new traps every day to set its inhabitants at loggerheads, sowing evil, enmity, exploitation, death? Or is this dream island, is our life there, more real than anything else? I defy anyone to answer that question. Who can say whether our true life is not in our dreamland, on that island of Menekşe?

What do you think, Fisher Selim? I wonder if he knows what went on in the coffee-house, if he is hurt, incurably wounded at this proof of men's viciousness . . . How will he act when we meet again? Will he turn and give me so much as one look, even unfriendly, out of those sorrowful deep-set blue eyes of his? I listened to but a small part of what was said about him. Who knows what those Menekşe folk have been inventing since? And, as sure as I'm alive, one of them must be retailing all the gossip to Selim day by day, watching with relish how his face changes from anger to pain, from disgust to despair. Or why bother to talk so much if Selim is to hear never a word? Does he know, then, does every remark relayed to him pierce his heart like a greasy bullet? Or does he give a contemptuous laugh, secretly rather flattered at being the object of so much talk, even if it is only malicious gossip? You never know with him, he talks so little, and even then it is not like other people. A sudden burst of words, and off he goes, head hanging as though ashamed of himself.

Well, anyway, I did not go down to Menekşe, but Mahmut came to see me several times. He seemed no different, cheerful as usual, but somehow subdued. We'd sit on the edge of the cliff and he'd talk about this and that. Then one day, without so much as a greeting, he said: 'Are you sore at me, brother?'

I did not reply. He sat down beside me. His arm touched mine. Involuntarily I drew away.

'So you *are* sore at me,' he said.

I only laughed.

'But Ilya also said things about him, and Tartar Ali and Father Hakki . . .'

'They'd never do that, Mahmut,' I said.

Mahmut was confused. His hands opened and closed. 'But it's true he's a coward,' he shouted.

'So are we all,' I said, 'you too, me too . . .'

He stared at me doubtfully. 'You too? Me too?' And then, bending his head, he murmured again: 'You too, me too . . .'

'All of us . . .' Silently, I cursed the whole world. If men were not such cowards, could they ever be so cruel, so hateful to each other, cheating, killing, enslaving, destroying? Humiliating others, browbeating them? Crazy, forgetting how to love and be

20

loved . . . Would the hand extended be so icy? Would they have lost all power of reasoning, only capable of aping others? Forever obsessed by death and never realizing the futility of the obsession? Would they be so insensible to the earth under their feet, to the sky, the stars, the streams, the flowers, the high mountain peaks, to light itself? How could they exist without love, affection, friendship, their hearts never stirred, never beating warmly like a bird's for a lover, for a faithful face?

'You're right, brother,' Mahmut said as if I had spoken out loud. 'Forgive me, but . . .' And he muttered something I did not catch.

'Speak out,' I said. 'I won't kill you.'

'Then, why . . . ?' He hesitated. 'Why didn't you . . . ?'

'Why didn't I do something?' I took the words from his mouth. 'Why, indeed?'

'I suppose a man gets carried away by the others, by what's going on about him,' Mahmut went on. 'You get confused, you can't think coolly . . .'

'That's how it is.'

'Still, I for one shouldn't have done this to Fisher Selim. He's always been kind to me . . .' He clenched his fists. 'Just let me hear them say one more word against him! By God, I'll scatter those people in the coffee-house to the winds.'

'It's no use,' I said. 'You'll never stop them. They can't do without their bout of gossip.'

'You're right,' he assented, crestfallen. 'They've always been like this about Fisher Selim.' He rose to go.

After a while I got up too and walked down the slope to Menekşe, passing under the bridge of the lopsided little railway station to emerge beside the sea. And there, sitting in his boat a little way offshore, was Fisher Selim, mending a net. He lifted his head and our eyes met. He looked startled at first, then he smiled.

'Hello, Fisher Selim,' I said.

He waved his huge hand.

'Have a cigarette,' I said.

Seizing the oars he drew the boat alongside the wooden jetty. The boards creaked and shook as I stepped up to him and held out the packet of cigarettes.

We smoked in silence. His eyes were fixed somewhere in the distance. At last he spoke, just one word.

'There,' he said, pointing in the direction of Hayirsiz Island.

'You don't say!'

'Certain.'

'But I thought there weren't any left.'

'Only a few. Here and there, like drunken creatures . . .'

'What a pity,' I sighed.

'Yes, but if I don't catch it, someone else will.'

'They ought to forbid it.'

'If only they would . . . But who listens to prohibitions! Dynamite fishing is forbidden too, but who listens?'

He was absorbed once more in his work and I sat on there, on the wooden jetty, legs dangling over the water. Several planes passed overhead to land at Yeşilköy Airport. The sea stretched out to the distant shores of Bursa, a glittering expanse. There was a smell heralding the *lodos* wind in the air.

'It won't rise,' Fisher Selim said without looking up from his net.

'What?'

'The *lodos*, of course.' He smiled and his strong white teeth gleamed. 'Sometimes it plays the coquette with you, like today.' He looked at me. 'So you like the sea? Why don't you come with me tomorrow? Who knows, you might be lucky and we'll see it.'

I was overjoyed. Certainly other people must have gone fishing with him before, but I felt somehow that I was the first to have been honoured with a genuine, heartfelt invitation. 'I'd love to,' I said with enthusiasm. 'I'm sure we'll find it.'

He seemed pleased at my eagerness. 'Tomorrow then, at three. Here.'

'All right,' I said.

He swung to the oars and rowed away, not stopping till he was in front of the presidential summer residence. I saw him bending over his net. The boat was swaying gently on the calm sea.

4

Excitement kept me awake that night. To think that Fisher Selim had actually invited me on to his boat!

The sea was only just paling when I left the house. In my garden the judas-tree, in full flower, shed a bright pink glow into the foredawn. A soft breeze, smelling warmly of the sea, wafted up to me as I walked to the shore. Fisher Selim was sitting in his boat by the wooden jetty. His huge shadow fell over the pale water and even from a distance the red sash he always wore gleamed in the blue starlight. He had drawn a green skullcap over his curly reddish-brown hair and when he saw me his face, his whole body, was suffused with pleasure. It was a profound gladness coming from the depths of his heart, such as I had not met with on these shores. The corners of his eyes crinkled as he smiled at me and I thought, now here is what we call friendship, love, fervour, if ever these things exist. But the next instant, as though he regretted having let himself go, he closed up again. The wrinkles on his brow deepened and his face grew grave. Still, his moustache quivered and he could not quite hide his pleasure as he grasped the oars.

'Jump in,' he cried.

He rowed out into the open. Then gently, with infinite care, he put up the oars, grasped the cord with his strong long-fingered hands and fired the engine.

We were heading for Hayirsiz Island, raising white waves on the smooth waters. The star-traceried sky shed a pale radiance over the sea and over the blue, smoke-veiled mountains on the opposite shore. We stopped off the island. The sea was calm. There was no swell, no sound from its bottomless depths. Yet, inert as it was, it impressed you as even more massive than usual, heavy as the earth . . . On an early morning such as this, all the world still pale, the stars fading in the sky, evanescent wisps of vapour rising slowly from the unruffled surface of the water, the sea seems to come into its own, displaying more than

23

ever its vast unbounded might.

I shrank from saying anything to Fisher Selim. It was as though, in the stillness of this wide expanse, an infinite weight was upon us and we were both loath to spoil something, afraid to startle the sea out of its profound slumber.

In the distance, sunk in shadow, its leaden domes, its minarets and buildings only vaguely discernible in the bluish haze, Istanbul was still asleep, its face hidden from the world. In a little while the city would awaken, with its buses, cars, horsecarts, its ships, steam launches, fishing boats, its *hamals* sweating under their loads of heaped crates, its streets and avenues overflowing, its apartment buildings, mosques, bridges, all surging, interlocking in a furious turmoil and, pressing through the tangle of traffic, wondering how this city could still move, was not entirely paralysed, people would be making superhuman efforts to reach their destination. Fish-vendors in their boats by the waterfront would be setting up their gear, lighting their coals or butane cookers, heating the oil into which they would drop the flour-coated fish, and soon the odour of fried fish would spread through the early-morning air right up to Karaköy Square, to the Flower Market and to the fruit-trading wharf. Hungry workers, tramps who had nowhere to sleep but had somehow got hold of a little money, carousers with a hangover, drowsy young streetwalkers, homeless children who subsisted by picking pockets, sneak-thieving or selling black-market cigarettes would line up in front of the bobbing boats to buy a slice of bluefish, a quarter of tuna, three or four pickerel or scad, sandwiched in a half-loaf of bread, and devour it hungrily, the fat dripping down their chins. And the dull heavy roar of the awakening city would reach us from across the sea, and gradually the domes and minarets, and also the ugly apartment buildings so out of keeping with the city, would emerge from the haze, and like a strange giant creature Istanbul would spread itself out in the light of day, down to its age-old battlements along the seashore.

Fisher Selim's curious gaze drew me out of my reverie. I turned to him, but he rose quickly, set the motor going again and moved to the tiller. In the distance a large white passenger ship, all its lights ablaze, its whiteness blending into the white of the sea, was sailing by. Fisher Selim's face lit up as his eyes followed the ship and he smiled, an irrepressible smile, as a primitive

24

savage might have smiled for joy.

As we were skirting the little island of Sedef, east of Büyükada, he rose and, shielding his eyes with his huge hand, scanned the sea all around. A few seagulls were swirling off the shore of Pendik. Fisher Selim's face was growing longer and longer. Finally, he came to a stop in front of Tavşan Island and his arms dropped despondently to his sides.

Suddenly I had to speak.

'It was here,' I said, pointing to Tavşan Island. 'Here that . . .'

'Well?' he prompted, and I realized he welcomed this diversion.

'It's nothing really,' I mumbled. 'Only that, once, we'd gone fishing over there . . . That's all.'

He saw that I had changed my mind about what I was going to say. 'You can tell me,' he said. 'I believe what's true.'

'Well, the truth is I caught a swordfish here once with a fishhook line.'

'Really?' He gave me a curious look.

'Yes, we weighed it and it came to fourteen kilos. I was with the engineer Mehmet Bey in his boat.'

'I believe you,' he smiled. 'But how?'

'How? First, I'd come up with about two dozen red sea-bream and I was doing very well when the next thing I knew the line went very heavy. I pulled and pulled . . .'

He was quite interested now.

'But nothing happened. The fish wouldn't come. "Give him some line," Mehmet Bey advised me. But the more I gave, the faster the fish went.'

'That's how it always is.'

'And then I had no more line to give. It was taut to snapping-point like the string of a violin. It frightened me . . .'

'Row on after him.'

'That's what we did,' I said. 'All the way from here to there. Then he must have tired, for I felt the line slacken. I pulled very slowly and he came. The line tightened again. I let go a little. And so it went on until, suddenly, I realized that he was coming up smoothly now. He was quite near the boat when he surfaced. Only for an instant, but I never saw such a blue in my life. His back, I mean, velvety blue, the blue of window-panes in the twilight. It flashed and was gone.'

'So what did you do?'

'I gave him some line again.'

Fisher Selim's face clouded and a frown contracted his brow. I had to wind up my story quickly.

'Well, anyway, this went on for three hours until he tired and I got him. It's true . . . Doctor Ibo was there in another boat and his wife, Beco, and her brother Muzaffer too . . . Fourteen kilos he weighed. A small swordfish . . . Out of the water its blue began to turn grey, then dulled entirely. The line had got tangled round his long upper jaw . . .'

'It's a month now I've been after him,' Fisher Selim muttered. 'He's a sly one, very quick. I've seen him. More than three metres long, he is. Three times I missed him, but I'll bag him yet. And then . . . A kilo of swordfish is worth a hundred and fifty lira. I'll take him straight to the Hilton Hotel, and if they won't pay the price I'll go to the Sheraton. Vehbi Bey has a hotel too, the Divan. He's very rich, Vehbi Koç, the richest man in Turkey. Wouldn't he buy my fish?'

'Why not?'

'What's seven thousand lira to him, after all?' His eyes were on me, questioning.

'Indeed, what?'

'I'll catch that fish. And when I've sold it, then . . .'

'What'll you do then, Fisher Selim?'

He only smiled, his white teeth gleaming, like a child with a precious secret.

'There was a time,' he went on, 'when this Marmara Sea teemed with swordfish, each one three, four metres long, weighing as much as six hundred kilos sometimes. But now all those fishermen, gentleman anglers, harpooners, dynamiters have killed them all off!' He was thoroughly launched now. Beware of those silent people. Once started, given a fair field, there's no stopping them. 'And the same goes for dolphins too . . . Dolphins who were the fisherman's best friend, his companion on the sea . . . I had a dolphin friend once. He would smell me out whenever I was putting out to sea, whether from the Bosphorus or Pendik, or from Ambarli or the Islands, and together with his family he would come over and accompany my old hulk all the way to wherever I was going, prancing, dancing, singing as he went. I knew him by his eyes that looked at me just like a human being's, by the scar on his back, by the torn end of his right fin. Yes, as God's my witness, he would jump for joy when he saw me, two metres up in the air, and plunge back, and in another instant he would reappear with his whole family whirling merrily round about my boat, his head popping out now and then to look at me. He'd speak to me too. Not me, *he* would!'

I could not help smiling. He didn't mind.

'Ah,' he said, pleased with himself. 'I sometimes talk to people too!'

It was a long-lasting friendship, this, between the dolphins and Fisher Selim. Like one family they were, sharing joys and sorrows. The dolphins would laugh out loud when they saw him. An animal laugh? Laughter, tears, the prerogatives of humankind? Hah, what fools men are! It is human beings who have forgotten how to laugh. It is human beings who are lonely, friendless, who cannot, will never ever enjoy the touch of a warm hand, the beauty of a loving gaze. It is human beings who are cynical, callous, indifferent to the beauty of the world around them, incapable of feeling the pure joy of being alive, of seeing the sky under which they live, the earth over which they walk, just blind wanderers in the midst of the majesty of nature. Dolphins, fishes, birds, foxes, wolves, even the smallest insects are those who enjoy our world to the full.

'The times we live in,' Fisher Selim sighed, 'an animal's far happier than we are.'

Nobody had ever loved Fisher Selim like this huge three-metre-long dolphin, not his mother, nor his father, not the comrades by whose side he had fought in the war, not his brothers, not the fellow-fishermen whose lives he had saved, only one other person, just one . . . Just let the dolphin not see Fisher Selim's boat for a few days . . . He would go mad, turning the vast Marmara Sea inside out, dashing at lightning speed from Yalova to the Bosphorus, from the Bosphorus to the Gulf of Saros, with all his family at his tail, frantic, grieving. He would approach every boat in sight, enquiring for his friend Fisher Selim, searching among the craft along the shore, tirelessly, ceaselessly. And the fishermen would come to Selim and say: 'He was beating about the sea again today, your pet, hey, Fisher Selim, looking for you!' And Fisher Selim, his heart swelling with love and pride, would think that there was some beauty, some hope left in being human.

On days of high wind and storm, the dolphin knew that Fisher Selim could not put out, so he would go on his way calmly after the small fry that he swallowed in shoals at one mouthful. Yet Selim was sure that even on such days, even if he did not show it, the dolphin pined for him. And didn't Selim pine too? He longed for the storm to abate, and after long days of separation, when at last the dolphin spotted Selim's boat, he would come tearing from afar, swishing up into the air every hundred metres, his joy radiating through the water to all the creatures of the sea, the fish and lobsters, the shrimps and crabs, and to the gulls too and the shearwaters and egrets. Round and round the boat he would swirl, then stop and gaze with bright adoring eyes at his friend.

'Don't call him an animal,' Selim said. 'Without words we'd talk and make up for lost time. He would tell me how worried he'd been, how he'd asked after me from all the fishermen and sailors he came across. And I would scold him for venturing so near the shore and explain how wrong it was, that one day these men would do him a bad turn. He'd promise never again to do such a dangerous thing. But I knew he couldn't resist, poor thing. Fish folk, once they get attached to you, are more faithful, more devoted than any human friend. Sometimes people would see us like this, facing each other, the dolphin and me, he in the sea, I in my boat, talking to each other, and they'd twit me: "Hey, Selim, what are you doing, sitting there with that fish in front of you?" They thought I was crazy. I'd take no notice of their gibes, but sometimes they'd provoke me into answering . . . "Doing? Doing! Are you blind, can't you see we're talking?" They'd burst out laughing and shout to each other: "Just look, folks, just see our Fisher Selim chatting with a fish when he won't talk with his own kind . . ." Fools, all of them! But what happened afterwards . . .'

He fell silent, pulled the cord quickly to set the engine running and headed west. As we came to Hayirsiz Island the sun dawned, a red orange rind above the island, mantling the pale clouds and edging them with fire. The white sea around us slowly turned blue, its shadows deepened and the reflections of the island and of the boat took shape. In the distance the blue darkened to purple and the far-off coastline grew grey. Long streaks and patches of blue, mauve, green and red chequered the sea. And for a fleeting instant a stream of light skimmed over the surface of the water in a lightning flurry, hardly seen, only sensed, a phantom of light, a shade, an illusion, transparent, invisible . . .

Fisher Selim jumped to his feet. 'Look, look!' he cried. 'Did you see it?'

'What's that?' I said.

'A weird light. It always comes at this time. As though it had never been . . . A light a man can see only with his blood.'

I gave him a quizzical look.

'But it's true,' he said. 'So many things happen like that in this world, movement, light, night, darkness, clouds, colour . . . Things a man can't see with his eyes, only with his blood, so tenuous . . . People don't believe me, they say I'm crazy. So I don't speak to them any more.'

'I understand,' I said quickly. 'I saw the light, but only just.'

'Of course you did,' he laughed, his wrinkled face opening up, relaxed now, all coppery in the sunlight. 'I knew it. Only just today, a little more tomorrow, and more and more, and in another year or two you'll blend with the light. It'll fill you with joy, set the blood tingling in your veins.'

Fisher Selim stretched out his arms as if to embrace the whole sea, then let them fall. 'Look what a chatterbox I can be if I find someone who understands me. Would they believe you in Menekşe if you were to tell them how I've been rattling on? Would they now, even if you swore on the Holy Koran?'

'They wouldn't.'

'Sure they wouldn't!' Then he looked at me hesitantly. 'And you,' he said, 'you write books, don't you?'

'That's right.'

'I've seen them,' he said, pleased. 'With a horse on the cover, orange on one, blue on the other, and with the rider holding a gun and the horse going at a spanking gallop . . .'

'That's right,' I said. 'I wrote those books.'

He smiled shyly. 'How could you find so many words?'

'There are no end of things to write about in this world.'

'True,' he said thoughtfully.

'Look at the sea here, teeming with life, the sky, the rumbling city over there, look at you, look at me.'

'Look at me . . .' He sighed. 'Still another day gone without my finding him.'

'Maybe someone else got him.'

He blanched. 'Impossible,' he cried. 'There's no man left in these parts who can hunt swordfish. No one. And that's a good thing. I need that fish. Very badly. No one but I must catch it.'

He stood up, measuring something with his hands and mumbling to himself as he scanned the coast, the islands, the headlands. Then his face cleared. 'All right,' he said, and we started off again, this time towards the city, the engine throbbing so hard that the whole boat shook and shuddered as though it would smash itself to pieces. When we stopped at last off Zeytinburnu, Fisher Selim's face was businesslike again, with no trace of that soft childish wonder of a while ago. He took some hooks out of a tin box and fastened them to the lines.

'See if you can find the right depth,' he said to me.

'I'll find it.'

'Red mullet it is.'

'I know.'

He gave me another of those curious looks.

'Lame Hasan . . .,' I began.

'Did you go fishing with him?'

'A few times.'

'He's the best fisher for red mullet in the world. Those huge-eyed little rascals even talk to him!'

'And you?'

'They wouldn't even so much as say hello to me, but I know their hiding-places and I catch them all the same.'

As he let his line down I watched him closely to see how many fathoms he would give. But his long arms had already speeded up and the line was coiling up again at the bottom of the boat while he leaned over, alert, his eyes on the water. Then I saw a red shape floating up to the surface. The bait was now level with the eyes of the mullet that flashed around it, incredibly red. In an instant Selim, extending his left hand, scooped it up expertly and threw it into the boat. Without another look at the madly floundering fish, but with manifest pride, he let the bait down again.

And so it went on till evening, his arms working machine-like and the boat filling up with red mullet, while I, in all this time, caught only three. Fisher Selim must have marked this particular spot long ago, after many trials, and kept it a secret too. No fisherman will ever reveal his special lairs and, anyway, very few go after the red mullet. Perhaps because it is difficult to catch. The red mullet swims in bottom waters and nests among rocks and weeds. A man must be familiar with every inch of the seabed to catch it.

The sun was setting when Fisher Selim stood up and stretched himself, a handsome figure of a man with his bushy moustache and pure blue eyes. A fresh evening breeze was rippling the smooth water, and the sun, a soft roseate mauve, sat on the horizon under a welter of clouds, orange, purple, green. 'Well, let's go,' he said, starting the engine.

The sun set and we were plunged into a blue radiance, an incredibly beautiful velvety blue in which the sky, the sea, the air all merged together. Overhead, shining white against the blue, a flight of gulls accompanied us as we headed back for Menekşe. The lights of the city stretched in a long bright line from Sarayburnu to Ambarli.

For some time after that I did not come across Selim. I had never been to his house, but I enquired and found it, a cottage painted chestnut brown, nestling under a mass of ivy and dog rose and with a porch all along the front. Near the door was an ancient Roman or Byzantine stone, inscribed with an unfamiliar script and embossed with a strange flower.

I knocked on the door, but there was no sign of life inside. A young girl popped her head out of the house next door. 'Abi,' she said, 'if you're looking for Fisher Selim, he hasn't been home for days now.'

'Where can he have gone to?'

'Oh, it's often like that with him.' The girl spoke with a pleasant immigrant accent. 'Sometimes he's away for months on end, sailing the seas. What d'you want him for?'

'I'm just a friend.'

She stared and smiled. 'So he does have friends,' she murmured, then blushed and hung her head.

'Yes, I'm one of them.'

'I'm so glad,' she blurted out. 'You know, they say Zeynel's going to kill him. That's why he stays away.'

'No one's going to kill him,' I reassured her.

'Some people say he's in love with a fish that he follows from sea to sea.'

'Oh, that was long ago . . .'

'But they're saying it now.' She made a face. 'What do people want with this man?'

'Who knows . . . ? Tell me, what's your name?'

'Nebile.'

'Well, Nebile, will you tell Fisher Selim I came to see him?'

'He doesn't speak to anyone. How can I tell him?'

'Doesn't he?'

'He's a good man, though,' she added. 'He looks straight at you, clean and clear.'

'He says everything with his eyes. Good, kind things . . .'

'That's true,' Nebile said, pleased.

As I left I heard her playing Ali Riza Binboğa's latest record on her gramophone.

Three days later I ran into Fisher Selim down by the Florya summer houses. 'Well!' I exclaimed. 'You quite vanished into thin air. I asked after you.'

'The girl told me. Thank you.' He waved a hand towards the sea. 'I just can't find him. Inside out I've turned this Marmara Sea. Nothing, nothing, nothing . . .'

'Where can he have got to?' I did not dare suggest that someone else might have caught him.

'I won't give up. I need him badly. Where can he be hiding, the son-of-a-bitch?'

'Well, the sea is very deep,' I ventured.

'Swordfish never lie near the sea bottom. That's their misfortune, the poor buggers. For the past twenty years they've been harpooned by every man jack that came along. They don't know how to hide. But this one does. That's why he's the only one left.'

'He's cunning.'

'Yes. Who knows how many harpoons he's got away with, how many hooks he's flattened out . . .'

'Is he so large?'

'Large!' Fisher Selim became excited. 'What do you mean? Six or seven hundred kilos he'll be weighing, I can swear to that. And then I'll be able to do what I've always wanted.'

What that was I didn't dare ask. Our friendship had prospered because I never put questions to him, or only those I knew he wanted me to ask. We walked on in silence.

'I'll find him yet,' he said at last.

'Sure you will.'

'Tomorrow, then. Before the early-morning *ezan*.'

'Three o'clock again?'

'Right.'

The dolphin, Fisher Selim's friend, the huge dolphin and his

32

family could have made him rich, as rich as Harun al-Rashid, had he been the man he now was, bitter, with his back turned to the world. Selim is not really a heartless man, full of hate and rancour, but he can take umbrage, not only against man and beast, but against the sea and sky and nature itself. He cannot help himself. He's been known to be angry at the sky when heavy rain prevented him from putting out to sea and then not to lift his head, not even on those bright-blue May nights, tingling with millions of stars. Why, he can be cross with the sea too, never giving it a look, not even when its briny smell drives him mad with longing.

The dolphin too, so staunch and friendly, could be touchy at times, like all warm-hearted creatures. The sea, the vast ocean, is touchy too. Only let it be provoked and it won't let anyone get a whiff of its fish or shrimps or lobsters. Yet it can be generous as well, relenting in the end, taking pity on people and pouring forth all the fish in its secret hideaways. Some days the dolphin, in a bad mood, would take himself off as far as possible from Fisher Selim, right up to the Çanakkale Strait, so as not to be tempted, not to be drawn back by his longing for his friend. But then, when Selim was angry, sulking, in a temper, it was something to see the dolphin performing all sorts of clowneries around the boat, trying to draw Selim out of his black mood, to make him laugh, the dolphin himself chuckling aloud like a human being. A strange phenomenon it was indeed, this relationship between the dolphin and Selim. The dolphin would find the finest nests of red mullet, lobsters and shrimps, and would then lead Selim to them. Selim's boat would overflow with the choicest fish, and when he went to sell his catch at the fish market the other fishermen would turn green with envy. And all the while Selim was hoarding money. He did not keep it in any bank. No, his hoard was elsewhere, growing steadily until the day when . . . Stingy, Fisher Selim? Niggardly? Well, when that day came people would see how generous he could be . . . For years now he had been hinting at something, yet no one had been able to discover what it was.

It was strange indeed that a man like Fisher Selim who had seen the world should scrimp and stint so . . . Why, in his youth there'd been none to match him in the taverns of Kumkapi for throwing a dagger, dancing the *lezginka* or singing in the weird tongue no one understood. In one single night he'd spend a

whole year's earnings, standing his friends to *raki* or wine as
though it was water, helping the sick and the poor. When Fisher
Selim's handsome figure with the fiery moustache rounded the
corner, the silver-nielloed Circassian dagger and the ivory-
handled Nagant revolver stuck into his red sash, all the folks of
Kumkapi – Turks, Kurds, Armenians, Circassians, Georgians,
gypsies – one and all would rise and stand at attention before
him. But something happened, something that made Fisher
Selim angry, and he never set foot in Kumkapi again. Without
him Kumkapi lost all its kudos. It was never the same again, not
until Blind Agop set up his small fish restaurant there. And even
then, according to Blind Agop, who himself had only one eye,
Kumkapi was half blind after Fisher Selim went away. Blind
Agop had no truck with customers who came just to eat and
drink. He was not in this world simply to cook fish and serve
raki to such boors. What he wanted was friendly talk, warm
comradeship, otherwise you might as well push off . . . Blind
Agop was a habitué of the horse races, betting to win or lose, no
matter. He loved horses, and even more loved talking about
them. He also bred roosters. He kept twenty-three pure-stock
Denizli roosters in the courtyard of the Kumkapi Armenian
Church. And friends brought the best fighting cocks from all
over Anatolia to match them with his own. What had the
Armenian priest to say about all these goings-on in his churchyard, what could he say, that good man, God's own beloved
creature, when his churchyard, usually empty on Sundays but
for Mad Serkis and a few old crones, was suddenly livened up by
Agop's world champion cocks? Why, the Armenian Patriarch
should have given Agop a medal for this service!

Yes, Fisher Selim never set foot in Kumkapi again. He broke
off all relations with the fishermen there and went to settle in
Menekşe. But here too people turned out to be false, double-
tongued, smiling to his face and talking behind his back. And so
Selim gave up. He made a shell for himself and retired into it.
Now and again he would drop in at the coffee-house and watch
the others, sometimes amused, more often pained, disheartened
by their perverseness, pondering on why they were like that, so
bent on making a hell of this lovely world around them. Human
beings are generous at heart, bright like the sea, like the sky, like
a fresh fragrant flower, alive, soaring with gladness and hope.
Why do they snuff these feelings out? Why, oh, why do they

drain themselves of joy and love? Why, oh, why have they grown so sad, so gloomy, so lonely? Why all this killing, all this destruction? The human being is pliant, kind, sensitive, loving . . . Then, why the anger, the rancour, the hate? Why when one is sated must a hundred thousand go hungry? And how can the one who is sated feel secure under all those watching angry eyes, how can he be so callous?

How can there exist a man like Skipper Laz Dursun? Who instilled such wickedness into him? Why did he and the other fishermen kill all the dolphins of the Marmara Sea? Without even realizing they were cutting off their own daily bread . . . For, as the dolphins roamed the Marmara in shoals, leaping and frolicking gaily, boon companions to birds and sailors, they stirred up the fish from the depths and herded them to the shores, so that in those times the catch was bountiful and the people of Istanbul could buy tunny for ten kurush and not, as now, a hundred lira the pair. The fish too were fatter, tastier. Something had happened to the Marmara with the extermination of the dolphins.

Nobody remembers what year it was, that accursed year when dolphin oil became a precious commodity. Foreigners were eager to buy it and one drop was worth a gram of gold. Fishermen flowed into the Marmara from everywhere, the Black Sea, the Aegean, even the Mediterranean, and soon a fierce hunt was on, more like a wholesale massacre . . . The cries of the dolphins still echo over the Marmara, the shrieking as they were caught – harpooned, dynamited or shot dead.

A few fishermen, like Fisher Selim, Lame Hasan and Skipper Sultan, pleaded with the others. 'Stop this killing,' they said. 'It's your own livelihood you're cutting off; we'll all die of hunger if there are no more dolphins.' But who listened! They only laughed. So Fisher Selim and his friends went to the Vali and put the matter to him. 'Save the Marmara, our sea, our bread, from these stupid vandals,' they said. 'Indeed?' the Vali said. 'Drying up the sea, are they?' He was looking at them queerly as though at creatures from some other, unknown world. 'So,' he repeated airily, 'they're drying up the sea . . . We shall look into the matter.' And he bent down over the papers on his desk. They waited uncertainly in that huge room which had once been the seat of grand viziers. Then a policeman signalled to them that the audience was over.

Next, they sent telegrams to the President of the Republic, the Prime Minister, to their representatives in the National Assembly, but with no result at all, not even an answer. In the end, discouraged, they gave up.

Only Selim would not give up. For days on end he talked and argued: 'Don't do this. There are so many other fish in the sea. The dolphin is like a human being, it *is* human. To kill it is worse than killing a man. Why, it is even holy – it protected our Prophet Jonah and kept him in its belly for forty days and forty nights . . .' And he always ended up with the same words: 'You'll anger the sea, you'll make her cross with all of us. After the wrong we've done her she'll never give us even a tiny sprat . . . She'll be cross with us . . .'

It was then that people gave him that nickname: Sea-Crossed Selim.

'Who's that again?'

'Who would it be! Sea-Crossed Selim!'

'The one who'll have the sea crashing over our heads.'

'The one who says the sea is drying up!'

'The man who's lost his heart to a dolphin!'

'Who's fallen in love with a dolphin and made a mate of him . . .'

'Copulating with a fish!'

'Sea-Crossed Selim!'

All along the shores of the Marmara Sea dolphins were being boiled in huge cauldrons and greasy clouds of smoke rose from every beach and cove. The sea itself smelled of burnt fish oil and all the land around, the trees and flowers, even the houses and people were impregnated with that same smell. Dead dolphins in hundreds strewed the waterside, waiting to be hacked up and thrown into the cauldrons. The oil thus obtained was scooped into barrels that were loaded on to foreign freighters anchored off Haydarpaşa or the Bosphorus.

Fisher Selim realized at last that all his efforts were in vain. Now his sole concern was how to protect his own family of dolphins, how to save them from this frightful carnage. He could not very well tie them to his boat. Sooner or later the five of them would fall into the hands of some fisherman or other. Each morning Selim would put out to sea, his heart in his mouth, and when he caught sight of his family, bounding over to him from afar, he would almost faint with relief.

One night, the sudden thought came to him that he might as well catch his own dolphins himself rather than let some bastard of a fisherman make oil out of them. The idea tormented him all night through, and when the next morning he saw them swimming joyously towards him from Büyükada Island, raising white foam over the sea, he reviled himself for the wicked thought. And that day, all day long, he talked to his dolphin, told him everything, and the dolphin spoke to him too, but what could the poor fish do? Sooner or later, he was bound to be caught . . . And when they separated in the evening Fisher Selim saw two tears in his dolphin's eyes. Yes, the dolphin was weeping, Selim could swear to it, and he too wept. It was as if they both knew the fate that awaited them.

There and then, he made up his mind to tackle all the fishermen, one by one. He would describe to them his own dolphin, the round black mark on his back, the broken tip of the right fin, the tail that was not upright like the others' but quite flat, and he would ask them not to hurt him or his family. He would plead with those dogs, those greedy low-down wretches who had the curse of God on them . . . He would do this for the sake of his family.

He started off at Pendik and the cluster of smallish islands around Tavşan Island, but there were no cauldrons boiling there. Then he made for the Gulf of Gemlik, and from a long way off he could see the smoke rising to the sky. He cast anchor in a small cove and rowed over in the dinghy to the group of men on the shore. Fifteen or twenty large dolphins lay there on the rocks. There were deep dark holes in their heads where the bullets had hit them.

Fisher Selim recognized Skipper Teslim in the group. He was an old acquaintance from his drinking days at Kumkapi, but Selim had never spoken to him since then. Skipper Teslim was hurrying up to greet him. 'Welcome, Selim. Welcome, my friend,' he cried as he embraced him and led him to where a pot of coffee had been set to boil. They sat down on a flat rock. Skipper Teslim could hardly conceal his surprise, for Fisher Selim would rather die than seek anyone out like this. He handed him a cigarette, then fixed his own cigarette in a large amber holder, picked up an ember from the fire and lighted it. Selim did the same.

'This is good business, Fisher Selim,' Skipper Teslim said.

'The dolphins are going to feather the nests of us poor fishermen. Those foreign freighters anchored in the port are ready to buy as much oil as you can offer them.'

Selim said nothing.

'If it wasn't for this dolphin business,' the Skipper continued, 'I'd have been obliged to sell all my boats this year and try something other than fishing. Think, only the other day I sold fourteen barrels of oil and got more money for them than I earned in all my fishing days!'

'But it's not good business!' Fisher Selim exploded. 'The sea will be angry. The dolphins are the beauty of the sea. Allah will be angry. The dolphins are his beautiful handiwork. And the Prophet Muhammed will be angry . . . And the Prophet Jonah. . . . The seas will turn barren. The whole world will revile us.'

'I know,' Skipper Teslim sighed. 'But if I don't hunt them others will.'

Five Mauser rifles were lined up against the cliff and magazines of cartridges lay about on the ground. Some deck-hands were putting up a large tent. Others were hacking at the dolphins with big butcher's cleavers and throwing the pieces into wide one-ton cauldrons. The strong penetrating odour of boiling fish stank in the nostrils.

Skipper Teslim was a tall, hawk-nosed man with a jutting Adam's apple, sunken cheeks and lips that seemed to have been cut with a razor. 'The whole of the Marmara Sea is like a battlefield now,' he said. Then he saw Fisher Selim looking at the Mausers. 'Those rifles,' he went on, 'I sold my new green boat to buy them. And I engaged one of those Kurds who can shoot a flying crane in the eye. We set out early in the morning. He lets fly without even taking aim, one, two, three, four, five. . . . In a couple of hours my three boats are packed full. Then there's nothing left but to boil the fish and sell the oil.' He laughed, showing his yellow, decayed teeth. 'At this rate we'll be able to buy apartment buildings in Istanbul, all of us Marmara fishermen . . .'

'Not with Allah's curse upon you!' Fisher Selim leaped to his feet, clenching his fists. 'Just you wait and see what'll hit you in a couple of years! D'you think there'll be any fish left in the Marmara once the dolphins are gone?'

'I know . . . I know the Marmara won't be the same without the dolphins, but . . .'

38

Fisher Selim seized him by the collar. 'Whoever kills my dolphin, my dolphin's family . . .,' he shouted. 'There are five of them . . . I'll make him wish he hadn't been born. I'll ask for blood! Blood for my blood.'

The deck-hands had stopped working and were staring at them.

'But Selim, my friend, for pity's sake, how on earth am I to tell which are your dolphins?'

Fisher Selim was stymied. How could he mention the black mark, the broken fin? Who'd wait to examine a fish when shooting at a distance and with a Mauser too?

'That's no excuse,' he yelled as he rushed away. A deck-hand was waiting to help him push out in the dinghy. 'These people are no longer human, Fisher Selim,' he whispered. 'They've gone mad.'

Back in his boat Selim stood motionless, his eyes narrowed against the sun, his mind in a whirl. Suppose he had a Mauser rifle too, three deck-hands, a couple of cauldrons . . . Suppose he too joined in the hunt . . . Wouldn't he make enough money in only a few months so to attain his heart's desire? Anyway, the Marmara would be emptied of dolphins and sooner or later, whatever he did, his own family would be killed by these brutes. Take Skipper Teslim . . . He wasn't a bad man, certainly not a brute . . . If a man's business is fishing, then he has to kill whatever he finds in the sea, even if it is his own father. Well then Fisher Selim, here's your chance. Will there ever be such a chance again in this accursed fishing trade? If you let this chance go by just because you say you want to be pure and human, then you'll never attain your heart's desire. Come Selim, don't be soft. . . . You're not getting any younger either, hey, Fisher Selim . . .

He could obtain a Mauser from Blind Mustafa, who had nine brand-new ones from Germany in his shanty house. And couldn't he engage Kurdish Cemil? Here, Cemil, take this rifle and shoot us some dolphins . . . Throw a coin into the air and he'll hit it every time . . . Then there's Laz Murat, the one they call the Algerian because he went fishing right up to the coast of Algeria. And what about Muharrem, the buffalo-drover? What about him for hacking up those human-eyed dolphins and setting them to boil? Why shouldn't Fisher Selim, too, hunt dolphins like everyone else? Those other fishermen, they didn't kill the beautiful creatures for sport, did they? All seafaring people love the dolphin. He is their boon companion, a delight to the eye on the solitary desolate seas. Doesn't every fisherman, every skipper, know that the dolphin drives the smaller fish in towards the coast, stirring them out of their nests, making it easy to catch them? Doesn't he know that with the dolphins gone the seas will dry up?

That night, in his house at Menekşe, Fisher Selim did not sleep a wink and at the crack of dawn he was at Blind Mustafa's door.

Mustafa could not believe his eyes. Fisher Selim! Visiting him! 'Welcome, Fisher Selim, welcome! Sit down and let me offer you a cup of our poor coffee . . . Woman,' he called, 'bring out some chairs and a table. Look who's here.'

'Who?' the woman called back indifferently.

'Fisher Selim!'

At this she appeared in the doorway. 'Fisher Selim?' she cried, astonished.

'Himself,' Blind Mustafa laughed. 'Fisher Selim himself come to visit us!'

His wife hurriedly carried out a couple of chairs and a little table. They sat down while she went in to prepare the coffee. For a while they did not talk. Selim was growing more and more uncomfortable.

'I'm going to do it too,' he blurted out at last. 'I . . . I . . . Dolphins . . .' His voice was strangled.

'So you're going out hunting the dolphin, eh? Well done!' Blind Mustafa congratulated him. 'Why, everyone's doing it! They say that all these fishermen are rich as Harun al-Rashid now. There's no end to the fish of the sea.'

'But there is!' Fisher Selim shouted. 'Such an end that there won't be a tiny wrasse left and all those Harun al-Rashids will die of hunger.'

'I wish I could buy a boat and go fishing too,' Blind Mustafa went on, 'but I've never been out to sea in my life, much less gone fishing. You know those German rifles of mine I hadn't been able to sell all these years? Well, yesterday a man came and bought the whole lot, ammunition and all. And he gave me so much money for them, five, six times what I was going to ask. "Agha," I said, "I hope that it's not a war that's been proclaimed . . ." The man laughed. "A war it is," he said, "a war between the

Marmara fishermen and the dolphins. And I'm joining this war with ten boats. All my fortune I've put into it, sold my land too."
Look, Selim, brother, if it's one of those German rifles you want, money's no problem. I'll give you one. I've still got one carbine left, brand-new. Why, I'd give you a thousand rifles to take away if I had them, I would. For a man like you it's nothing.'

The lines on Fisher Selim's brow deepened and his face darkened. His hands were trembling.

'Look, Selim, brother, don't you worry about the money. I'd do anything for you. That man said you can get rich in six months hunting dolphins. "Once we've finished with the Marmara," he said, "there's always the Black Sea. The world's full of seas . . ." '

At that moment a warm aroma of coffee spread through the fresh morning air and the woman came up to them, her hazel eyes gleaming, her cheeks glowing, swinging her hips and carrying on a silver tray the coffee in old-fashioned red-striped cups without handles.

'Here you are, Selim Agha,' she said. 'Welcome to our house.'

With quivering hands Selim took the cup, spilling some of the coffee into the saucer. Quickly, he lifted the cup to his lips and swallowed the whole lot at one go. Then he leaped to his feet, mumbling, 'Thank you, thank you,' and walked swiftly down the slope and on to the shore. He was sweating profusely.

Next he burst into the coffee-house, shouting, 'I'm going to hunt the dolphin too. I'm going to bore black holes in their heads with greasy bullets. They'll cry out like babies, they'll weep . . . Let them weep . . .'

'You should have done it long ago,' Süleyman said.

'Other people have been earning bankfuls of money all this time,' one-armed Zühtü complained.

'Only our Menekşe fishermen have stood idly by,' said Rüstem the pedlar.

'Don't talk like that,' Laz Hamdi admonished him. 'Which of us has a rifle to hunt them with? Or cauldrons, or for that matter a boat large enough?'

'Let Fisher Selim go,' they said.

'I will! I'll kill all the dolphins in the Marmara Sea,' Selim said vindictively. He ground his teeth. 'The sea will be red with their blood.'

Suddenly he rushed out of the coffee-house like a madman,

gasping for air. The minute he was gone, they started deriding him.

'Go, then, you lazy good-for-nothing! As if there are any dolphins left by now . . .'

'Well, I never!' young Özkan cried. 'Fisher Selim talking to us!'

'He'll talk twenty to the dozen when he's in a tight spot, he will, the stuck-up fool,' Süleyman hissed spitefully. 'What is he anyway that he won't speak to us? Only a common fisher!'

'Thinks he's a king, that one,' Zühtü chimed in. 'Giving himself airs as though he was lord of all creation.'

'But now that he's in a fix . . .'

'Now that others have snapped up all the fish in the Marmara Sea . . .'

'Now that he's missed the boat . . .'

'He comes babbling to us about shooting dolphins!'

'That man who never deigned to look at us!'

'But Fisher Selim always does what he says,' Özkan protested.

'That he does,' some others upheld him.

'You'll see how he'll catch heaps of dolphins and sell barrels of oil to those foreign tankers and build himself a palace right here in Menekşe.'

'Go on!'

'Yes, he will. He's going to make a paradise of Menekşe.'

Suddenly the crash of breaking glass filled the coffee-house as slim-waisted glasses full of hot tea were flung at Özkan. The large window-pane behind him smashed down over his head and he was spattered with glass splinters, tea and blood. With difficulty two men dragged him out of the coffee-house cursing madly. 'Bastards, rats, jellyfish! Call yourselves fishermen? Just you watch Fisher Selim, how he's going to catch all the fish in the Marmara. And all the dolphins too. You'll see, you low-down jealous dogs . . .'

The two men who held him, Bomber Kemal and Swanky Vedat, were trying to stop his mouth to keep the quarrel from spreading further, when they caught sight of Fisher Selim at the door of Fevzi's restaurant. 'Shhh, look who's coming,' they warned Özkan, who sobered up on the spot.

'Let go of me,' he whispered. Fisher Selim scanned him from a distance, then swung angrily towards the coffee-house and stopped in the doorway. The men inside froze as his steely blue

42

gaze, huge now, transfixed them. Suddenly, he turned away in disgust and strode off towards Çekmece.

First he went to the *kebap* restaurant which Çakaloğlu had established after being thrown out of his job some months before. This man, young as he was, had been arrested because he had formed a trade union and incited the workers to strike. He had stood fast under the most terrible tortures during his interrogation by the police at the notorious Sansaryan Han. Fisher Selim did not know what took him to the restaurant, for he barely had more than a nodding acquaintance with him. The trade unionist greeted him warmly. He showed him to a table and ordered coffee for him.

Fisher Selim started speaking even before he had sat down. 'I've got myself a rifle from Blind Mustafa,' he said. 'Brand-new . . .'

'He's got plenty, that one,' the trade unionist interrupted him. 'Those Laz fishing boats smuggle weapons in to him all the time and he squares the transaction with the police. Don't let yourself be deceived by that shanty-house he lives in, nor by his bland ways. He's from Antep, the head of a large contraband network. There's no counting the men he's killed or had killed. He was the most notorious border smuggler in all the provinces of Urfa, Mardin, Diyarbakir and Antep. But the smugglers fell out with each other and began fighting to kill, so he sought safety in Istanbul. His name's not Mustafa at all, but some much more well-known name . . .'

Fisher Selim listened with only half an ear while Çakaloğlu recounted Blind Mustafa's exploits, how he was buying up land and property all over the country, how he already owned six apartment buildings in Istanbul itself. Suddenly, he looked the trade unionist straight in the eye and shouted: 'I'm going to buy still more carbines from him. I'm going to hunt the dolphin, and kill and kill until there are no more left. The Marmara Sea will turn red with their blood, red, frothing . . .'

The trade unionist was smiling. 'You're not a man to kill dolphins,' he said calmly. 'It's not everyone can do that.'

'I will! I will . . .'

'You are Fisher Selim,' Çakaloğlu said softly. 'You'd kill yourself before you killed a single dolphin.'

'Then I'll kill myself. But first I'll kill my own family of dolphins, one by one. First I'll hack my own family to pieces and

43

boil them in cauldrons. Then all the other dolphins, all of them.
. . . Then I'll kill myself, kill, kill . . .'

'Oh come on, Fisher Selim,' the trade unionist implored. 'Stop this. What's come over you?'

Fisher Selim sprang to his feet. The coffee brought in by a waiter stood untouched and cold on the table. He ran out and burst into the coffee-house next door. 'I'll kill them,' he began, 'first my own family, then all the other dolphins in the sea, and then myself too . . .' Frantic, beside himself, he wandered all over Çekmece like a living lament, and when he had exhausted all the restaurants and coffee-houses there, he jumped into a taxi and made for the Çiçekpazari, the so-called Flower Market up in Beyoğlu.

The closed market smelled of flowers, of fermenting beer, of shrimp and crabs and fish and lobster. On a table in the centre a mound of shrimps, small lobsters and crayfish shone bright red under the glare of the bare electric bulbs. Barrels serving as tables crowded the market. There were beer glasses and plates of fish on them and people sat drinking and eating all around them. At the entrance the *kokoreç*-vendors had set up their stalls and were busily swivelling the skewers of their broilers in a swirl of fumes, their hands working machine-like, slicing the roasted *kokoreç*, sprinkling it with parsley, onion and tomato and inserting it into sliced loaves of bread which they handed out to customers without even lifting their heads. The odour of burnt *kokoreç* fat filled the whole market and even permeated the beer and fish, the white cheese and the almonds which, blanched yellow and piled on trays, were carried around by small boys or old men who themselves looked like small boys.

Selim plunged into the tumult and found himself seated with some men at a barrel, drinking first beer then *raki*. Did he know them, were they friends of his? He simply could not remember. All he knew was that they listened to him all ears, with an occasional encouraging word: 'Kill them, kill them. Don't let a single one escape alive. Get rich and come here and get drunk with us. Here's to you . . .'

The swarming market was spinning around him, the naked bulbs, the odours, the flowers . . . The sea too, and blood and slow-creeping lobsters . . . Golden glittering lights, motor cars, voices, *kokoreç* fumes, street sellers, car horns, reeling drunks, oaths and curses and vomiting, half-naked huge-eyed women in

44

the show-windows, fish-stands with rows of swordfish and sturgeon, clusters of green salads, the Cumhuriyet Restaurant, fruit-stands, oranges, tangerines, apples, and again all along the street displays of fish, gleaming, and bunches of parsley, green peppers, and dangling in the windows of butchers' shops pheasants, quails, golden orioles, woodcocks, hares with gashed necks, turkeys, chickens, and overflowing out of the street right up to the British Embassy and down to Tarlabaşi Avenue barrows of vegetables and fruit and piles of melons and watermelons, some sliced open for display, bright red, yellow, muskmelons, one of which alone was enough to drown Beyoğlu in its fragrance . . . All spinning round and round . . . And Lambo's tavern . . . Lambo's smiling face, his wise tolerant eyes, the way he holds the glass as he hands a customer his drink, a little tighter and the glass will be crushed, yet polite, gentle, everyone's friend . . . 'It won't do,' he was saying, 'you'll never forgive yourself if you do this, Fisher Selim. I know you, my friend, I know you can do it, but you'll kill yourself afterwards. All right, you'll get rich, And then? You're much better off as you are . . .' Dimly Fisher Selim sensed that this gentle, earnest man was right, but he could only mutter over and over again: 'I'll kill them, I will, all the dolphins . . .'

Up and down Beyoğlu he wandered, reeling, bumping into people, and came again to the Flower Market. It was less crowded. A man was playing the accordion. A group of fishermen friends from the old days was there. They jumped at his neck, made him sit at their table and plied him with drink. He drank whatever was put before him, babbling away unconsciously all the time. 'I'm going to make the Marmara a barren sea. I'm going to sever its life-giving artery, drain it of all its blood. I'll tear out its heart, its lungs. I'll twist its balls so it never spawns again, so it doesn't even smell like the sea any more.'

Suddenly he got up, lunged at the accordionist and yanked him by the collar into the centre of the market. The Laz vendor there hurriedly pulled his stall of shellfish out of the way.

'Let go of me,' the accordionist cried. 'It's a *lezginka* you want of me, isn't it? Let go and I'll play it for you.' He was delighted to see Fisher Selim again. 'Such a *lezginka* I'll play tonight, the very paving stones of Beyoğlu will rise up and dance with you!'

'I want no one tonight,' Selim yelled. 'Tonight all the seas will

45

die.'

People made way as Selim threw himself into the dance, faster and faster, lost in a trance. The market began to fill up again. One or two people joined in the dance. Then others . . . More and more . . .

Eminönü Square, Ahirkapi, Kumkapi, Narlikapi, Topkapi, Bakirköy . . . The sea, the stars, the moon, the sun, roads, trees, Çamlica Hill, the Princes Islands, lights and clouds and boats, a loud voice, the reflection of tall minarets on the water, of Süleymaniye Mosque, of the Valide Mosque, of the oil-trading wharf, Azapkapi Mosque, Sultan Ahmed Mosque, Topkapi Fountain . . . The leaden domes wavering in the haze, seabirds, swallows, street lamps, vagabonds . . . All helter-skelter, slithering over the sea, gliding on a greasy tightrope . . . Lambo's voice, a little hurt, 'Don't, don't do it, Fisher Selim . . .' White clouds flowing over the city, white seagulls on the red-tiled roofs . . . Laz fishing scows coming into port, yellow, blue, green, orange, crowding side by side in front of the Fish Market at Azapkapi, mermaids carved on their prows, or huge-petalled roses, or dolphins, a bearded man on a dolphin, the Prophet Jonah . . . Millions of glittering fish scales . . . Lights, winds, stars, minarets, the stinking Golden Horn . . . Pell-mell. Stars in the Golden Horn . . . Its fetid waters bright with stars, gleaming with the green, red, blue reflections of neon lamps, the Golden Horn, a long, very deep, dark well . . . A great stormwind is shaking the Süleymaniye Mosque, the bridges, Rüstem Paşa Mosque . . . A raging sea, thundering, sweeping away Topkapi Palace, Sarayburnu, uprooting the plane trees from Gülhane Park, sweeping them on, a dishevelled mass, the whole park sliding into the sea, the flowers, the trees . . . Thousands of seagulls screeching, clamouring, thousands. Soaring up into the sky, swooping back over the sea, dripping with blood . . . Red, blood-red gulls, and dolphins . . . Dolphins raising foam, minaret-high, blood-red foam, shrieking . . . Screaming gulls, screaming dolphins, blood-red, all in a jumble in the churning sea, red breakers staining the shore . . . And, pouring from the blood-red sky, red frothing blood, dolphins scattering blood . . . All blood-red . . . Dark.

Up above Menekşe railway station, Fisher Selim had propped a little mirror in a cleft of the plane tree in front of Yahya's

46

restaurant and was shaving in the half-light of the stars. He was going to put out to sea. Yet he was afraid. What if he never came across his family again?

He finished shaving and went down to his boat. Steering along the little stream, he got off at Çekmece and bought five cans of diesel oil and a dozen loaves of bread. He had three good harpoons in the boat, and his fishing lines and nets were stacked in the hold under the prow. Then he made back downstream and out to sea, heading for Silivri, but even before he got there he encountered a Laz fishing boat and caught sight of the dolphins heaped on the deck, their blood flowing like a fountain. The boat must have met with a whole school of dolphins and now they were being taken to that little creek near Ambarli to be hacked up and boiled. Fisher Selim averted his eyes.

All day long he wandered about the Marmara Sea. Perhaps the dolphins had taken flight and sought safety in the depths of the sea . . . Dolphins are canny creatures. Why shouldn't they be able to think of that? At Eregli, Fisher Selim turned back. His head was numb. Only flitting images were rushing through his mind. Electric lights, ships, minarets, a queer poisonous green, a saffron yellow, the Flower Market, lustrous red lobsters, fumes and odours, and a sea illuminated from deep deep down, the sun shining upwards from its far depths, irradiating the waters, everything crystal-clear, turbot lying over the sandy bottom, their noduled backs spangled, their shadows hitting the surface of the water, red mullet casting bright-red reflections up above, red coruscating scorpion fish, combers, pickerel, humble scads, swarming crabs, long-bodied dusky perch, John Dorys, translucent green, mackerel, their backs all a-shimmer, the loveliest of blues, speckled tuna, flashing cerulean swordfish, jellyfish, red and white bream, oysters, sea urchins, all moving in the surge and swell, whirling in a thousand and one vortexes, changing shape and colour from one moment to the next, growing brighter and brighter, drowning the sky in a flood of light, houses at the bottom of the sea, all alight, cars, trams, pale green and yellow, creaking along, and people swarming, scrambling over one another, Süleymaniye Mosque, Haghia Sophia, Topkapi Palace, the subway, and Beyoğlu, reeking of ammonia, of beer, of sour fermenting unbaked bread, the corpse of a dog, bloated, its blood streaking the asphalt, a vast forest under the sea, orange leaves, and dolphins, hundreds of them, their great white bodies clinging to the trees, rocking in a flood of light, then hurling themselves down one after another, their fins held low, spraying sparks high into the sky, spuming light as they fall and shatter in a steely blue radiance. Raindrops, blood-drops, roll over the blue radiance, and flowers of blood ripple in the cold wind . . . From deep down under the sea, from its farthest depths, the sun is dawning. Ships and boats, large and small, are caught in a maelstrom, spinning, churning in smoke, funnels, sails, masts, cranes, whirling whirling . . . Cracking, breaking, pitching into each other . . . The sea in a cataract like blue ice-cubes . . . The sea tossed up like blue sand . . . A great storm of blue swirling, splintering, blustering . . .

There, in the middle of the sea, its engine at a stop, Fisher Selim's boat was wheeling as if caught in a whirlpool and from the shore drifted the smell of boiling fish. A burst of gunfire made him jump. He heard a long shriek as of a child being slaughtered. Unthinkingly, he set the motor purring and headed towards the sound. After a while he found himself in a forest of fishing boats. Hundreds of guns were blasting away and the sea was red with blood. Smitten dolphins shot up into the air screeching like children, splashed down into the water and surfaced again, white belly turned up, bleeding. Some, screaming, dived out of sight only to rise a little later, white belly up, bleeding. Others tossed and turned, squalling frantically, squirting blood, then lay still, white belly up . . . And the fishermen, with hooks and ropes, hoisted them into the boats.

As Fisher Selim stood there blinking, at a loss, he was hailed by one of the skippers. The voice was familiar, yet he could not make out who the man was, with that long pock-marked face and those green-streaked grey eyes. Some old comrade from his youthful flings in Kumkapi he must be; but who, looking at him so mildly, with concern, with affection even? Suddenly, behind the pock-marked face there hovered a snow-white nurse's cap with the badge of the Red Crescent, no sooner seen than gone in a wisp of smoke. Long golden tresses, sometimes braided, spreading curtain-like over the water, and a pair of large blue eyes brimming with love, faintly glimpsed behind the curtain of hair. Fisher Selim stood staring at the bleeding dolphins, at the sea foaming with blood, at the sailors struggling with the dying animals, heard the shrieks of children being butchered, and tried to recapture some forgotten thing that eluded his mind. As the sailors hauled the dolphins on to the decks, the boats sank lower and lower into the water. The pock-marked skipper, his hands on his hips, his legs set wide apart, smiled at him. Selim smiled back. In an instant his own boat was loaded with a big pile of dolphins. He set out for Sinan village. There he borrowed a large cauldron from Mad Nuri and with the help of Nuri's three sons he boiled the fish in the bay of Sinan village. The oily stench seeped into his very bones. He could never forget it, nor the man with the pock-marked face, though he never found out who he was. Then the long freighter flying an Italian flag, loaded with barrels. The grating of winches . . . And afterwards, as though in the grip of some hectic fever, the money burning his hands, Fisher Selim rushed off to lose himself in the city . . .

The Fish Market, the crowds crossing the bridge, the barges on the Golden Horn, the swarms of seagulls, the masses of turbot, the cases and cases of gurnards . . . Gurnards flying bright red through the air from the boats on to the wet grey wharf, picked up by practised hands and stacked in neat heaps, all eyes pointing the same way . . . Piles and piles of fish eyes . . . And the seagulls, wing to wing, weaving a curtain over Süley-maniye Mosque, seething, hurtling down with mad bitter cries at each fish that was thrown. The tall slim minarets appearing and disappearing behind the mass of wings . . . A yellow dog stretched on the pavement, asleep, head resting on its paws . . . Fisher Selim's head is burning, on fire, as he watches a crimson sun dawn between the minarets of Sultan Ahmed Mosque. The waters of the Golden Horn are thickly skimmed with dust and dirt and oil. The Golden Horn stinks. Floating on its surface are dead seagulls, driftwood, empty tins, tomatoes, green peppers, corncobs, water-melon rinds, dead fish, all swaying sluggishly, mantling the turbid muddy water.

5

The events of that night I only know by hearsay.

It was well past midnight when Selim became aware of a pair of eyes at the window. Suddenly, the muzzle of a gun flamed. Six times the gun exploded before dropping to the floor. Selim had caught hold of the man's wrist. It was Zeynel. He was struggling to free himself, writhing like a snake at the bottom of the wall, yelling, cursing, his eyes starting from their sockets. Fisher Selim screwed up his face as though some foul stench had offended his nostrils.

'Go, damn you,' he said. He switched off the light and got into bed without another look at his attacker. Yet for the first time in days, he thought about Zeynel and suddenly he felt strangely disquieted.

Zeynel had been ten or eleven years old when he turned up in Menekşe, all alone, and took shelter with some fellow-countrymen of his. That was nine years ago. In his home, somewhere on the distant Black Sea coast – maybe up on the mountains of Rize, neither Zeynel nor his countrymen had ever once mentioned where – Zeynel had in one night witnessed the murder of all his family: his father and mother, his brothers and sisters, his uncles and their wives and children. Even Zeynel's six-year-old brother had not been spared. Zeynel could never forget the sight of him, sitting in his bed against the wall, bathed in blood, both hands clamped to his mouth, his eyes frozen in a wide lifeless stare. Somehow, Zeynel himself had escaped without a scratch. Maybe he had been in the barn during the raid. Maybe he was a sleepwalker and had been wandering in the tea or hazelnut gardens. Or perhaps he'd gone out to make water under the plane tree and had clambered up into its branches at the sound of shooting. In the morning some neighbours found him in his bed, huddled in a ball among the gory corpses, all his limbs trembling. For days afterwards he remained coiled up, rigid, his eyes tightly closed, refusing food and drink. Try as they might, the strongest men could not prise his mouth open. When at last his teeth loosened and food was put before him, he gobbled it up like a wild animal, his eyes rolling with fear, ready to fly at any moment. Some distant relatives had taken him in, but he did not stay there more than a month, and even then he vanished during the day and only glided in cat-like at night. He lived in dread of everything. A bird, an ant, the faintest rustle of a leaf startled him into flight. And then one day he turned up in a boat in the port of Trabzon, far from his home, huddling in the bilge water between two ribs of the hold. The sailors plied him with questions, but could not get a single word out of him, and when they tried to put him ashore he clung to a mast and all the crew together could not tear him away, short of killing him. So they gave up and set a large bowl of soup and a loaf of bread in front of him, but he would not even glance at the steaming mint-scented soup until he was sure the boat had weighed anchor and was way offshore.

'Here,' the captain tackled him, 'take this spoon and grub up. Look, we're as far from port as can be and I've no intention of going back just for you.'

With the instinct of a wild creature Zeynel sensed that no harm would come to him from the captain. He crept up to the soup and gulped it down quietly, still casting fearful glances around like a caged beast. And so it went on until the boat came to Istanbul, the boy cleaving to a mast at every port, uttering desperate howls if anyone so much as made to touch him. In Istanbul he went straight to Menekşe, to the home of Laz Refik, a former neighbour from his home village. For six months he never stepped out of the house, and when he did it was only to run back if anyone spoke or even looked at him. Then suddenly at the age of sixteen or seventeen this timid lad turned into a veritable hellion. Wherever there was trouble, a fight, a robbery, Zeynel was sure to be there. In the space of a few years he became the worst troublemaker this side of Bakirköy.

A crowd had gathered outside the house. Fisher Selim heard the sound of many feet and Zeynel's voice raised above the roar of the surf. So it's the *lodos* wind again, he thought.

'Let me go!' Zeynel was yelling. 'I'm going to set fire to his house. I'll put a bomb in it. If you love your God don't stop me. This world has no use for the likes of him . . . That dog . . .'

The tramp of feet and the rumble from the crowd grew louder.

'Throw that dynamite, Zeynel! You're as good as dead anyway. D'you think you'll get off alive after what you did? Throw that dynamite, then, and rid us of a bad lot. Let go of him, you fellows . . .'

Zeynel's voice rose still higher. He was carried away by the feeling of power it gave him to swear and curse at Fisher Selim and so prove himself a real man. Fisher Selim guessed how it was and so he waited calmly in his bed for Zeynel to spend himself and go away. Yet, after a while, he began to have doubts. That confounded lad was lashing himself into a frenzy. What if he did indeed have a stick of dynamite with him?

Fisher Selim rose, switched on the light, drew on his trousers, picked up the gun from the floor and opened the door. The railway station lamps lit up the little garden which was packed with men in pyjamas or underclothes and women in night-dresses and curlers. The hubbub died down, the crowd fell away and Zeynel stood transfixed, like an owl pinned by a strong light, as Selim bore down upon him with the gun.

'You fool!' Selim said quietly. 'Take your gun and go. You'll have the police on you any minute.'

Zeynel turned on his heels and fled, disappearing down the steps that led to the seashore.

It had begun to rain, and still the crowd remained there, staring.

'Get a move on, you people,' Selim said. 'What on earth d'you think you are going to find in my house at this hour of the night?' And he slammed the door in their faces.

The next day, I was down on the seashore very early. A blanket of smoke lay over the sea, so dense that not a single boat was to be seen and just the tips of the Islands and the mountains opposite emerged. There was no trace of last night's *lodos*, only a warm caressing dawn breeze, bearing an odour of iodine, refreshing, invigorating, infusing you with an exhilarating sensation of being born anew, of bliss at being alive.

Fisher Selim was already on the wooden jetty, repairing a blue fishing net. His hands moved at lightning speed and he was so absorbed that he never even heard me approaching.

'*Merhaba!*' I called.

His eyes lit up when he saw me. '*Merhaba!*' He beckoned me to his side and went on with his work.

'What time is it?' he asked after a while. 'Must be about four, but that rooster hasn't crowed yet.'

'It won't be long,' I said. 'It's ten to four.'

'I wasn't wrong, then,' he said. 'When the shadow of that tree there hits this white stone at this time of the year, it's four o'clock.'

I stared at him, wondering whether this was some kind of joke, for I could not make out any shadow in the dawn light, but he was already gathering up the net and carrying it to his boat.

The smoke blanket over the sea was gradually retreating.

'Jump in,' he invited me. 'Today we'll hunt for that bullock again. You never know but he might spring up under our very nose before we reach the clump-of-trees landmark.'

We struck out west into the receding smoke and stopped at the clump-of-trees landmark which is between Ambarli and Çekmece, a mile and a half out from the old Menekşe weir. The sea here this morning was mauve, shading to pink and blue and purple in places, and deep down there was a long trail of purple lengthening into the open sea.

'We'll cast a net here for mullet and pick it up on our way back. Tell me, have you ever been to the Fish Market very early in the morning?' he asked as he began to lay out the net.

'Only once,' I replied. 'At seven o'clock.'

'That won't do,' he said. 'It's at five you should go, provided you can find the market wharf under the gulls.'

'The gulls?'

'Yes. In the early morning they gather like a vast cloud over the wharf and the whole of the Golden Horn too. They swarm down on the incoming fishing boats for the portion that every fisherman sets apart for them. Not to do so, not to give these poor city vagrants their dole each morning at the Fish Market, brings on the worst of bad luck. It's a well-tried thing. The fisherman who neglects to do that can't sell his fish that day. For a long time afterwards he never catches any fish at all. Many a fisherman has seen his engine go on the blink, his oar break, his sail tear, a hole in his hull . . . And sometimes the boat sinks too. Yes indeed! Every creature in this world must get his due, the fish in the sea, the bird in the sky, the ant on the earth, and man, above all man . . .'

'Yes,' I said, 'man above all.'

'I know,' he said with a broad smile. 'I know about you, why you were thrown into prison. Yes indeed . . .' He raised his voice as he dropped the end of the net with its float into the water. 'Above all man's due. Cheat a man out of his due and sooner or later it'll stick in your throat. Look what happened to Laz Mazhar, the commission merchant who used to bleed all us fishermen white. He took his last count at the age of twenty-seven. Yes, above all man's due . . .'

'It'll stick in their throats.'

'When?' he asked wistfully.

'Soon.'

He laughed. 'Of course. Soon. Those young people are doing something about it. One night . . . You remember that Laz youngster, the small one with fair hair, one of those whom they killed later? Well, I ferried him secretly to Şarköy one night . . . Ah, they're killing them all, one by one . . .'

'Yes, but they won't get away with it.'

'Children of poor humble families, they are, all of them. If only I'd had a son,' he sighed. 'Even if they killed him . . . I would have gone like the others to the Gülhane Morgue to recover his body, with his comrades in thousands accompanying me . . .'

'Didn't you ever have any children?' I asked.

His blue eyes clouded. 'No,' he said.

'Why not?'

'I never got married,' he replied, his face softening, his hand on the tiller quite still now.

The sound of some late-crowing cocks floated over from the shore. Way off Büyükada Island a brightly lit passenger ship was gliding by in all its glory. After a while its wake reached us and rocked the boat. Selim stirred. He looked at me, then bent his head. Quietly the words dropped from his lips into the sea. 'But I will get married . . .' His voice was so strange that my flesh crept. 'Let's go now,' he went on as he started the engine. 'We'll pick up these nets later.'

He didn't say another word until we came to Kumburgaz. His eyes were scanning the sea, hawk-like. All around us tiny baby fish popped out of the water and plopped back, again and again, as though they were racing our boat.

'Look,' Selim remarked, 'they're running for their lives.'

'Who from?'

'Why, from Jumbo Dentex of course! Just look at the poor little things! Almost ready to fly in the sky to escape being gobbled up. But Jumbo Dentex is hungry too . . .'

'Let him eat poison,' I said indignantly. 'As though there's nothing else for him in the sea but these tiny baby fish.'

'He just has to open his mouth and swim around,' Fisher Selim said. 'Masses of things for him to swallow in the sea . . . Like the human dentex . . . The world is full of food. All men could have their fill, but most of them go hungry . . .'

We were sailing past the little port of Silivri, a hazy blue streak along the coast with a few lights blinking here and there, when Selim veered off towards Marmara Island. And suddenly, without warning, our boat heaved. I started up and there, only a little way ahead of us, I saw the crystal blue back of a huge fish. It flashed and vanished.

Fisher Selim grabbed the harpoon. 'There he is,' he yelled. 'Ya Allah!'

The back of the fish flashed again. Selim waited. For the third time the fish surfaced like the gleaming curve of a wave, razor-blue. Then it was as if Selim's body had leaped out in the wake of the harpoon and swung back. The rope went taut, only for an instant, then slackened.

'Curse it!' Selim cried. 'He's escaped.'

'But the rope went taut. The harpoon must have pierced him . . .'

'Just his tail. My hand wasn't steady enough.'

'Won't he die of the wound and sink to the bottom of the sea?'

Selim laughed. 'Swordfish don't die from such a small wound and the salt sea will quickly heal it. Besides, a dead fish doesn't sink. It surfaces and the gulls and other fish devour it.'

'Next time . . .'

'Next time, I'll get it,' Selim vowed. 'I know him better now. My hand won't tremble next time. Then we'll take him to the Hilton.'

We turned back. Flecks of light, pink, mauve, blue, green, danced on the sea and the tip of the sun appeared in a sudden blaze, accompanied by a surge of sound from the sea-depths, from the Islands, from all around us. The city lights went out and the domes and minarets floated out of the haze. The Bosphorus Bridge, a long strip of light in the distance, faded into a fragile grey line like a bow of smoke. A breeze blew in from Yakacik, ruffling the surface of the sea, and shoals of fish splattered on the water.

Fisher Selim broke into a joyful song that made you want to

stand up and dance. The words were in a tongue I had never heard before. But after a while the song grew melancholy and all the way to the Islands he sang on in this doleful vein.

'Let's stop here,' Selim said, 'and watch the city. See how it wakes like a huge angry monster . . .'

The world of the sea, too, was coming to life with the light of day. The sun lit up the seabed with its rocks and fish and algae. Scorpion fish flashed rainbow-like. A fat dentex swam up and nosed into the weed-covered rocks. At the sight of him all the other fish darted away and he remained alone, cruising majestically in the green-tinged blue water.

'Look,' I said, 'let's cast a line. He's as good as hooked.'

'No,' Selim said. 'I don't like catching a fish who's so exposed. He's out enjoying the fine morning, just like us.' He laughed, pleased with the thought. 'How could I drop my line over him now, take him off his guard? Think of him swallowing the bait, struggling for his life, screaming. Like he's been struck by lightning . . . I can't do that . . . I . . .'

'Yes?'

'I can't get married . . .' Then quickly, 'No, no, I will, I must get married.'

Clouds were gathering fast from over Yalova. North too the sky over the Black Sea was lowering, and the west, which only a moment ago had been bright as though another sun had dawned there, became black.

'We'll be caught in the rain before we reach the shore. We'd better be going.'

'I like the rain,' I said.

'Well then, you'll be well served in a minute. We're in for a good soaking before we get to the nets.'

'All the better. We'll be washed clean, inside and out.'

His eyes brightened. 'That's true. The rain does cleanse a man inside too . . .'

The sea had grown dark and choppy. We pressed on to reach the shelter of Menekşe Bay, the waves splashing into the boat, the clouds churning black above. Tall breakers foamed on the shore of Büyükada Island and over the Kumkapi breakwater. Soon the rain was driving down, hurled by the wind this way and that in sheets, lashing at the sea. The sky assumed a lurid ashy hue, while over the mosques hung a nebulous glow as though water was being squirted from all sides on to that one patch of light.

In an instant we were both soaking wet. Water flowed down Fisher Selim's cap, the reddish tuft of his brows, his bushy moustache, and filled even the wrinkles of his face.

The storm died down as suddenly as it had arisen, leaving the sea calm and smooth as a mirror.

'Let's stop awhile here,' Selim said. The rain had thinned off into a bright crystal blue, soft as velvet, and the clouds were turning from grey to pale green. Selim, his head bowed, was lost in thought. Then he looked at me. Obviously, he wanted to say something, but did not know how to begin. That was why he had stopped here, in the middle of the sea. Our eyes met. He smiled humbly.

'You see this?' he said, opening his shirt to reveal the scar of a deep wound that had shattered his left shoulder. 'It's a bullet wound, a dumdum bullet. Haven't you noticed how my left shoulder always droops?'

'No, I haven't.'

'Well it does. And d'you know where I got this wound?'

'Was it in one of the Kumkapi taverns?'

'No, nothing like that.'

'Well, I'm curious to know.'

He flushed to the tips of his ears and when he spoke it was in a low murmur, as though to the bilges of the boat, to the sea, in a dream.

'On Mount Ararat,' he said. 'I got this wound on Mount Ararat. The Kurds there were up in arms and, at the time, I was serving in the army at Erzurum.' He lifted his head. 'Have you ever seen Mount Ararat?'

'Yes,' I said. 'I climbed it once.'

He stared. 'You mean to the very top?'

'Not quite. There's a flat stretch just before you get to the summit and from there you can see three small peaks. One of them is the highest point, so they say. Well, I got to the flat spot, but I simply couldn't scale that last hillock. They told me it was only about sixty metres to go.'

'How can they measure that?'

'There's a special instrument for that. So you were on Mount Ararat?'

'I fought against the Kurds. Brave people and crack shots too. I used to hold my cap out on the end of a stick and in an instant it would be pierced by half a dozen bullets. Our commanding officer was a certain Salih Pasha . . . An unpleasant man he was, though they say Atatürk liked him . . . Every time one of his soldiers was killed by the Kurds, he'd go mad with rage and order the nearest Kurdish village to be set on fire and all its men shot. He simply couldn't understand that these illiterate peasants, who didn't even speak Turkish, should rise up against our Atatürk. We had orders to shoot every Kurd who fell into our hands. Why, if we'd listened to him there wouldn't have been a single Kurd left in Turkey today. But what did we soldiers do? We sometimes let the Kurds go. After all, weren't we brothers in the same faith? By God, if the Pasha had got wind of this, he'd have had the whole army before a firing squad! Some of our soldiers got quite rich, charging one gold piece for each life they spared. The Kurds had plenty of money, plenty of gold. But I never took a mite from those Kurds I set free, for you can't do that to a human being. Where I come from there is no price for a life . . . Every soldier had in his sack some gold ornaments, chains, bracelets, anklets, nose-rings, all of gold. Kurdish women wear anklets and nose-rings, you know . . . Then in the spring we laid waste the foothills of Mount Ararat, burning, killing, razing villages to the ground. When it was all over Salih Pasha summoned those Kurdish Beys who had collaborated with us, and made a night of it in his tent, drinking, belly-dancing and all. I was there. In those days I didn't talk much, you know. Why, I've never talked so much in all my life as I've been talking to you.'

'I know,' I said.

'Yes, yes,' he went on hurriedly, as though afraid the words would be taken from his mouth. 'So we continued mopping up the last of the Kurds. Those who came down from the mountain to surrender we'd kill to a man, I mean those who had no gold . . . And one morning we encountered resistance on high rocky ground. There must have been fifteen of them concealed behind the rocks and shooting at us, but not to kill, obviously, or they would have finished us on the spot, for we had no cover at all. Even if they'd been firing at random, they would certainly have killed some of us, but such good marksmen were they that they aimed unerringly at a leg, an arm, a shoulder, but never to kill. Night was falling and a blizzard blowing up when I felt the burn in my shoulder and fell to the ground. I never knew how many days it was before I opened my eyes again . . . '

The rain had dwindled to a stop and a dazzling sun emerged from the clouds. A wide rainbow encompassed the sky, and along it a second rainbow, and a third and a fourth . . . Their reflection hit the water, forming a perfect circle over land and sea. We were plunged into a deluge of brightness, lights and colours whirling all around us. Another world, another dream, a paradise of colour, filling us with joy, lifting us up into the heart of the rainbow. The air smelled warmly of salt sea and earth, a soft smell as of the rainbow itself. A honey-bee settled on a board of the boat, panting, resting its wet wings. Seagulls, gleaming white, swooped in and out of the rainbow at lightning speed with shrill mad cries.

'I opened my eyes and what should I see? There I was, in a bed with clean white sheets. And beside me, leaning over me, a nurse . . . With clear blue eyes . . . Wide blue eyes . . . A pure creamy face . . . A lovely nurse with flaxen hair falling to her shoulders . . . Holding my hand, looking at me . . . Her beautiful eyes smiling . . . Her hand so warm . . . In all the years of my life no one has ever held my hand like that, so warm . . . Bending over me, smelling of roses, yes, there's no other word for it – roses! Her breath on my face, and something stirring in me, lifting me up . . . I am alive, a new lease of life . . . The days go by and I'm mending fast. Every day she holds my hand. Her eyes, blue, huge, like blossoms, there's no other word . . . Her breath so sweet, smelling of roses . . . And I praying to God: Please, God, don't make me get well too quickly . . . "What is this place?" I ask her. "Cerrahpaşa Hospital," she says. So I'm in Istanbul! "But Cerrahpaşa's a civilian hospital. What's a soldier doing in a civilian hospital?" I ask. "You're not a soldier any longer," she says. Her voice, so soft, caressing my very heart . . . Gently touching my heart . . . '

Along with the seagulls we drifted in and out of the rainbow. And the passing ships, too, were lifted into the rainbow, above the water. The sea, bright and sunny on one side, was still dark on the other and the ships glided high up in the air, now bright and gleaming, now grey like the clouds, the smoke curling up tremblingly from their funnels.

'The day draws near. I'm going to be discharged. She sits on the side of my bed, her eyes on me, pleading, ah, pleading . . . Her hand holds mine, warm, so warm, burning my heart . . . She

59

holds my hand to her heart, and my hand is on fire . . . Her hair brushes my cheek, her sweet breath . . . I shall die if I have to leave . . . And still she looks at me, her face now flushed, now pale, and she never lets go of my hand on her heart. Never have I told this to anyone. I became mute after that, speechless, silent. . . . "You're quite well now," the doctor says. "We're discharging you today." And I am dying . . . Her white cap with the red crescent, her white uniform, her flaxen hair with the ever so slight whiff of medicines . . . And she is holding my hand. "Selim," she cries, "ah, Selim, Selim, you've wounded me, wounded me. How can you go away and leave me like this, Seliiim?" Maybe she didn't call after me like that, maybe she didn't weep, maybe I imagined it all . . . My hand too . . . But no, no, no! She did hold my hand. I can still feel her warm touch. But how could I, tell me, how could I take her with me to Kumkapi? I, Selim, a down-and-out bum in Kumkapi . . . She should live in a palace, with soft white sheets, golden necklaces . . . Selim, Selim, Seliiim! How many years ago it happened, I don't know. I still hear her, wherever I go, whatever seas I sail on. Above all in the springtime, when the sea blooms like a blue flower, when flocks of storks wheel cloud-like over the sea . . . And, again, on autumn days I hear her voice calling after me. Now, at this very moment, I can hear her, the first time it has ever happened when someone else is with me. "Selim, oh, Selim, accursed Selim . . ." '

The rainbow was gradually melting away and the sky darkening again. A warm rain-heralding gust ruffled the surface of the water. Large raindrops began to plop down and the gulls skimmed low over the sea.

Fisher Selim's face was changing. He shot me such a black look that I shivered. 'You're the only one in all the world to know of this,' he uttered as though flinging a knife at me. 'You and God and me . . . Twenty years, more, an eternity I've been keeping this inside me . . .'

Didn't you ever go back to Cerrahpaşa, I wanted to ask, but I didn't dare. He answered as though I had spoken aloud.

'How could I? How could I even go near the gate of that hospital, me, Fisher Selim, a ruffian, a daredevil, rowdy, foul-mouthed, down-at-heel, stinking of fish, filthy, homeless, destitute . . . I said to myself that one day . . .' He looked at me forlornly as he drew a dirty handkerchief from his pocket and wiped his face. 'When I have a house . . .' He sighed, then rose and busied himself with the engine. 'Let's go, brother. That's what you call a friend in the Chukurova, isn't it?'

'So you've been to the Chukurova too?'

'Let me tell you. They said there were tons of money to be made in that Chukurova where you come from. So I went, and all I got was a crippling malaria fever. For three years I trembled like a dog . . . After that, I tried everything, but everything, to make money. I even went to America as a sailor . . .'

'But you haven't lost hope?'

'Never! You know, that swordfish is my last hope.'

'You'll catch it . . .'

'I will,' he said. 'And now to our nets. They should be full of red mullet by now.'

6

For three days and three nights Fisher Selim never emerged from
Beyoğlu, drinking himself senseless and falling asleep wherever
he was. Then he went to Yeşilköy and stayed for several nights
at the *kebap* eating-house near the lighthouse which was run by
Mad Memed from Adana. During the day he scoured the coast
between Yeşilköy and Florya, but kept away from Menekşe. For
hours he sat under the huge plane tree at Florya, his eyes fixed on
the sea and the Islands. The halcyon weather filled him with
dread. He longed for a gale, a tempestuous *lodos* wind, a heavy
sea. If only he could once see his dolphin cleaving through the
waters, arching like a bow as he leaped into the air, hurrying to
reach him, bursting with joy . . . How could he possibly recognize his dolphin from such a long way off? Fisher Selim would
take an oath on it, he would know not only his dolphin, but his
dolphin's shadow from seven days' distance.

So he waited, his heart in his mouth, wandering up and down
the shore, working himself into a passion of anxiety. What if
that fool fish had ventured near the boat of some son-of-a-bitch
fisherman, what if he had got plugged with a bullet in his brain?
There were times when Selim derided himself for his obsession
with a mere fish. He who had never liked his fellow-men, who
had turned his back on all his relatives, that he should feel for
these dolphins as though they were his real family! But then . . .
Who said that Selim did not like his own kind? He did, he did!
He would give his life for a cordial handshake, for one of those
too rare loving looks that make you warm and glad inside. But
why were people so callous, so craven, so suspicious of each
other, selfish, scheming, ready to gouge each other's eyes out for
a few pennies, caring only for their own small family, and
sometimes not even for them? Why was a human being so blind
to the world around him, to the sea, the clouds, the fish, the
birds, the bees, the horses? Friendless, confined in ghastly
darkness, hiding his face in his hands, shutting out the light?

Obsessed by the curse of death, mad, hopeless, terrified . . . Yet the same human being is also capable, in the marrow of his bones, with all his soul, of feeling music and songs and kisses, the dawning day, the blooming flower, eyes shining with love, the white radiance of the sea before sunrise, the smell of earth and falling rain, a warm embrace, the coming together of a man and a woman as one being, melting in sensual pleasure, the shimmering softness of an animal's fur, that ecstatic instant when you have the whole world tucked into your heart . . . There are many, many people like this, and there always will be, as joy, happiness, hope will always be. Since time began man's song has been a paean of thanks to nature for the blessing of existence, for the earth and the rising sun, the glittering sea, for springtime in flower, for pain and darkness and wickedness even, for things of beauty, lost and found again, for the joy of reunion . . .

Perhaps Fisher Selim could never have put these thoughts into so many words, but he could explain the secret of his relationship with the dolphin family very well. He was not ashamed of it. Why should he be? If those gloomy people who had forgotten how to sing and dance, to laugh and weep, could be like his dolphins, he would be friends with them too. With what joy the dolphin greeted him! What somersaults didn't he turn in the air at the sight of his boat! There must be human beings like that too somewhere, but not crammed into apartment buildings, hemmed in by concrete and iron and asphalt, poisoned by the fumes of petrol. There must be humans who are not ashamed of weeping freely like a morning shower, of laughing sunnily like an almond orchard in bloom, of bestowing compassion and love, of offering their heart with open hands . . . Oh, yes, there must be many like that in this world and if we have fallen far from them, alien now, it must be our fault . . .

One morning when the sea was still white and the light of the stars fell over the clustering white clouds, Fisher Selim at last summoned enough courage to put out to sea. He steered towards Hayirsiz Island where the dolphin had so often come to meet him in the past. The sea was smooth, empty all the way to the coast of Yalova. He turned west towards Silivri, then back again to Menekşe. And suddenly, like a miracle, like a dream . . . The large dolphin in front, the others following . . . There they were, streaming up to him, tracing luminous arcs in the air as they leaped in and out of the water! And a turmoil of light, of joy, of friendship seemed to break over the whole wide sea.

After this, his mind at rest, Selim went fishing every day, and every day the dolphin would greet him with the same unabated effusions of delight.

Then the *lodos* wind erupted and for three days waves as high as minarets pounded the shore, flooding the point of the Seraglio and making it impossible for boats to put to sea. The morning of the fourth day dawned calm and bright. The sea was transparent, fish and crabs and weeds clearly visible on the bottom. Red gurnards, swimming near the surface, shot flame-like through the blue waters.

Fisher Selim made straight for Büyükada Island. He waited and waited, but there was no sign of the dolphin. Round and round the group of islands he circled, Hayirsiz Island, Sivriada, Burgaz, Heybeli. Then he headed south towards the coast of Yalova, but there was nothing, nothing at all ... After this, Fisher Selim became a ladle and the Marmara Sea a cauldron. He never stopped. He would not give up. He ran out of water, of food, of fuel. Quickly he replenished the boat and was off again, his black forebodings increasing every minute. At the end of five days he knew it was all over and he set out in search of the dead fish, scouring all the bays and beaches along the Marmara Sea. 'Have you caught a dolphin with a family of four, a huge one, maybe three metres long, with a broken wing and a mark on his back?' he enquired of every fisherman he came across. Some only laughed, others turned him away with rude mocking words.

At length he encountered Skipper Dumpy Osman, a friend from his old Kumkapi days. 'Dumpy Osman! Dumpy Osman!'

Skipper Osman stopped his engine at once. It was many years since Selim had been known to speak to anyone from Kumkapi. 'Fisher Selim!' he exclaimed. 'Is that you, Fisher Selim?'

'Yes, yes, Osman, it's me. Wait!' Fisher Selim steered his boat alongside Skipper Osman's and jumped in. The deck was piled with dead dolphins. Fisher Selim inspected them all, one by one. 'No,' he muttered at last. 'Mine's not here.' He ground his teeth. 'Whoever ... I'll kill him!'

Osman offered him a cigarette. Fisher Selim smoked it fiercely, sucking in his cheeks. Then he came out with his story, eyeing Osman suspiciously for any sign of ridicule or scorn. But

Osman, a worldly-wise old fisherman, understood Selim's feelings. He expressed his sympathy and Selim was grateful to him.

'Do you know Skipper Dursun?' Osman asked. 'Bald Dursun, the Laz?'

'Yes . . .'

'Well, he's been out with fifteen boats, a real plunder, and he's piled up all those dolphins in Zargana Bay at Erdek, high as that hill there. Nine huge cauldrons he's set up, boiling away day and night. God knows, your dolphin may be there . . .'

No sooner did he hear this than Selim was in his boat and off full tilt for Erdek.

As he entered Zargana Bay and saw the swirling smoke and caught the rank odour of fish oil, Fisher Selim felt suddenly faint. Pulling himself together, he cast anchor and rowed over rapidly to the shore. The beach was piled with dead dolphins, each with a black hole in its head. He walked over to the tallest heap, his feet crunching over the shingle. The sailors stared at him curiously as they went on slicing up the dolphins and dropping them into the soot-blackened, bubbling cauldrons under which huge logs were burning. After having carefully inspected the first heap of dolphins, Fisher Selim passed on to the second, then to another lot behind a jutting rock. Suddenly his heart beat faster, his head whirled and his eyes went black. There, only two paces in front of him, was his own dolphin. The mark on his back was growing darker and the broken wing beating faintly.

Fisher Selim stood rooted to the spot, swaying on his feet. 'Which is Skipper Dursun?' he managed to ask after a while.

A grey-bearded, hawk-nosed, goose-necked man with a slight hump came forward. 'I am,' he said. 'What do you want?'

He had hardly spoken before Fisher Selim was at his throat. The sailors rushed up, yet not one of them could prise open Selim's vice-like grip. It was Kurdish Remzi who saved his life. The Skipper was at his last gasp, eyes bulging, lips purple, when Remzi grabbed Selim's testicles and twisted them. Touched to the quick, Selim relaxed his hold. The sailors had a hard time dragging him away and getting him to cool down.

'I'm going to kill you, Bald Dursun,' Selim stated at last, with cold fury, 'just as you killed my dolphin. I'm going to plug seven holes into your head. Just wait a couple of days and you'll see what's coming to you. So long as I live, I shan't let my dolphin's blood go unavenged.'

The steely determination in his voice made Skipper Dursun's blood run cold. 'Get going, lads,' he moaned, as soon as Selim had left. 'The man's raving mad. He's off to get a gun and he'll be back in no time to attack us. Either we'll kill him and go to jail or he'll kill us. Hurry up, we're going straight back to the Black Sea. Damn the man and damn his fish. I've got a family . . . If we stay here in the Marmara, he'll find us wherever we are. It's not a man we're running away from, it's a maniac.'

The oil from the cauldrons was quickly poured into barrels, the fires extinguished, the remaining dolphins stacked into the boats, and in no time they had steered clear of the bay and sailed away in the direction of the Bosphorus.

Before dawn Fisher Selim was at Blind Mustafa's door.

'Wait,' Mustafa called to him. 'Let me put something on.'

'I can't wait,' Selim said dully. 'I want a rifle quickly, and as much ammunition as you can spare . . .'

'Aha! I told you so, Fisher Selim, didn't I? There's no time to waste. All those fishermen from Kumkapi, Samatya, Bandirma, the Black Sea, all of them have been making fortunes out of dolphin oil. There's no time to waste at all . . . I've got a German carbine that'll shoot you every dolphin you find in the pupil of its eye . . .'

'Bring it!' Selim shouted.

'All right, all right, I'm coming. I know, I know. You're in a hurry. You're afraid the others have finished all the dolphins in the Marmara Sea. But you're so skilful you'll get some too, whatever's left of them. You'll be rich too one day . . .'

'Enough!' Selim thundered.

'I'm coming, I'm coming. Of course you must make haste. Everyone's been hunting the dolphin for months now, while you . . .'

Blind Mustafa was soon back carrying a shiny German carbine and a large bag of ammunition. 'Here you are,' he said. 'You'll pay me later, whenever you wish. I can give you some more carbines if you want. And bullets too, cases and cases . . .'

'This'll do,' Selim said. 'You'll get your money next week.'

'At your convenience . . . Whenever you wish . . .'

The stars glittered overhead as though ranged in the sky by a magic hand when Fisher Selim arrived back at Zargana Bay, nursing the German carbine on his lap.

The bay was deserted. A few logs were still smouldering and, at the foot of a rock a single dolphin lay stretched on the sand. Fisher Selim drew near and saw the mark on the dolphin's back, faded and grey now. He looked and looked, then walked away. A swarm of bees that had fled at his approach returned to drone over the dead fish.

His feet dragging, sick to death, he regained his boat, took an old blanket out of the hold, wrapped himself up in it and, laying his head on a board, fell asleep.

The sun was quite high when he awoke, the air warm, the sea, the earth, the spring day smelling of a pleasant sunny smell that filled a man with gladness. Gentle white-crested wavelets broke on the shingle. Fisher Selim cast one last glance at his dolphin. The bees were still whirring above the dead body, very low. He set his engine going and, without another look back, steered on towards Istanbul.

7

—◄•►—

Many a tale was told in Istanbul about the dead dolphin and
Fisher Selim. It was the one topic of the day, retailed with a
wealth of embellishment from the Bosphorus to Pendik, from
Pendik to Silivri, from fisherman to fisherman, boat to boat, all
over the Marmara Sea and as far up as Şarköy, Gelibolu and
Çanakkale.

'He went mad, poor Fisher Selim, stark staring mad when
they killed his dolphin.'

'Poor man, poor, poor man!'

'He wandered up and down the Marmara Sea, all by himself,
searching for his fish . . .'

'His beloved . . .'

'Like one possessed . . .'

'Enamoured of a fish!'

'How can you make love to a fish?'

'It has no breasts.'

'It's cold too . . .'

'It can't speak . . .'

'It has no arms to embrace you . . .'

'Yet he was in love with this dolphin.'

'In the middle of the market-place in Erdek he got Skipper
Dursun by the throat, the bald one who killed his fish, and he
squeezed and squeezed . . .'

'All those people in the market couldn't drag that bald skipper
from his hands!'

'And when they did, he was half-dead.'

'At his last gasp he was, Bald Dursun.'

'Serve him right!'

'What did he want with Fisher Selim's beloved fish?'

'Fisher Selim should have cut his throat.'

'Gouged his eyes out . . .'

'Skinned him alive!'

'Such a beautiful fish it was, a man couldn't help falling in

68

love with it.'

'They say that Fisher Selim would talk with it . . .'

'The fish would come to meet him in the early morning . . .'

'It would jump into Fisher Selim's boat and take up a mirror . . .'

'Don't spin us yarns, mate, we're all Muslims here!'

'Who's spinning yarns, man? People have seen this as sure as I see you now.'

'It must be true, or why should Selim suddenly lose his heart to a fish?'

'In the old days, not now, not in these degenerate times we live in, was there a fisherman on this Marmara Sea who hadn't seen a mermaid?'

'There aren't any now.'

'How could there be?'

'What business have mermaids with the likes of us now? Bastards, depraved, dissolute, base, wicked, adulterous . . . Hitting defenceless apprentices, trawling fish we don't need just for the fun of it and casting whole netfuls back into the sea, dead and putrid . . .'

'Lying, scandal-mongering . . .'

'Betraying our closest friends . . .'

'Scheming to destroy each other . . .'

'Oppressing the poor . . .'

'Laying waste the sea . . .'

'What business have mermaids in a place like Istanbul is now?'

'In a world where the underdog is always crushed . . .'

'Fisher Selim's quite right to shun people.'

'Still, there was this one mermaid left in the Marmara Sea . . .'

'Oh, come off it, man!'

'Let your whore of a wife come off it!'

'Your brothel-keeping mother . . .'

'Well, stop telling fish tales . . .'

'Let your pandering cuckolded fag of a father stop!'

'One mermaid, one only, remained in the Marmara Sea and it was Fisher Selim who found her!'

'Each morning before sunrise the mermaid would swim over from Emerald Bay at Büyükada and climb into Fisher Selim's boat. She'd take a mirror and comb her long shimmering yellow tresses. And then . . .'

'Then she would go into the cabin and lie on the bunk, waiting for Selim, all afire with desire, until he came to her. The mermaid was very jealous. If Selim looked at a human woman, if he so much as touched her hand, the mermaid would smell it out and she would raise such a storm on the sea that it would fare ill indeed for Selim.'

'Mermaids are the most jealous of creatures . . .'

'And that is why Fisher Selim never speaks to human beings, never.'

'He had three children by that mermaid, two girls and a boy . . .'

'They say the girls were the spitting image of their mother.'

'Selim took the boy to his own family. And there the boy grew up . . .'

'But that boy sits all day long on the shore, without food, without water, gazing far out over the sea . . .'

'He'll avenge his mother. He'll kill that bald Skipper Dursun.'

'No other human being's ever coupled with a fish. Only Fisher Selim . . .'

'Who knows what a strange, pleasing sensation it must be . . . ?'

'Look here, Selim's not the first one . . .'

'Ever since the time of the patriarch Noah men and fish have had intercourse with each other. Ever since the Flood mermaids have seduced the handsomest males at sea.'

'Oh, come on, man, don't talk rot!'

'Don't let me start on Selim and his dead fish-woman!'

'Shame on you! It's a sin to make fun of a man like this.'

'You'll be struck down by a spell.'

'You never know who's who in this world.'

'I wonder if mermaids have monthlies like human women.'

'But they have breasts, that's for sure.'

'Is it wide enough down there?'

'Warm . . .'

'Can they hug and kiss?'

'Did Selim . . . ?'

All this talk reached Selim's ears in the end. People made sure of that, if only to annoy him. Those who were afraid of him, who would not have dared approach him otherwise, took a malicious pleasure in making bawdy insinuations and conjectures, especially before women and girls. Fishermen are the worst scandalmongers in the world and in those days the fishing community of Kumkapi and Menekşe was no exception to the rule.

For a long time afterwards, no one saw Fisher Selim, neither in Menekşe nor Kumkapi nor anywhere else. And finding nobody to get their teeth into, the gossips finally tired of repeating to each other every day the adventures of Selim and the mermaid.

And when Fisher Selim returned to Menekşe with a red dolphin painted on the prow of his boat everything was forgotten and the embers had long turned to ashes.

8

———— <•> ————

Zeynel was waiting at the Sirkeci train terminal. His gun thrust into his belt, the very way he walked different now after his exploit, he paced up and down, erect, with stiff unbending knees, on the look-out for Hüseyin Huri and the other vagrant boys.

Hüseyin Huri was now in his twenty-first year. Long years ago his father had gone off to work in Germany and when his mother died soon afterwards he was left on the streets. A whorehouse madam took him in and he grew up pampered by prostitutes who vied to mother him with all the repressed yearning for the children they could never have. Nothing was denied him, so it was no wonder that at the age of nine Hüseyin Huri decided to be a globe-trotter. Frontiers, passports, police stations were no obstacle to him. Footloose and fancy-free he roamed from country to country and his adventures made the headlines in the press for days on end. One day there would be a large photograph of him in Germany, standing on the boarding-ramp of an aeroplane among fur-clad ladies and men in elegant overcoats, a broad smile on his full lips, his mischievous black eyes gleaming, and the papers would set aside all other matters to speculate on how a nine-year-old urchin could have boarded that huge plane. Another day, news agencies would be sending in photographs of Hüseyin Huri in London, still smiling, and the papers would vie with each other in surmising how this miracle boy could have found his way to London. Next, he would turn up in South Africa, having travelled as a stowaway in a ship, and there would be statement after statement by the authorities about him. He became quite notorious and it so happened that many rich families felt it an interesting proposition to take him under their wing. So, now in Germany, now in Switzerland, wherever Hüseyin Huri set foot in his peregrinations, a wealthy couple would press him to stay with them and as good as adopt him. They would deck him out more splendidly than their own children and have themselves photographed in the public squares of Munich, Berlin and other well-known spots, holding the boy's hand with a great show of affection. There was one photograph in particular, taken in the Swiss Alps, that made you wonder if this was really Hüseyin Huri or Riza Pehlevi, the son of the Shah of Iran, so alike did they look, the black eyes, the pointed head, the hair parted in the middle, the skis, the ski-suit. Even the bashfulness that lay under the cocky gaze . . .

And then one fine day, Hüseyin Huri was back in Istanbul. He'd had his fill of travelling. No more Munichs, Berlins, Bonns, Genevas . . . Finished the Londons, Cape Towns, Cairos, Beiruts, Stockholms, Oslos, Madrids, the sleek golden mothers and chic fathers, the pearls, diamonds, furs, the heady perfumes, the pleasure cruises in luxury yachts, the Swiss Lakes, the Italian operas – yes, Hüseyin Huri had even been taken to La Scala in Milan and for the first time this gregarious child had felt ill at ease in such an assembly, all stiff as scarecrows, the hand-kissing, the waves of heat, the heavy scents mingling with foul breaths, the fluttering furs, the jewels, the strangely attired fellow on the stage with horns and long ass's ears, bellowing and sobbing at the top of his voice, the garish colours, the spectators pretending to watch while carrying on whispered conversations with each other – all in the past, the circuses, the casinos . . . Hüseyin Huri had broken away and come to rest at the Sirkeci railway terminal, joining a gang of street waifs who slept wherever they could, in Gülhane Park, in the hollows of the old city ramparts, in empty railway cars, and spent their days picking pockets, thieving, drinking and gambling. Then one day it came to the ears of one of the stalwarts of the Democratic Party, a self-made man who had managed to acquire three factories in only six years, that Hüseyin Huri had fallen among some dissolute youths and he felt it behoved his new status to make a gesture of humanity, especially as this was the famous Hüseyin Huri who had so often held the headlines and been compared to the heir to the Iranian throne. A peremptory instruction to the police to find the boy and, no sooner said than done, the next morning the newspapers featured pictures of a tall man with pommaded hair embracing an impish ragamuffin whose bold black eyes stared straight into the camera. There were long articles on how the wealthy industrialist, Fahrettin Çoksoylu, had decided to adopt Hüseyin Huri. After that the

73

papers and popular magazines regularly published photos of the two with captions that reflected the importance of Hüseyin Huri's new father. And in all these photos, whether in the winter resorts of Abant and Uludag or in the warmer regions of Izmir and Adana, Hüseyin Huri was always attired in a ski-suit. The last photo of Hüseyin Huri and his new father was taken in the Alps with a tall snowy peak in the background. There was a new blonde mother too and all three wore ski-clothes. Hüseyin Huri looked somewhat crestfallen. His eyes were sad and his full lips pouting.

Less than a month later he was back in Sirkeci for good. For a time he wandered aimlessly about the town, still in his ski-suit. Maybe he liked it. Besides, everyone recognized him in this outfit. All heads would turn to him as he strutted up and down Beyoğlu. The trouble was his new father, Fahrettin Çoksoylu, had never thought of buying him any other clothes, not even a shirt or a pair of underpants. He wore that expensive ski-suit next to his naked body. Still, it kept him warm, and when the weather grew too hot he sold it for a pretty good sum to a sports dealer.

His acquaintance with Zeynel dated back quite some time. About a year after arriving in Menekşe, Zeynel had been sent to sell fish at the Fish Market in Istanbul and, as he was waiting for the train home at Sirkeci station, he met Hüseyin Huri, then still in his shining sports outfit. After that, Zeynel went back to Sirkeci every month or so and there he got to know Hüseyin Huri's gang of street arabs, though at first he did not take part in any of their exploits. Boys came and went, but Hüseyin Huri was always there, guiding the newcomers from Anatolia or the poorer quarters of Istanbul in the art of pickpocketing, gambling, black-marketing and all kinds of petty pilfering. He was on the best of terms with the police. Only recently he had killed one-armed Salman, the cigarette black-marketeer, and thrown his body on to the railway tracks in full view of any number of witnesses, but he was not even apprehended by the police, nor was he disturbed in the scraps and gambling games he organized under the walls of the railway station facing the Bosphorus.

Zeynel was growing impatient. There was still no sign of Hüseyin Huri. He walked over to the entrance of the station and looked towards the landing-stage of the city-line ferries, then left, to the rise that led to Cağaloglu. Some boys were selling black-market cigarettes in front of the station gates with shrill shouts . . . Marlboro, Kent, Dunhill . . . Zeynel began to stride up and down again with stiff firm steps. I am like my name, he thought, Çelik . . . Iron . . . Zeynel had chosen this family name for himself because he said he had forgotten his own name, and perhaps he had, perhaps he had never even known it. He liked his new name. Çelik. Iron. A man of iron, hard, inflexible . . . Not like Zeynel . . .

Zeynel, who a few months after his arrival in Menekşe had been eager to do odd jobs for all and sundry . . . Washing down the rowing-boats drawn up on the banks of the Çekmece stream, keeping an eye on the nets spread out to dry on the little bridge, helping the old people, Ilya, Tartar Ali, Jano, to weave nets, unwinding the skeins, attaching the bobs and corks to the nets, tirelessly toting everyone's fishing gear or extracting the fish from their meshes, lending a hand to Japanese Ahmet who repaired and painted the boats . . . With time Zeynel had grown proficient at a whole variety of jobs. He could weave nets, whitewash walls, repair taps and engines, he could do anything that came to mind, and if anyone were to offer him money he would hang his head bashfully. 'It's nothing,' he would demur, 'don't mention it . . .' And the readier he was, the more people took advantage of this silent, timid lad. Many a time on snowy winter evenings was Zeynel woken up and dispatched to Çekmece just for a bottle of wine. Even the dope addicts, when in trouble, would have recourse to Zeynel and give him their hashish to hide. Zeynel never refused anyone. He would accept every job with a smile. When a fisherman badly needed a deckhand, Zeynel would be there, ready to go out to sea any time, and if given his share of fish he would take it as though ashamed, not knowing what to do with it. If one of the women fell ill, he would wash and cook for her and carry water from the village fountain to her house. In fact, he carried pails of water to every house in Menekşe. And for all his pains, people only disparaged and sneered at him.

One person there was, though, for whom Zeynel refused to do anything, and that was Ihsan, the good friend and bodyguard of Meliha who ran that illegal brothel on the road between Menekşe and Çekmece. Ihsan was one of Istanbul's notorious thugs, never without a pair of Nagants at his waist, ready to whip them out at the slightest provocation. It was common knowledge that he had killed four men and served years in prison for it, so people were careful to keep on the right side of him. Fishermen would offer him the pick of their catch and Ihsan would pay or not, as he pleased. He extorted a levy from every casino and house of ill fame all along the coast from Florya to Sinan village and spent the rest of his time gambling or swaggering up and down Menekşe, his jacket slung over his shoulder, spitting into the sea. A large man with a long yellow moustache and a double chin, he sported garish ties, a new one every day, and trousers of the most expensive cloth, cut wide at the leg and pressed sharp as a sword's edge. In one incident in Menekşe, Ihsan had let fly at three men, leaving them lying in a pool of blood and maimed for life, and had somehow got away without even being charged. It was about a week later that the encounter with Zeynel had taken place. 'Here boy,' Ihsan had called to him, holding out a bundle of fish, 'take these home for me.' Zeynel did not move. He stood stock-still on the little bridge that led to the beach, his head held high, his eyes fixed in the distance. It was as though he never even heard Ihsan shouting at him. 'Damn the boy,' Ihsan said in the end. 'He's just a good-for-nothing idiot.' And he handed the fish over to someone else who was only too glad to do the gangster's bidding.

Once in a while Zeynel would vanish for two, three months on end. No one knew where he went or what he did. Many a job on hand came to a standstill then. Boats to be repaired or painted, engines to be cleaned, tholes or oars to be made, stoves to be dismantled and put together again, all had to await his return.

His brand-new blue jeans, very tight about the buttocks, making his small bottom seem even smaller, were wide at the legs and fell over his yellow shoes. He wore a red shirt with a bright blue tie, and a red handkerchief was thrust into the breast pocket of his navy-blue jacket. His yellow hair curled down to his collar and his reddish moustache hung thinly, as though only newly sprouting. He chewed it nervously as he watched the stream of people hurrying to the trains, the screaming street pedlars, the itinerant vendors of *lahmacun*, meatballs and *ayran*, the cars and taxis either massed in front of the station or struggling to pierce their way through into the street, all in a blare of sound of every pitch and tonality. Zeynel Çelik had come to know Istanbul quite well, but his most familiar haunts were around Menekşe and Sirkeci. These were like home to him. Yet, for the first time, it struck him how noisy Sirkeci was. The rumble of incoming and outgoing trains, the roar of the crowd, the ear-splitting honking of cars and hooting of ships' sirens, the cries of hawkers and newsboys, the swearing and cursing . . . And all the dust and smoke that burnt the throat, the greasy fumes of meat and onions fried over coals, the ground strewn with paper, fish bones, orange peel and dirty rags, the urine at the foot of the walls in pools exuding an acrid ammonia smell and swarming with black flies, the spittle on the cracked, uneven pavements, the man-deep holes left yawning all the year round with the earth piled beside them . . . How was it that he had never seen all this so clearly before? And the Konyali Restaurant across the street from which emanated the spicy odour of *döner kebap* and other heavenly foods . . . Not once had Zeynel ever set foot there. God willing, he would do so just once, before being thrown into prison . . .

At last he caught sight of Hüseyin Huri entering the station building. Hüseyin Huri spotted Zeynel at once and ran up to greet him.

'I've killed a man,' Zeynel announced, pointing to the gun at his waist.

'What! Who?'

Zeynel hung his head. 'Ihsan,' he said humbly.

'Not Meliha's Ihsan?'

'That's right,' Zeynel said with a deprecating shrug.

'Well, good for you!' Hüseyin Huri exclaimed. 'If you kill, it should be someone like Ihsan so as to make a splash in the world . . . Did he scream a lot?'

'I don't know.' Zeynel thought it over. 'Perhaps . . .'

'Mine raised the roof, the son-of-a-bitch, as he was pegging out. He bellowed like an ox when I plunged the knife into him.'

'God knows, Ihsan didn't scream so much. Perhaps not at all . . .' Zeynel was trying to recall how it had been.

'What are you going to do now?' Hüseyin Huri asked. 'Will you give yourself up?'

'Never! I've still got things to do.'

'Then, let's get out of here. Somebody might recognize you.'

'You go. I'll join you in a couple of hours.'

'Don't be later than midnight,' Hüseyin Huri said, 'or I'll start worrying.'

Zeynel stood looking after him as he walked away past the ancient, crumbling edifice on the shore and disappeared beyond the point of the Old Seraglio. Then, with trembling legs, he crossed the street and entered the Konyali Restaurant. He was no sooner inside than he repented his temerity, but the head waiter was already at his side, ushering him to a table. Zeynel went hot and cold and the only thing he remembered afterwards was the menu being handed to him by an elderly waiter. How had he ordered the food, how had he plied his knife and fork, or had he eaten with a spoon, was there bread on the table, how had he paid, had he tipped the waiter, or had he not paid at all? He found himself outside at the ferryboat landing, bathed in sweat.

Slowly recovering, he spat three times into the water and his legs took him to the antiquated Sansaryan Han that housed the Istanbul Security Department. Two policemen were on guard at the entrance of the ugly edifice, blackened by time and with its plaster flaking off in places. Zeynel's hand was on his gun, which could be seen clearly under his unbuttoned jacket, as could the bullets that filled the pockets of his jeans. Without looking at the policemen, he strode over to the wide, timeworn stairs and rushed up to the top floor, bumping into people, then clattered down again at top speed. He burst in and out of rooms as though looking for something, his hand always on the glinting butt of his gun, never stopping, never answering a word when questioned, his face tense, terrible, his eyes huge with fright, unseeing . . . And in a trice, slipping out under the startled gaze of the crowds there, he was far away in front of the Valide Mosque in Eminönü.

Pigeons rose and fell in black clouds over the courtyard of the mosque, pecking at the grain that the vendors, small boys or old people, kept scattering around. Street sellers with loudspeakers tied to their necks, hawkers of black-market goods, cigarettes, radios, television sets, cameras, had spread their wares under the arcade and between the cars parked along the east flank of the mosque, overflowing right across the street to the Iş Bank and rendering it well-nigh impossible for pedestrians to make their way through. On the side of the mosque facing the Spice Bazaar, a man was trying in vain to make a lethargic snake perform a dance so as to attract customers for a new brand of poor-quality razor blades. Further off, a conjuror, proud of his skills and casting an occasional mocking glance at the snake-charmer, was producing doves and rabbits out of a hat. He was selling engraved wooden mortars, old gramophones with loudspeakers, pocket watches, painted Konya spoons, chased Erzincan copperware and a whole array of very ancient Tokat bells of all shapes and sizes. Another wonder-worker, with flames starting from his mouth, was thrusting a long sword down into his stomach. He had stationed himself below the Eminönü footbridge where the traffic got jammed at all hours of the day, buses, cars, trucks, horsecarts, tankers, all in a tangle with the straggling throngs of pedestrians, and there he stood shouting out the merits of some old-fashioned cut-throat razors, trying to make himself heard above the din of motors, car-horns, boat sirens and yelling drivers, and such a piercing voice he had, the wonder-worker, that if he had called out from the top of that minaret there, hand held behind his ear like a muezzin, his voice would have carried right up to Taksim Square or even across the sea to Kadiköy and Moda. Beside the razors were a towel, a shaving brush and soap, and the wonder-worker kept praising his razors and belittling those newfangled coxcombs who used safety razors. Next he picked up as many as ten cut-throat razors and started passing them from one hand to the other, the naked blades sparkling in the air. And the taxi drivers looked on in admiration, while their fares were glad rather than restive at being stuck there.

Zeynel was calmer now. He wandered about gazing at the street sellers and conjurors and drifted into the Flower Bazaar. There in a large cage was a rabbit with timorous red eyes, crouching in a corner. Something stirred in Zeynel. He thrust a finger through the bars and touched the rabbit's pink nose. The rabbit never even moved.

'It's only in its first year,' the shopkeeper said. 'A fine specimen. You can use it for drawing lots. Rabbits bring luck, you know. And it's cheap too, only a hundred and fifty lira. Look at its eyes . . . Like coral . . .'

Zeynel stared at him, blanching. Suddenly he took to his heels and rushed away towards Galata Bridge. And as he ran he remembered that eagle of long ago. It was a huge coppery eagle with a wingspread of maybe three metres, a powerful beak, a head large as two fists, crooked talons and large streaked eyes, opened wide in a mad furious gaze. The eagle's owner, a short man dressed in a conical Turcoman felt cap, a frazzled fox-fur

79

coat and soft Circassian boots, carried on his back a large board pierced with dozens of holes into which were inserted slips of paper bearing fortunes which the eagle would draw out for customers. The board would be set up regularly on crowded market-days in Çekmece under the plane tree in front of the smithy. The little man would place his eagle upon it and, taking up the megaphone that hung from his neck, would start shouting.

'Roll up, roll up, folks! Come and see the golden eagle that was captured on Mount Kaf. The golden eagle hatched by the Phoenix who lives on the mountain . . . Only one egg in a thousand years does the Phoenix lay, and from that egg this eagle . . .'

At this precise moment the eagle would fling out its broad wings and flap them three times, and the large bells tied to its legs would jingle.

'Yes, folks, indeed, here you see the offspring of the Phoenix! Ninety-two years old it is, and has travelled as far as Mecca and Medina and visited the shrine of our Holy Prophet. Eagles like this never fail to visit our Holy Prophet. It will be nine hundred and eight years before another such immortal eagle appears on this earth. So we are fortunate indeed, my friends, to have this one here . . .'

The people jostling about the market-place would leave off their shopping and press up to look at this marvel which came into the world once in a thousand years.

'Golden eagles born of the Phoenix circle the globe sixteen times as soon as they break out of their egg. And their eyries are on the snowy peaks of the Altai Mountains, and also on the snowy peaks of the Himalayas. The Phoenix never lays its egg anywhere but on Mount Kaf and for seven years it sits on this egg without stirring, neither to eat nor to drink. It is nourished by the Almighty. Such a bird is the Phoenix . . . In olden times, it was the Phoenix that crowned and girded kings and sultans, shahs and beys, Jenghiz Khan, Lame Timur, Süleyman the Magnificent . . . So now, do you understand who this eagle is?'

'Yes, yes, we understand,' the entranced onlookers would shout.

'Well, this eagle, who has seen both Hell and Paradise, who still bears the odour of Paradise on its wings, can tell a man's past and forecast his future. And by laying it in the palm of his hand too! Such a mirror it will hold up to you that in it you will see your whole life, past and to come. Here, on these slips of paper, everything about you is inscribed. Perhaps you will object, you will say that all this was written long ago, long before we existed . . .'

At this point the eagle would lean down towards him, as though listening.

'Look, my friends, look how this noble bird is giving ear to us! Yes, you are right, these things were written down long before you were born and taken to the Kaaba on the wings of this eagle, there to be immersed in the holy Zemzem water and brought back again . . . And of this you may be sure: it is this great holy eagle who wrote these things, after its manner, giving us news of those who are no more, bending its thoughts to the fate of all mankind . . . And in this time and age, people's fate, their past and future are one. We are all alike, my friends, rich or poor . . . Eagles are alike too, and doves . . . So here, my friends, lies all our past and all our future. They say a man's past and his future have three hundred and sixty-two modes at the most. But here I have seven times that number, just to be on the safe side, because there are still many unfathomable things in a man's life . . .'

Here the eagle would spread its wings again and remain rigid in that position.

'And now let us begin, friends. Only two and a half lira! For just two and a half lira you will hold the mirror to your fate, you will know what will befall you all the days of your life! See how this great holy eagle is waiting for you with outstretched wings . . .'

The crowd would line up, while the eagle, its wings folded tight, a strange elongated bird now, waddled over the board, picking out slips of paper with its strong hooked black beak and putting them in the hand of the little man, who presented them to the customers. This went on till evening, the eagle growing more and more tired, its wings drooping, its neck thinning out, its feathers quivering, lustreless, wet, and there were days when its trembling legs would flag and it would drop down unable to get up again, stretched out over the board, motionless, its eyes half-closed, veiled with a white film. Then, the fortune-seller, seized with grief and fright, would gather the eagle up in his arms, throw the board on to his back and hasten away, followed by angry looks, gibes and curses from those people who had been waiting to have their fortunes drawn.

It wasn't only in the Çekmece market-place that the fortune-seller produced his eagle. His sphere of activity included all the principal places where markets were held in Istanbul, Yeşilköy, Hasköy, Balat, Kadiköy, Beşiktaş, Feriköy, Cağlayan . . . It was rumoured of this glabrous, shabby man that he owned property in the best quarters of the town, a huge mansion on the shores of the Bosphorus and partnerships in a factory and a bank, all of it earned by the eagle.

'Good for the man!'

'Every single thing that eagle tells comes true. Such a mirror it holds up to you that your whole future, your life, your death, all are laid bare.'

'It's a service to mankind that fellow is doing. He's got every right to the money and houses he makes out of it.'

'Who knows what trouble it was to him . . . ?'

'They say he went himself to Mount Kaf.'

'Seven years he waited there for the Phoenix's egg to hatch! Seven years!'

'In that rocky wilderness!'

'Seven years on that mountain! It's easy to say it!'

'How could he know, poor man, when the egg would hatch?'

'So he waited there a full seven years.'

'There's patience for you . . .'

'With patience sour grapes can be turned to sweet helva.'

'The dervish who waits attains his heart's desire . . .'

'So our little man armed himself with patience and waited on the lofty peak of Mount Kaf . . .'

'In the winter snow and blizzards . . .'

'Waited so that he could serve mankind.'.

'He's earned every house, every mansion, every farthing of that money.'

The shrill grating of brakes made Zeynel jump. He was in the middle of the traffic on the bridge and a 1960 Dodge had just avoided running him over. He flung himself on to the pavement against the iron parapet while the driver hurled anathemas at him. Unnerved, he hurried down the staircase to the landing below the bridge. The noisome stench of the Golden Horn assailed his nostrils, mingling with whiffs of the fresh smell of the sea. Children, old people, retired bureaucrats had cast their lines there and one and all had their eyes fixed hopefully on the dirty water which was coated with rotting tomatoes, eggplants, green peppers, onions, rubber balls, chips of wood, paper and all kinds of rubbish. His eyes went to a boy concentrating with all his being on a blue nylon fishing line he was hurriedly drawing up. When the fish popped out at last, tossing and pitching, and the boy finally held it in his hand, its blue back shimmering under the sun, an ecstatic expression suffused his face. His hands, eyes, hair, his whole body were the very picture of delight. The fish was twitching in his hand, the blue of its back rapidly fading. A few faint spasms, a couple of jerks and it was quite still. The boy could not take his eyes off it and Zeynel, too, found himself sharing his joy.

After a while the boy unhooked the fish and threw it into a plastic basin filled with water and there the fish seemed to come alive again in spite of its torn, bleeding mouth. The boy looked gratefully at Zeynel who had shared his joy and pride. 'Take it, it's yours,' he said with a bright friendly smile. 'It looks like I'm going to catch a lot of bonito today. This is a good start, isn't it?'

'Yes,' Zeynel replied, 'but let it stay there. A fisherman should never give away his first catch or his luck will run out. Don't you ever forget that.'

'Pity,' the boy sighed. 'Who knows how many more I'll bag by this evening? You could have taken this one home and made a nice meal out of it.'

Zeynel laid his hand gently on the boy's shoulder. Something warm was stirring within him, a tender glow deep in his heart, bright as a polished pebble. In the green basin the fish, dead now, floated with its white belly up, doleful, alone, cut off from the world. 'I have no home,' Zeynel murmured sadly as he watched the boy baiting his line. 'I've never had a home . . .'

'Then why don't you come to us this evening and let my mum make you a bonito stew? You're not the only person without a home in this world . . . My mum's a Laz from the Black Sea. Father left us. He went with another woman . . . But my mum cooks the best bonito stew you've ever tasted. You'll eat your fingers with it, you will . . . Please come this evening, Abi.'

The boy was prattling on happily. 'And if you don't have a home, what matter, we've got one. And you look as if you're from the same part of the country as Mum . . .'

'I'm from Rize,' Zeynel said. 'What's your name?'

83

'Kemal,' the boy said. 'Dursun Kemal Alceylan.'

'What a nice name!' Zeynel exclaimed. 'Who gave you that nice name?'

'My father . . .' The boy could not hide his sorrow. 'Mum's from Rize too. Father was sorry afterwards. He came back, but Mum wouldn't take him in any more. There's no one like my mum for making bonito stew, no one . . .'

'Dursun Kemal,' Zeynel said, 'do you know that I've killed a man?'

Dursun Kemal stared at him. Then he smiled. 'You don't look like . . . Not at all like . . .' He laughed, showing a set of white pearly teeth. 'What a joker you are, Abi! What's your name?'

'But I did kill a man,' Zeynel said. 'My name is Zeynel. They used to call me Little Zeynel in Menekşe . . .'

The boy suddenly noticed the gun at Zeynel's waist. His hands trembled and the fishing line he was unwinding got all tangled up. 'With that?' he stammered, indicating the gun with his eyes. 'Is it true then? But . . . What had he done to you, this man?' The tackle dropped from his nerveless hand and began to slide rapidly into the water. He grabbed it just in time and started winding it up again. 'Blood,' he mumbled stupidly. 'Was there a lot of blood?'

'The floor, the man's face were bathed in blood . . .'

'Run,' the boy cried in sudden alarm. 'Run, Abi. The police . . . Run! It's full of cops around here . . .' All the while his hands were working mechanically and he never noticed the end of the line until the hook came and stuck in his palm. As he pulled it away, blood spurted out.

Zeynel blanched. Quickly, he drew out his red handkerchief and pressed it over the wound. 'Close your fist tight,' he said.

The boy's eyes were fixed on him. 'You don't look at all as if . . . ,' he whispered. 'A man who's killed wouldn't simply stand here, talking to a little boy.'

'What would he do?'

'Run away.'

'Not me.'

Dursun Kemal's eyes went to the milling crowd pressing under the bridge. With a wide, frantic gaze he looked round and round, but everything was just as usual. The rowing-boats alongside the quays with the fishermen frying their fish, slotting them into a half-loaf with a sprinkle of parsley and onions, and offering them to passers-by, the live fish frisking in plastic basins, their vendors hawking their wares at the top of their voices, occasionally changing the water to freshen them, the costermongers, the sellers of *simits* and books and newspapers, all shouting, the shoeblacks sitting at their boxes, swinging their stained hands vigorously at the foot in front of them, the shoddily attired, pomaded young spivs at their accustomed vantage-point on the Islands landing-stage where they shot lewd remarks at the full-bottomed rich island girls, the drunk swaying to and fro against the parapet like a flapping wing, the saliva trickling down his greying beard and his voice raised in an old Istanbul ditty . . . All as usual . . . As usual, Necati, the handsome policeman, a Kurd from Urfa, on his regular beat from the police station to Karaköy Avenue and from there to the coffeehouse under the bridge . . .

'No, Abi,' the boy said almost pleadingly, 'it's not at all as though you'd killed somebody.'

'Why not?'

'Because you . . . The bridge . . . All these people, everything . . .'

'But I did kill Ihsan. And what's more I killed him every day for the past ten years. Every day . . . Three times a day. This is only the last time . . .'

'Run!' Dursun Kemal shouted suddenly. 'Quick! Look, they're here.'

'Shh!' Zeynel clapped a hand to the boy's mouth. Three policeman were just passing by. 'D'you want to betray me?'

Dursun Kemal drew back. 'No, Abi,' he said. 'Here, take this line and do some fishing until I come back. There's a lot of bonito today . . .' And off he walked towards the Valide Mosque.

It never even crossed Zeynel's mind as he plied the line with expert hands that the boy might be going to the Security Department to sell him out.

Dursun Kemal passed under the Valide Mosque arcade into the Flower Bazaar and made for a large cage where hawks of every colour and size were on display. These hawks came from the mountains of Thrace, the Istranca range, and from the rocky crags of Rize province, and Dursun Kemal was in the habit of counting them every day to find out if any had been sold or new ones added to the cage. This time he counted thirty-six. So there were five new ones today . . . Then he went on to the rabbits.

There was one that always laughed at him with its coral-red eyes. This rabbit was a jolly, friendly little creature. Who knows, poor thing, how much jollier he'd be if only he weren't in a cage? After the rabbits, the quails, the tiny snow-white mice, the minute iridescent fish in their aquariums, the many different flowers spread out like a garden, the potting soils, the lovebirds, best of all the lovebirds, bright blue and green and red and yellow . . . Dursun Kemal would watch them for hours, laughing delightedly at the way they kissed. And always the peculiar smell of the Flower Bazaar, pleasant, bitterish, intoxicating . . . but not everywhere, not if you turned towards the mosque and stood facing the minaret on this side . . . Then . . .

Almost every day Dursun Kemal would pay a visit to the Flower Bazaar, inspecting the place meticulously. He knew exactly how many flowers had been sold the day before, how many birds, mice, fish . . . And afterwards he would enter the Spice Bazaar, sniffing the many scents – cinnamon, lime tea, sage, sumac, naphthalene, mint, hot red pepper, so pungent, so bitter, black pepper, *pastirma* – and walk through to the seaway entrance, arched with red stone, and there stop and watch the never-ending throng and the shadow of the minaret stretching out over them, until something would make him go and step on the very tip of the minaret's shadow.

He slipped into the courtyard of Rüstem Paşa Mosque which smelled of shoemakers' leather, tinsmiths' burning ammoniac and chestmakers' lath, and where in the dim shadows the tiles of Rüstem Paşa glowed and glittered in a riot of colour that rose up even in the night, flitting out towards the bright city lights. In broad daylight too, many a time had Dursun Kemal seen the tiles leave their wall and glide away over Istanbul, a spangled rainbow of seven thousand colours . . . Many a time late at night, Dursun Kemal had witnessed these same tiles flowing silently like a gentle breeze towards the Golden Horn and dropping starlike over the gilded blue darkness. Who else but Dursun Kemal knew of the marvellous doings of these tiles? Who but him would remain huddled behind the carved wooden shutter of that window, forgetting home and mother, food and drink, returning to this corner day after day, month after month, in a dreamworld, never taking his eyes off the tiles? Who but him had seen them tint the sunbeams that filtered through the window or drown the Istanbul night in a thousand and one

86

dazzling colours?

But now he cast only a cursory glance into the mosque where half a dozen boys and a very old man, all wearing skullcaps, sat cross-legged, each before a Koran stand, swaying back and forth as they recited the Koran. He walked across the road to the oil-trading wharf. The red tiles of the market roof were white with seagulls. Stopping on the edge of the wharf, he looked down at the turbid brownish water, wrinkled with mud, a stagnant sea, never stirred into waves now, then at Galata Bridge, the mosques, Karaköy Square on the opposite shore, the Laz fishing scows moored to each other and almost covering the whole of the Golden Horn, the little steamboats whose funnels folded back as they passed under the bridge, loaded with vegetables and fruit . . . Something was escaping him. Yet, he thought, nothing has changed, nothing, everything's just the same . . . Then he gave a start. There, only a few steps away, five policemen had materialized out of the blue and one of them was a sergeant. Dursun Kemal turned away quickly towards Eminönü and what should he see but another policeman advancing along the wharf. And, oh, had he been there before, that gendarme posted at the entrance to the Spice Bazaar? And those three policemen in front of the vegetable market? Dursun Kemal was thoroughly flustered. Whichever way he looked he saw policemen and he felt naked, exposed, in their midst.

Dursun Kemal was not yet twelve. On waking up every morning the first thing he did was to run to the mirror and see if his moustache had sprouted in the night . . . There are a hell of a lot of cops today, he thought. I must look sharp. Another one was just coming up from Unkapani. He passed him by and turned into the narrow street that led to Mahmutpaşa, the six-pointed star badge flashing in the sun. Now the road was clear. Dursun Kemal could walk on, but . . . Ah, he wasn't born yesterday! That policeman must have posted others there under the bridge. On the other wharf, one of the five policemen, the one in top-boots, rocked to and fro, his legs splayed wide, scratching his bottom. They had no intention of going away, these policemen, and anyway the place must be crawling with plainclothesmen. So what was Dursun Kemal to do, trapped here between Rüstem Paşa Mosque, the oil-trading wharf and the sea? Traffic in the street was jammed as usual and the hooting of car-horns rent the skies. What if he tried to edge his way out, unseen, through the tangle of trucks heaped high with vegetables, the oil tankers, the cars and the *hamals* toting their piles of vegetable and fruit cases, bent double, the sweat dribbling from their noses and black moustaches? Could he reach Adem Usta's workshop safely? Impossible, he thought, they're sure to nab me . . . Just look at them there! And that sergeant spitting into the sea all the time, it's a wonder he's got any spittle left. Suddenly, he trembled as though caught in an electric current. Two new policemen were approaching down Unkapani way, arguing and waving their arms, apparently absorbed in each other, but Dursun Kemal was not to be fooled, ha-ha, no, you dumbbells . . . Quickly, he slid through a hole in a wooden palisade and, his eye to a slit, began to observe the two policemen who disappeared under the bridge, still wrangling loudly. Breathing a sigh of relief, he cautiously emerged from his hiding-place and, never taking his eyes off the other group of police, crouched behind an old delivery truck. Ah, if only those policemen would take themselves off too . . . And there now! That black-hatted man with the thin moustache and sunken cheeks, a plainsclothesman if ever there was one . . . Dursun Kemal had seen plenty of police from his fishing-post under the bridge. He could tell one at a glance. And that fatty . . . Come now, he reproved himself, who's ever heard of a fat policeman? But what about that slant-eyed, tonsured fellow with the air of a film star? Look how he scowls at you as though ready to kill . . . If Dursun Kemal had not thrown himself into the tinsmith's just in time . . .

The tinsmith was alarmed at the sight of this boy dropping into his shop like a wounded bird. 'What is it, child? What's the matter with you?'

'The police,' Dursun Kemal panted. 'The police, uncle . . .' His heart was beating as though it would break through his ribs.

'What have the police to do with you, son? What have you done?'

This brought Dursun Kemal to his senses. He stared at the kind, bearded face of the smith. 'That's true, what have I done that . . . ?' Suddenly he smiled, wiping the sweat from his brow. 'I haven't done anything at all! So why . . . ?'

He stepped out of the shop and returned to the wharf. A nauseating smell emanated from the Golden Horn. The swaying policeman was still there, scratching his bottom, spitting constantly into the sea, and the others throwing ribald jokes at each other.

'But I haven't done anything to them . . .'

One of the policemen was looking at him, he was sure of that. He had thin lips, as though slashed by a knife, and this made his mouth look like a dark pit. Yes, his eyes were fixed on him. Insistently . . . Dursun Kemal took to his heels. The sight of another policeman standing before the Central Bank at Unkapani made him turn back at full speed. He was hardly aware of bumping into a horse-drawn cart and a *hamal*, and found himself in the Vegetable Market, bathed in sweat, threading his way through mounds of tomatoes, onions, oranges, radishes, leeks, apples, crashing into empty cases, beating about as though caught in a trap. Everywhere he turned he saw a policeman. He was encircled, there was no escape. The circle was tightening about him. The fearful din of a thousand and one feet, the dust, the *hamals*, the horsecarts, the gunnysacks that barred his way . . .

'Master! Master . . .'

'What is it, Dursun Kemal?'

'Nothing, Master, I just ran too fast.'

'I've been waiting for you.'

Adem Usta was one of the last remaining makers of *yazmas* in Istanbul. He was well over seventy now, an indulgent, pleasant-faced man with a flowing snow-white beard, which he was in the habit of coiling and thrusting into his shirt to avoid staining it when he pressed the block-print to the cloths. He had long, very long fingers, and that was the first thing you noticed about him, together with the snow-white beard. And then his eyes arrested you, beautiful, clear, light eyes, like the sunlit bed of a pool.

'Here, my child,' he said and handed Dursun Kemal a square orange kerchief. 'Print this one.' He pointed to the pots of paint and the wooden blocks at the foot of the wall. 'You can choose the stamp and colours for yourself.'

Dursun Kemal had been Adem Usta's apprentice for some time now. They got on well together. It was the Master who had told the boy about the tiles in Rüstem Paşa Mosque and of their glowing colours and so made an addict of him.

The boy set to work. In a short time he had decorated the orange cloth with green cranes, blue trees-of-life and right in the centre a black deer with tall antlers.

'D'you like it, Master?'

Crinkling his eyes the Master considered the cloth, then sighed with pleasure. 'It's beautiful, child, bless you. How well you've composed it. Here, there's plenty of time till evening, why don't you dye a few more?' He handed him a roll of cloths. 'Choose from among these.'

This time Dursun Kemal selected a wide blue cloth, maybe three square metres, and spread it on the floor. Then he took his pick from the rows of wooden stamps and, dipping into the pot of orange dye, he impressed it over the blue cloth. When he lifted it, there was an orange gazelle speeding over a vast boundless desert. Kemal followed it with the imprint of a billowy white cloud. This block Adem Usta had carved long years ago in his youth and it had taken him three months to finish. On the other side of the cloth, Dursun Kemal printed a flower, a red magic flower such as had never been seen on this earth. Perhaps the gazelle was trying to reach this magic flower . . .

'Well, Dursun Kemal, you're a master hand now! Does a man vanish into thin air and neglect his work for days on end once he's become so skilled?' The Master's voice sounded hurt.

Dursun Kemal cast about for some excuse that might earn him forgiveness. 'It's my mum . . . She said to me . . .' He faltered and decided to tell the truth. 'There's such a flow of bonito just now . . . The sea's crawling with fish . . . Fish . . .' He stopped short, his hands arrested. Then, dropping the stamp on the blue cloth, he streaked out of the shop, down Mahmutpaşa slope, knocking into people, bringing down invectives on his head, until he came to the landing-stage under the bridge and stopped, transfixed at the sight of Zeynel, still there, leaning against the parapet, the fishing line hanging from his hand into the water.

'Zeynel Abi . . .'

Zeynel looked up. 'Where have you been, Dursun Kemal?' he said calmly. 'It's nearly evening.' At his feet were four large green basins with bonitos swimming in them.

Dursun Kemal stared at him in awe. 'Did you catch all these?'

'There's such a lot of fish today,' Zeynel said. 'I tied the line to the parapet here while I nipped off to buy three more basins and when I returned that large bonito was hooked on it.'

Dursun Kemal whistled. 'Well, what do you know! What a

90

marvellous fisherman you are, Zeynel Abi . . .'

'Never mind that now. Go and sell some of these bonitos. What are we to do with all this fish . . . ?'

With difficulty Dursun Kemal carried three of the basins to the end of the bridge near the Kadiköy landing-place. He was back in no time waving a wad of money. 'I sold the lot to a fishmonger, Abi.'

'Then, put that money into your pocket.'

'Abi,' Dursun Kemal said pleadingly as he stuffed the money into the inside pocket of his jacket, 'let's go now.'

'Where?'

'Home. Mum's going to cook a stew for you . . . And look, this place is crawling with policemen. Let's get out fast.'

'Let me catch another fish first. To make a seven.'

Dursun Kemal tugged at his sleeve. 'Six is quite enough, Abi. Look . . . The police . . . If they recognize you . . . That one there, that man . . . And that other one, they're all policemen.'

'Really?'

'I know them all. The plainclothesmen . . .'

'Don't worry.'

'But I'm hungry . . .' Dursun Kemal hung his head piteously.

Zeynel drew in the line with yet another blue-backed fish. Then they gathered up the tackle, stacked the basins into each other with the fish in the top one and made for the street to wait for a *dolmuş* to take them to Beşiktaş. All the cars seemed to be going elsewhere and it was half an hour before they piled into one, with the driver breathing fire and fury at the slowness of the traffic and chain-smoking all the way. Getting off at Beşiktaş, they hurried up the steep Serencebey slope and came to a rickety little wooden house with soot-blackened boards coming loose in places and with pink, blue and red ivy geraniums hanging from its windows. It was in a side alley so narrow that doors and windows almost touched each other.

'Mum! Mum!' Dursun Kemal had started to shout as soon as they had turned into the alley.

A white-kerchiefed head poked out of a window. 'Huuu . . .'

'Look, look, look!' Dursun Kemal held up the basins as he ran, while all the neighbours clustered at their windows. 'Look at all this fish Zeynel Abi's caught with my line, Mum! I caught some too, but he's a real crack fisherman. The fish came up as fast as he cast for it . . .'

'Come in, Zeynel brother,' the woman said, greeting him like an old friend. 'You're very welcome, I'm sure.'

'Mum, you'll cook him one of your fish stews, now, won't you, Mum? I said to Zeynel Abi that he'll eat his fingers too with it, he will . . .' The boy prattled on excitedly while his mother replied: 'Yes . . . Of course . . . How nice . . . Certainly.' She was a woman of dazzling beauty, with coal-black eyes, a clear golden complexion and full breasts and hips.

At their windows the neighbours, all eyes, were commenting to each other with secret signs on the visit of this fair-haired stranger. The woman promptly shut the door in their faces. This little alley was like one house, like one room even. Everyone knew everything about everyone else, what they did, what they ate and drank, how many times a night or week they made love, who had a lover, who went to the brothel, who made money by devious means, who sweated out his life like a fool working in a factory, which of the women and girls came with a shriek and which made as though they took pleasure in sex when not once in all their lives had they felt anything at all, which girls managed to preserve their maidenhood intact while keeping countless men at their beck and call, going to bed with them too. People here even knew what others had forgotten about themselves, had wanted to forget or didn't even know. At this very moment it would not take them long to learn who Zeynel was, how he had come to Istanbul from Rize and grown up destitute in Menekşe, how in the end he had killed the gangster Ihsan for no apparent reason and then met Dursun Kemal on Galata Bridge. By what wondrous means these things became known was an unfathomable mystery, but this close-packed little street which had not changed one whit since Ottoman times was informed of all that went on in Istanbul – even in such wealthy families as those of Vehbi Koç, Eczacibaşi and Erol Simavi. Every morning Geçermiş Street read the palm of Istanbul's hand and told its fortune. If you should feel like it, go and spend a couple of days there, and all of Istanbul with its slums, its posh districts, the villas of the rich in Polonezköy or on the Islands, the suicides and murders, the gambling and smuggling and prostitution, the pleasure trips to Switzerland, Paris, London, all will be laid bare for you to read like a great open book. Geçermiş Street is the key to Istanbul, this inscrutable magic city. The inhabitants of these tiny clustering wooden houses, painted a honey colour years ago but now black and cracked, live through every phase of Istanbul life, its excesses, its slovenliness, its dirt and slime and stinking rottenness, its ruthlessness and hatreds, its merry-making and joys and beauties, its warm and generous love and friendship, its integrity, its rebelliousness, live it all many times amplified. In the back alleys of Beyoğlu too, in the outer quarters of Kumkapi, Kasimpaşa, Elmadag, Istanbul is experienced just as intensely. People like Kerami Usta who makes the loveliest nacre-inlaid shoeshine boxes, yet who never in all his life has taken a step out of Bakirköy, or like Blind Agop, the tavern-keeper in Kumkapi, or like Hüseyin Huri and the other vagrant boys in Sirkeci, these are the ones who live Istanbul to the full.

The woman was bustling about at the sink. In no time she had cleaned the fish and was chopping an onion. Clitter-clatter went the sharp knife as she hummed an old Istanbul song to its rhythm. Putting the onion to simmer in a little water, she sprinkled it with salt and black pepper, then turned up the flame and laid the fish in the pan. Now and again as it was cooking she added some herbs. Over a round table she spread one of those gilt-embroidered Istanbul tablecloths, worn but snow-white, with three matching napkins, knives and forks, and an ancient gilded carafe and its glasses. Finally, in the middle of the table she placed a mauve-blooming fragrant Istanbul carnation in a slim spun-glass vase.

And all the while she darted curious glances at Dursun Kemal and Zeynel who were whispering to each other, their faces alternately brightening and darkening. They fell silent when they realized she was watching them and sat there staring at the wall where, high above the divan, hung three gilt-framed photographs of uniformed, large-eyed, moustached officers, the one in the middle with frowning brows obviously of higher rank, a pasha maybe, but all three wearing fezes with tassels falling to the right. The white divan cover was embroidered with large roses, green leaves, mauve and yellow pansies, black-eyed narcissus and a coppery grapevine. Against one of the flaking, yellowing, limewashed walls was a seascape in a sooty frame, an imitation of Ayvazovski. A couple of very old Bukhara carpets were spread on the floor, torn and threadbare, but the colours still fresh as if they had been woven that very day. The windows were hung with clean white curtains, silver-embroidered. In a corner, reaching almost to the ceiling, was a glass-paned walnut cupboard carved with roses, antlered deer and swans. This large room served both as living-quarters and as a kitchen. Under a counter topped with a cracked slab of black-veined marble were a whole array of objects, plastic basins and pails, engraved copper bowls and ewers, old Istanbul candlesticks, tin pots and pans, a huge bronze brazier burnished bright, a capacious copper cauldron, a small pumpkin of an unusual red colour, a gilded pink Sèvres dish with a rose on the lid, an old Chinese vase with a blue dragon, broken and stuck together, funny little tables of wrought bronze, a beautiful pair of bellows with silver-nielloed ivory handles. The white marble slab was the kitchen corner and on it a gas stove was burning bluely. On the wall to the left was a gold-hafted sword, its gold all blackened now.

The woman slid a green, blue and brown Kütahya coaster on to the table. 'My name's Zühre Paşali,' she said.

Zeynel's eyes were suddenly arrested by the swaying of her hips. Ashamed, embarrassed as though caught red-handed, he just managed to blurt out: 'Thank you, sister . . .'

Her cheeks dimpling, her black eyes curious, she gazed at this young man with the parched face and blistered lips. There was something strange about him, but what? She turned away, her hips moving as though she wore nothing under her skirt. Zeynel felt his throat tightening. Something was spreading through the room from the woman's hips, like a mist, like a heady smell, overpowering, and in that instant his penis rose, pushing at his trousers. She was now placing the steaming pan on the coaster, again diffusing that strange something from her body that appeared suddenly stark naked in the fumes of the pan. Zeynel broke into a sweat. His face red, he stared vacantly at his penis which was growing harder and harder. Zühre's eyes, too, were riveted on his penis. Her cheeks had grown pink, her dimples deeper, her face moist.

Dimly, as from a great distance, he was grabbing like a famished wolf at the furry mound between her bare legs, then flinging himself out of the house, the woman at his heels, catching up with him, down a slope, over a garden wall, the warm fragrance of a lime-tree around them, the woman unbuttoning his shirt, Dursun Kemal's wide stare frozen in unbelief, the woman seizing his penis, never letting go, dragging him on, the odour of crushed lettuce, the mud, the thick-trunked tree under which she fell upon him and wrenched the jeans off his legs, her moaning as she came, the searing through his body, his entering a warm maddening place . . . All far away, like a blurred twilit memory . . .

Dursun Kemal was running after him, carrying something in his hand, something he wanted to give him . . . The Beşiktaş boat landing-stage, green neon lights, the dark night . . . Through the red, green, blue, orange neon lights he rushed and on to the ferry, his penis still erect, moist. Dursun Kemal, his eyes still frozen in that wide stare, vanished slowly, just a dark green spot in the raw green of a neon lamp . . .

Suddenly Dursun Kemal's voice rang out and in that instant Zeynel recovered his senses. He was at the point of the Seraglio. Like lightning he leaped behind the empty pond, his revolver already aimed.

'Don't move or I shoot!' He raised the revolver a little above the policemen and fired three times at the lamppost. 'Throw down your guns!'

The policemen did as they were told.

Zeynel's penis was down at last. He was glad of that. Then he spotted Hüseyin Huri behind the policemen, a gun in his hand. 'You too, throw that gun down, you son-of-a-bitch.' Hüseyin Huri dropped his gun. 'Hands up, all of you . . . Kemal, go and bring those guns to me.'

The boy, who had been standing by like a shrivelled tree, moved at last. He picked up the guns.

'Now get their ammunition, their money, whatever they have.'

With great care Dursun Kemal went through the pockets of the policemen and of Hüseyin Huri and brought everything to Zeynel.

'So, Hüseyin Huri, you low-down fag, you asshole, you wanted to turn me in, eh? I'm going to kill you.'

'Don't kill me! I've been a fool. I'll never do it again, I swear. Never! I'll help you. May my two eyes drop out if I don't, may I see my mother dead and my father too . . .'

'All right, then. Get these chaps' belts and tie their hands behind their backs.'

Hüseyin Huri obeyed with alacrity.

'You, Kemal, take this gun and go with Hüseyin Huri to bring some ropes from our hideout. Hüseyin will lead you, but don't let the dog out of your sight. If he tries to run, let him have it. And don't get too near him, he's very quick. He'll jump on you and take your gun away.'

'He won't, Zeynel Abi!'

Hüseyin Huri, with Dursun Kemal following, vanished into the darkness of Gülhane Park. They were soon back with the ropes.

'Now, both of you, make these cops lie down and truss them up properly.'

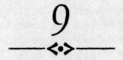

9

The sea was still pale when Fisher Selim reached Hayirsiz Island. He dropped anchor six hundred metres west and cast his line. He was tired today, stretching himself and yawning till his jaws ached. His mind was preoccupied with other things. Land prices were going up every day. If he wasn't quick about it, he would never in all his life be able to buy that land he'd had his eye on for so long and if he didn't buy it he could not attain his heart's desire . . .

Soon he had forgotten the sea, the fishing line, the world around him, and was adrift in that happy, exhilarating dream of long ago. Often on mornings like these when the sea lay all pale about him, he would give himself up to the thrill of that dream, and if a fish bit the hook, he would not even feel its tug and the fish would remain dangling like that at the end of the line.

A group of nurses in white uniforms, white stockings, white shoes, white caps, all flaxen-haired, all blue-eyed . . . Selim was passing in front of them. His shoulder hurt him. That old bullet wound . . . Something drops in the midst of the group of nurses and they scatter away out of sight. And Selim is lying on an iron bed in white sheets smelling of soap, the bullet still in his shoulder, tormenting him. He is delirious, seeing those far-off mountains he has never known. There, on the steep mauve crags, among rippling brooks, they were fleeing . . . Behind, the pounding of cannon, the crackle of rifles . . . Crossing a defile . . . So many dead, so many many wounded . . . The sniping coming from the crags . . . His father erect on a white horse, a hawk-nosed fair man with an Adam's apple jutting from his long neck and bright, very bright moss-green eyes, a Circassian dagger at his tight nielloed belt, his leather boots worn and scuffed . . . His mother, so beautiful, her waist so slim . . . Bitter, never smiling, forever keening for her three brothers who had died on the march . . . Now and again one of the horsemen fell to the ground screaming, hit by a bullet. The human flood pressing behind picked him up, laid him on a rock on the edge of the defile if he was dead, threw him over a horse if he was still alive. It was a long trek, a long battle there on the craggy heights. His father too was hit and slipped from his horse, but his mother helped him up again. The blood gushed out of him as from a fountain. His beautiful mother was steeped in it. This battle that he had never seen, Selim still lived through it, so many times had he heard it told, every detail, every instant, even the smell of gunpowder. They stopped on a plain, a wide expanse of green, bounded on the far horizon by a thin dark line that was the forest. And there on the plain, in front of the tents, the Circassian girls and youths danced the *kazaska* for joy at having come out alive from the war. Horses were being sacrificed in thanksgiving. A tall, lean, white-bearded man was the oldest of these people who had survived fire and death, a very old man with a slow pensive gait. As the smoke of the dying camp-fires floated low over the plain they saw the old man making towards the mountains whence they had come. All the people followed him. He came to a river. There was a burst of rifle fire and the old man fell into the water. In an instant the river had swept him away, out of sight.

Far, very far now, the tall snow-clad Caucasus Mountains . . . His father had knelt down facing the lofty peaks. White clouds were floating half-way up their slopes. Three times he had kissed the mossy earth. Perhaps we shall never, never ever see you again, oh, our mother, our mountain . . . He had prayed there, a long farewell prayer to his native land. And afterwards, as they trekked down south, the plains heard their long-drawn-out plaints. Selim heard them much later in the rocky foothills of the Taurus Mountains, the shrill razor-sharp cries, the never-ending keening of these war-stricken migrants for their dead, for the high mountains, for the homeland they had been torn from, heard them all over their wanderings on many mountains, Ararat, Süphan, Nemrut, Erciyes, Hasandağ . . . Heard them on the burning poisonous earth of the Chukurova where half of them perished. Then they came to Uzunyayla, and there built beautiful houses and once more raised noble horses, once more fashioned Circassian saddles and silver-nielloed daggers. And there Selim was born. And from there ran away, on the death of his father, straight to Istanbul . . .

For him, it was a time of gallivanting with girls. Especially with the Greek girls of Samatya . . . Many a one lost her heart to Selim, falling for his tall figure, his fair hair, his long reddish moustache, his deep blue eyes . . . All gone from his mind now, save perhaps that willowy Greek lass with the black eyes and sunburnt legs, for the love of whom Selim renounced his rowdy ways and took up fishing, determined to lead an honest life and to marry her. But one day when he had gone to see her as usual he found the house deserted. The mother had taken her daughter and fled to Athens. This was too much for Selim's pride. He fell back again into his old wild ways. The girl would not have left him, he knew; it was the mother who had spirited her away, and for a long time he nursed the idea of going to Athens to bring her back. And then, without warning, he was conscripted and sent to the east. There, in the midst of the snowy mountains, he remembered his mother and his child-hood home at Uzunyayla. She must be alive still and he had brothers and sisters too. They must still be there, farming and raising horses, still singing those nostalgic laments for their lofty Caucasian homeland, still dancing the *lezginka* at those endless wedding festivities. An irresistible longing to see them, to hear again his native Circassian tongue, gripped him and he swore to himself to return as soon as his service in the army was over.

He opened his eyes in a large ward of Cerrahpaşa Hospital in Istanbul, a harrowing pain in his shoulder. He moaned and she was there, with her flaxen hair and clear blue eyes, bending over him, holding his hand in a warm clasp. Three days later she had him transferred from the crowded ward into a two-bed room. She never left his side. She held his hand always, so warm, her flaxen hair caressing his face, her sweet smell enveloping him. Even now, in the middle of the sea, Selim could sense it, as fresh as long ago. He did not even know her name, not that he had forgotten it, but he had been too timid to ask and she had never told him. Or perhaps she had in those first days when he was so sick, and he had not heard, not understood. But what did her name matter? She was there in Cerrahpaşa Hospital, waiting for him, waiting till the end of time . . . Her flaxen hair a little wet with perspiration, her serious face . . . Her warm hands stroking his hair, binding his wound . . . Her eyes on him, adoring, her clear blue eyes like lucent pools, the sky distilled, so beautiful . . .

Beneath him the deep wide sea was swelling gently. Fisher Selim had forgotten the line he had cast. He was dreaming of a mild sunny winter day on the Galata Bridge, that one time when he had come face to face with her, how they had stood there, mute, motionless, while the crowds flowed past them ... The insistent hooting of boat sirens, the shrill calls of itinerant vendors, the squalling of seagulls ... As though enchanted, as though tied to each other ... How they had come apart, how lost one another in the crush, Selim never could tell. Why hadn't he clasped her in his arms? Why, oh why? He never saw her again. One year, two years, maybe three, Selim had waited for her every afternoon outside Cerrahpaşa Hospital. Even on rainy, snowy winter days he never moved from the gates of the hospital. In vain ... Perhaps he could have found her had he wanted to, but he was afraid, trembling, bathed in sweat. Whenever he caught sight of a fair-haired, white-capped nurse he would take to his heels, his heart tearing at his chest, and rush off to Kumkapi, jump into his boat and put out to sea, regardless of waves high as minarets. And later ... Later he could not bring himself even to go near the hospital.

Thereafter everything happened in his mind. Those flaxen tresses, he caressed them every day, every night, even out at sea, awake, asleep ... those soft hands, he held them always. Warm, oh, so warm ... A lifelong sunny dream ... Waiting for that day, imagining how it would be ... Their house should be by the seaside, under a great thick-boled plane tree, a house all of polished timber like that villa at Çengelköy on the Bosphorus, bright flowers blooming in the garden, a green lawn blending into the blue of the sea. That was the house he needed, nothing less would do ...

'I can't,' Selim would say to himself. 'Not like this. And, anyway, won't you wait for me? Won't you wait if it takes a thousand years?'

'I shall wait for you.'

'Our house will be on the edge of the sea. Even if it costs me a million lira I'll buy that land, and if Halim Bey Veziroğlu won't sell I'll kill him, I will. The land shall be mine and you, as a bride, shall enter the most beautiful house in Istanbul. My mother will come from Uzunyayla and so will all the Circassians. A magnificent Circassian wedding it'll be ... Everyone in their old native costume ... Circassian horses racing ... Yes, that's how it must be, that's how it's going to be.'

'But if we can't ... Does it matter? Is it worth waiting so long?'

'It is, it is! Didn't you say you would wait?'

A gentle breeze stirred the line in his hand. Slowly he awoke from his dream and took a firmer grip. The line was taut. As he started to pull it in he felt how heavy it was and how the fish was struggling deep down. An expert fisherman knows the size and weight of a fish the instant it is hooked and some can also tell unerringly what kind of fish it is.

'Come along, old father dentex,' he said gleefully, wide awake now. 'Let's see how beautiful you are.'

In another instant a largish dentex was splattering the smooth surface of the water. 'I'll build that house under the plane tree yet,' he vowed as he unhooked the fish and threw it into a tin can. He bent down to rinse his bloodstained fingers, then cast the line again.

There were times, and very often too, when it crossed Fisher Selim's mind that the girl might have married, was old now, with children maybe, that she might have forgotten him. 'She's married, she must be,' he would tell himself. Such was his relief then, as if a heavy load had been lifted off his back, that he sincerely believed this. But then ...

First her hand would rise out of the water, followed by the white cap with the red crescent, the flaxen hair blowing in the breeze, the large deep-blue eyes reproachful, fixed on him. 'Foolish Selim, coward,' she would cry. 'You're afraid, afraid! Here I am, right under your nose and you're afraid even to see me. As for me, I have loved once and for ever and I shall wait. I shall wait ...'

'I'm afraid,' Selim would say. 'You're right, Gülizar, I'm afraid. But I have no home, nothing, not a stitch on my back. How can I bring you here to this miserable stinking fishing boat? How can I touch you, Gülizar, how can I let my hand even graze your hair?'

That's what he would call her, Gülizar, when he was pleased with the way their conversation was going.

He hauled in another fish, a dentex again, and his heart lifted as he felt the swell of the sea deep down with its massive weight of billions of tons. Seagulls were fluttering above. On an impulse he let down a paternoster line on the other side of the boat and in no time he brought up half a dozen scad which he threw to the gulls. Screeching, they swooped down over the water.

The day was drawing to a close when Selim unhooked his last fish and tossed it on to the planking. It tossed and twisted, then lay shuddering between two ribs. He wound in his line and scanned the sea. There had been no sign of the big fish today, the fish he must capture and sell, so he could go to that wretched man and buy the land with the plane tree.

Just let him say it again: 'I won't sell.'

'What d'you mean, you won't sell?'

'I won't, that's all. It's my land, isn't it?'

'So you won't sell, eh? D'you think I've lived on dry weeds and rotting fish all these years and scraped and scrimped just so that in the end you should refuse me that land? Just so as to be branded a skinflint, a miser?'

'But I don't want to sell! I'm going to build a seven-storey block there with twenty-eight flats that'll sell at more than two million each . . .'

Just let him say it this time . . .

'You won't, eh? Look at me, my hair turning white already, the wrinkles on my brow so deep you can sink a finger into them! How did I get to be like this? For twenty-five years I didn't eat or drink, dry bread and water was my lot. I had my eye on this land before you even bought it. For twenty-five years I've made that plane tree grow, caressing it with my eyes. Hey, Halim Bey Veziroğlu, you own land galore from Pendik to Izmit, from the Old Walls to Tekirdag, you own seven housing estates that bring in a goodly rent. You own commercial buildings, hotels, factories . . . Look, Veziroğlu, that land's mine. You just name the price. Look Veziroğlu, we're the same age, you've got children and grandchildren, all I have is a pair of blue eyes, wide, eager, watching and waiting for me . . . Waiting for me, flaxen-haired, no one's ever touched her . . . Look Veziroğlu, you've got everything the world can give, but it's you who are wanting . . . I'm a fisherman, I know all about the infinite variety of the sea, of its many creatures, of its moods and currents. What do you know but how to count money, to swindle and cheat and lie and amass still more money and land? Look Veziroğlu, those olive trees along the sea, it was I who planted them on that land twenty-five years ago. How could I have known you were going to buy it? Get this, Veziroğlu, nobody's going to put a stone, a stick on that land without first taking my life. Here's all the money I've saved . . .' Veziroğlu counted the money quickly, then sat back in his armchair, threw back his head and laughed. 'No, no, what you've got here wouldn't buy fifty square metres of my land . . .'

A couple of years later Selim had saved some more, especially that last year when bonito sold for fifty lira the pair. He went to Veziroğlu again. But Veziroğlu laughed still more. 'It's a bare twenty-five square metres you could get with this money now,' he said. Selim insisted, even pleaded with him, then stuffed the money back into his pouch and stormed out of the room. A few more years and he was back. He had caught a lot of fish, saved a lot of money. 'Look Veziroğlu, those olive trees there, I planted them. I've waited this long for that land. It's crying for a house, a bride, flaxen-haired. I've staked my life on it . . .'

'Get along with you,' Veziroğlu scoffed. 'This money won't buy ten square metres of my land at present-day prices . . .'

'I'll buy it, see if I don't,' Selim swore wrathfully, and he left, heaping curses upon Veziroğlu. No, he would never give up. If only he could catch the big fish, ah, then he'd go to him one last time, to that ruthless man. Let him refuse then . . . Just let him dare! Large yellow roses he would plant in the garden. There would be blue hydrangea blooming in the shade of the rocks, and a bed of poppies . . . In the little bay three fishing boats, all equipped with radar . . . Even in the stormiest weather he'd put out to sea and she would wait for him, her hand on her heart, dying of anxiety. Yes, her flaxen hair blowing in the fierce northeaster, she would be there as Selim's boat left the shore to brave the raging waves . . .

'Let him refuse this time! Just let him!' Angrily he spat into the sea, pulled the cord to set the motor going and steered for Menekşe.

The sun was sitting on the sea when he made land, a very pink sun, mauve-tinged, dyeing the surrounding clouds mauve-pink. From the west three planes glided through the sky like three drops of gold, blending into the pink, emerging again, leaving a golden vapourous trail in their wake.

Three plainclothesmen were on guard in the coffee-house, working on the theory that a murderer always returns to the scene of his crime. They sat there, taking turns day and night, waiting for Zeynel. They were all three country lads and had been taken into the police force because, so they were informed, they were pure-blooded, unalloyed sons of a noble race. Convinced of this privileged condition, they nursed a strong animosity towards all Circassians, Kurds, Lazzes, and more particularly Jews, Greeks and Armenians. They felt a special hatred for Zeynel because he was a Laz. Just let them get their hands on him, they'd skin him alive, that Laz, fill his mouth with bullets ... They never exchanged a word with the fishermen in the coffee-house. Casting supercilious looks at them, they sat apart in a corner, talking in whispers about how one day they would kill all the socialists and purge the noble blood of the Turkish nation. They had the strength for that. In the police force alone they numbered twenty thousand, avenging eagles every one of them, of pure and noble race, sworn enemies of those Kurds, Lazzes, Circassians, Jews and immigrants, especially the immigrants, and the Salonicians, those turncoat Jews ... Yes, it was those people of impure blood who were ruining this country. But the Great Leader would soon give the word, and then ... A very sound reckoning by their Great Leader and his Grey Wolves: three million people had to be killed, another five million banished, and thus Turkey would be redeemed. And then the true Turks would be brought over from Central Asia, in particular the descendants of our Kirghiz forebears.

It was Mustafa Çelikdağ mostly, the tall fair-haired one with trousers pressed like a sword's edge, who was talking, his mouth foaming as he did so. Before enrolling in the police force he had been a day labourer in Adana on the orange plantation of one of those self-proclaimed patriots, Türkoglu. The skin of his hands was still in shreds from the orange spikes.

'Three million! Three million!' he repeated, almost choking with excitement, his eyes bulging, the veins in his neck swelling.

Ali Sarpoğlu was cool and mild-natured. He did not speak much. Only once he burst out as though struck by a fit of epilepsy. 'Let me get at those leftists and you'll see how I'll cut their throats ... One thousand, two, five, ten thousand ... Very slowly, with a blunt saw ...'

Durmuş Yalinkat came from the barren Tektek Mountains of Urfa. For years he'd made a six-hour journey every day, toting water to his house on his back with never a murmur. Then his mother died. A whole week she remained in the house in the summer heat with a stunned Durmuş watching over the bloated, putrefying body, until some neighbours, alerted by the smell, took her away by force. Without his mother, Durmuş was left utterly at a loss, not even eating and drinking. In the end, the village agha managed to get him employed as a shepherd on the Ceylanpinar State Farm. Later he was conscripted for military service and then passed on into the police force, a promotion due to his pure blood . . . That was when he began to count up the people he would kill when the time came. First, he had a grudge against the agha who had made a mere shepherd of him. Then he dreamed of killing all the aghas in the country. The farm overseers and the tractor drivers who had looked down on him were also on his list, and even the other labourers, but the shepherds would be made policemen. He confided these ideas to a student at the crafts school who had the rank of captain in the secret organization he belonged to. This man had been arrested after killing a leftist student, but released on the spot. Very good, the captain had approved, those workers are all communists anyway, they should be wiped off the face of the earth . . . Yes, that's what Durmuş Yalinkat would do. And this family name he hated, he'd soon change that. Yalinkat . . . Singlefold! Which low-down headman had saddled his family with a name like that, a name for paupers? To be poor was a despicable thing, all poor people were evil, all communists. They must be done away with. That's what they had taught him on the police course. So he was waiting patiently, secure in his faith, for the day when those three million communists would be exterminated and the country purged at last.

'Are you Fisher Selim?' Durmuş Yalinkat asked sternly, when Selim entered the coffee-house. He fixed a frowning gaze on him as he had been taught on the course and as if Selim was one of the three million who had to be killed. He had learned all about Selim here in Menekşe.

'Yes,' Selim answered without looking at him.

'You're to go to the police station tomorrow to make a deposition.'

'All right,' Selim said.

'And you too,' Durmuş Yalinkat said, turning to me.

'All right,' I said.

Just then Hasan Bey came in with his billowing mane of white hair. The policemen could not bear to look at him. How could they, when he headed the list of those they were going to kill soon, very soon? Hasan Bey, a poet who had been living for twenty years now in a shack in Menekşe, was their chief enemy, his name one of the first on the list of communists they had been given on the police course, and so they were the more astounded at seeing him here in Menekşe, loved and respected by all. How could these people speak to such a man so freely, unafraid?

His hands trembling with excitement, Durmuş produced a notebook from his pocket and began writing down the names of the fishermen who greeted Hasan Bey.

'What are you doing, Durmuş?' Mustafa Çelikdağ asked.

'I'm going to report these people to the chief of police.'

'What good would that do?' Mustafa Çelikdağ sneered. 'It's clear now how this man's got away with everything all the years he's been living here! You must put that police chief at the head of your list.'

'I'm going to give this list to the Great Leader,' Durmuş Yalinkat said, 'so that when the time comes they shouldn't forget these people here who dare to talk to that man. They're all fishermen here, aren't they, without a penny to their name, and that man's been poisoning their minds all these years . . .'

Mustafa Çelikdağ said nothing. What did it matter, let him report these miserable paupers, he thought. If they'd had any spunk, they wouldn't have remained poor fishers all their lives anyway. Let them be killed too and the fatherland purged once and for all!

'Tomorrow at ten o'clock!'

'All right,' I said. And I left with Selim, not even stopping for a glass of tea. We went to sit on a bench in the Municipal Park.

'Did you notice the eyes of those cops?' Selim said. 'They're crazy.'

'Funny,' I said. 'I had the same impression.'

'I've seen eyes like that before,' Selim said. 'They're the eyes of a killer. I was scared. And for Hasan Bey most of all.'

'I was scared too. What's more, they've got the backing of the ruling party . . .'

'You don't say.'

'It's the truth.'

'If I'd had a son,' Selim mused, 'these fellows would have

killed him. Still, I wish I'd had children. To be childless, that's the worst of all. That Zeynel now, these people'll gun him down the minute they see him, the poor lad.'

'But Zeynel tried to kill you too, that night.'

'He wouldn't kill me. He could have done it that night if he had really wanted to.'

'What makes you think that?'

'Because he doesn't fear me. He's the kind who only kills when he's afraid. He was afraid of that Ihsan . . .'

'But what did Ihsan do to him? Nothing.'

'That's not the point. Who knows what particular thing, what event can arouse fear in a man?'

'Maybe one of Ihsan's rival thugs or black-marketeers put Zeynel up to it . . .'

'No, Zeynel's not the kind to plan anything. Never mind. Let's go fishing tomorrow, after the police station. Perhaps we'll come upon my fish. And then . . .'

'We'll go straight to the Hilton, won't we?'

'Just let Veziroğlu refuse to sell me that land then!'

IO

———— ‹•› ————

'Have you trussed them up tightly?'

'Yes, yes,' Hüseyin Huri stammered.

'So, Hüseyin,' Zeynel said, 'you were going to turn me in, eh?'

'Won't they catch you anyway?'

'Never! See these guns here? I'll fight the cops to the last bullet. I won't die before killing them all. As for you . . .' He bore down on Hüseyin Huri, who backed away. 'Don't run, you dog. Answer me. Is it normal among the likes of us to set a trap for a comrade?'

'No, but . . .'

'Then haven't I got the right to kill you?'

'But I was only going to have you arrested to save you from the gallows.'

'Isn't death better than prison for me when I've no home, no family, nothing?'

'No, it isn't,' said Hüseyin Huri. 'I was locked up many times and I survived, didn't I?'

'Yes, but they raped you in there.'

'You're too old to be raped,' Hüseyin Huri said.

'I'd die of hunger.'

'No one who's killed a notorious thug like Ihsan goes hungry in prison. Why, your fame's spread to all the prisons of the town by now. And anyway, there'll be an amnesty soon . . .'

'Who d'you think you're fooling, you whoreson? We had an amnesty only the other day!'

'There'll be another one soon. No murderer stays locked up more than five years now. Come on, Zeynel, give yourself up . . .'

Dursun Kemal stood on tip-toe to reach Zeynel's ear. 'Let's tie him up too. He's sure to free those cops the minute we're gone.'

'You're right,' Zeynel said. 'Lie down!' he shouted to Hüseyin Huri. 'Quick!'

He trussed him up, then checked the other policemen, found

the ropes loose and tightened them with strong fisherman's knots. 'Let them stay here and freeze till morning,' he laughed. 'By then we'll be way off in Ankara. Take these guns, put them into their holsters and tie them to your belt. The cartridges too . . .'

In no time Dursun Kemal had collected all the guns. 'Look, Abi, I'm just like a policeman now!' he cried.

The policemen were pleading and threatening in turn. 'I'll make mincemeat of you,' their chief yelled. 'You bastard Laz, untie me at once. I'll show you what a Turkish policeman can do!'

'Zeynel brother, set us free, we shan't do anything to you . . .'

'Look, Zeynel, if you untie me I'll help you get out of the country.'

'Look, Zeynel, I swear I won't let them beat you up at the police station. Word of honour.'

'D'you think you'll get away with this, you whoreson?'

'I'll skin you alive the minute I get my hands on you!'

'Let's go,' said Zeynel. 'These people are making me mad. I'll shoot them all if I stay here another moment.' He strode up to the policemen. 'Shut up!' he raved at the top of his voice, stamping his foot. 'Be quiet! Don't force me to bloody my hands . . .'

'Abi,' Dursun Kemal appealed to him, 'may I take one of these policemen's caps?'

'Yes, but hurry up.'

Dursun Kemal began trying on one cap after the other. 'Not one of them fits,' he said at last, crestfallen.

'Never mind,' Zeynel said. 'I'll find a cop with a narrow head for you and then you can have his cap.'

They crossed the Gülhane Park bridge at a run and came to Eminönü where they hid behind the tarpaulin curtain hanging over the door of the Valide Mosque.

'Well, I'll be damned!' Zeynel exclaimed. 'My good friend Hüseyin Huri! It was touch and go. A good thing you thought of tying him up too. If we hadn't . . .'

'He'd have set those cops free at once.'

'And we've got three guns too, a good haul. Where shall we go now?'

'You said Ankara on purpose, didn't you?' Dursun Kemal asked.

'Of course! To put them on a false track.'

'Hurray!' Dursun Kemal cried. 'Let them hunt for us in Ankara now.'

'We must hide these guns somewhere.'

'I know the very place,' Dursun Kemal said. 'In the mosque, behind the *mimber*. There's a cache there. You just have to draw out a tile. I know it because I went to a Koran course here for three years.'

'But the door?'

'The *imam* used to hide the key in a crack here . . . . Here it is!'

'Good for you, Dursun! Why, with the two of us working together, all the police in the world won't get the better of us, God willing.'

'God willing,' Dursun Kemal said proudly, as he inserted the heavy key into the lock. The door snapped open and they crept in. The cache was under a window behind the *mimber*. They lifted the tile, thrust in the guns and closed the hole up again. 'Quick,' Dursun Kemal whispered fearfully. 'There may be someone inside.'

Zeynel held his hand as they made for the door. With difficulty Dursun Kemal locked it again and put the key back in its hiding-place. 'Let's get away from here,' he said in a trembling voice.

Lifting the heavy tarpaulin curtain they emerged on the seaward steps of the mosque. The sea was choppy, Eminönü Square deserted. Only the lights of landing-place number two were shining. At this time of the night Eminönü was like an abandoned camping site, strewn with garbage and invaded by foraging stray dogs. They came in droves from Gülhane way, snarling at each other, dogs of every description, degenerate wolfhounds, hunting dogs, shepherds, emaciated greyhounds, mongrelized lapdogs . . . The fetid smell of the Golden Horn floated over the square, warm and nauseating.

As they were walking past landing-place number four, Dursun Kemal grasped Zeynel's arm. 'Look,' he said, his voice choking with fear. 'Over there! They're coming this way.' He pointed at the arcade of the mosque, then at the gate of the Spice Bazaar 'Look Abi, look!' Policemen were emerging out of the darkness like cockroaches. Zeynel and Dursun withdrew into the shelter of Galata Bridge. Some street pedlars were asleep there, curled up at the feet of their handcarts. A bunch of street waifs, their heads resting on each other's bodies, huddled together, also fast asleep. There they would remain until some nightwatchman chased them away.

Out of nowhere policemen appeared in ones and twos under the bridge, holding their guns at the ready.

'Abi, they're going to kill us . . . Look, they've drawn their guns!'

Zeynel seized the boy's hand and rushed up the steps on to the bridge. On they ran, past the Kadiköy landing-stage and into a side street where the street lamps gave out less light than a barn lantern. But at Necatibey Avenue their way was blocked by another lot of policemen and they turned back. The whole area was crawling with policemen.

Shrill police whistles . . . Blaring ships' sirens . . . The massive old Galata Tower with its circle of crude green lights at the top, reflected in the Golden Horn, warped and broken . . . The Golden Horn, a noisome, nauseating dark well, yellow, red, mauve, the many crude colours of the neon signs stirred by its swell . . . The Golden Horn, that deep well surrounded by huge ugly buildings and sooty factories, spewing rust from their chimneys and roofs and walls, staining the water with sulphur-yellow rust, a filthy sewer filled with empty cans and rubbish and horse carcasses, dead dogs and gulls and wild boars and thousands of cats, stinking . . . A viscid, turbid mass, opaque, teeming with maggots . . . A strange musty creature, the Golden Horn, a relic from another age, battered, agonizing, rotting away, yet still restless . . . Lengthening, undulating, weaving into each other, the neon lights danced over this dark fathomless well. Seagulls whose stock went back to old Byzantium, weathered seagulls, wing to wing in the darkness, glided in and out of the multi-coloured neon lights, screeching, their cries mingling with the police whistles.

They managed to reach the sheds of the Karaköy fish market. It was dark and full of cats. Their feet brushed against mounds of soft warm fur. On they pressed through narrow alleys, the whistling growing louder, nearer. They took refuge in one of the boats moored to the quay. Seagulls fluttered frantically over their heads and the police began to close in on them again. They fled, jumping from one deck to another, all along the fishing boats that were strung out in close formation right up to the middle of the Golden Horn. At their heels the police, in their ears a thundering roar . . . In a hull smelling of tar a brawny, bushy-bearded man grabbed Zeynel by the neck, lifting him up like a rabbit. 'What's this in the middle of the night, you scapegraces?' he said. 'Where d'you think you're going?'

Then they slept, the neon lights sweeping over them, staining them yellow, green, red, blue. The ring of bulbs at the top of the Beyazit fire tower glowed a bright blue far up in the sky, higher than any minaret.

Zeynel's nose, his mouth, his hands were bleeding and he was pounding away at something with his fists. Dogs were dragging a carcass along the street that led from the timber mill to the Central Bank. On, past an old ramshackle wooden house lean-ing precariously against a concrete wall . . . A woman emerged from the house, heavy-breasted, dressed in black, with large languid eyes and wide hips billowing way behind her. Zeynel went up to her, his mouth still bleeding. And all around the police, closing in again . . .

Menekşe . . . Day was dawning over the sea, a pure white satiny sea, smelling sweet and fresh. Özkan straightened up in the boat he had been sleeping in. He rubbed his eyes, drank a draught of water from a bottle. He reeked of fish even more strongly than Fisher Selim. His whole body, his clothes, bed-ding, even the rusty engine of his boat were impregnated with the smell. Fish scales and skins were stuck to his hair, eyelashes and clothes. It was as though he had lived for years in a fish stack.

'Özkan, Özkan . . . It's me, Zeynel, and this is Dursun Kemal, my friend. I've just trussed up half a dozen cops and left them lying at the point of the Seraglio . . .'

'Run!' Özkan cried. 'Get out of here quick. The place is full of cops, lying in wait for you. Run!' All in a dither, his eyes white with fear, his face glassy, white as chalk . . . 'Run, Zeynel, run!'

Cocks began to crow, dogs barked, police whistles blared, bullets whizzed, cleaving through the darkness. The smell of powder was everywhere. On the steps of Menekşe railway station three policemen were waiting.

'Help, Fisher Selim, save me . . .' And as he said it he froze, arms, legs, mouth locked tight, teeth clamped to breaking, a stiff mass steeped in blood. The policemen were running up, their guns drawn.

'That way,' said Fisher Selim, pointing to the crooked little station building. 'They've gone that way.' And the policemen took up their old positions on the steps of Menekşe station.

Zeynel and Dursun Kemal were locked together, but Zühre Paşali, Dursun's mother, spreading that maddening woman's odour around her, approached and tried to pull them apart. In front of Azapkapi Mosque the Golden Horn stinks of rotten flesh . . . Zühre Paşali is sheltering them under her large breasts . . . Zeynel breathes in that moist, acrid, misty odour, his limbs slowly loosening. Masses of seagulls are fluttering over the closely moored boats that hide the sea, most of them serving as dwellings, with children emerging from the boats as from antholes, playing and jumping from one boat to another, the largest boat serving as a football field. On and on Zeynel and Dursun Kemal sprinted along the moored boats . . .

'Stop,' Zeynel said. They stopped, they ran, they sprang into a bus going to Beşiktaş.

'Mum, Mum! Listen to what we've done! Eleven cops . . . We took their guns. Everyone's afraid of Zeynel, all the cops . . . We went to Menekşe too and we saw Fisher Selim!'

'Shh! Are you crazy, both of you? Don't let the neighbours hear you. Besides, they know all about Zeynel. This place was crawling with police. They've gone away now, but they'll come back. They'll kill you, you crazy fools. Run, Zeynel. Go away . . .'

That misty female smell was spreading again like smoke through the house. Zeynel heard nothing, saw nothing. The smell was enveloping him, powerful, binding . . .

'Dursun, you stay here by the door,' he said. 'Don't stir a step. If the cops come, give a cough and I'll escape through the window.'

Trembling, he seized her hand. It burned him. He let go and, hanging on to the old wooden banisters, dragged himself up the stairs, faint, beside himself. She followed and began to undress him with quivering hands. Naked, yellow, his ribs standing out, he stood there, hunched, his penis erect, bonelike, pointed. She threw off her clothes and drew him over her on the bed. Zeynel was paralysed, trembling, unable to do anything. 'Not like that, not there,' she moaned. 'No, no, here . . . No, wait, here . . .' With a cry Zeynel found himself locked into the woman, almost unconscious, lost in her moist flesh, her breasts, the feel of her body moving under him. He was regaining consciousness, breathing in the odour of their mixed sweat, when the whistles sounded. Dursun Kemal was coughing loudly, insistently, Zühre Paşali was up and dressed in an instant and Zeynel too, quickly, in the darkness. She jumped out of the back window, he followed, and holding hands they slipped away, a loud uproar in their wake, whistles blaring, cocks crowing, dogs barking, women screaming, a tumult that resounded down to the Bosphorus. They raced through an abandoned mulberry orchard and the pebbly courtyard of a school. Zühre Paşali was leading him somewhere. They slid under an arch, only just avoiding a volley of shots. Swiftly she pulled him down and they rolled over to the door of an apartment building.

'You must go away. Leave me,' Zeynel whispered. 'The police will kill you too.'

'I can't leave you like this. Is it the first time, tell me, is it? The first time you've been with a woman?'

'Yes,' Zeynel said humbly, 'the first . . .'

'How can I leave you? You're only a child, a child! The police will kill you.'

They crept down to the basement of the building. It was like the bottom of a deep well here. The place smelled of mouldy bread and urine. They heard the tramp of police boots above them, thump thump thump, and held each other close. Zeynel was breathing in that heady odour again, drowning all other smells. Of their own accord, his hands were on her breasts, between her legs, caressing. Abruptly, she jumped up. 'Come,' she said, 'we must get out of here.'

Outside, it was raining. The street lamps were extinguished, the darkness complete. From Zühre Paşali's quarter of Beşiktaş came the faint murmur of voices. They ran down a slope, tumbling in the mud, climbed over a wall into a vegetable garden and their feet sank into soft warm soil planted with cabbages, radishes and lettuces and also with fragrant marigolds. There was a well there, its white stone distinct even in the pitch darkness. Somehow the rain had not touched this garden. Suddenly, they made out shadows advancing towards them from a corner of the garden. They fled, breathless, and it began to rain again. In front of them was an imposing iron gate. 'Here,' Zühre whispered. She heaved herself at the gate and it broke open. 'This is the Ihlamur Palace,' she said. They walked in and came to a small pavilion that smelled of dry grass. Zeynel flung himself upon her and tore off her clothes. They rolled on to the dusty floor.

When did they get out of the pavilion, what happened to Zühre Paşali, when did she leave him? He had no idea. He was in Beyoğlu in the first half-light of day, his penis still erect, wandering past uncollected dustbins, assailed by foraging dogs and cats, past ageing whores and huge-moustached sleepy garbage collectors with horse-drawn carts, through the warm fumes of milk and baking bread issuing from basements, his hands in his pockets, a feeling of ineffable well-being inside him, his body fresh and light as air, Zühre's odour in every pore of his skin, dreaming . . .

He spotted a small boy who looked like Dursun Kemal and approached him. The boy's eyes widened and he took to his heels. Zeynel was surprised. What had come over the child, what could have frightened him so? He walked on towards Tünel, looking into people's eyes, and one and all avoided his gaze and shrank from him. From the gates of the Underground a sleepy silent crowd emerged. Never had Zeynel seen a crowd so silent, so hushed. He looked at the sky. It was overcast. A warm rain-heralding wind, smelling of gasoline, licked his face. Leaning against the wall of the Swedish Consulate, he scraped the dried mud off his clothes, then strolled back to the Hachette bookstore and paused in front of the window to contemplate his long, slim figure reflected over the many-coloured books in the window. He could not see himself clearly enough, so he passed on to another, darker window. Stroking his moustache, he decided it was just like Fisher Selim's. He was as tall as Fisher Selim too, or just about . . .

At Galatasaray he stopped short before a large bank and stood staring as though mesmerized. Passers-by were jostling him, stepping on his feet, pushing him this way and that, but he paid no attention. Rousing himself from his trance he ran to the Underground, bought a token and got on the train. He was soon out in Perşembe Market. There he bought a good-sized nylon bag, then searched through the market until he found a rusty iron ball that looked just like a bomb. He shoved it into the bag and quickly turned back towards Beyoğlu. Unseeing, oblivious of all around him, bumping into people, he planted himself again in front of the bank, unable to take his eyes off the cashier's desk. The entire façade of the bank was made of glass.

With a superhuman effort he darted across the street and shot into the bank, making straight for the cashier's desk.

'Hands up!' he cried. 'Hands up, all of you!' He opened the bag and rolled the iron ball towards the entrance. 'This is a bomb,' he announced as he drew his gun. 'I want you to put all the money you have into this bag. If you leave a single kurush in the cashbox I'll touch off that bomb as I leave. It's powerful enough to blow up the whole of Beyoğlu.'

Several bank employees lost no time in stuffing thick wads of money into the bag.

'That's all,' a young man with long hair said at last. 'There's not another kurush left . . .' His face was ashen.

Zeynel was pale as a sheet too, in a worse state than the bank employees. He heaved the bag on to his back and went to the door, his finger on the trigger of his gun. A crowd had been gathering outside. Panic-stricken, he fired. The crowd backed away hastily, scrambling over each other, and Zeynel, still firing, crossed the street and dashed down the Boğazkesen slope. It was raining again and the day had grown dark. Some people were after him, a policeman, two watchmen . . . He turned, aimed his gun at the policeman's belly and shot him down. The others threw themselves to the ground. Swerving into a narrow alley, he darted into a carpenter's workshop where a young boy, who looked to be about sixteen, was working. At the sight of him the boy screamed. Zeynel swooped upon him like an eagle. 'Be quiet,' he hissed, 'or I'll pump you full of lead.' The apprentice shut up at once. 'Don't you make a sound! I've just robbed a bank. I'll give you some money too.' On the spur of the moment he picked up a coil of rope that was lying around and bound the boy's hands. 'Is there another room here?'

'Yes,' the boy said, quite at ease now, as though this were some sort of game. 'Look . . .' He pushed open a small door into a recess that was full of sawdust.

'I'm going to lock you up in here. Where's your boss?'

'He's gone home. He won't come back today.'

'What's your name?'

'Mutlu.'

'Well, Mutlu, you'll have to stay in there for a while.'

'All right,' the boy said, secretly thrilled at this adventure. 'Did you bag a lot of money from that bank?'

'A lot,' Zeynel replied. 'Now, get in there.' He was just closing the door when he drew it open again. 'I ought to gag you really. What if you shout when you hear someone come in?'

'I'd be a stinker if I did, Abi,' Mutlu declared. 'We're men here. A man doesn't give another away, especially a big brother who's robbed a bank!'

Zeynel closed the door upon Mutlu. He took the bag of money he had left lying near the entrance and shoved it under the workbench. Then he slipped on one of the aprons hanging on the wall and, seizing the largest plane he could find, started planing a board on the bench. He went on with this till nightfall. The board had been planed to the thinness of a sheet of paper when he left off. He opened the door to the little room and switched on the light. Mutlu was lying on the sawdust, fast asleep. Who knows, Zeynel thought, how hard this child must work, how tired he must get that he can sleep so soundly . . . The room smelled of pine, a heady, dizzying smell. He knelt beside the boy, thinking of the many many times he himself had dropped asleep like that, tired out, insensible as a stone. He could not bring himself to wake him. Putting out the light he closed the door and crouched down, overcome by an intense weariness. If he let himself go he could drop off right there and sleep for three days and three nights without stirring. Struck with fear, he leaped to his feet, took a wad of money from his bag, opened the door to the little room again and turned on the light. Mutlu was still lying on his right side, his lips pouting, breathing peacefully. His heart swelling, Zeynel stuffed the five-hundred-lira banknotes into the boy's pocket and turned off the light, leaving the door open. A big blue apron on the wall caught his eye. He took it down and wrapped the bag of money in it. Then, still wearing the other apron, he went out. Threading his way through narrow side alleys, he came to the Kabataş boat landing. A battered old taxi was driving down the hill from Galatasaray. He hailed it. 'To Topkapi,' he said.

The driver, a seasoned old-timer, sized him up. 'I can't take less than a hundred and twenty-five,' he said.

'I've got a hundred lira,' Zeynel countered. 'Not a kurush more. What does a carpenter earn these days, anyway, boss . . . ?'

'Hop in, hop in,' the driver said magnanimously. 'Carpenters make a pretty good penny, I know. Still, I'll let you off with a hundred lira, carpenter-lad!'

'Thanks, boss.' Zeynel sat down beside the driver, wedging

the bag between his legs and the door. 'You can pick up others in the back if you like to make a *dolmuş.*'

In this manner they reached Pazartekke, picking up at one time or another a traffic policeman, two women, four shaggy-haired youths whose breath reeked of *raki*, two stooping old pensioners and a very upright former army officer who talked all the time in imperative tones. At Pazartekke, Zeynel got out and walked on towards the Old Walls.

A light rain was falling almost imperceptibly. Zeynel knew exactly where he was going, to an old hideout of his at the foot of a huge portal. On the right of the portal, a little way inside a cemetery, was a large fig tree that hid the entrance to a small vaulted crypt.

The rain was gathering strength and he was quite drenched by the time he reached the portal. Agile as a cat, he leaped over the cemetery wall, ran to the fig tree which was barely discernible in the darkness, and passed under the vault into the crypt. An acrid smell of dust, wet stone and moss made his throat burn. He coughed. The very sound of his coughing frightened him and he swallowed hard. With a chisel he had taken from the carpenter's shop he started digging into the soft earth. When he had dug to an arm's length, he opened the bag, took some money out, and shoved it into the back pocket of his jeans. He then wrapped the bag up again in the blue apron, took off the one he was wearing, laid it over the bundle and lowered it into the hole. Then he shovelled the earth back, stamped it down and smoothed the surface with his hands. No one could ever find his money now. Street children were much too afraid of the cemetery to come here and the crypt had long been forgotten by everyone else. And even if someone chanced this way, how could he suspect that there was money here in that hole, deep as a grave? He patted the ground once more and went out. It was raining as though the sky had been rent asunder. He went to the Samatya railway station and waited for a train. From there he would go and have a few drinks in Kumkapi and then he would find old Lame Hasan and give him three thousand lira. Lame Hasan was the one person in Menekşe who had always treated him well . . .

II

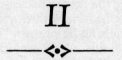

A tempest was raging off the coast of Menekşe. White breakers
tearing in from distant Büyükada Island pounded at the shore,
shaking the houses, the roads and the earth. Sheets of rain
slashed through the night, cold, razor-like. In the coffee-house
the three policemen were sitting in a corner playing cards and
talking desultorily. Menekşe had just gone through another of
those eventful days since the murder of Ihsan and everyone was
commenting on the exploits of Zeynel Çelik and his gang. Three
times Zeynel had riddled Fisher Selim's house with bullets,
rousing the whole neighbourhood. Finally, the night before, he
had set fire to the house. It had blazed up in an instant like
kindling wood, the wind fanning the flames high up over the
railway station. The house had been reduced to cinders so
quickly that no one could believe it. If Selim had not been such a
light sleeper and so quick on his feet as well, he too would have
been ashes by now.

The loss of his house did not particularly grieve him, but he
felt angry at Zeynel. The lad was turning out to be a dangerous
roughneck. He had killed Ihsan out of some secret fear, but now
this fear had assumed such proportions that it must be affecting
his mind. Anyway, that very day Fisher Selim bought some
timber and fibreboard and other necessary material and started
rebuilding his house, assisted by Mahmut and Özkan. Soon the
whole of Menekşe, even those who had been so hostile to him,
were lending a helping hand. Some brought sand and water,
panes of glass, taps, pipes, others mixed the sand and cement or
planed the wood. This kind of shanty is generally built by
teamwork. It draws people together and enmities are set aside.

The newspapers were full of the exploits of Zeynel Çelik, but
each gave a different version of Ihsan's murder and not one of the
photographs printed bore the faintest likeness to Zeynel.
Mostly they depicted a tall, broad-shouldered, hawk-nosed man
with glowering eyes under knit brows, holding a sten gun. One

newspaper had spread a large photo of Zeynel over half a page, with steep mauve crags in the background. Another had Zeynel with his whole gang, the caption reading: 'Here you see Zeynel Çelik with the gang he formed three years ago on arriving in Istanbul from Erzurum, his home town.' There were also varied accounts of Zeynel's life which even the Menekşe folk had begun to believe. And why not? Zeynel, they argued, had been quite a grown man when he came to live in Menekşe and that was ten to fifteen years ago! Besides no one knew what he had been doing all those years, where he had been. As for the photographs, well, after all, a man could change quite a lot after so many adventures . . .

That morning, Menekşe had been astir exceptionally early. Some boys had been dispatched to get the newspapers from Küçükçekmece. Even Ibo Efendi had loosened his pursestrings for once and ordered three newspapers. When they arrived, groups assembled on the beach, in the coffee-house, outside the houses, and the account of the murder was read aloud and commented upon. Though this differed from one paper to another, there was one point on which they were all in accord. Zeynel and his gang had fired at the houses all night long, had even fired at the sea and the fishing boats. One paper related how Zeynel had burst into the Menekşe coffee-house with nine men, grabbed hold of that notorious thug Ihsan, who had a clean eleven murders to his credit, and after torturing him for some time had shot him three times in each eye and then had slashed off his tongue and penis before coolly leaving the coffee-house. Alerted, the police had surrounded the gangsters, but Zeynel, that old-timer, so bold and swift, had managed to break through and escape. The Menekşe folk believed it all. Very likely, they said, when Zeynel broke into the coffee-house his gang was waiting outside, but what a pity they had not seen the police surrounding him on sea and on land, as the paper wrote. Yet how could the paper say the skirmish had gone on for days and nights when that was not true at all?

Then there was the incident of the trussed-up policemen, which had made a great sensation in the press. The police, having received a tip-off, had set an ambush for Zeynel at the point of the Old Seraglio, in front of the statue of Atatürk, but instead they found themselves trapped in a hail of bullets. 'I don't want to kill you,' Zeynel Çelik shouted, 'but that's what

I'll do if you don't surrender.' The police had no choice. Zeynel Çelik bore a grudge against policemen in general and, after tying these ones up, he taunted and tortured them and took all their guns and money. Never before had the Istanbul police had to deal with such a ruthless gangster. Besides, the papers intimated, there was an even more powerful gang behind it all.

Then came the bank hold-up in Beyoğlu, followed by the burning of Fisher Selim's house. Here was a windfall for the newspapers! Now they could fill up their columns every day with the epic doings of this dangerous gangster, and Istanbul, its hand on its heart, would be waiting for the morning papers with growing eagerness every day.

One journalist had by pure chance, he wrote, come upon Zeynel only the day before, drinking whisky in an unnamed casino on the Bosphorus and Zeynel had granted him a long interview. Splashed over the front page of the paper were various pictures of Zeynel posing beside the journalist. Here Zeynel was a tall handlebar-moustached brave and the journalist said that he originated from Tunceli. First, at the age of eleven he had joined a large smuggling network, but it took him only a few years to realize he did not like black-marketeering. He defied their chief and killed him. Policemen he hated. Wherever he saw one he had pledged himself to truss him up and next time he would send his gun to the Chief of the Security Department. Zeynel, the article went on, was about thirty, cool and self-possessed and quite modest too. The reason he had shot Ihsan was because the man had murdered Zeynel's brother. As for the bank hold-up, well, the gang needed money. They couldn't be expected to go hungry, could they? And nothing was easier than to rob a bank. Three more he had to rob in order to secure his material independence and then he'd never touch another man's property again. Thieving and plundering were downright sinful when you had enough money to get by anyway . . . Among the football clubs Zeynel was an ardent Fenerbahçe fan, and had been ever since his youth. His favourite foods were black cabbage soup, croquettes made of madimak, a herb unknown in Istanbul, and special meatballs made of mincemeat and bulgur. He also liked *kebap*, Antep style. He was a bachelor, but he had a girl in mind, a girl who had just graduated from university, and he intended to marry her very soon. The girl had a soft spot for gangsters, for wild men of character, and she had fallen in love with Zeynel at first sight. The journalist had wanted to know how good a shot Zeynel was and Zeynel had whipped out a gun and aimed at an electric bulb on the far side of the casino. The bulb had burst into shivers and without another look Zeynel had got into his car and driven off in full view of all the people in the jam-packed casino.

That was it. After this, in a very short while, Zeynel Çelik's gang had grown to redoubtable proportions and events gathered speed, a second bank hold-up taking place in Beyoğlu, a third in Şişli, a fourth in Sirkeci. At the Harem boat landing-place the corpses of three men were discovered, all three shot in the nape of the neck and all three with their trousers and underpants lowered to the knees. These were identified as three merchants from the provinces and it was thought that the trousers business was just a false trail to give another aspect to the murders. And, soon after, a couple of new corpses, mother-naked this time, were found in the underpass in Aksaray. No one doubted but that all these murders were the work of Zeynel Çelik's gang. Every new day brought a fresh murder, another burglary or hold-up in this or that quarter of Istanbul, and also a whole spate of photographs of Zeynel, holding now a machine-gun, now a Mauser rifle, a carbine, a sword . . .

The police had tracked Zeynel Çelik to the house of that convicted sexual pervert, Rifat Ardiç, in Unkapani. The skirmish lasted through the night. Towards dawn, as the firing from the house had ceased, the steel-vested policemen charged in with a volley of machine-gun fire and came upon Rifat Ardiç, steeped in his blood, lying on the floor, one hand clasping the door-knob. And that wasn't all. Inside, hunched over an automatic pistol, lay a girl, her head blasted to bits, her brains stuck to the wall, her crumpled blood-drenched skirt dried stiff as a tarpaulin. She was clasping the automatic pistol, so one paper said in the caption under her photo, as though it were her lover. A dark, long-necked, curly-haired boy of about fifteen was slumped in a corner. His blood had run along the floor to gather in a pool on the threshold. Two more persons, huddled under a sideboard, were moaning in pain, obviously hit by the last volley as the police burst into the house. They were swiftly transported to hospital, but their case was hopeless and they died on the way.

Members of the press had been present at this last operation.

Of course they were rather disappointed to find that Zeynel Çelik had somehow escaped, but they had plenty of material with the photographs of all those other bloody corpses. Besides, Zeynel Çelik had lost the most valiant member of his gang, the gangster girl who was known as Thompson-Toting Fatoş. On the whole, it was much better from the journalists' point of view that Zeynel should have got away, and in such a spectacular manner too, jumping from rooftop to rooftop. How could the police have foreseen that he would break out of the house through the roof? Next time, they would put a watch on the roofs as well . . .

The Istanbul police were being showered with tip-offs. It seemed as though the citizens had nothing else to do. Only yesterday morning, at the very same time, twenty-three Zeynel Çeliks had been spotted in Samatya, thirty-seven in Beyoğlu, nine in Tarabya, ninety-six in Bebek, three in Eminönü, seventy-one in the Spice Bazaar, one in the Vegetable Market, forty-six in Eyup, one in Menekşe, three in Florya and twenty-seven in Aksaray. And so it went on, the police doing their best to follow up all these leads. One day, in Dolapdere, they managed to capture alive and without a scratch five members of the gang, but again Zeynel Çelik slipped through their fingers with the cunning of a fox. The men sang like nightingales about their bank robberies, about what kind of person Zeynel was, but of the stolen loot there was no trace. How could there be? Would Zeynel let anyone have even a whiff of a single kurush? Another time, in Kasimpaşa, the police cordoned off a house and subjected it to a barrage of fire. Six members of the gang fell into their hands, wounded, but not that fiend Zeynel Çelik. Again, in the neighbourhood of Umraniye the police arrested fifteen men belonging to Zeynel Çelik's gang and they all confessed to their crimes. Every one of them worshipped Zeynel. He was brave, he could never be caught, he was larger than the largest champion wrestler, a very devil. There was something magic in his eyes. Just one look from him and a man was mesmerized and, were he the Chief of Police himself or the Minister of the Interior, he would find himself at Zeynel's beck and call . . .

Once, the police came upon Zeynel Çelik in a car near the Karagümrük Stadium, but before they even had time to draw their guns a crowd had gathered, forming a protective circle around the car, and both gangster and car disappeared into thin air. That night, the inhabitants of that quarter were soundly beaten up at the police station, but of Zeynel Çelik there was not a trace.

All over Istanbul the police were hunting Zeynel, leaving no stone unturned, organizing raids every day, every hour, making up to a dozen arrests daily, killing a few people, but for some mysterious reason Zeynel always eluded them.

Zeynel Çelik was the topic of the day in every coffee-house in Istanbul. In Menekşe people talked of nothing else. Here all kinds of stories were being told. What a good fisherman he was, what a marvellous shot . . . How once, when Arapoğlu's skiff had sunk off Hayirsiz Island, Zeynel had swum all the way from there to Menekşe, and in a raging tempest too. How he never went out without his two guns at his waist, how he could shoot a sparrow from a tree with one shot, without even taking aim . . .

A wind of panic was sweeping over Menekşe. Not one of the people here had ever been kind to Zeynel. They had sent him out fishing in freezing weather without paying him anything. They had made him work for nothing, ordering him about like a servant. And now they lived with the constant fear that Zeynel Çelik's gang would come in the night and set fire to their houses, shooting down anyone who attempted to get out.

'You, Duran! You heathen, didn't you try to rape the boy that time you took him with you fishing? An innocent harmless child fresh out of the Rize Mountains! And you a fellow-countryman of his too! The boy bit your hands and legs and fought till you had to give up. And you came to the coffee-house and told everyone about it, your mouth watering! D'you think the lad will let you live on after that?'

'You, Temel! A relative of his! Didn't you throw the mite of a boy out of your house into the mud when he was sick and almost dying? If it hadn't been for Fatma Abla he'd have been dead now. All you can hope for is that he'll let you choose your own death!'

'As for you, Süleyman . . .'

'I never did anything bad to him! Why, I gave him bread once when he was hungry . . .'

'What about the time only a few years ago when we had that exceptional run of bluefish in the Bosphorus? Didn't you take him out in the snow and a raging northeaster, didn't you step on his hand with your hobnailed boot, breaking the bones? It's you he should have killed, not Ihsan! Bless Fatma Abla, she took the poor boy to a bonesetter and he saved his hand. Think Zeynel Çelik'll spare you?'

'But it wasn't my fault! How could I know his hand was there? It wasn't on purpose . . .'

'Shame on you, Süleyman! I was there. You got mad at the boy because he wasn't pulling in the net quickly enough, so you stamped the heel of your boot down on his hand. He very nearly fell out of the boat from the pain. He could have drowned . . .'

'Well, I gave him some money . . .'

'You didn't give him one kurush!'

'And what about you, Fahri Bey? What are you going to do? Wasn't it you who had Zeynel taken to the police station, accusing him of stealing your fishnets? Wasn't it you had them beat him up there a full forty-eight hours?'

'God, what shall I do now? He'll kill me, Zeynel, he'll skin me alive . . .'

'Run, Fahri Bey, get out of here, go to Switzerland.'

'Well, my friends, I for one never did anything to him. Now tell me, did I? Once, on a Bairam day he came to kiss my hand, so I gave him twenty-five kurush. He'll remember that, Zeynel will. He wouldn't forget, now, would he?'

'No, no, he never forgets anything.'

'There's not another one like him.'

'And to think that we treated him so meanly . . .'

'The famous Zeynel Çelik, growing up destitute, sleeping winter and summer in whatever broken-down boat he could find! When we all had warm homes, he . . . In the cold . . .'

'One morning I came to open up the coffee-house and what should I see! Zeynel, crouched against the door, numb with cold. I took him in and brewed some tea. Yes, it's true, piping-hot tea I gave him. Zeynel would never forget that! He's got a heart, he has. His teeth were clamped fast and he couldn't open his mouth. So I took him on my lap and rubbed him all over and when his limbs relaxed I held the tea to his lips and made him drink it. Thirty-six hot glasses of tea he drank that day, Zeynel, and I never took one kurush from him . . .'

'What a tale! You wouldn't give a free glass of tea to your own father, not even if he were at his last breath! Liar!'

'It's you who's a liar, dog, and all your brood too! When I think of all the teas you've drunk here for nothing . . .'

'Wait! Stop! Don't quarrel. Zeynel may be here this very night

with his gang of thirty-six men. You can remind him then of
how many teas you gave him and how you saved him from
freezing to death!'

'He'll burn this whole neighbourhood, that's for sure . . .'

'But Fatma Abla? He likes her . . .'

'He liked Fisher Selim too, but that didn't prevent him from
setting fire to his house, did it?'

'Well, Fisher Selim shouldn't have spit in his face!'

'They say that Zeynel invaded the Security Department the
other day with his thirty-six men and had all the cops lined up in
front of him. No more forcing bribes out of the poor and needy,
he said. And with one voice the cops all swore they wouldn't
ever again. Neeever! No more firing on poor shanty-houses,
pulling them down, killing the inhabitants . . . And again the
cops pledged their oath. Nee-ever . . . Zeynel made them swear
to many many things. Never open fire on strikers, he said,
they're your brothers. And the cops vowed they wouldn't. Neee-
ever . . . Very well, Zeynel said, then I won't kill you this time.
I'll spare you for your families, for your children . . . Thank you,
Zeynel brother, the cops said. What's more, he said, from now
on you must stop chasing me, because you'll never catch me
anyway, and if you don't keep your promises I'm going to plant
forty kilos of dynamite under the Sansarayan Han and blow you
all to kingdom come. So keep that in mind, he said, and went
away . . . Elusive Zeynel, they call me, he said, remember that!'

'They'll never catch him.'

'Even as a boy, it was clear how he would turn out.'

'Once, I locked him up in the beach toilet and two minutes
later there he was, outside!'

'Once he'd pilfered a tray of fish from me, so I trussed him up,
the pig's ball – you know, his ankles bound and thrust through
his arms, also bound. No, no, it was Osman my deck-hand who
did it. No one can extricate himself from that knot when I do it –
I mean when Osman does it . . . Then I took him to Kumkapi,
plumped him down in Agop's fishing boat and returned to the
coffee-house here. And what should I see: Zeynel there before
me, large as life! "Sorry, Zeynel," I said. "Forgive me . . ." '

'All the policemen in the world will never be able to catch
him.'

'Yes, but what are we going to do?'

'We must go to Fatma Abla. Only Fatma Abla can soften him,

if anyone . . .'

'Once he'd been arrested, but I can't remember why.'

'Never! Not even once . . .'

'But yes, you know nothing about it.'

'Well, anyway, what happened then?'

'They clapped double handcuffs on his wrists. And on his ankles too . . .'

'And then? And then?'

'They locked him up in the deepest dungeon with an iron door. But it was Zeynel Çelik they had to deal with, a real lion! When the policemen looked in after a while, the cell was quite bare, save for the shattered pieces of the handcuffs on the floor.'

'No, no, they can never lock him up.'

'They say he's been giving away the money from the bank hold-ups to those people whose shanty-houses have been pulled down.'

'Good for the lad! He always had a kind heart. You could do anything with him, he was so meek . . . And look at him now! Those awesome photos in the papers, those eyes flashing like lightning . . .'

'He wouldn't do anything to us . . .'

'After all the years he's been eating our bread . . .'

'You see if he wouldn't! He'll come . . .'

'If not tonight . . .'

'Why, man, you made him spit blood all these years! Blood!'

'Well, we didn't kill him, did we?'

'It was no more and no less than what every other working lad has to bear.'

'If every one of them were to start burning houses . . .'

'But Zeynel's different. He'll do it all right.'

Zeynel had become the embodiment of all their sins. In their minds he was a mixture of all things: smuggler, saint, madman, gangster, good, bad, generous, cruel, courageous, timorous . . .

Not only in Menekşe, but in all the coffee-houses of Istanbul, Zeynel's adventures, his past life were commented upon and fresh details added, varying according to the temper and character of the talker. And all these new elements of the Zeynel Çelik legend somehow got into the newspapers and into the police reports and were read again, magnified a hundredfold, all over the town. Already itinerant story-tellers had taken up the legend. With just a cursory look at the newspapers of the day and at the photographs of Zeynel, they were off, relating with enthusiasm the exploits of the gangster.

How this wondrous, fearful adventure would end nobody knew, nobody wanted to know.

12

The crumbling whitewash of a wall was the first thing he saw on waking. Then the spider dangling on a tenuous thread and creeping to its web in a corner of the ceiling. Strange, Zeynel thought, that it should make its own thread and use it to go wherever it wants. He could not for the life of him recollect where he was. His aching head fell back on the pillow.

Suddenly he remembered the night before. He had been drinking in Yani's tavern. A hundred lira he'd tipped the waiter and indulged in all sorts of tomfoolery, drawing his gun and shouting: 'I'm Zeynel Çelik! Zeynel Çelik, they call me!' And Yani, the wise old tavern-keeper, had taken him by the arm, saying, 'Everyone's Zeynel Çelik these days,' and had led him off to the railway station to prevent him from making any more trouble.

'I *am* Zeynel!' Zeynel was yelling. 'Zeynel Çelik! Is there anyone who dares to look askance at me? It's me who killed Ihsan, me who robbed the bank, trussed up all those cops, me me me!'

'All right, son,' Yani had said soothingly, removing the gun from his hand and shoving it back into his belt. 'You're whoever you say, the greatest thug in Istanbul. You're Zeynel Çelik . . .'

'But I *am* Zeynel Çelik. Don't you believe me?'

'Yes, yes, I believe you.'

'Then why don't you turn me over to the police?'

'Because the police will break every bone in your body if they take you for Zeynel Çelik. That's why, my little lion,' Yani had said and left him there, sitting on a bench at the station.

Dimly Zeynel recalled getting into a train and out again at Florya, wandering through the woods, tumbling into the mud, being caught in a flood of neon lights, yellow, green, white, purple, floundering this way and that, dazzled, frightened, desperate, yet still yelling like a madman: 'I, I, I am Zeynel Çelik, you bastards! Why won't you believe me?' Buttonholing whoever he came across. 'Why are you laughing at me?'

'Zeynel Çelik's a giant of a man – you could hew three of the likes of you out of him!'

'I am Zeynel Çelik, I, I!' He pounded his chest. 'It was I killed Ihsan. Everyone in Menekşe saw me.'

'Pish! That's a tall one!'

'Those policemen . . . It was I . . .'

'Pish!'

'And the bank too . . . Look, look at this! This is what you call money . . .'

'Pish!'

'But I am, I *am* Zeynel Çelik . . .'

'You, Zeynel Çelik? Ha-ha!'

'Everyone calls himself Zeynel Çelik these days, son, or takes himself for Zeynel Çelik. Why, there must be dozens shouting in every quarter of the town that they are Zeynel Çelik . . .'

'But it *is* me, I swear it!'

'You poor lad! Don't you ever read the newspapers? Zeynel Çelik trussed up fifteen cops, single-handed. He's not an ordinary person. That bank now, single-handed! And Zühre Paşali . . . Single-handed! He's a man who's got the whole of Istanbul in a tremble. You can't be Zeynel Çelik, lad, nor can anyone else we know.'

'I *am* Zeynel Çelik, I tell you.'

'Oh come off it! Stop pulling my leg.'

'Look, those photographs, they're not the real Zeynel Çelik . . .'

'Piss off, will you?'

The thundering of the sea sounded in his ears. His clothes, the revolver, the bullets in his pocket were all wet, as though he had plunged into the sea. The police were at his heels, Hüseyin Huri leading the chase. Those neon lights forming a circle, so blindingly bright, was it the Golden Horn? He fell right into the centre of the neon circle, into its darkest core. The police were firing away. Trapped, breathless, he tried to escape, but only banged his head against the wall of neon lights. 'Here, here . . .' Hüseyin Huri's voice and the footsteps drawing nearer . . . Beyond the glare, pitch-black darkness and the crackle of gunfire. Again Hüseyin Huri's voice. 'Here, he's here! I swear I saw him. Perhaps he's jumped into the sea. He can stay under the water as long as he wants to and swim like a seabird.' Zeynel

was scrambling up the wall of light, slipping, trying again . . .
Then he was in the courtyard of a mosque. The scent of jasmine
drifted to his nostrils. In the darkness he broke off a sprig from a
bush. It was an elder. The white flower of the elder is delicate,
not to be touched even lightly or it will darken and fade . . .
Zeynel crouched behind the tomb of some holy man, the sprig of
elder he was afraid to spoil in one hand, the gun held ready in the
other, trembling in all his limbs, determined to shoot down the
policemen if they so much as stepped through the gate. The
neon lights were far away now, but his eyes still ached as though
they had been burnt. The darkness flowed over him, heavy,
stonelike. He was still panting, a loud raucous rattle. My breath
will give me away, my breath . . . Son-of-a-bitch Hüseyin Huri!
To do this to me, your best friend . . . But I'll get even with you, I
will!

The footsteps went past the mosque. They had not heard his
loud breathing, they had not even looked in. Zeynel broke into a
sweat. The sweat streamed from his pores as though it would
never stop. He heard it fall from his hair, drip drip, over the
marble slab of the tomb.

When at last he ventured out into the street, an icy wind was
blowing. His sweat dried in an instant and he shivered. Quickly
he sprinted off downhill towards Ayvansaray, where large Laz
fishing scows lay in the dry docks. Once there, he felt more
secure. Three men were sitting at the foot of a lamppost, bent
over some work they were doing. Zeynel lifted his hand to his
nose to smell the elder flower, but it was empty, only the scent
still lingered on his fingers. It vexed him to think he must have
crushed it as he ran.

One of the men in the pool of light sprang to his feet. 'Who's
that?' he cried.

Zeynel did not move. 'Only a fisherman,' he said.

'Oh, we thought it was the police.'

'Yes, there are a lot of cops around here . . .'

'You look as though you are from the Black Sea too . . .'

'I am.'

The man spoke with an even more pronounced Black Sea
brogue than Zeynel. 'Are you looking for some place to sleep,
lad? Or is it the cops you want to avoid? Here, get into this boat.
You can hide in one of the cabins and get some sleep. Nobody'll
find you there in a dozen years.'

'But the cops . . .'

'Don't worry, they're only after the gangster Zeynel Çelik.'

Without another word Zeynel climbed into the dilapidated old hulk and drew the ladder up behind him. The smell of tar and pinewood mingled here with that nauseating Golden Horn stench.

He was roused at dawn by the blaring of boat sirens and the clangour of hammering that shook the boat, the air, the whole of the Golden Horn, boom boom boom . . . He was dead tired. His body ached as though all his bones were being torn apart. The noise of hammering, the barking of dogs, the shouts of the caulkers, nothing could stir him out of his torpor.

When he woke up at last the din at Ayvansaray was deafening. Thoroughly bewildered at first, memory returned and he took fright. The pit-like centre of the neon lights, the miry nauseating Golden Horn . . . There was an islet, a morass, lately formed right opposite Eyup . . . Should he go and hide there? In that small hut in the middle of the islet? Could he swim through this swamp-like water? Wouldn't the bog drag him down? Hüseyin Huri's voice, the pale, elongated faces of the policemen, all wet through, water dripping from their capes . . . Three times lightning flashed over Süleymaniye Mosque. One bolt forked into four streaks, flooding the mosque with light, only for an instant, the wet dome growing larger, rising higher in the sky, gleaming darkly. Only for a fraction of a second . . . A dog came sniffing around his feet, then started away with a yelp.

Zeynel let the ladder down the side of the boat. The place was crammed with vessels ready for caulking and the fumes of burning paint, sharp, scorching the throat, drowned even the foul carrion stench of the Golden Horn. He threaded his way between the hulks and the hawk-nosed men, steeped in grease, their faces black with soot, and emerged on the muddy street. Nobody paid any attention to him. At Hasköy he got into a *dolmuş*, then changed to another one going to Beyoğlu. Stroking his moustache, he fretted at how sparse it was. It would surely grow thick soon, but it would never be black like the one in the newspaper photographs . . .

In Beyoğlu he stepped into one of the large ready-to-wear stores and stood looking about him, a little diffident, though not half as shy as when he had entered the Konyali Restaurant.

'Can I help you, sir?' A young man about his own age, with a long, pointed, yellow moustache, was at his side. Zeynel smiled. Ah, if only this young man knew who he was! How frightened he would be!

'We've got some suits here just your size. If you'd care to look.' The young man led him to a counter and produced three different suits. Zeynel looked at them, then at the young man.

'You don't like them?'

Zeynel shook his head. The other drew out some more suits, but none seemed to please his client. Suddenly, he had a brainwave. 'D'you like mine?' he asked. 'We've got one exactly like it. Let's see now, are we the same height?' He came to stand beside Zeynel. 'Straighten up, please. Don't stoop, hold back your shoulders. Yes, by Jove, the very same size! I'll get it right away. Identical cut, identical pattern . . .' He ran off to another department and was soon back with a suit just like his own. 'Here we are, this one'll fit you like a glove, it will.' He opened a door into a tiny cubicle lined with mirrors. 'This way, this way, you can try it on in here.' Almost pushing Zeynel in, he shut the door on him. Inside, Zeynel felt more confident. He took off his clothes, but when it came to the shoes a fetid odour filled the cubicle. I must buy some socks, Zeynel thought, and under-clothes and . . . He put on his shoes before opening the door.

'Like a glove!' the fair-haired salesman exclaimed, turning him this way and that. 'As if it had been made to measure . . . And you look so well in it too.'

Zeynel gave him a grateful look. He had taken a liking to this fair-haired smiling-faced young man, who was just about his own age and size.

'You can keep it on, if you like. I'll make a parcel of your other clothes. You'll be needing some shoes too, won't you?'

Zeynel nodded.

'Look, there's the Goya store just across the street. They make the best, the most solid shoes in all Istanbul. Give my name to the salesman. Tell him Kaya sent you.'

'All right,' Zeynel said, and added softly: 'Thanks, brother . . .' He paid his bill, picked up the parcel containing his old clothes, the pockets of which he had carefully emptied in the cubicle, and went over to Goya's and from there to another shop where he bought underclothes and socks. The new shoes were beauti-ful brown ones, but the smell from his socks had made him want to sink to the middle of the earth. He had forgotten about that or he would never have gone in without washing his feet. When the salesman had asked him to take his shoes off, he had broken into a cold sweat and bought the first pair he tried on without taking them off again, without even knowing how he paid for them or how he left the shop.

And now he was rooted before the window of a toyshop, unable to tear himself away, oblivious of the jostling stream of people about him, a strange look in his eyes, smiling, muttering to himself, leaning down to look closer at a toy, stepping up to the door of the shop to peep in, then springing back and standing outside the window again. Suddenly, he shot into the shop, so fast that the salesgirls took fright.

'That one,' Zeynel said, pointing into the shop window. 'That one too . . . And that one . . .'

A salesgirl, recovering from the shock, took the toys out of the window. One was a pink elephant sitting in a wooden cart, its front legs held out stiffly. The second a monkey clinging to a tree and the third a long-necked, long-legged spotted giraffe.

'Pack them in a box,' Zeynel ordered, producing a five-hundred-lira note. The girl indicated the cash register. His hands trembling, Zeynel took the change, collected his parcels and rushed off, away from the crowded street, down the stairs that led through the Technical University Park to Dolmabahçe pier. There, by the waterside, he took his shoes off. Even in the open, his feet stank to high heaven. He flung his old torn socks as far out into the sea as he could, then washed his feet and dried them with tissue paper from one of the parcels of toys. The new socks smelled good and fresh from the factory. This evening he would go to a *hamam* and get himself scoured clean, not to the small dirty one he'd been to once, but to the large famous Cağaloglu Hamam. With beating heart he took the elephant out of its box. There was nobody about. Trembling, he took hold of the string and drew the cart from the iron railings of Dolmabahçe Palace to the wall of the mosque opposite. Glancing again to right and left to make sure he was quite alone, he ran back, the cart with the large pink elephant rattling behind him. Soon he forgot everything. Ever more quickly he ran up and down the pier, pausing now and then to laugh at his elephant, to caress it, to feel its white pointed teeth, to talk to it.

Tired at last, he stopped to catch his breath, and what should he see . . . A whole crowd there on the pier, people in cars, on foot, all looking at him, laughing . . . For just a moment he stood there, riveted. Then, snatching up his boxes and parcels, he dashed off along the avenue lined with plane trees behind Dolmabahçe Palace and did not stop until he came to Beşiktaş Square.

A noisy group of children were playing football, and a few younger ones, boys and girls, sat on a low wall, watching the game. Zeynel scrutinized their faces, one by one, their shoes and attire, but none seemed to take his fancy. The children, for their part, stared wide-eyed at this strange man with a toy elephant slung over his shoulder.

Zeynel turned away and walked up the hill towards Yildiz. Everywhere, in even the tiniest open space, there were children playing football. Zeynel took stock of them all. Finally, he came to a tumbledown wooden house, its time-blackened boards mouldering and coming loose, its windows fixed with plastic sheets instead of glass and an ancient marble slab, worn hollow, on the threshold. In front of it were two small children, a boy of ten and a girl of nine. The boy's trousers were patched, sagging at the knees, and he was wearing a pair of cheap rubber shoes. His scraggy neck hardly supported a wobbly head on which the hair stood out like spines. The girl wore a peasant dress and the same cheap rubber shoes as the boy. Her long hair was braided into two thick pigtails. Both of them had long curling eyelashes and huge wondering eyes. The instant he saw them, Zeynel's heart fluttered with joy. He stood there a while, overflowing with a strange mixture of love and pity.

'Come here, children,' he said softly, his voice so warm, so full of love it sounded alien to him. As the children hesitated, he walked up to them. 'Here,' he said, smiling at the boy, 'take this elephant. It's a toy for boys.' Then he removed the monkey from its box and held it out to the girl. 'And this is a girl's toy.' The giraffe he set down on the marble slab by the door. 'And this one is for both of you. You can play with it each day in turn. Or you can both play with it together if you like . . .'

The children stared at him, dumbfounded. The girl's eyes were growing wider and wider, wavering between fear and joy. A lump rose to Zeynel's throat and his eyes filled with tears. 'Go ahead, play,' was all he could say before rushing off down the slope and out into the avenue.

There he hailed a passing taxi. 'To Cağaloglu,' he said, and added: 'To the historic Cağaloglu Hamam . . .'

When he emerged from the *hamam* he felt light as a bird. At first he had been at a loss what to do with his gun and ammunition. Then he had wrapped them up in his soiled smelly underclothes and placed them beside his shoes.

The street outside was jammed with cars, horse-drawn carts, trucks, buses, hardly moving at all, desperately tooting their horns in unison from time to time, then falling silent again. He crossed over at a leisurely pace, walked past Haghia Sophia and down along the Topkapi Palace walls to the Ahirkapi lighthouse. Quickly he sprinted across the highway, for here the traffic flowed fast, and sat down on a flight of steps that led to the sea. On the opposite shore were the imposing old structures of Selimiye Barracks and Haydarpaşa Lycée and over them a very white cloud hovered against a bright-blue sky. Zeynel took his gun and bullets from the bundle of dirty underclothes and replaced them at his waist and in his pockets. Then, screwing up his face in disgust, he hurled the bundle of stinking linen as far out as he could into the water. It fell with a plop like a stone and a flock of seagulls flashed up into the air.

From here, the new Bosphorus Bridge was just a finespun line, hardly visible, a rope strung out as a make-believe bridge. A very long copper-coloured freighter was passing underneath and everywhere the small city-line ferries scurried this way and that in a whirl.

Suddenly Zeynel froze and his mouth went dry. Five policemen were reflected in the sea in front of him, etched on the very bottom of the still stagnant water. He tried to move, to get up, but he was unable to stir a limb, as if he had been turned to stone. There, right above him, the policemen stood talking for a while, then they went away, but Zeynel still remained frozen to the stone steps. It was already dark when he came to himself. He rose, stretching himself until his bones cracked. From the restaurant under the Ahirkapi lighthouse came the odour of fish being broiled over a coal fire and all of a sudden he felt a gnawing hunger. He walked into the restaurant and stopped abruptly. The five policemen were sitting there at a table, drinking *raki*. He hesitated, but there was no help for it. He must go in now. Besides, he didn't look at all like that handlebar-moustached Zeynel Çelik . . . He sat down at a table only a little way off. The policemen did not give him a glance. They were busy talking about Zeynel Çelik.

'What will you have, sir?' a waiter asked him.

'Grilled bonito,' Zeynel said, his voice shaking.

'And to drink?'

'Beer . . .' Zeynel's throat was dry. 'Bring me some mineral water too. And also Albanian-style liver, a carrot salad, toast, and . . .' All these he had seen in Fevzi's Restaurant at Menekşe, but there was another thing he could not remember, something the customers always ordered . . . '*Cacik!*' he said triumphantly, forgetting all about the policemen for a moment.

'Very good, sir.'

In its corner of the ceiling the spider spread its web wider and wider, then, gathering itself into a ball, moved away from the centre of the web and quickly slid down a tenuous thread, stopping in the middle of the room. Zeynel heard Lame Hasan's hoarse coughing voice.

'Zeynel! Zeynel, are you awake?'

'Yes, uncle, what is it?'

'Quick, get up, get dressed.'

Zeynel started up at once. 'What is it, uncle?' he said again to the old man who had entered the room.

'The cops are all over the place, searching for you, Hüseyin Huri at their head . . .'

'The son-of-a-bitch!' Zeynel hissed. Quickly, he got into his clothes, took the gun from under the pillow and stuck it into his waistband. 'I'll never give myself up. I'll fight them.'

'They'll kill you, my lad. You're only one. There are twenty-five of them out there, all with steel vests too.'

Zeynel stopped and stood despondently in the middle of the room. The spider swayed gently on its thread near his head.

'Get out!' Lame Hasan cried. 'Fast. They'll be searching here too. Get out by the back door and try to reach the station. Mix with people, get into a train and go as far from here as it goes. Only don't stand there dawdling.'

Suddenly, Zeynel ran to the back door, opened it carefully and slipped out, cat-like.

13

Years ago, when the weir still stood in Menekşe Bay, it was the custom at the close of winter and in the early spring, and during the first days of autumn as well, to light fires all along the beach. Homing fishing boats, spying the smoke from afar, would steer into the bay as close to the shore as possible, and cast some dozen or more fish on to the sands, according to the kind and size of their catch. Especially in the spring, at the time of the bonito run, when the boats were full to the brim, the fish really rained down on Menekşe beach. Swiftly, with well-whetted knives, they would be cleaned, washed and salted, then laid upon the piles of glowing embers. Soon a mouth-watering odour of fat, sizzling bonito would fill the whole bay. The poor folk, the children, the loners and the sick would be waiting, each with a large loaf of bread sliced through the middle. The crisp, sea-smelling fish would be boned and inserted into the loaves and devoured in large hungry mouthfuls, the grease trickling down chins and fingers.

So it used to be on spring evenings, all along Menekşe shore, heaps of glowing, starlike embers and the heavy fumes of sizzling, burning oil. The whole village would be replete and children's faces wreathed in smiles.

As a child Zeynel never could afford a loaf of bread and no one thought of giving him one except Kadir Agha. The old man would watch out for the boy, then fetch the loaf he had kept for him in his boat, select the choicest fish, shake it by the tail, removing the spine at one go, press the fish into the bread and hold it out to Zeynel, who would snatch it and run off to one of the empty beach cabins to savour his fish slowly, all by himself. And Kadir Agha would watch from a distance, smiling proudly.

Kadir Agha hailed from Rumania. He had come to Menekşe many long years ago, when no one yet had settled here, when those slopes there were covered with bushes under which nestled clusters of fragrant wild violets that had given the village its name. A wide, swampy reed-bed stretched right into the bay and in front of where the factory now stands the rushes were so thick and tall a tiger could not have penetrated them. After Kadir Agha, the sand-dealer Sait Bey came to settle in Menekşe and then, in no time, the place was full of people. How and when they came, Kadir Agha doesn't remember at all. Lame Hasan, for instance, who caught the most beautiful red mullet here, exactly twenty-six centimetres each, exactly! If the mullet was shorter by only a millimetre – Lame Hasan had the measure marked out on the side of his boat – he would cast it back into the sea, saying, 'You've still some time to grow, laddie,' or if it was longer, 'You're a little past your prime, chum, just go on laying eggs and breeding plenty of young mullet . . .' Those red mullet that were the right size he would put into his fish tank in which he changed the water every fifteen minutes, and watch them swim around, entranced. Lame Hasan would not dream of selling his catch to any Tom, Dick or Harry. He had his own select clients, old aristocrats who lived in Florya, Yeşilköy and Bakirköy, gourmets who could appreciate what he brought them, not like those new real-estate millionaires who would bargain half an hour for one single fish. Why had Lame Hasan quit fishing and taken to just raking up flotsam and jetsam these last years? Because those gourmets who appreciated his red mullet at their real value do not exist any more in Istanbul, because they are dead now, or impoverished, because nowadays people are incapable of truly savouring fish.

As for Kadir Agha, never in all the fifty years since he had come from Rumania had he seen the inside of a house, or even of a hut or a tent. Summer and winter he slept in his boat. Perhaps he had been born in a boat and most probably he would die in one. It was Kadir Agha who pioneered fishing in Menekşe. He was not finicky like Lame Hasan about what he caught and sold. Any kind of fish and fishing was good enough for him. He would dispose of his catch wherever he could and then hurry up to Beyoğlu, to the Flower Market, for a bout of drinking with his fellow-fishermen, after which he would pay a visit to his lady friend in that notorious Abanoz Street. His greatest feat whenever he came into town was to clamber up the parapet of Galata Bridge and stand there, drunk as he was, without losing his balance, without even swaying, to pee into the water.

'There's a good sun today,' Lame Hasan commented. 'Just the

right weather for fish.'

'No more fishing for me,' Kadir Agha declared. 'My eyes aren't as good as they were.'

'With me, it's my ears,' shouted Lame Hasan.

'So it is, so it is . . .'

'Besides,' Lame Hasan went on, 'there's no fish left to speak of in the Marmara Sea.'

'Ah, they've bled the sea dry,' Kadir Agha mourned. 'They've sinned against the sea.'

'It's because they killed the dolphins, the criminals. The fish were angry then and took themselves off. To Greece, to Russia . . . Even Fisher Selim – he was only a boy at the time, well, a lad anyway – he swore he'd never go fishing again after the dolphin carnage, but he didn't keep his word. So the fish went away, angry with us, with the sea. Angry . . . Gone . . .'

'Serve us right,' Kadir Agha growled.

'They scorn us now, the fish of the sea,' said Lame Hasan. 'It's the worst thing that could happen, to be scorned by the fish of the sea . . .'

'Let them go,' Kadir Agha said. 'Let them never come back.'

'And what about that Zeynel lad?'

'He did well. Everyone here in Menekşe treated him a thousand times worse than they treated the fish. Not me . . . I always gave him fish to eat. Everyone else cheated him out of his deck-hand's due, he was beaten and spurned by all. Many a cold winter's night he could not find even an old hulk to sleep in and I took him into my own boat. We'd squeeze in somehow.'

'I gave him a lot of fish too,' Lame Hasan said.

'Be quiet, you heathen!' Kadir Agha shouted. 'You wouldn't give anyone even the trimmings of your little fingernail, let alone a fish . . . Hah, all your fish were for the fine gentlemen of Yeşilköy, your red mullet . . .'

For the fraction of a second when a fish emerged from the water, struggling madly at the end of his hook, Lame Hasan would hold it up in the sun, gazing adoringly at the flashing, glittering lump of red. 'Who knows what bastard's going to eat you this evening, my beauty?' he would mutter to himself as he unhooked the fish and measured it, and if it was not exactly the size he wanted his face would brighten. Gently he would touch his index finger to the fish and slide it back into the sea. The truth of the matter was that Lame Hasan would have liked to do this with every single fish he caught. It made his heart bleed to think of his lovely red mullet being eaten by those rich *raki*-swilling bastards, may they eat poison . . .

'No,' he said to Kadir Agha, 'you've forgotten. I gave that orphan child many, many red mullet . . . But the papers are writing very bad things about him.' His round wrinkled face grimaced bitterly and his lips shrank inwards still more.

'Very bad,' Kadir Agha said. 'They say he intends to set fire to Menekşe and kill everyone.'

'Let him!' Lame Hasan flared. 'Who was ever kind to him here? Even that Aslan who's supposed to be a relative of his . . . One winter he stripped the boy naked, doused him with water and whipped him without mercy. I saw it with my own eyes.'

'And Kurdish Resul? Three years he had Zeynel toiling as his deck-hand, then gave him the sack without paying him one kurush.'

'And Ali? Bald Ali from Eskişehir? Who knows what he did to Zeynel that the lad should tremble at the mere sight of him? No, he'll burn this place all right, he will!'

At this moment, young Taner, the fisherman, came into the coffee-house with the day's papers.

'This way, Taner,' Kadir Agha called out to him. 'Let's see what those papers have to say today. Sit down here and read it all out to us.'

'Right away, uncle! It's for you I got the papers, all of them.'

'Well, go ahead, then, read,' Lame Hasan urged him. 'Let's see what our lad's been at again . . . I mean that gangster,' he added quickly with a furtive glance around him. Lame Hasan had been living in fear for days now. He thought everyone must know how Zeynel had slept in his house that night. Yes, they knew it, but they were a sly, underhand people, these fishermen. They were keeping mum, so as to blab to the cops when Zeynel was arrested, to tell them it was Lame Hasan who, without a thought for the authorities, had hidden a gangster, a murderer in his house, and for five days too . . .

'Not five days,' Lame Hasan muttered aloud. 'One day, only one short night . . .'

'What are you talking about, Hasan, for God's sake?' Kadir Agha cried.

Lame Hasan started. 'Nothing, nothing,' he said, mopping his brow. 'Go on, Taner my boy, read.'

'A new order has been issued to shoot to kill the gangster Zeynel Çelik . . .'

'Indeed!' exclaimed Kadir Agha.

'Poor lad, they're going to kill him,' Lame Hasan whispered.

Taner went on reading. 'Last night in Unkapani the police closed in on Zeynel Çelik as he was trying to abduct a workgirl from the Cibali tobacco factory, but the gangster, firing on the police, broke out of the trap and escaped, leaving the girl behind. "Nobody raped me," she said, in her statement. That man was just someone from my home town. His name? Zeynel . . . I don't know his surname . . . Çelik, you say? Ah, yes, Çelik . . ." ' Taner unfolded another newspaper. 'Look,' he cried, 'here's a photo of Zeynel with a woman beside him, a very smart woman. It says that she's Zeynel's sweetheart. But does this man look like Zeynel to you?'

Lame Hasan took the paper and scrutinized it carefully. 'Allah, Allah,' he exclaimed, as he passed it on to Kadir Agha. 'How's it possible? A man can't change so in a couple of days.'

'I couldn't say,' Kadir Agha said. 'My eyes aren't so good.'

'Selim, Selim! Come here,' Lame Hasan called out to Fisher Selim who was standing on the little bridge that led to the beach. 'Take a look at this paper. Is this fellow here Zeynel? How can a man change . . . ?' He was going to say, 'It's only a couple of days since I saw him, this isn't Zeynel, this Zeynel Çelik's someone else.'

Fisher Selim glanced briefly at the paper Taner held out to him. 'Of course it isn't Zeynel,' he snapped and turned away.

'But if it isn't,' Kadir Agha objected, 'why should they publish just anybody's photo like that? Tell me, why?'

'That moustache,' Taner commented. 'The thick jaw, the large shoulders . . . This fellow doesn't look like Zeynel at all.'

'Perhaps it's a disguise,' suggested Lame Hasan.

'But the man's quite different,' Taner said.

'Well, you go on reading, Taner.'

Taner picked up a newspaper. ' "Zeynel Çelik is very nimble, very quick," says the chief of police, "it's going to be quite difficult to catch him, but we will, and very soon too. Our men are   on his track. We've got hold of several leads that we're following up . . ." '

'They'll never catch him,' Lame Hasan declared. 'Go on,

Taner, read.'

'Zeynel Çelik and his gang were traced last night to a Laz fishing scow at the Ayvansaray repair docks, but under the cover of darkness the gangsters managed to get away. A very fast motor-launch was waiting for them, moored to a pier on the Golden Horn, so fast that although the police gave chase it was way away on the Marmara by the time they had reached Galata Bridge. This motor-launch was found later off the Kalamiş coast, abandoned, strewn with pistachio shells. The gangsters had eaten a great quantity of pistachios as they fled.'

'Go on, Taner, go on.'

'Gangster Zeynel Çelik's new murder: The dangerous gangster has now committed his seventh murder since the killing of that other gangster Ihsan in a Menekşe coffee-house. His new victims, a multi-millionaire and his wife, were shot in the nape of the neck after having been lashed to each other in their fifty-three-million-lira villa in Bebek. It is believed that the gangster and his men forced their way into the villa at one in the morning and, after killing both husband and wife, made off with one and a half million lira in money and jewellery to the value of four million. The servants arriving in the morning discovered the bodies lying in a pool of blood.'

'Now, that's not good!' Lame Hasan exclaimed. 'That was a cruel, bloodthirsty thing for him to do . . . Well, well, well, but what a very rich man that was!'

'And young too,' Taner said. 'Look at their photos.'

'They probably inherited all that fortune from their families,' Lame Hasan sighed.

'The poor lambs!' Kadir Agha cried, peering at the paper. 'May your hands wither, Zeynel!' At once he regretted having spoken like this. What if it reached Zeynel's ears? 'Who knows?' he said. 'Maybe they did something to Zeynel, perhaps he had a grudge against them.'

'Listen,' Taner said. 'It says here that the man made all this huge fortune in only ten years.'

'H'm,' Lame Hasan commented, 'there's something fishy about that.'

'Yes, very fishy,' Kadir Agha concurred.

'Not that much!' Taner said. 'Istanbul's full of young self-made multi-millionaires like the one Zeynel killed and they've all made their fortunes by shady means . . . Listen, there's a great

143

deal more about Zeynel's doings in the papers. He's the terror of the whole town and he's got the police so they don't know whether they're on their heads or their heels.'

'Who'd ever have expected it of that puny lad?'

'Like an undersized, thin-bellied, hungry greyhound he was . . .'

'Last night . . .'

'Are you reading from the newspaper?'

'Yes . . . Last night the police surrounded Zeynel Çelik in the de luxe residential district of Arifpaşa Grove on the Bosphorus. As our newspaper was going to press, reports were still coming in of a violent clash with the gangsters. A responsible police officer stated to our correspondent that they would get Zeynel this time, dead or alive.'

'It's all up with him then,' Kadir Agha said. 'Who can hold out against so many policemen?'

Taner smiled broadly. 'I know Zeynel, uncle,' he said. 'We grew up together. No one can catch him. Mark my words, you'll read in tomorrow's papers that Zeynel Çelik's broken through the pincers again.'

'İnşallah!' Kadir Agha said. 'Let's hope so. I gave him a lot of fish as a boy . . .'

'And I . . .' Again Lame Hasan held his tongue just in time. If these people only knew that it was he, Lame Hasan, who had saved Zeynel from the police the other day . . .

The coffee-house was in an uproar, with everyone shouting, arguing and swearing all together.

Süleyman slipped away unseen and ran all the way to his house. 'Woman,' he said to his wife, 'pack up a few things and let's get out of here. That monster's running wild, killing whoever he comes across. Last night he butchered a millionaire and his wife in Bebek. If he does this to an innocent millionaire, what will he do with me! If only I hadn't stepped on that dog's hand . . . It wasn't on purpose at all.'

'Don't deny it, Süleyman,' his wife said rancorously. 'It was on purpose. You did the same to me when you made me sort fish from your net on a bitterly cold day. Well, let's see you save your sweet life from his hands, let's see you!'

'Not a word to anyone, not a word! Get ready, quick. And the children . . . While I fetch a car . . . He'll come after me if he finds out where we're going. First to Ambarli and then we'll take a bus to . . . Quick, quick!'

He rushed out and was back five minutes later with a 1950-model Chevrolet. 'Are you ready?' Taking his wife by the hand he hurried her and his two children into the taxi. Only then did he relax. 'To Ambarli,' he ordered the driver. 'Now let those Menekse folk worry, let Fisher Selim worry, the bastard! Let him figure out how many pieces Zeynel's going to hack out of him! Does a man in his right sense spit on the likes of Zeynel? Hah, he's in for it all right, that Selim!'

The next morning dawned, bright and warm. Menekşe smelled of the sea and was bathed in sunlight.

'Zeynel didn't attack us last night,' Hatçe commented as she sat knitting a jumper for her husband, the fisherman Kemal. She was a long-faced woman with one of her front teeth missing. Two thin braids of hair hung down her sagging breasts. Over a pair of green trousers she wore a short skirt of flowered calico and her head was bound in an orange kerchief pinked with large mauve flowers.

'He'll be coming the night after tomorrow.'

'How d'you know?'

'That's my business.'

'It's what the newspapers say! Zeynel said, "I can't live as long as that Menekşe stands there . . ." '

'He said, "I'll never give myself up before setting fire to that place and shooting down every one of those people, children and all." It was in the papers.'

'You know what he did the other night to the police? He stripped them all mother-naked.'

'Yes, indeed! It was in the papers.'

'Then he tied them to each other, chucked them all into a Laz scow and left them way out in the middle of the Marmara Sea.'

'Only three days later were they rescued, hungry, naked, fainting . . .'

'Yes, indeed! It was in the papers.'

'Zeynel had warned the police, "Don't come after me or it'll be the worse for you . . ." '

'He's got quite a gang now.'

'And all of them crack shots . . .'

A group of Menekşe women had gathered under the willow trees where the fishing nets were spread to dry and from every side came a fresh surmise about Zeynel.

'Süleyman's cleared out!'

'What else could he do? It's a matter of life and death.'

'Fisher Selim's taken himself off too.'

'Fisher Selim wouldn't do that!'

'Look, there he is, standing on the bridge, gazing at the sea.'

'Let him gaze away, he'll see what's coming to him!'

'He'll find out what it costs to spit on the likes of Zeynel in front of everyone!'

'One day, I remember, Zeynel was passing by our door, back from fishing, soaked, his hair ruffled like a wet kitten's. "Why, my poor child, my little Zeynel," I said, "you're freezing!" And I gave him a large chunk of spinach pie.'

'Zeynel wouldn't set fire to our house, never! Why, I knitted that sweater for him that he's still wearing . . .'

'They say Zeynel's bought himself a mansion on the shores of the Bosphorus.'

'Nonsense! What would he do with a mansion?'

'They say Zeynel's engaged to the daughter of the millionaire, Osman Tuzlu . . .'

'He's been seen riding in a huge sky-blue limousine . . .'

'He shoots down anyone he doesn't like the look of . . .'

'How could we have guessed he'd turn out like this, our mousy Zeynel?'

'Poor lad, he was so meek . . . "Go catch that snake with your bare hands," you could tell him, and he'd do it.'

' "Get me a shark from the depths of the sea . . ." And he'd do it.'

'They say he cleared a clean two and a half million in those bank hold-ups. And he's still at it, stealing even more.'

'What's he doing with all that money?'

'Why, everyone knows the answer to that! He went straight to Ümraniye where they pulled down the shanties the other day. "Take this money," he said, "it's all yours." Yes, he gave every penny he'd robbed from the bank to those poor homeless squatters.'

'Zeynel's going to buy a brand-new boat for Kadir Agha. With radar too!'

'Radar?'

'Yes, so as to be able to spot all the fish at the bottom of the sea.'

'And he's going to buy an apartment for Fatma Abla . . .'

It started to rain, gently at first, a soft patter on the ground and over the sea. Then a strong gust blew in, tossing the branches of the willows this way and that, tearing off the leaves and sending the women scurrying to the shelter of their homes.

14

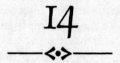

It was always at three o'clock that I used to meet Selim on the little jetty. He would be waiting in his boat, busy with his nets. 'Jump in,' he would call in a pleased voice and I would walk along the shaking boards of the rickety jetty to the far end where his boat was moored.

We would set out at once in the direction of Hayirsiz Island where he'd look around for the big fish, then steer for one of his seamarks. There we would cast our lines down into the secret depths of the murmuring, translucent, emerald-green sea.

Fisher Selim's clothes, his hair, his hands were invariably covered with fish scales. On entering the coffee-house he would be preceded by a pleasant odour of the sea and he himself always smelled strongly of fish. It was Fisher Selim who said that the man of the sea carries his smell with him wherever he goes.

'And his scales too . . . ,' I said.

He smiled. 'Yes, his scales too.'

First, he had worked as a coachman on Büyükada Island. The owner of the carriage was a Circassian, and Selim's job was to look after the horses and drive his fares, mostly elegant ladies, around this pleasure island. But ever present in his mind was the thought of his mother. I must go and see her this winter, he resolved. For some reason he did not do so. How old was he at the time? He had no idea. Why had he run away from home? He never told me. The second summer he quarrelled with the Circassian and found another job with a Greek greengrocer on neighbouring Burgaz Island. All through that summer he carted cases of vegetables and fruit, always with the idea of setting out for Uzunyayla as soon as winter came. But instead he got work on board a fishing boat, thinking that in another year he would have saved even more money. That winter he discovered the tavernas of Beyoğlu and tasted his first *raki* and his first woman too. He developed a passion for fishing. The master of his boat was a Greek, Hristo, a jovial fellow who spent all his earnings carousing in Beyoğlu or with his lady friend, Despina. Selim had got to like Hristo. For three years he worked for him, the two men on the best of terms, sharing work and pleasure alike, though Selim still nursed the plan of going to Uzunyayla.

One day, Hristo, blind drunk as usual, was quarrelling with himself, which he often did when he had had a drop too much, scolding and swearing for all he was worth. A keen northeaster was blowing. It was freezing, and raging waves were beating at the island, coming half-way up the houses along the shore. Hristo jumped into his boat, which was moored in the little bay, and steered for Yalova. Selim ran after him, but it was too late. In vain he waved and shouted, up to his waist in ice-cold water. Hristo did not so much as glance back and three days later his boat was found aground off the coast of Yalova. He was never heard of again, neither alive nor dead. After this, Selim could not stay on in Burgaz Island, but as Hristo had no relatives that anyone knew of, his boat came to Selim. It was a good solid craft with a powerful engine, a Volvo Penta. Selim decided to go to Kumkapi. In those days there was not another boat like this one in all of Kumkapi. That winter Fisher Selim caught a lot of fish and made a pile of money. Next spring, he vowed to himself, I'll go to Uzunyayla to see my mother . . . But that was the year he was conscripted and sent to Mount Ararat where he fought and was wounded, ending up in Cerrahpaşa Hospital in Istanbul. And there he met the fair-haired nurse . . .

Ever present in his mind was a promise, her promise that she would wait for him until her dying day. His mother, his brothers, Uzunyayla, gambling, drinking, all were set aside. He knew that one day, yes, he was sure of it, he would be reunited with her. On that day, that is, on the day when he'd built a house, a house to match her beauty, he would go straight to the hospital, take her by the hand and bring her home. They would be married at the Beyoğlu registry office, the bride almost invisible in the profusion of flowers . . .

So all these years he had scrimped and saved for this house. He was still saving for it and, as time passed, the girl's image was growing even clearer in his mind's eye. On those days when he had made a lot of money and put it away in his special hiding-place, he would dress in his best clothes and set out to find a plot of land for his house. The first place that had caught his eye was in the Maden quarter of Büyükada Island. Without finding out who the place belonged to, he planted seven pine trees on it and went back again and again to watch them grow. After a while he grew dissatisfied and found a place more to his liking on Burgaz Island where he also planted a few trees. This too, in time, seemed not good enough for his fair-haired love and he opted for a spot near the sea at Florya. There he planted three plane trees. Next it was Yeşilköy that took his fancy. This time it was lime trees he put in. This also palled in a few years. Finally, one day when he was out fishing in the Bosphorus, he came upon a plot of land with tall shady plane trees. This is it, he said. He went straight to the Beykoz nursery and bought seven olive saplings which he promptly planted there. This land belonged to a retired official from the Revenue, who had inherited it among other property from his grandfather, a rich pasha. Fisher Selim considered the land reserved for him once he had planted trees on it. So he never thought of paying a deposit to the white-haired, scraggy-necked old man whom he would see each time he went to Çengelköy, sitting under the venerable plane tree in the seaside café and smoking a nargileh. So sure was Selim of his land that he had long ago engaged masons, carpenters and other craftsmen and had for years now been discussing with them every detail of the house he planned to build.

'Well, Selim?' Haydar, the master craftsman would call out whenever he passed the fisherman's door. 'When are we starting on that house of yours?'

Selim would get all flustered. 'Soon, very soon, master . . . Will you be free in a few days?'

'I'm free any time for you, my friend.'

'Thank you, master, thank you,' Selim would say hurriedly, avoiding any further commitment.

Everyone, the carpenters, the masons, the fishermen, all of Menekşe were waiting for that happy day when Selim would build his rich mansion.

It had been the same with Selim's old flame, the Greek girl. For her too Selim had planned a house in a garden with huge trees. He would keep talking to her about it, changing the location and shape of the dream house each day. 'Vre, Selim!' the girl had said to him one night after their love-making, 'all you do is talk! Vre, it's castles in the air you're building, not a house!' At this, Selim had gone away in a huff, slamming the door behind him. That was the last he saw of his Greek sweetheart before her mother whisked her off to Athens.

Whenever this incident came to his mind, he would be deeply troubled. What if his fair love, like the Greek girl, grew tired of waiting? What if she said, 'Damn your land and damn your mansion, Selim, I'm an old woman and those plane trees you've planted have reached up to the skies by now'? What if she just went away like the other one? No, this one would never do that, he'd tell himself every time. She's too much in love with me. This year, yes, this year, this very spring I'll build that house . . . Just have a little more patience, my rose, my beauty . . . Look, my love, how Master Haydar's ready to start the minute I give the word. And Leon, the best bricklayer in Istanbul . . . And the glazier Cemal from Sivas? 'I'll fit all your windows with crystal, Selim,' he tells me. The masons, the craftsmen, they're only waiting for me to say go and then they'll build me a mansion in a mere couple of months. Just let me save some more money, only a little more . . .

Then one day news reached Fisher Selim that made him fly to Çengelköy. The owner of the land, that white-haired patrician, had died and all his estate had been bought up by Halim Bey Veziroğlu! Selim went straight to him.

'That plot of land there with the plane trees, it's mine,' he said. 'See, I've planted seven olive trees there.'

Taken by surprise at first, Halim Bey Veziroğlu had some papers brought to him and consulted them with meticulous care. Then he turned to Selim, who had remained standing. 'We have no record of your owning land anywhere around here. That place you're speaking of is ours. There never had been any dispute over it. Isn't there some mistake?'

'No mistake,' Fisher Selim replied. 'That land's mine. Seven olive trees I've planted on it. You can go and see for yourself. And how they've grown too!'

'But you can't take possession of land by just planting trees! Have you got the title deeds? Have you effected any payments at all?'

'I'm going to build a mansion there.'

'A mansion?' Halim Bey Veziroğlu collected himself. 'So it's a mansion you have in mind? Won't you take a seat, sir?' And as Selim perched gingerly on the edge of the leather armchair: 'May I ask what your business is, sir?'

'I'm a fisherman.'

'A skipper?'

'A fisherman.'

'Oh . . . Where?'

'In Menekşe.'

'But there must be some mistake.'

'No mistake at all. I was going to buy the land from that old man. I'd been looking for such a place for years. It's just right for her, just right . . .'

'I see,' Halim Bey Veziroğlu said. 'Well, there's no harm done. We'll see what we can do for you, sir. Will you have a cigarette?' And he held out a chased-gold case. Fisher Selim took a cigarette and lit it from the flame of Halim Bey's massive gold lighter. 'Don't worry yourself, Skipper. The land's yours whenever you want to buy it.'

And with that assurance Fisher Selim left Veziroğlu's office, his heart at rest.

The sea undulated gently beneath us. We must have been on one of Selim's most prolific seamarks for, as soon as our baited hook was down, the line tautened and we kept pulling in fish after fish. Here and there the blue of the sea turned to purple and to green. Little white clouds were scudding swiftly on towards Istanbul, casting their shadows over the water. Fisher Selim was deep in thought, his nostrils flaring like a horse's after a fast gallop.

Suddenly, he fixed his steel-blue gaze on me. 'This spring,' he said, 'I'm going to buy that land, and if he doesn't sell it to me I'll kill him.'

'Killing the man won't get you the land,' I remarked.

Selim was irritated. 'I know that,' he said. 'But Veziroğlu has to believe I'll kill him. Then he'll sell.'

'He might, indeed.'

He shook his head. 'Ah, but he's a sharp one, that Veziroğlu. Wouldn't he know that I could never kill a man?'

'He would . . .'

'What can I do then?'

'Nothing.'

'Seems to me that in the end I'll have no choice but to kill the man.'

'God forbid! What kind of talk is that? We can find other places just as good, if not better, provided we have the money.

What about trying right here in Menekşe?'

He looked at me hopefully. 'With a view of the sea? And with plane trees? Large enough for me to plant some olive trees?'

'There's one already planted with olives . . .'

'You mean Zeki Bey's?' He was delighted.

'Of course. Or part of it, at least.'

'That part with the clump of plane trees.'

'Zeki Bey would willingly sell to you.'

The sun had sunk over the horizon, a glowing purplish pink globe, drowning sea and sky in a purple radiance. Now and again an aeroplane would shoot through this purple glow, a golden starlike droplet, leaving a long pink scintillating trail in its wake.

'Are you game?' Fisher Selim said, laughing.

'Yes,' I said. 'For what?'

'I cast out some nets this morning before you came, for goatfish. Want to help me draw them in?'

'Of course.'

It did not take long to reach the nets and we set to work at once. The nets were teeming with fish, frisking, dancing, leaping back into the water.

'We did well not to put this off. Fish shouldn't die in a net.'

'But they're dropping back into the water.'

'Never mind. There'll still be more than enough for us.'

Fisher Selim was silent as we started back for Menekşe. Above us a group of seagulls, wings outspread, were racing us to the shore. A snow-white steamer, all its lights ablaze, was gliding on towards Çanakkale.

'It has to be the coming spring . . . Under those plane trees . . . White it shall be, my mansion, and bright like that.' Selim pointed to the ship. 'Like the first day . . . Yes, the very first day, that's how it'll be.' I didn't ask what first day. 'I'm getting on,' he continued. 'If I don't do it this spring . . . You can't expect a girl to . . .' He sighed. 'Five years or six at the most . . . Next spring . . .'

'Why not now?'

'The land . . . Now . . . Will you come with me to Veziroğlu? Then we'll try Zeki Bey.'

'All right,' I said.

I had always wondered but never asked Selim whether this boat was the one that had belonged to Hristo. It looked so new and the engine ran like clockwork. If I had asked, he might have answered confidently, with pride even: 'Of course it's Hristo's. See how I've cared for it all these years? Like the apple of my eye, so that if Hristo were to come back one day and ask, "Where's my boat?", "Here, Hristo, I'd say, take your boat. Like the apple of my eye I've looked after it . . ." ' Why hadn't Selim sold this boat and built the house he longed for so much? Even now it would bring in a goodly sum. But Selim would never do that, not if it was Hristo's boat. He would never betray a trust. So, for years, Fisher Selim had been waiting for Hristo. He was not dead, Selim was sure of it. He was alive, in Athens. He would return one day, yielding to his yearning for Istanbul. Selim knew those Istanbul Greeks. They so missed the city that they always came back here to die. And so would Hristo one day.

'There's an abundance of fish this year.'

'It's going to be a good year for fishermen.'

'Come the spring . . .'

15

Hüseyin Huri, that bastard, lost to all sense of comradeship, was leading the police search for Zeynel. A gun at his waist, a police cap on his head, he went prowling through the town just like a foraging dog, sniffing at the foot of walls, bushes and trees, under bridges, in empty fishing boats and railway wagons, in hollows of the old city walls, in burnt-down palaces and ruined houses, abandoned mosques, forgotten Byzantine churches, underground cisterns, crumbling aqueducts, unfrequented woods on the Bosphorus hills, city-line boats, in short, all the haunts of vagrant city waifs. He knew every one of Zeynel's habitual resorts and it was he who had tipped the police off about Lame Hasan's house. But for Lame Hasan's quickness, it would have been all up with Zeynel. Yes, it was that bastard, that treacherous snake, Hüseyin Huri . . . How Zeynel regretted not having killed him!

Every morning Zeynel bought the newspapers and read word for word the account of Zeynel Çelik's adventures, thrilled to the core, admiring the handsome, broad-shouldered man in the photographs, the wavy hair, the hawk nose, forgetting that this was not Zeynel Çelik at all, then suddenly freezing at the realization that the gangster they were talking about was he himself, the Zeynel Çelik who had killed that husband and wife in Bebek, who had led a gang of twenty-one men all armed with automatic weapons, who had held the police in check at the Harem landing-stage for exactly four and a half hours and only escaped when troop reinforcements arrived, who with his men had raped four young girls in Çemberlitaş, who had a sweetheart in Beşiktaş . . . That's what they said, a very beautiful woman of noble stock, the daughter of pashas. Zühre Paşali was her name. Her son had told the police that Zeynel was so madly in love he'd be sure to come for her before skipping across the border to Greece or Bulgaria. Two other mistresses Zeynel had, one in Aksaray, the other in Menekşe, and the police had the houses of all three watched day and night, particularly Zühre Paşali's. The police had also been given important information about Zeynel by Hüseyin Huri and by those of the gang who had been captured. And also by the son of his sweetheart who went by the name of Durmuş Ali Alkaplan. Yes, the police would soon get hold of that bloodthirsty gangster who was also involved in the smuggling of arms and narcotics . . .

Who was this Zeynel Çelik? Who was the man in the photographs? Could there be two Zeynel Çeliks operating in Istanbul? The woman in Beşiktaş, that was true, the bank robbery, that was true too. And trussing up the police . . . But Durmuş Alkaplan, that was wrong, it wasn't the boy's name . . . What about the couple murdered in Bebek? That must be the work of the other Zeynel Çelik, as must be the clash with the police at the Harem landing-stage. And what about the police-men reported wounded in the fight at Ayvansaray? They had indeed given him chase that night among the Laz scows docked for caulking. Hüseyin Huri had been at their head like the police-dog he was, but all Zeynel had done was to lie low between the boats, while they shouted and fired at each other in the dark, until he could slip away to hide in the lumber depot behind the Cibali cigarette factory, the one place Hüseyin Huri did not know about. It was the girl, Mido, who had shown it to him one night. There he had slept peacefully all through the day among the pleasant smells of pine and cedar and beech, just as if he were up in the high mountains, and as soon as darkness fell he had slipped out, cat-like, through the heaped lumber and made straight for the Lale tripe restaurant in Beyoğlu.

Strange. While he, Zeynel, did nothing but stroll around the city, unmolested, that other Zeynel Çelik was hard at it, killing, robbing, raping, smuggling, visiting his mistresses, making the whole of Istanbul tremble.

Suddenly, his eyes fell on a headline in one of the tabloid newspapers. 'Gangster's hoard uncovered.' Without stopping to read the rest, he started up and hailed a taxi. 'Quick, quick, to Yedikule, near the bus terminal,' he said. Luckily the road was free of traffic and they were soon there. His hands in his pockets, whistling nonchalantly, Zeynel joined the motley crowd milling around the bright-coloured buses. The terminal was drowned in a cold, dizzying radiance. Coloured neon signs flickered above the bus line offices. The noise of engines, of many voices, of hawking vendors, all merged in a booming resonance. Somewhere near the entrance six policemen stood in a group and one of them was watching him covertly. Without changing his stance, Zeynel walked on, still whistling, past the six men and into the Edirne bus office. He emerged a little later with the same unconcerned air and made his way to the gates. Once outside he broke into a run and came to the wall of the cemetery, at the back of which was the Golden Gate, the largest in the old Byzantine ramparts. A sea of tombstones, long, short, slanting, tumbledown, inscribed or bare, stretched from here to the gate. Suddenly, he caught sight of the policemen again. They were crouching behind a cart. He did not stop, but kept to the road leading to the sea. At the railway workshops, he turned in towards the carpet-cleaning plant, and retracing his steps along the wall of Yedikule Castle dungeon he came again to the cemetery wall. The policemen were still there and inside, under the vault canopied by the fig tree, something stirred and a brass button glinted briefly.

'God!' Zeynel said. 'Oh God, my money's gone . . .' No one but Hüseyin Huri knew of that crypt beneath the vault in the old walls. Of course, he must have blabbed to the police about this, their most secret hideout. Why, oh, why had he been such a fool as to put all his money in that hole? Hüseyin Huri was a sharp one, he could ferret out the devil himself from his lair. Hadn't he already combed through all their other hideouts? And where would the gangster Zeynel Çelik keep his two and a half million but in one of his secret caches? He didn't have a father who had safe-deposit boxes, did he?

Worried, bitterly dispirited, he made his way down to the shingle on the shore. Ah, you blockhead, you stupid Laz, he reproached himself, ah, you crazy idiot, to go and hide your money just where Hüseyin Huri would be sure to find it! When you could very well have entrusted it to Lame Hasan. But no, no . . . At the sight of so much money Lame Hasan would have had a fit, especially when he learnt it was the loot from the bank. And what about Fisher Selim? Why, he'd accept the money and then sit upon it. Entrust Fisher Selim with money! He would at once buy land with it and plant a few trees, yes, as much land as that money could buy. Some said he had quite a pile put by, that he had killed the Greek, Hristo, and taken all his money and his boat too . . .

Zeynel had robbed a bank, all right, but who would know it was him? Wouldn't everyone attribute this to the other Zeynel, even the murder of Ihsan? A good thing the fellow's name was Zeynel. But for him, it would have been all up with this Zeynel. What about the folks in Menekşe? Would they go to the police when that other Zeynel was caught and say, 'That's not the one who shot Ihsan, who robbed the bank'? No, no, they'd be much too scared. If that Zeynel was to be feared, so was this one. Hadn't he killed Ihsan in full view of all of Menekşe? Just let anyone try to denounce him!

Hüseyin Huri . . .? He stopped short on the shingle. If the money wasn't there, the first thing he'd do was to kill him. Killing Ihsan had been easy. Just a cry and he'd dropped from the chair and died. With Hüseyin Huri he would make a real killing of it, ripping out his bowels, slashing his throat . . . And as for the money, he would just go and rob another bank. Weren't there bank robberies every day in Istanbul? Suddenly, he shivered. Could he ever even go near a bank again? The very sound of the word made his blood run cold.

He turned back and ran all the way to the Golden Gate. The cart was still there, but the policemen had gone. He flew over the wall and in an instant he was at the entrance to the vault. Something made him start. Like lightning he whipped out his gun.

'Throw down your guns or I shoot,' he hissed.

Three voices rose from the deepest corner of the crypt. 'We surrender, Zeynel Abi . . .'

'Who the hell are you?'

'Don't you recognize me, Zeynel Abi?'

With his left hand Zeynel drew out of his pocket the tiny torch he had bought that morning and shone it in the direction of the voice. There, in the corner, three little boys were huddling on top of each other, their eyes blinking with fright.

Zeynel was relieved. 'For a moment I thought it was the police,' he exclaimed.

The oldest of the boys stepped forward. 'D'you know why we've come?' he said. 'Hüseyin Huri's squealed on you.'

The two other boys drew nearer.

'He's told the cops about all your secret places . . .'

'And, what's more, he's set all the boys after you.'

'The cops have given them money . . . Sweets . . .'

'They don't beat us up any more when we sleep at the railway station.'

'They've promised to give a thousand lira to the one who finds out where you are. And a new suit and shoes too . . .'

'What about you, Rifat?'

'Well . . .' Rifat hesitated.

'Me too,' Ali blurted out.

'Me too . . . ,' Celal murmured.

'And which of you would get the thousand lira?' Zeynel asked.

'Me,' Rifat said.

'Why you?'

'My grandmother's sick,' Rifat said. 'Bedridden. There's no money at all for the doctor, for medicines. I was going to give it to her.' His clothes reeked of urine.

'Where are the cops?'

'They've gone now. Four of them were guarding the gates, two were under that fig tree and seven more in that big tomb out there.'

'And you?'

'They gave us some money . . .'

'What am I to do now? If I leave you here, you'll be with the police in a moment.'

'No, Abi, I swear to God that . . .'

'No, Abi, may my two eyes fall out if . . .'

'No, Abi, would we ever squeal on you?'

'Listen. I'm going to take you into the cemetery and tie you up there. I'll give you a lot of money, much more than the police, if you do as I tell you. All right?'

'Oh, yes, yes!' the boys cried joyfully.

'You'll say I took you prisoner. I'll have to gag you, though. Have you got handkerchiefs?'

'Yes, we have. Gag us, Abi. Tie us up too.'

'We need some rope though.'

They pointed to their trousers, which were held up by cords instead of belts.

'All right then, let's go. No trying to escape, mind, or I'll shoot you down.'

'For shame, Abi! We're your prisoners now, and you're giving us money too. Why should we escape?'

'But who's going to set you free after I've gone, if no one comes along?'

'You just tie us up, Abi. We'll see to the rest,' Rifat said. 'Anyway, the cops will soon be back.'

'What! Why didn't you tell me that? Damn you, you wretched little bastards, damn you, take this . . . And this . . .' Beside himself, Zeynel hit out at them blindly with his gun. 'Rifat,' he said, dealing him a final kick, 'take the cords off these little buggers' trousers and tie up their hands and feet.'

'As you say, Abi . . .'

Zeynel held the torch on the boys whose hands and faces were running with blood, while Rifat cut each boy's cord in two with a penknife and bound their hands and legs.

'Tie those handkerchiefs round their mouths too . . .'

When this was done, Zeynel proceeded to bind and gag Rifat in his turn. Then he lugged all three boys out into the cemetery. There he hesitated a minute, then drew a wad of money out of his hip pocket. They were all five-hundred-lira notes. He selected a batch and hid it in the hole of a tombstone. 'Here,' he said. 'A thousand lira for your grandmother and the rest to be shared between you three. Don't tell the police or they'll take it away from you. Goodbye.'

He was laughing to himself as he went back to the crypt. The money was there, he knew it. He had felt the earth with his foot while he was talking to the boys. His heart beating, he dug up the sack, swung it on to his shoulder and, leaping over the tombstones, ran into the street. There he drew up short. It wouldn't do to be seen running. Whistling, he strolled down to the seaside and sat down at the foot of a tall pile-driver that towered on the embankment like a fairy-tale giant. Its very hugeness made him feel safe, as though he was in the heart of an iron mountain.

And now what was he to do, where was he to hide all this money? He went on sitting there, seeing nothing, hearing nothing, and when he was roused by the billing and cooing of a pair of lovers right behind him it was already dark. His hand went to the money sack. It was there, where he had put it. Tucking it under his arm, he staggered out on to the main road and hailed a taxi. 'To Unkapani,' he said. There was nothing for it. It had to be the lumber depot again. He could think of no other place where he could get some sleep.

It had begun to rain. After a while they found themselves

locked in a traffic jam, with policemen blowing their whistles, cars honking, people yelling, all to no avail. Suddenly the city lights went out and in the darkness the confusion became even greater. All the cars hooted their horns in unison. His own driver too was honking away non-stop. As they reached Unkapani Bridge at a snail's pace, the lights came on and all the cars sounded their horns together again, exultantly this time. He got off in front of the Central Bank and made his way round the Cibali cigarette factory to the lumber depot. Just as he was about to jump in through the window, a hand grabbed him by the nape of his neck. He struggled, but could not shake off that strong grip. Then – how it happened he did not know – the bundle of money was under his left arm, the gun in his right hand, glinting under the street lamp, exploding, and he was free, on the opposite side of the street, all in an instant, and in his wake people shouting and the long strident blare of whistles. Just then the lights went out once more and in the stonelike darkness the rain gathered strength. He rushed uphill, past Lame Mustafa's restaurant and into the Priest's Garden. It was Mido again who had shown him this garden. Ah, if only she were with him now! What a bold gallant girl Mido was . . . The noise of running feet, guns firing, police whistles was coming nearer. Zeynel ran for all he was worth, bumping into walls and trees, tripping over brambles, cold with sweat, wet through, the bundle of money held tight under his jacket to keep it from the rain, taking care all the time not to fall into that dry well Mido had taken him to once. Finally he came upon the well. It was more of a large cistern and not nearly as deep as he'd thought. There were several cavities in its walls. Shining his little torch at one of them, he stuffed the sack of money in and closed up the aperture with some stones. After this it was only a matter of minutes before he had slipped out of the garden and reached the Bozdoğan Aqueduct. Crossing under the passageway, he came to the Aksaray buffet and ordered three *lahmacuns*. He was wet to the bone and the money he drew from his pocket had turned to pulp. With trembling hands he managed to extract a hundred-lira note and handed it to the buffet man.

Under an awning nearby a man with a drooping moustache was broiling corncobs over glowing, coral-like embers. Zeynel drew nearer to the brazier to catch a little of its warmth. The *lahmacuns* he devoured in an instant. 'Broil me a nice fat one,' he said to the corncob man, wiping his mouth with the *lahma-cun* wrapping-paper. 'Right-ho,' the man said and he selected a good-sized corncob to put on the fire. 'You're very wet, brother. Where have you been in this weather?'

Zeynel was upset by the question, but only for a moment. 'I've been having a fling in Beyoğlu,' he said, assuming a self-satisfied air, 'and with all this rain I couldn't find a *dolmuş.*'

'And where are you from?'

'From Rize,' Zeynel answered.

'It sticks out a mile,' the man said.

'How's that?' Zeynel said, piqued.

'Your native accent, that's how,' the other laughed. 'And also that Black Sea nose of yours.'

Zeynel's hand flew to his nose, then he burst out laughing too.

'What d'you do for a living?'

'I'm a fisherman,' Zeynel said. 'What a drencher this is! And what's your name, then?'

'Abuzer,' the corncob man said. He spoke with a strong Kurdish accent.

'Malatya?' Zeynel guessed.

'You've hit it on the nose,' the man laughed.

Zeynel was studying Abuzer closely. Could he risk it, could he say to him, 'Will you put me up tonight? I'll pay you as much as you ask . . .'? But look at those eyes, Zeynel thought. He's a sharp one. He'll catch on in a minute and go straight to the police. Without a word of farewell, he rushed off down the boulevard to the seashore and sat down on the shingle. The rain was beating down with all its force. Across the sea the lights from the Princes Islands twinkled feebly. For a moment he entertained the idea of taking refuge there, but that would be like stepping into a trap. His leg ached. Feeling it, he realized his trousers were torn. Suddenly the thought of his money made him jump. What if the police had discovered the hiding-place in the cistern? He sprinted up the steps and along the Aksaray Boulevard, then veered towards Topkapi to avoid being seen again by the corncob man. Aksaray Square was almost deserted at this hour. Some itinerant vendors still stood around with their barrows of oranges, apples, bananas and melons. There were also a few *kebap*-sellers, making ready to pack up. But at his meatball barbecue-car the old Tartar man was only just firing his coals. Clouds of smoke swirled out of the stovepipe as from the chimney of a factory. Zeynel halted in front of a *çöp-kebap*-vendor who had fixed his apparatus on a cart mounted on four bicycle wheels. On the side of the cart was the legend: 'The Desert Gazelle Breadearner'. The tall-chimneyed brazier was very wide and heaped to the brim with glowing embers.

'Sixteen skewers,' Zeynel said.

'Right away,' the vendor said, pleased. He was a very old man with a short white beard, a long sallow face, shrivelled pouches under his eyes and a knife scar on his forehead. His wide shoulders were hunched, giving him a lopsided gait. Sprinkling the tiny little cubes of skewered lamb with salt and pepper, he laid them over the embers which he fanned with a piece of cardboard adorned with the picture of a naked woman. In a moment the odour of burning fat spread through the square and thick fumes smoked greenly in the neon lighting. Dextrously the man slipped the meat cubes off the sixteen skewers into a bread loaf and added half a tomato and a sprig of parsley. 'Here you are, sir,' he said.

Zeynel was gratified at being called sir. Munching his bread and meat, he sped on under the rain, impelled by the vision of the police, under the guidance of Hüseyin Huri or even Mido, discovering his cache and taking away his money. Breathlessly, he swallowed the last of the bread, now reduced to a pulp by the rain. If only he could get a drink of water somewhere ... Anyway, tomorrow the first thing he would do was to go to Beyoğlu and buy himself a new suit from that big store. No, no, not that one! Wouldn't the salesman wonder how he'd got his clothes so messed up in only a couple of days? He would go to that other store opposite. And the shoes he would buy in Beyazit. Why, he could buy a hundred pairs if he wanted! He had tons of cash now. Then his heart sizzled and he hurried on to the Priest's Garden.

He was about to step in when he caught sight of shadows stirring in the direction of the cistern. He turned and fled. As he stumbled down the slope, windows and doors were flung open, then slammed shut again. Three men lunged at him from behind a minibus. Quickly, Zeynel slipped under a vine trellis into a side alley where two rows of old wooden houses tumbled over each other. Their windows were all dark. The few street lamps shone dully and dripped with rain. Under a lamppost was a man with a drawn gun in one hand and the long hair of a woman twined about the other. With much kicking and cursing, he was trying to drag her along with him, while she, for her part, stood fast, her feet planted firmly on the ground. Zeynel caught a glimpse of her bloodstained hands and ran for all he was worth, stopping a few streets higher up. Suddenly he saw two nightwatchmen marching his way from in front of the Orthodox Patriarchate, obviously suspicious of him. He staggered up to them, more dead than alive, his clothes clinging to his body, in a piteous state. 'He's killing her,' he panted. 'My big sister . . . He's murdering her, that man down there.' And he clutched at the arm of one of the watchmen as though he were going to faint. The watchman shook him off and he and his companion rushed down into the lower street, while Zeynel dashed into a side alley and found his way back again to the Priest's Garden. Three shots rang out from the street below, followed by a long piercing scream. Zeynel heard the tramp of many feet ringing through the street. Quietly, he glided along the wall, not daring to look back. From behind him, the yellow neon light of a giant billboard fell over a half-rotten plane tree whose hollow trunk had been filled with cement. Drowned in this yellow light, he heard more loudly now the pounding of hob-nailed boots. He whirled round the broad trunk, steeped in yellowness, and whirling with him very slowly were a group of yellowed, elongated figures. Another long scream from down below, and Zeynel flung himself over the wet wall, leaving those long, resonant shades still wheeling round the thick cemented tree-trunk, captive in the dense yellow neon light. He bumped into trees, stumbled over bushes and fell spreadeagled over a long slab of stone. Some figures clustered above him and nightwatchmen began to blow their whistles, shriek after shriek. He jumped up and dashed on along the wall, nearer and nearer the cistern . . . Up to his neck in water, almost drowning . . .

The next morning was sunny in Eminönü Square. Wet, ruffled pigeons, torpid and silent, huddled on the steps of the Valide Mosque, drying themselves. The shadows of the minarets reached all the way to the Vegetable Market in front of Rustem Paşa Mosque. Zeynel was dying of thirst and he still could not bring himself to get up, so tired was he. His knees ached as though they were being torn apart and the soles of his feet were burning. All the bones in his body cracking, he rose from the steps of the mosque and staggered up the footbridge and down to the buffet near the boat landing. He asked for a fizzy lemonade. It was ice-cold and he gulped it down at one go. All around him small boys were selling black-market cigarettes with shrill cries. Most of them he knew. They were from the Sirkeci gang. He ordered a bottle of mineral water and drank that too, but it only made him thirstier. He had to get away from here quickly, before one of these boys recognized him. He asked for some water. This he drank very slowly, looking warily about him. Then he slipped into the waiting-hall, out through another door and took a taxi for Beyoğlu.

First he went into a shoe-shop and chose a pair of high-heeled shoes with platform soles, such as he'd dreamed of for years. He kept them on and had the muddy ones packed into a parcel. Next, he entered the fanciest ready-to-wear store in town and, more confident than ever, took the lift to the men's department.

'What can I do for you, sir?' A very pretty salesgirl greeted him without a look at his torn, muddy clothes. Again, it was the suit of his dreams he hit upon. In the little mirrored cubicle he fastened the gun under his armpit as Ihsan the gangster always used to do.

'I want to buy an overcoat too,' he said to the salesgirl. She led him to the coats department and handed him over to another girl.

'Will you look after the gentleman?' she said.

The new girl was even prettier.

'One of those,' said Zeynel, indicating some coats. And at the third one he tried on: 'This one.'

The salesgirl smiled. It hadn't taken long.

Zeynel paid for his purchases on the ground floor and left, carrying all his old things in parcels. He felt rather wobbly in his new high-soled shoes and it seemed to him that everyone's eyes were on him. At Galatasaray corner he turned into a side alley. Making sure no one was looking, he deposited his parcels in a corner and walked out again into the high street, where he took a taxi to Cibali. He got out just in front of the lumber depot. The air here smelled of tobacco from the cigarette factory and also of the all-pervading rotten stench of the Golden Horn. He examined the spot where he had shot the man the night before. There was no blood on the pavement, no trace of anything. The bullet must have only grazed him he surmised as he walked slowly up last night's streets. He longed to get to the cache more quickly, but it would not do to be seen running in broad daylight.

He came to the rusty iron gate of the Priest's Garden and pushed it open fearfully. Inside, near the old cistern, a group of children were playing football, shouting shrilly at each other. Very slowly, looking warily about him, he approached the well. Suddenly he caught sight of the girl Mido. She was sitting there on the wall in close embrace with a youth whose hair was as long as the girl's. This gave him a real shock. He retraced his steps at once. Was it possible? Had Mido found the money? And, worse, had she given it to the foppish fellow she was smooching with? If so, they'd see, those two, how Zeynel would make mincemeat of them!

His legs wobbling, he wended his way down the slope. Mido and that dandy must be lying in wait and the moment those children were gone they would grab this stupid Zeynel's money and spend it as lavishly as Vehbi Koç himself, while he, Zeynel . . . It was not to be borne. He must go back and do away with them both. Up the slope again he went, at a run, and back into the Priest's Garden. The children were still at their noisy ball game and Mido and her long-haired swain were still engrossed in each other, lost to the world. Zeynel's tight hold on the butt of his gun relaxed.

Mido was only fourteen years old, but there was not a male in all Sirkeci that she had not lain with. She would gladly have gone with Zeynel too. And it was with this intention that she had brought him here last year when they had first met. They had climbed down into the cistern, but there Zeynel, seized with panic, had gone quite limp and this had made him so mad that he had almost killed the girl. And now she was necking with that fellow and as soon as the football players were gone they would make for the cistern and Mido would throw off her clothes and lie on her back, stark naked, her legs wide open . . .

He drifted down the slope, but stopped at the bottom of the street. The time-worn cobbles shone in the bright sunshine as though polished. He could not tear himself away. Up he rushed again. The football players were still there and so was Mido with the young man. Relieved, he turned down the street, yet having reached the bottom of the slope his feet dragged him back. Again and again he found himself at the garden gate, weary, exhausted, thoroughly dispirited.

It was nearly evening. Apartment buildings, houses, roads were all in the shadow now. Only the spires of the minarets shone in the fading daylight. A smoke haze was slowly settling over the Golden Horn.

'Mido can't have found the money. She hasn't even looked for it, lusting as she is after that long-haired fellow. I'll just wait till it's dark . . .'

He hailed a taxi for Beyoğlu. There, in the Flower Market, he bought three brightly striped nylon bags, then quickly returned to Cibali.

Darkness was falling when he reached the Priest's Garden. It was completely deserted. His heart pounding, he hurried to the cistern, jumped in and removed the stones from the hole. The sack with the money was right where he had put it. His whole body quivered with joy as he lifted it out. Such a lot of money . . . Sitting down on the stone, he began transferring the banknotes to the new nylon bags. Two of them he filled to the brim, and the third almost. He stuffed half a dozen wads into his pockets. The trouble was he needed a newspaper or something to cover the top of the bags so the money would not show. That newspaper-stand under the plane tree . . . It should still be open, he thought. He twisted the handles tightly together and set off. There was one last paper on the counter. He took it and left some change. In a secluded nook behind the factory, he covered the money with the pages from the newspaper so that the devil himself could not have guessed that these three shopping-bags held anything like banknotes.

Emerging on Unkapani Avenue he hopped into a taxi. 'To Beşiktaş,' he said. He directed the driver up the Serencebey rise and got off at the mouth of the alley that led to Dursun Kemal's house. He had hardly taken two steps when someone touched his arm. With a bound he was round the corner, his gun in his hand. Then, looking back, he recognized Dursun Kemal.

'It's only me, Zeynel Abi,' Dursun Kemal said in a mournful tone. 'They've got the whole neighbourhood surrounded. I've been waiting here for you ever since that day. Come this way. There are no cops in that alley.'

'What's wrong?' Zeynel asked.

'Father . . .' Dursun Kemal blurted out. 'He's killed my mum.'

167

He choked and burst into tears.

Zeynel tore off into the darkness. Dursun Kemal fell after him. On they rushed, Zeynel in front, the boy following, through dark alleys, bright streets, leaping over ditches, fences, walls, into a garden with very tall trees, where the sound of voices made them sprint off, north this time into a pool of light, and away into a field. Zeynel's foot caught in a bramble and he sprawled to the ground. A whiff of wet turf rose to his nostrils. His heart was pounding in his chest, in his neck, legs, belly, through his whole body.

'Wait, Abi,' Dursun Kemal panted. 'Let's stop here. There's no one. It's quite deserted . . .'

After a while Zeynel was able to speak. 'Why did he kill your mother?'

'He killed her,' Dursun Kemal said brokenly. 'With a dagger. Stabbed her twenty-one times . . .'

'But why?' Zeynel insisted.

'He killed her,' the boy repeated. 'He was going to kill her for years anyway. The neighbours told him you'd been to our house, and also that you were Zeynel Çelik.'

'Where is he now, your father?'

'At home. Crying . . . Crying, he says, because you've killed my mum . . . So the police are lying in wait for you. I heard them. They're going to kill you the minute they see you, without warning. That friend of yours, he was there too, that maniac, what's his name – the one with black eyes and thick eye-brows . . .'

'Hüseyin Huri.'

'That one. The police questioned me too. They wanted to know where I'd met you. "On the bridge," I said, "as I was fishing." . . . So don't go anywhere near the bridge. It will be crawling with plainclothesmen. Sirkeci too . . . Everywhere . . . Ready to shoot you on sight, they're so afraid of you.'

The boy talked on, but Zeynel heard nothing. He saw only a room spattered with blood. Crimson blood all over the place and a dagger stabbing again and again, craunch, craunch . . . And he heard the woman's screams, rending the skies.

'Father dragged me to the back of the house, without the police or anyone noticing. He held the bloody dagger to my throat. "Speak," he said,? "you saw it, didn't you? With your own eyes you saw Zeynel Çelik kill your mother. Or didn't you?

If you didn't, I'll kill you . . ." "I saw it," I said, I lied. The police questioned all the neighbours. All of them said you had killed her. I'm afraid. He's going to kill me, my father . . .'

Zeynel sprang up and dashed away. Dursun Kemal rushed after him. 'Go back, go back!' Zeynel kept shouting at the boy. 'Don't come after me, don't! They'll kill you too, along with me . . . Please go . . .' The boy paid no heed and stuck close to his heels.

Suddenly they emerged into a brightly lit square. As though stunned by the light they both stopped short. Zeynel looked back and met Dursun Kemal's eyes, wide with fright. 'Don't . . . You mustn't come with me,' he gasped out. 'They'll kill you . . . Kill you . . .'

'I'm afraid,' the boy said in a moan. 'My father's going to kill me . . .'

Zeynel produced three wads of banknotes from his pocket and thrust them into the boy's hands. 'Look, take this. It's a lot of money. You can go anywhere you want with that money.' And he was off again.

Dursun Kemal tucked the money into the inside pocket of his jacket which he buttoned up carefully, then he scurried on after Zeynel.

'Are you still there?' Zeynel spoke in a tearful voice. 'Look, they're going to kill me and you too with me . . . Go back, you goddamn fool!'

Dursun Kemal only stood there, five paces away, as though riveted to the ground.

'Look, I'm begging you. Stop following me. If the cops see us together they'll know at once that I'm Zeynel . . .' And off he ran.

Dursun Kemal hesitated a little, then spurted after him as fast as he could. It was pitch dark. They went trampling through a cabbage patch and came to a hothouse, a long structure in which a stove was burning and carnations bloomed. Zeynel ran round the hothouse and down to a wooden fence which he pushed down with a crash. Dursun Kemal shot through the opening and suddenly realized they were in Yildiz Park. 'Stop, stop, Zeynel Abi!' he called as loudly as he dared. 'The cops . . . All the cops of Istanbul . . . They're here! Here in this park!'

Zeynel stopped in his tracks. 'Where? Where?'

'There! Down there in that house,' Dursun Kemal whispered.

'They sleep there, a thousand cops, two thousand, three thousand . . .'

Zeynel ran to the gates of the park. They were closed. A hubbub broke out. They escaped up the dark slope along the wall. By what route they reached the broad, tree-lined Ortaköy Boulevard, he never knew. It was raining, a misty drizzle.

The Beşiktaş boat landing . . . A brightly lit ferry . . . Zeynel was inside. A web of light streaked by, another boat with the dark shadow of the Bosphorus Bridge falling over it. Houses like fairy lights all along the shore . . . Their reflections in the water, torn apart by the boat . . . All eyes on him, wide, insistent . . . People from the four corners of the boat converging upon them. . . . Run, go away! Gimlet-like, the searchlight boring into the night, illuminating the curtain of misty rain . . . Water gushes over the deck. The boat is sinking, rising . . . Slipping, slipping, the three striped nylon bags gripped tightly in his left hand . . . A wide net of misty rain, a far-distant net, swaying vaguely behind the curtain of misty rain, a vast blue moon-net from Rize town, hung out between two huge plane trees . . . And behind the net three ship's lanterns. The boat, its prow uplifted, is heading for the Black Sea. A wooded village . . . A rocky coast, the thundering Black Sea, the racing waves pounding the shore, madly . . . And the quails, tired, dead, falling in hundreds into the nets, into the water, into the light, into the dark night . . . All over the Black Sea, basketfuls of quails . . . Lured as they are crossing the sea, hastening to get to the lights with a supreme effort of their weary wings, often unable to reach land, dropping into the water. . . . As they strive to cross the boundless billowy remote Black Sea . . . Fuming embers, fires dotting the shore, star-like . . . The greasy odour of roasting quails floating in the wind . . . A yellow motor car . . . Charge what you like, but just drive on, brother. Thousands of headlights, thousands of cars, shrill whistles, the city lights suddenly extinguished . . . On the Bosphorus a boat, shimmering bright, a single boat in the pitch-black dark . . . And Hüseyin Huri's eyes, huge, glinting blackly in front of the policemen . . . Stop! Stop there. If you come after me again I'll shoot you. Think they won't kill you all the more if you stay with me? Are you mad? My God, it's full of cops everywhere I go. . . . The boat is gliding through the night like a ray of light, through the misty drizzle, the quails raining down upon it . . . Run, Dursun Kemal, they're going to kill you!

'Look, don't come another step, Dursun Kemal!' Zeynel whipped out his gun. 'I'll kill you too like . . .'

Like I killed your mother. Killed her, killed her . . .

He stopped a passing taxi. Dursun Kemal jumped in after him.

The police again at Kumkapi, firing their guns . . . And the fumes of grilled meatballs . . . I'm dying of hunger, Dursun Kemal whispered. Die dammit, die, Zeynel hissed.

'There! Hüseyin Huri! There . . . Kill him!'

Three guns exploded simultaneously under the Ahirkapi lighthouse. Zeynel and Dursun Kemal shot away uphill towards Topkapi Palace. The door of an old wooden house was open. They barged in and a dog scurried out, barking in fright. It was quite empty inside and they sank into a corner.

The house leaned against the walls of Topkapi Palace. In front of it was the courtyard enclosure of Haghia Sophia and the rumble of the city resounded deeply from the walls of the old basilica, as though against a craggy mountain. Suddenly, Zeynel was on his feet, running. 'They'll find us here. They're bound to.' Only when he was in front of the Sultan Ahmed Mosque did he stop. Walking over to the Egyptian Obelisk in the old hippodrome, he sat down on its railings. Dursun Kemal came and perched opposite him on the iron railings of the park. As soon as he saw him, Zeynel streaked off round the back of the mosque.

'Don't come after me. I'll kill you. Go away!'

'I'm afraid . . .'

In the lumber depot they fell asleep on the piles of planks and boards. On waking and sitting up Zeynel banged his head against the zinc roof of the depot, which reverberated long and loud. The bundle of money was clamped in his hand. He had not loosened his grip even in his sleep. He gasped when he saw Dursun Kemal beside him.

'Go away,' he moaned, 'go, don't follow me any more. They're going to kill me and you with me. Run, save yourself at least . . .'

And taking his head in his hands he tried to think.

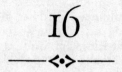

16

The sea had not yet paled when Fisher Selim set out that day. A delicate dawn-heralding breeze was softly blowing, to fill a man with joy. Fisher Selim's heart tingled. The old familiar seagulls accompanied his boat, gliding with outstretched wings above him. Day would be dawning by the time he reached Hayirsiz Island and the sea would then become snow-white, luminous. It was not always like that before sunrise, but that's how it would be today. Selim knew it from long experience, from the mountains opposite, the clouds, the haze over Istanbul city, the swell of the sea, its special hue, the reflection of the star-studded sky.

Sitting at the tiller he gazed at the city trembling behind the smoky haze, its shores and hills, domes and minarets, apartments and neon lights, now vanishing, now floating into view.

As he came to Hayirsiz Island the sea began to whiten. It stretched about him, a boundless snow-white expanse, perfectly smooth, without a wrinkle. At such moments, Fisher Selim would remain motionless, his whole being blending into the sea, the mountains, the fading night sky, never stirring until the first rays of the sun beamed up from behind Selimiye and Üsküdar, illuminating the bronze crescents of the minaret tips. Afterwards the east would turn purple, then pink, and finally in a blaze of light the sun would appear and the leaden domes and the windowpanes would flash and flare. In an instant Istanbul would be drowned in brightness. And as the city with its tall minarets was stretching and rousing itself Fisher Selim would get ready his baits and hooks, casting his first line when the sea turned gradually from white to mauve to a luminous blue, prepared to wait for the first live creature to strike the sharp, crooked, merciless steel.

A pinkish-blue light licked the surface of the water like a breeze and died out. Today there was no bursting radiance over Istanbul. The light sprung out from over the Bosphorus, Leander's Tower, Moda promontory and, spreading over the sea like a slow sheet of liquid, passed beneath Fisher Selim's boat with a violent thrust, moving on towards Silivri and Tekirdag.

Fisher Selim began reciting the magic prayer learnt from his grandmother in that very ancient Caucasian tongue, a prayer he had never really fathomed, which spoke of eagles, steep crags, noble horses. It was not a prayer he resorted to often, only when he was in a tight spot or when he wanted something very badly, and always before going to Halim Bey Veziroğlu. Today he said it very slowly as he selected the most attractive, sweet-smelling bait he could find and fixed it on his largest hook.

There was a slow swell in the sea now, a breathing that came from deep down, and its colour was changing gradually from blue to green, a rich green that glistened like lush spring grain waving in the sun. In all these years I've been fishing, Selim thought, only very few times have I come across such a sea . . . Green grain, billowing, a crystal sea hit by the sun, breaking, reflecting, glistening, breaking again, a spangled undulation shedding its light into the sky, a riot of sparks . . . The rocks of Hayirsiz Island too were drowned in the sparkling green brilliance. So was Fisher Selim's face, his hands, the fishing line, the mosques and minarets, the whole of Istanbul city, breaking, shattering, swimming behind a green haze like a dream.

Fisher Selim concluded his prayer and let the line run gently through his fingers into the green water. This was not a hook for small or even medium-sized fish. Today he was expecting his own fish, the very large one. Today the weather, the sea were just right for the big fish. Today the sea was a bountiful field of grain, growing knee-high, rolling, flashing in the sunlight.

Halim Bey Veziroğlu, that grasping son-of-a-bitch, may earth fill his eyes! Those dull eyes . . . Shrivelled like those of a dead sheep, eyes that bode no good, that carry the symptoms of some fatal disease . . .

Selim's practised hands gave the line a few gentle tugs. If he caught it today . . . Last time, the hook had been too small, the line not strong enough. But this time there was not a fish in the Marmara Sea that could resist his line. He would have the right amount of money then. And Halim Bey Veziroğlu must get it into his head that after this fish . . .

Halim Bey Veziroğlu . . . Death was stamped on that sallow face. The yellow, elongated, lifeless hands, the sagging trousers, the purple lips, even the hairy ears, purple . . . The balding head

with one or two wisps of hair combed across the bare patch . . .
Lethargic, tired of living, yet at the mere mention of land those
dead sheep's eyes come to life, they gleam, and it is as though an
entirely different man has taken his place. Each time, he takes
the money, counts it, counts it again, makes a few reckonings,
stares at it, then with a deep sigh, 'Oh dear, Selim Bey, land
prices have shot up again and your money's not nearly enough.
I'm terribly sorry, Selim Bey, but how can I sell you that land of
mine, every inch of which is worth its weight in gold, for the
paltry sum you offer? Let's just wait a little longer. Oh, I
understand how it is! Well, you can root up those trees of yours
if you wish. But I'd be sorry about that, Selim Bey, very sorry.
How beautifully they've grown! I went there yesterday and saw
them, green, bursting with life. Yes, Efendi, it's a pious deed to
plant a tree, especially an olive tree. They're so long-lived and
their fruit is said to be one of the fruits of Paradise. What trouble
you must have taken, how you must have toiled to raise them!
And I was told – you know, I've just bought another piece of land
– that the trees on it were also planted by you! Yes, I know your
love for trees, and very proper it is. To breed a tree is as good
as breeding a child. Well, then, let's be patient, Selim Bey. I
don't say I won't sell to you. It's just that I don't usually sell
land. I only buy it. I like to buy land, Selim Bey. I own the best
in Istanbul, all with tall grown trees, and sometimes I wonder whether you've planted them all. We'll see, Selim Bey, the
land won't run away, don't you worry, and I won't sell to anyone else . . .'

A little breeze ruffled the green surface of the water. The
sunlight reached deep deep down, a welter of light billowed on
the sea bed, dark green in places, flashing bright in others. Fisher
Selim could see his white line all the way down.

The hospital . . . Her soft breasts, slightly downy, warm
against his face . . . The very memory was enough to drive him
into the wildest ecstasy. Especially on such days, floating on a
calm sea, his line deep down in wait for the big fish . . . Letting
himself drift into a warm paradise . . . How many many times
had he tasted this bliss . . . His greatest joy in life was these
moments when he could summon up the memory of her flaxen
hair, her blue eyes, her woman's smell. And his worst torment
was when something broke the spell and the dream receded. Yet
even then, like wine whose dregs have settled, like a shimmer-

ing mist, the dream was enhanced by distance. Sometimes for a month or two the flaxen-haired vision eluded him and he would turn frantic. For once a man has had this dream he will be the happiest of creatures all his life. He will not see the light, nor the sea, the blue, women, fish, the smell of fish, of the sun, he will not see or smell or feel these things, he will blend into them with his whole being, smelling of sun more than the sun itself, such wild intoxication that he will never sober up in a whole lifetime. Bewitched . . . This was Fisher Selim, caught for ever in a spell, his back turned on reality, safe in his dream . . .

'Who wanted this of you, Selim? Ah, Selim . . . Who asked for a house under a plane tree, a garden? Perhaps a shanty, a single small room would have been enough for her . . .'

Hadn't Selim considered this in all those years when he was deceiving himself, waiting at the gates of Cerrahpaşa Hospital waiting, waiting, then taking to his heels as the white-capped nurses began to troop out, rushing down the street as though a savage beast was after him, jumping into the first taxi he encountered, putting out to sea as far as he could get? Of course he had, but he could not forsake that dream of paradise, that ineffable thrill. A white bed, smelling clean of soap, and she sitting beside him, naked, her breasts white and firm, the curve of her hips, his hand on her belly . . . She is stroking his hair, leaning over him, warm, redolent, embracing him, embracing Selim, burning . . . That is why Selim is always alone, solitary, on his fishing expeditions, talking to no one, unwilling to allow his dream, his sacred vision, to be spoiled, still determined to build his house there, under the plane tree at Çengelköy, to buy the land from Veziroğlu and, if not, from Zeki Bey. Yes, he will build it and, if nothing else, fill it with her warm fragrance.

A screeching turmoil of seagulls over Hayirsiz Island roused him from his reverie. Hundreds of gulls were wheeling round and round in a large swarm above the rocks, and more and more gulls were joining them, their mad cries growing shriller and shriller.

'Something's up,' Selim muttered. 'A school of large fish must be after some smaller prey.' And indeed he soon spied a glittering flurry way over there in the water, thousands of fish leaping into the air, vanishing, reappearing a little further off, sparkling in thousands, fading, then up again in a quivering scintillation on the green sea. 'Yes, something's up. We'll see soon enough.'

And he kept his eyes on the fleeing, frisking shoals, alert now, for these were no small fry, but quite big fish, jumping perhaps as high as one metre out of the water.

Abruptly, the gulls ceased their frenzied clamour and dispersed, scattering this way and that, to reassemble again in a long row stretching from the island far out into the distance. The sun was quarter-high now. The silently swaying sea had changed from green to grey, then to blue, and the brightness of its depths had died away.

'There's something strange today,' Selim muttered, as though addressing the gulls. 'Something out of the ordinary . . .' And he fell back into his dreamy state. No fisherman should do that, ever, and certainly not with his line down in the water.

Long white ships, heading for Istanbul or for the Çanakkale Strait, floated high above the sea, suspended in the brightness. Thus it is in such weather, when daylight melts into a vaporous haze. From a distance the ships appear to be hovering far up in the smoky sky. Perhaps, Selim thought, it's the *lodos* wind coming. Perhaps . . .

Suddenly his arm jerked. The boat, the sea, the gulls, everything reeled and he was almost swung overboard. In an instant, the gulls were thronging over the island's point, wheeling crazily with piercing cries. Selim's practised hands at once began to let out the line. This isn't a fish, he thought as the cord slipped rapidly through his fingers, it's a monster . . .

What should he do when the line gave out? He must decide quickly. Should he run the engine and follow it quietly or should he let the fish pull the boat? The nylon cord was strong, no ordinary fish could break it. If this one had swallowed the bait whole, then it could tow the skiff as long as it liked, it would tire and surface in the end. Swiftly, he lashed the line to one of the bronze tholepins and felt at once how the boat was drifting along after the fish. From over Hayirsiz Island the gulls swooped down in a mad screeching swarm and began to fly above his boat, wing to wing.

And so they sailed on, now more slowly, now gathering speed, the squalling gulls above dashing back and forth between the boat and the fish. After a while Selim noticed the line slackening. He picked it up. It was limp and floating on the water. His heart sank. Could it be that the fish had cut it and escaped? He pulled and pulled and still it came. Then without warning, as though the fish had been playing with him, the line tensed, he lost his hold and found himself sprawling on the prow. Before he could gather his wits, the boat was lurching and dipping dangerously. Water filled the keel and Selim, drenched, stunned, could only watch helplessly as the fish continued to drag the boat on with all its strength. Up down, up down went the prow, then the rolling abated and the line slackened again. Selim seized it and started winding it in, but on his guard now, very very slowly, and indeed there was a violent tug and the skiff speeded on inland towards Hayirsiz Island, though not so fast this time.

This fish must be even larger than the one, the last of its kind, that Selim had been after all these months. Surely it must weigh three hundred kilos, maybe five hundred, and, no doubt about it, it was a swordfish. There could be no larger fish in the Marmara Sea, neither the big tuna nor the shark. Hurray, swordfish, he rejoiced. But the boat was heading steadily for the rocks of Hayirsiz Island. What if the damn creature drags the skiff on to those rocks, Selim thought. Should I run the engine? This fish is a sly one . . .

As they neared the coast, Selim primed the engine, but just then the fish changed its course. Tracing a half-circle, it swam on ever more rapidly around the island. 'It couldn't break my line!' Selim shouted, his heart pounding. 'And it won't. It'll soon tire itself out.' But the fear in him was shouting too. 'It's got the line taut to breaking, quivering, hissing . . . It'll break . . . It can't take any more.'

What if it tugs the boat down, he thought with dread. His hands quivered as he strained and pulled in vain at the vibrating line. Then, no, he told himself, the boat's too big, no fish, however large, can drag it down. Yet all kinds of fearful misgivings assailed him. There is no knowing how strong a fish may be. Even a little fish struggling on the end of your line will unexpectedly snap it and fly back into the water. It can sometimes have your large boat tossing as on a rough sea . . .

Sighing, Selim revved up the motor and steered the boat carefully after the fish. And still it never loosened the line, nor lessened its speed. On it went, even faster now, on a perfectly straight course, neither plunging nor rising nearer to the surface. The sea, flat, blue, smooth, overflowing with sunlight, undulated gently beneath them. But for the whooping turmoil of gulls flying low between the boat and the fish, it was as though nothing untoward was taking place. Who knows what a great fish this was! Perhaps it wasn't a fish at all . . . Whatever it was, it must be a brave, splendid creature. The line was stretching ever more tightly, so Selim revved up the motor, but the faster the boat went, the more the fish gathered speed.

A little further in front of them, the sea was turning purple and beyond that was a white streak. The fish passed the purple stretch and struck against the current. This forced it to swerve east, towards Büyükada Island. It was going even faster now and the joy that had been welling up inside Selim burst into the open. It was a magic being, a miracle that he had before him, a creature that never tired, that never would tire even if they went on like this for days, an uncanny being.

Suddenly, the fish must have paused, for the line sagged over the water. Selim grabbed the rudder, then hastily switched off the motor. The boat was nearly above the fish. Just then the fish gave a long pull, the prow dipped and straightened and the line became taut again. The fish had managed to get clear of the current. Selim felt a resurgence of joy. He seized the line and heaved, but the fish held fast. Then it must have given a toss of its head, for Selim was yanked forward and barely avoided being flung headlong over the prow. He felt a burning in his palms as the cord slid through his hands. The bronze tholepin vibrated as though it was being wrenched off. Rushing to the motor, he started it up again and steered after the fish. The line was still rigid, but the tholepin did not grate any longer.

Stand fast, my lion, stand fast, was the mad scream rising inside Selim, though what he meant by that he did not know. The skiff circled Sedef Island and skimmed in front of a city-line ferry. White clouds rising from the north were gathering swiftly over the sea, swelling, brightening . . .

Now they were sailing straight for Yalova, on the opposite coast. In the distance, a luminous patch on the sea, like a well of light, reflected the sun in blinding radiance. The sea smelled deliciously of the sun now. Selim's hands hurt a little, but his whole body was alert, vibrant. That Halim Bey Veziroğlu, if he could be convinced that Selim would kill him – such old men hold their lives very dear – perhaps then he might surrender the land, perhaps without even taking any money . . . He must be made to feel fear, to believe Selim would kill him. And for that

Selim had to believe it himself . . .

The line slackened again. Was the fish diving? Down, down, down went the line under the boat, it tightened, the boat floundered, but not so badly this time, a sign that the fish was tiring. Selim felt a pang of pity. Surely it would not be long now before it surfaced and lay there, its white belly exposed in the air . . .

But here it was, tugging again! The line straightened, a good part of it shot out of the water. Then it went limp. Again and again it tightened and loosened, water spurting up high all around. On they streamed, the sea beneath them now white, now green or mauve. Ahead, white waves were billowing and when they reached them the fish shook the boat again, then dived deep down, slowed and accelerated. And Selim followed its every move, rejoicing, losing heart, rejoicing again. He could not understand himself, sorry for the fish when it tired, relieved when it plucked up its strength . . .

Now it was pressing on madly, the line steady and taut above the water. Never had Selim come across such a fish. Certainly he had hooked others and kept up the chase for four hours, five, seven even, tiring his game, bagging it in the end, but never one that could tow his boat as though it were no heavier than a nutshell. What if this one dragged him all over the Marmara for three days and three nights, what if he ran out of fuel and the fish, straining at the line, broke it at last and got away? Yet, if he caught it . . . The thought made him tremble with joy, but at the same time there was an ache in his heart.

The gulls seemed to have gone mad. Back and forth they coursed from the fish to the boat, a whirling, tossing mass caught in a violent storm, their cries amplified to a fearful ululation. And the more they churned above, the faster went the fish. The shadows of the white clouds raced over the ever-changing surface of the water.

Selim's mind wandered from the fish to Veziroğlu, to the trees he had planted on that land, to the lofty Caucasus, to the flaxen-haired one in Cerrahpaşa Hospital, to the scent of her breasts, to the hazy domes and minarets of distant Istanbul city, while his practised hands mechanically steered the rudder according to the fish's course.

He was roused from his reverie by the sharp grinding of the bronze tholepin. They were opposite Hayirsiz Island again and the fish, straining with all its might, was swimming round the island. It's going to break away, Selim thought, elated. Twice the fish circled the island, then it slowed down.

'No fish, however strong, can sever this nylon cord, thick as a finger,' Selim muttered despondently as he gathered in the slackening line. 'It can't get that huge hook out of its mouth either. It'll never break away, never be free again, the poor thing . . .' The fish seemed to have abandoned the fight. 'Come, then, come, come to me,' Selim murmured like a lament. 'Come, sonny, prince of the high seas, come to me. How quickly you've surrendered in spite of your mighty size! Come, then, come quick . . .'

But even as he spoke the fish revived. The line in the boat skidded back into the water and tautened, and they were circling the island once more, the boat tossing up and down, spewing white foam all around it. The madly screeching gulls swarmed over more thickly in a dizzy, jumbled whirl, their cries deafening now. Suddenly, the line tightened to breaking-point, water spurted from it and an enormous fish appeared on the sea, tensed like a bow, its back a rich radiant blue under the sun. Then the shimmerng mass sank back. Selim sat spellbound, but even before that glistening splendour had faded from his sight the fish flashed up again, drowning Selim, the boat, the water, the whole world in a radiant blueness. It arched and disappeared. The third time that huge glistening mass of blue rose to the surface, Selim was ready. With his sharp fisherman's knife he slashed at the line. In the same instant the fish ducked, leaving a frothing ferment in its place. Selim's arms fell to his sides. For a long time he stood staring after the fleeing fish, the deep-blue radiance still flashing through his head.

When he came to himself the sun-drenched sea shone with a different brightness and a serene, quivering gladness enveloped him. He set the rudder for Menekşe and sank down, weary yet rested, light as a bird inside.

What if the fish can't get the hook out of its mouth? he was thinking as the boat slowly chugged on towards the coast. What if it swallows it? Will it die? Then, no, he told himself his heart trembling with joy, no hook can really hurt such a big fish. The flesh will form an envelope over it, that's all. As for the line, well, it'll find a way to cut it . . .

Every old fisherman knows this from long experience.

17

From the Vegetable Market opposite Azapkapi Mosque to almost half-way across the Golden Horn a whole array of derelict Laz scows are moored, smelling of tar, clustering larboard to starboard, stern to bow, and it was in the murky, stuffy hull of an empty scow that they had slept, snuggled against each other, to be woken at dawn by the blaring of boat sirens. People lived here in these old scows, bachelors, seasonal and unemployed workers, all in perfect accord and particularly respectful towards the women. The drug addicts on the shore, the black-marketeers, the thieves and cutpurses had no place here. And all around was the huge miry swamp, the Golden Horn, nothing but a cesspit now, a garbage dump, full of carrion, dogs, cats, huge rats, gulls, horses, a stagnant sea with never a wave, its flow forgotten, bleakly reflecting the neon lamps, car lights and the dull hazy sunlight, strewn with deadwood and the sweepings of hundreds of kilos of vegetables, tomatoes, eggplants, oranges, leeks, melons and water-melons from the Vegetable Market, torpid, its surface skimmed with years and years of acid-stinking burnt oils from the surrounding factories, reeking with a noisome nauseating odour like no odour in the world.

And now, weary, dirty, ghastly, the Golden Horn was waking together with the rest of Istanbul. And Galata Bridge and Unkapani Bridge were also slowly stirring, soon to become an inextricable tangle of cars, a maddening traffic jam lasting for hours, exuding a continuous odour of exhaust fumes, all veiled in a thin but stifling haze.

Rowing-boats and motorboats, cleaving drearily through this thick water, were crossing from one shore to the other. Small steamboats passed under the bridges, folding back their long painted funnels. In the Kasimpaşa dockyard, ships' hulls, stern to stern, extended to the middle of the Golden Horn. Here was a world of iron rust, forming a raddled slimy layer over the water. Blue blazing flares of blowtorches, razor-sharp, fulgurating, cut through the city, through its lights and ships and noise and rain. All the gulls of the Golden Horn were assembled here, a white blanket over the dome of Azapkapı Mosque and the red-tiled roofs of the houses and apartment buildings, slumbering in the first light of dawn. In a while, as the fishing craft arrived at the Fish Mart, they would wake, shrieking, and swarm down over the water and the incoming boats, diving at lightning speed after the fish thrown away by the fishermen.

On the hills around the Golden Horn Istanbul town was waking too, its muddy, pot-holed streets strewn with garbage, rotting fruit, broken plastic objects, scraps of old shoes, the limbs of carcasses, bloody bones, its air viscid, poisonous, deathly ... Soon the neon lights of the billboards over the buildings would go off and the Golden Horn would close in upon itself, drowned in dense factory smoke and fetid smells, the brief flashes of the welding torches and its weak lights fading into the day, and from Karaköy the city-line ferries would belch out their black smoke, spreading a lowering pall over sea and land.

Zeynel and Dursun Kemal had woken up in this tarry hull on the miasmic Golden Horn, stiff, staring blankly at each other, all that had taken place the night before a blurred jumble in their heads.

And in Istanbul city, people were killing, gouging each other's eyes out, robbing banks, running, choking under pelting rain, choking with the ghastly corrosion, the sewers, the refuse heaps, falling on the garbage like screeching rapacious seagulls, crazed, a ravenous, despairing horde assailing the city. Half-naked tramps, itinerant vendors, small-time black-marketeers, murderers, rapists ... And de luxe motor cars, elegant shops, painted bejewelled women, no longer human, smelling of mould ... One single car selling for three million, an apartment for seven million ... The rent alone sixty thousand lira ... Gardens planted with flowers imported from far-off Japan, tended by gardeners also trained in Japan, villas, luxurious yachts, gambling dens ... Black-marketeers selling smuggled cigarettes, whisky, electronic machines, spending money like water, shedding blood like water too ... And the starving ... Driven to suicide by hunger ... Three hundred thousand prostitutes ... The destitute, the homosexuals ... And the police, present at every corner, in every brothel, extorting bribes, killing like any other network of thugs, letting murderers off scot-free and laying the blame on their victims, swinging their truncheons and shooting in blind frenzy not at the killers and racketeers, but at the slain, the underdogs . . . All intermingled, the jewels, the furs, the hunger, the dirt, the sewers, the night-clubs, the haggling, the trafficking in human flesh . . . Corrupt, the Golden Horn, ever since bygone Byzantium, the people, the carrion, the factories, the filth, the nakedness . . . Corrupt, Beyoğlu, Galata, the merchants, the Genoese tower, the buying and selling, the glittering Ottoman gold coins . . . Corrupt, a medieval city always and for ever, until the day it wastes away and goes to ruin . . . And, wallowing in mud, the squatters, fleeing the country in droves from hunger and want . . . Zeytinburnu, the pocket-sized dwellings of clapboard, sheet metal, old packing cases . . . Scanty light, a trickle of water from a fountain . . . Gültepe, Fikirtepe, Kuştepe, all the hills ringing Istanbul, crowded with ramshackle hovels, rape and abuse, jealousy, bloodshed . . . Corrupt, the proud domes and minarets, the tall apartment buildings, insolent, sickening, extravagant, chaotic . . . All that is beautiful and good and human destroyed long ago . . . The few remaining trees chopped down. Corrupt, perishing in a noisome stench of decay, a swiftly disintegrating aged city, Istanbul. Its heart crawling with millions and millions of maggots, the water, the earth, the people rotting away, the very stones and steel putrefying, a garbage heap, a body ripe for devastating plagues and pestilences . . .

Zeynel stretched himself leisurely, picked up his nylon bags and without a glance at Dursun Kemal vaulted up on to the deck, then over into a scow alongside. A woman was kindling some wood in a tin can. He stopped and sniffed at the fumes of the burning wood, then passed on to the wharf. At the Valide Mosque he went up the steps and turned on one of the ablution taps. The water gushed out. Quickly, he set his bags aside on the stone pavement and carefully washed his face and hair and hands. As he straightened up he saw Dursun Kemal on his right, bending over another tap and washing with exactly the same movements as himself. He did not speak to him.

Eminönü Square, the streets around the mosque and the Spice Bazaar were slowly filling up. Itinerant vendors with pale, drawn faces, wearing rubber shoes and clothes that floated on their bodies, youths with long hair in high platform-soled shoes, their buttocks rippling in tight blue jeans like American

Negroes, men with bushy village-style moustaches in indeterminate attire, neither country nor city, women in colourful peasant frocks worn over long trousers . . . Meatball-sellers were pushing in their carts mounted on old bicycle wheels and swirling with the mouthwatering fumes of burnt fat. *Börek*-vendors in soiled aprons had already set up their glass cases. So had the *lahmacun*-sellers, and the wooden churns of the *ayran*-vendors were swinging away busily.

Soon the place was teeming with every conceivable kind of goods: cheap shoes, trousers and shirts, underwear, pullovers, second-hand coats, plastic pots and plates, mugs, pails, flasks, aluminium utensils, glassware, artificial flowers, brooms, poultry in cages, baskets of eggs, barrows of melons and watermelons, small motor trucks full of lemons and oranges, tomatoes, parsley, radishes, and even rugs and carpets and sheep.

By mid-morning a milling crowd had completely encompassed carts and trucks and booths, on which the vendors had clambered to shout their wares, many of them using loudspeakers. The hawkers were mostly women and children. One scraggy-necked little boy of ten or eleven, his eyes starting from his head, stood on top of a stall and kept up a continuous babble, while his father below was selling orlon, nylon and woollen sweaters all of them green. A yellow-haired woman on the steps of the mosque, swaying her hips like a night-club dancer, her heavy breasts swinging, was singing the praises of a new brand of nylon stockings. Her skirts were hitched up and she kept putting on a pair of stockings and stripping them off again. And pressing all around her was a tight circle of blue-jeaned goggling youths with long unkempt hair and muddy shoes and trouser-legs. On the top step an old man paced up and down, hawking some things wrapped in red paper that he held in a string bag. 'Come, friends, come this way, this way,' he shouted ceaselessly, beads of sweat on his brow, though what he was selling it was impossible to tell.

An ill-dressed crowd it was. People's bodies were misshapen, their faces drawn and sallow, their hair unwashed, their hands lifeless, their eyes hungry, resentful, sullen . . . A degenerate, different species it was that thronged the square, bumping into each other, stepping on one another's feet, screaming, swearing, bargaining, a flurried mass stretching down to the shore where rowing-boats and city ferries came and went, cleaving through the garbage-strewn water.

In all this turmoil, snake-charmers, conjurors, sword-swallowers, fire-eaters were exhibiting their prowess, and at the foot of the Spice Bazaar wall were lined up the fortune-tellers with their pigeons and rabbits trotting out of their cages to pick out a scrap of paper and put it into the hand extended to them.

Zeynel and Dursun Kemal were at the hub of the crush, drifting wherever the crowd was the densest. If it thinned out around them they hurried into its very centre again. They felt afraid, naked and abandoned without all these people round them. Somehow it had occurred to them to buy a *börek* each. They were munching away with huge hungry bites and drinking fruit juice from a stand nearby.

Over in the east above Haghia Sophia an eagle was wheeling. Its wings spread wide, it vanished into the clouds and reappeared gliding over the Bosphorus Bridge. The next instant it was over Leander's Tower, tracing a wide circle from there to Fenerbahçe and the Ahirkapi lighthouse, and then once again it took up its position between the minarets of Haghia Sophia, hovering in the face of the north wind, its rufous wings glinting in the sunlight.

Küçükçekmece, on market days, was like this, aswarm with a thousand and one feet, and on such a day the fortune-teller with the eagle had set up his board, large as a door, with the many holes into which were inserted the red, green, yellow, blue, purple slips of paper inscribed with fortunes. The great coppery eagle, alert, its wings tightly closed, its crooked talons knife-sharp, paced up and down the board, its hook-beaked head held high, pausing now and again to pierce the crowd with its fierce gold-ringed eyes, while its owner shouted out tales about his magic eagle and its oracular powers in a sing-song voice, beside himself, ecstatic, his hands and feet, face and hair and eyes, his whole body adding to the telling of it.

'This eagle,' he was saying, 'this wondrous eagle is the off-spring of the Phoenix that only lays one single egg in a thousand years up on fabulous Mount Kaf. For years and years it has been divining. Thousands, millions of people have heard it and not once has it gone wrong, everyone's future has been laid bare before him like an open book. Come, folks, now's the time for your fortune, before night closes on you!'

He was a tiny little man, but as he talked he gained stature, his bow legs straightened and his small hairy face with the wedge-shaped slanted eyes and the high scar-marred cheekbones took on a strange beauty.

A long line of people, men and women, young and old, had queued up while the eagle picked out the folded scraps of paper from their holes with its strong crooked beak. Up and down it went over the wide board, stopping now and then to stretch its powerful neck and spread its huge wings, glaring at the crowd with its keen yellow, white and mauve striated eyes, only to resume its coming and going ever more quickly, as though performing some age-old eagle dance.

One after another, those who had received their scraps of paper turned away, reading and re-reading their fortune as they took themselves home, their hearts at ease, with fresh confidence in the future, as though entering a new and brighter world, grateful to the eagle if only for one night's dreams of paradise.

As the day drew to a close and the market-place emptied, the slant-eyed little man would take the exhausted eagle from the now empty board, set it on the ground, then heaving the board on to his back and putting his arms through its leather straps he would pick up the drooping eagle and set out, his pouch of money in his hand. Crossing the old Küçükçemece bridge he would emerge on to the London Highway and, blinking his tiny wedge-shaped eyes, would turn either left towards Istanbul or right towards Avcilar.

A gentle drizzling rain was falling that evening. The setting sun, huge, mauve-pink, was poised poplar-high above the sea and reflected on the water, a perfectly round disc. Banks of swelling clouds, deep mauve, were whirling on the golden line of the horizon.

The little man with the great eagle in his arms was climbing the rise of Avcilar, leaving Çekmece Lake behind, and after them went Zeynel. How old was he then? He could not remember, but for some time he had felt a fascination for the eagle and its owner and he followed them whenever he could. The great eagle had come to represent security, a kind of safeguard for him. And if he happened to have a little money his greatest treat was to have the eagle draw a lot for him.

The little man now descended the cliff to the edge of the sea, set down the eagle, leaned his board against the cliffside and hung the money pouch on it. Then he opened the large bag slung over his shoulder and took out a dead pigeon. Squatting under a tree at the top of the cliff, Zeynel watched as the little man began plucking the pigeon, while the eagle, suddenly perking up, rubbed itself against his legs like a cat and flapped its wings. The little man flung the plucked pigeon on to the shingle and the eagle, slightly lifting its wings, wobbled over to it eagerly. At that moment a man appeared round the cliff and came striding over to the little man who was trying to kindle a fire with a few sticks and brambles. The little man leapt to his feet. Zeynel had recognized the newcomer. It was Ihsan the gangster . . . They began to talk. Then the talk turned into an argument. Zeynel could not catch what they said, but they were shouting and swearing angrily. Soon they had come to blows, the little man holding his own against the huge and awesome gangster, pounding at him with increasing force as the fight went on. Twice Ihsan stumbled and fell, as the little man, nimble and swift, ran round him, pummelling away and hurling stones at him. From a distance the great eagle, flapping its wings, hopping and lunging, was taking part in the fight too. Zeynel, struck dumb with fear, cowered under the tree, his teeth chattering. Suddenly, he saw a long knife glinting in Ihsan's hand. It flashed briefly and Ihsan's arm went up down, up down. The eagle's owner bellowed and slumped to the ground. Ihsan stooped over him and stabbed again and again. At last he lurched over to the board, seized the money pouch, then turned back to the dead man, ransacked his pockets and stuffed some things into the money pouch. The eagle was standing there forlornly at the dead man's feet. Ihsan dealt it a kick. The bird uttered a long cry, fluttered over to the shore and came and stood again beside the corpse. Suddenly, it rose high into the sky, then swooped down and with outstretched motionless wings began to wheel above the body.

The next morning at dawn some fishermen discovered the corpse on the shore. The eagle was still whirling up above and Zeynel still crouching under the tree, frozen stiff. An ambulance arrived and removed the body to the morgue near Gülhane Park. And the eagle followed the ambulance all the way. Everyone in Menekşe was talking about it, about the eagle that kept gliding a poplar's height above the ambulance and how, as the body was carried into the morgue, it came and perched on the plane tree in front of the entrance gates. No one appeared to claim the body. It remained there in the morgue slot for quite a while and all day long the eagle was seen wheeling above the morgue and round about – Haghia Sophia, Gülhane Park, Topkapi Palace. Several times a day it swooped down upon the pigeons of Valide Mosque, snatched one up and soared off, disappearing for an hour or so, then turning up again, ceaselessly circling the sky above Haghia Sophia, now and again alighting on the ancient plane tree in the middle of the street. Finally, it was the Municipality that took the body away to be buried and with it the eagle vanished too, only to reappear a few days later in its accustomed place on the plane tree or in the skies above Haghia Sophia.

To this day Zeynel had never told a soul that it was Ihsan who had killed the eagle's owner . . .

Way over Azapkapi Mosque a mass of seagulls swirled up and down as though caught in a whirlwind. The crowd enveloped Zeynel and Dursun Kemal like a warm blanket. They were not hungry, but still, when they saw a barrow heaped high with fresh cucumbers, they bought one each. It seemed as if the whole of Istanbul had gathered here today, all the neighbouring slum areas of Kazliçeşme, Zeytinburnu, Taşlitarla, and the denser the crowd, the better Zeynel felt.

It was near the old enclosed fountain that his eyes lighted on the newspaper at the stand there. He stopped short, electrified, bought a paper and, dashing over to the mosque, sat down on the topmost step. Then he saw Dursun Kemal planted right beside him. 'You go and sit over there,' he ordered, pointing to the far end of the flight of steps. Setting the money bags down, he unfolded the paper with trembling hands and stared as though he could not believe what he saw. Splashed over a whole page was a colour photograph of Zühre Paşali, stark naked, sprawled on a bed, her full breasts, the hair of her pubis and armpits, every part of her exposed. The white sheets, her face and belly were spattered with red blood. Yes, this was Zühre Paşali herself, and her large beautiful eyes had remained wide open . . . Zeynel recognized the bed, the embroidered sheets, the pillow-case trimmed all round with pink roses. Under the photograph, in red characters as big as a finger, running from one side of the page to the other was the legend, 'Cut-throat gangster Zeynel Çelik's latest murder', and beneath, in smaller type, blue this time, 'The police in a state of alert . . . Orders to shoot on sight.' All the blood left Zeynel's face and the paper slipped from his nerveless hands. Dursun Kemal made a dash to retrieve it. 'Stop,' Zeynel shouted. 'Don't touch that paper.' The boy dropped the paper at once.

It's shameful, Zeynel was thinking, the poor boy mustn't see his mother like that, stark naked . . . Suddenly, he felt himself in a void, alone, exposed, transfixed by countless eyes. He plunged down the steps into the crowd. Dursun Kemal was at his heels.

'Quick,' Zeynel whispered to him breathlessly, 'go and have a look around. See if there are any cops with Hüseyin Huri on the watch for me at the landing-place and round the corner of the mosque. I'll wait for you here, near this fountain.'

Dursun Kemal sprinted away and the first thing he saw as he rounded the mosque was a group of five policemen. He made himself scarce in the crowd and cowered under the arcade. The policemen were walking in the direction of the fruit-trading wharf. He got up and followed them. On the wharf the same policemen he had seen the other day were there again, even the one who kept scratching his bottom and the other one who spat endlessly into the sea. And from the Unkapani underpass two policemen came running towards him. Dursun Kemal turned to flee and met two jet-black eyes under thick brows, Hüseyin Huri himself, standing there looking at him maliciously. He made a dash for the entranceway of the Spice Bazaar, but there, too, a pair of glittering black eyes, exactly like Hüseyin Huri's, were fixed on him. Dursun Kemal did not know which way to turn. Hüseyin Huri seemed to be everywhere and with him a whole lot of policemen. At the fruit-trading wharf Hüseyin Huri grabbed him by the collar. 'It was you who killed your mother,' he shouted, spitting into the sea. All the policemen were spitting too. 'You! Not Zeynel! Not your father, you! You caught her whoring and so you killed her!' Dursun Kemal shook himself free and darted up the slope leading to Süleymaniye Mosque and into smelly narrow alleys where small children were playing in the mud. Here too he came upon policemen at every turning. Finally, he made for Mahmutpaşa Street which, as usual, was thronged with shoppers and crammed with a whole array of goods, clothes, shoes, kitchen utensils, glassware, all overflowing from the shops on to the pavements. He plunged into the crowd and disappeared.

Sitting at the foot of the fountain, his three bags of money beside him, Zeynel was reading the papers. He had bought them all and each contained the same news. Zeynel Çelik was to be killed on sight, with no warning or chance to give himself up. Every time he read this, Zeynel's blood ran cold. One paper said that the police were on Zeynel Çelik's track. For the past three nights the gangster had been seen prowling around the house of Zühre Paşali, his victim, a revolver in his hand, and at his heels his slain mistress's eleven-year-old son. What could the murderer be after now? Another newspaper printed a long account of his relationship with Zühre Paşali and a whole array of photographs of her, large and small, including a wedding photograph in which Dursun Kemal's father, sweating, his eyes bulging in a wild glare, held the bride, a plump girl all in white, as though afraid she would run away from him. That man's a killer, Zeynel thought . . . Printed in all the papers was a colour photograph of a moustached Zeynel Çelik. Only in two papers were the photographs different. In one, Zeynel Çelik held a long-barrelled gun, his arm extended as though firing at something. He was wearing shiny top-boots and breeches, a sash at his waist, a red tie, and a handkerchief in his breast pocket. The man in this photograph bore no likeness at all to the moustached Zeynel Çelik and the paper carried a heart-rending account of the love affair between Zühre Paşali and Zeynel. The second paper, badly printed, not one of the colour tabloids, had a few faded photographs, one of a group of bandits lined up at the foot of some tall crags, with an arrow indicating Zeynel Çelik, a Mauser rifle in his hand and rows of cartridge belts all over him. This Zeynel had no moustache and his eyes squinted slightly. There was a long story about Zeynel's childhood, how he grew up in a village and on reaching manhood killed the man who had murdered his father, and then eloped with the most beautiful girl in the neighbourhood, how they both fought against the gendarmes up in the mountains, how, when his sweetheart was killed, Zeynel left for the town and there met Zühre Paşali, how he took her away from her husband, how she taught this mountain outlaw the ways of the big city and made a redoubtable gangster of him and how for three days now he had been raining bullets on Zühre Paşali's house in order to get in and retrieve his hidden booty . . . Other items of news were that Zeynel Çelik had been sighted in Beyoğlu the night before, but had whipped out his gun on the spot and disappeared, that he had wounded a taxi-driver, that he had intercepted the seventeen-year-old belle of Nişantaş who, recognizing him, had fainted away and had been saved from the gangster's hands only by the arrival of the police. The inhabitants of Menekşe were living in fear. Those who had maltreated the gangster during his childhood were abandoning their homes, resolved not to return until he was captured or killed. Zeynel smiled as he read this. The cowards, he muttered, the lowdown fools . . .

The police had captured three more members of Zeynel Çelik's gang. One of them, known as the Üsküdar Monster, had described Zeynel as the bravest, the most bloodthirsty, the most elusive of the Istanbul thugs. He knew the city down to its innermost recesses, he had a girl in every neighbourhood, he never missed a shot, he had the devil's own charm, a mild smiling countenance, but when angered could even kill his own mother and father, and indeed his first murder had been that of his sister and her lover. It was after that he had come to Istanbul. Zühre Paşali was a close relative of his, a cousin maybe. Anyway, he had a tendency to fall in love with every pretty girl he saw. The police had therefore decided to use young girls as decoys in order to trap him.

Zeynel Çelik was filled with admiration for one of the photographs featuring a mountain of a man with a bushy moustache and hawk-like eyes. He felt a pang of pity at the thought that he would soon be killed. He imagined the police closing in and riddling him with bullets. He saw the huge man toppling over on the lawn of Gülhane Park like a felled plane tree, bellowing, the blood gushing from him . . . He swore to himself never to set foot in Gülhane Park again. Suddenly he shivered. What if they took him for that other Zeynel Çelik and riddled him with bullets too? He jumped up, seized his bags and flung himself into the crowd. Then, terror-stricken, he made for the fountain again. Something was up, he was sure of it, he was surrounded, he, the real Zeynel Çelik. Crazed with fear, he floundered this way and that, his eyes bulging, his hand on his gun, expecting a shower of bullets at any minute. Just then, Dursun Kemal came running up.

'Hüseyin Huri,' he gasped. 'The cops . . . They're all over the place . . .'

Zeynel dashed off to the arcade.

'Wait,' Dursun Kemal cried, rushing after him. 'Look! There! Hüseyin Huri . . . The cops . . .' He grabbed Zeynel's arm and together they ran back. At the corner of the Sümerbank store, Dursun Kemal held Zeynel back again. 'Look . . . There!' They swerved into the street of the Central Post Office and struggled through the throng of street sellers hawking radios, tape-recorders, postcards, posters, stationery, shoes, walking-sticks, coloured plastic flowers, oranges, apples, bananas, and again at the end of the street Dursun Kemal glimpsed Hüseyin Huri and a group of policemen. The street opposite led to the Security Department. It was crawling with police, but there was no Hüseyin Huri, so they struck into it and emerged in front of the boat landing-place. It was full of policemen too.

A trap had snapped shut upon them. They would never be able to break loose. The milling crowds of a moment ago were thinning out, the street pedlars, the conjurors, the loudspeakers had disappeared and people were gradually taking themselves off home. And still the two of them wandered about helplessly, exposed, already holding their arms protectively over their heads against the rain of bullets they were expecting at any moment. In the end, Dursun Kemal dragged Zeynel to the wooden palisade he had once hidden behind and Zeynel wriggled through the hole. They emerged on to an empty muddy patch, crossed it and came to the old building where Dursun Kemal had been apprenticed to the cloth-printer. It was dim inside and empty by this time. There was only an aged janitor, sweeping the floor with a long-handled broom, and coming towards them as he swept.

'It's all right, Zeynel Abi,' Dursun Kemal whispered. 'That's only Halo Misto, the best man in the world. You'll see, he'll brew some tea for us at once. He always does it for everyone, even for those who can't pay.'

As the old man drew near, sweeping away, he lifted his thick grey eyebrows that almost hid his eyes and recognized Dursun Kemal.

'Why, Dursun my child, where have you been?' he cried lovingly. Then in a stricken tone: 'Ah, my poor child, I'm so sorry. So they killed your mother? My poor poor child . . . Is there anyone like a mother, is there anything worse than to lose one's mother? It's like dying once yourself before you die . . . Come, let me make you some tea.'

With a wave of affection Zeynel looked at this boy whose mother had been killed, who had been clinging to him out of fear, yet risking death at his side. He leaned over and stroked the boy's hair with a burning hand. Dursun Kemal's eyes filled with tears. He huddled up to Zeynel and hugged him fiercely.

18

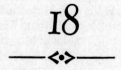

Fisher Selim tossed and turned in his bed and the bedsprings creaked and groaned under him. From outside came the muted sound of the sea and the whirring of insects in the night. Now and then a plane roared down into Yeşilköy Airport, but the last train from Halkali to Sirkeci had long trundled past. Out in the darkness, dogs were howling.

'I'll kill him this time, I will!' Selim vowed. He had been saying this over and over again for the past few days now, trying to work himself up into believing he really would kill Halim Bey Veziroğlu.

The man was wicked, cruel, bloodthirsty, treacherous, the brains behind all the thieves and black-marketeers in the country . . . For long years he had directed the traffic in hashish, heroin and opium and invented a variety of ways and means of smuggling. He was ruthless, he stopped at nothing to attain his ends. Countless homes had been ruined by him, countless children orphaned. Veziroğlu was a surname he had adopted later on. Nobody knew his real name, nor where he came from. There were people who had known him when he operated a gang of thugs in the gambling dens of Beyoğlu, exacting as much protection money as he could. After a spell in jail, he married the daughter of the biggest manufacturer of heroin in Istanbul. And then it was as if Allah had given him a free rein. He donated millions to various political parties, while remaining above politics himself, and when any one of these parties came to power they did not forget his good services. For thirty years the name of Halim Bey Veziroğlu had hung over Istanbul like a pall of fear. He made fortunes and lost them too. Once he was forced to scuttle his ships laden with millions' worth of contraband, another time to blow up his trucks filled with precious black-market goods. On another day he snapped up a large grounded freighter, flying under the Panamanian flag and full to the brim with smuggled cargo, for no more than the price of a motor car.

Over all the coasts of the Marmara and the Black Sea, he set up an iron network of police, gendarmes and gangsters, so that his ships could unload their cargoes of weapons, whisky, American cigarettes and electronic devices in perfect safety under the cover of night. If everyone in this country carries a gun at his waist nowadays, it is largely due to Halim Bey Veziroğlu. And if villages and homes are equipped with automatics and machine-guns the Turkish Republic owes it to him.

Halim Bey Veziroğlu never allowed anyone to pronounce his name without that distinctive 'Bey' in the middle and no one would have dared to do so. He was a close-fisted man who would haggle to the death over one kurush, yet at times spent his money lavishly. Especially when he was entertaining, no one could be more extravagantly generous. All Istanbul knew of Halim Bey Veziroğlu's shady doings and only respected him the more for it. He was the most honoured guest in high society, admired by all, particularly women, and his name came up every day in connection with some scandal or other.

'I shall kill him!'

Halim Bey Veziroğlu's best quality was his ability to pick his men, to attach them to himself, to portion out his gains equally among them and also to protect the high-placed persons and the authorities with whom he dealt, to keep their identities secret, never to breathe their names to anyone. No one had ever been able to ferret out Halim Bey Veziroğlu's contacts.

He owned a number of factories in various branches of industry, two farms, one in Adana, the other in Izmir, and partnerships in several enterprises. He had long ago renounced his other shady activities. One day he cut himself off from them as though with the stroke of a knife. Or maybe it had not happened as quickly as people thought. Maybe he had done it gradually year by year, eliminating one traffic after another until he himself must have been surprised to find that his former illicit dealings had stopped completely.

And now, for the past few years he had stepped up his purchases of land. This was his hobby, his passion. He could not hear of a good tract of land for sale without snapping it up on the spot.

'The man must be done away with, the world cleansed of his filthy presence . . .'

Halim Bey Veziroğlu also had a predilection for very young

girls. Each year he had to have a certain number of girls, eighteen or nineteen years old, neither younger nor older, to deflower. Among his countless business preoccupations, that was his only relaxation. Is that too much for such a man to ask? Why, Istanbul was full of girls ready to give up their maidenhood to Halim Bey Veziroğlu, who always rewarded them bountifully . . .

At least once a month, either by land in his motor car or by sea in his motor launch, he would cover both shores of the Bosphorus and purchase whatever mansion or empty plot struck his fancy. He rarely haggled over the price, but if the owner refused to sell, ah, then it was the turn of firearms to talk . . . Once, he had set his mind on the courtyard of a mosque because he liked the plane trees there, and it was all his men could do to make him renounce his project. After all, it was good money he was paying. He could have bought the mosque itself if he wanted and these people could go and build themselves another mosque on top of Kandilli hill, which was a much grander spot for a mosque . . .

Thus Halim Bey Veziroğlu acquired the choicest land on the Bosphorus and the Islands, in Pendik and Yakacik, and even as far afield as Yalova, Kumburgaz and Tekirdag. And from Antalya, Marmaris or Bodrum on the Mediterranean, to Şile, Akçakoca or Amasra on the Black Sea there was no place that escaped him. The land he bought for fifty thousand today would be worth ten million three years hence, or sometimes even thirty or forty million. He would sell only a tiny fraction of these lots and then buy some more, which again brought in a thousandfold a few years later.

'I shall kill him, kill him! He's bought up the whole earth, that man! Why, he owns enough land to build large cities! But that tract is mine. It was I who planted those trees on it years ago, I who toiled on it. Where was he then? I'm going to build my house on that land. She wanted this of me . . . There, she said, in Çengelköy, under that plane tree . . . She's been waiting all this time for me . . . Enough! I've grown old. I'm long past my prime. And she . . . She? No, she's just the same. Women don't age, they remain fresh as the sea. The sea doesn't grow old, nor the sky, the clouds, the stars . . . Only human beings wither and die. . . . I shall kill him if he doesn't give me my land. I'll shoot him straight in the forehead. If a chit of a child like Zeynel can fell that mountain of a man, surely I can kill Halim Bey Veziroğlu? Who cares if he's got the authorities, the police, the gangsters behind him? I'll kill him, cut him to pieces. I'll do it if it costs me my life. I'll take that miserable puny life of his . . .'

He tossed heavily in his bed and gnashed his teeth. 'What's this!' he cried aloud. 'What I've had to put up with from this man! Each year I go to him with a whole bagful of money and what does he say? "Ohhooo, is that all you've brought, esteemed Selim Bey? You couldn't buy three square metres of my land with that money. No, no, I'm not refusing to sell, it's simply that your money's not enough. Last year? Ah, my friend, land prices are twenty-eight times higher now. Yes, indeed. I'm sorry, dear Selim Bey . . ." '

That sallow, elongated face, repulsive, porous, sagging . . . Those eyes . . . The eyes of a sheep that has been bled to death . . .

'Enough! I'm going to kill you, to rid Istanbul of your tyranny, to take revenge for all those homes you've destroyed. I'm going to kill you, kill, kill . . .'

They're all his, the woods and valleys and streams of the Bosphorus, all Halim Bey Veziroğlu's, the age-old plane trees. He's going to cut them down, uproot the woods, level the valleys, dry up the brooks and fountains. A ravaging fire, an ill wind blowing over Istanbul, this Halim Bey Veziroğlu, turning into a hurricane. Filling the lovely shores and wooded valleys of the Bosphorus with ugly apartment blocks of a hundred or two hundred flats . . . And the waters of the Bosphorus will be strewn with refuse from these buildings and, like the Golden Horn, the Bosphorus will become nothing better than a stinking swampy marsh.

It's easy enough to get into Halim Bey Veziroğlu's presence and to shoot the dog, but how to get away afterwards? Maybe it can be done . . . Just screw up your courage, cast away all doubt, believe it in your very heart, tell yourself this: I can't live on if he doesn't die . . . It's death for me as long as he's alive. And with that conviction take your gun and go and face him. Don't worry about the rest . . .

Fisher Selim got out of bed in the grey dawn. He dressed and, taking a cake of soap, went down to the public fountain. Holding his head under the streaming water, he soaped his hair and vigorously washed his face, neck and ears. Then, sprinkling water to right and left, he ran back to his shanty, dried himself, donned his jacket and combed his hair and moustache in front of the old mottled mirror. After this he made straight for the coffee-house where a few sleepy men were already sitting and drinking tea. He bought some cheese and a warm loaf of bread from Tahsin the grocer, sat down at a table outside, ordered his tea and began to eat his breakfast.

A gentle south wind was blowing and the mountains of Bursa on the opposite shore seemed so near you could hold out your arm and touch them.

Fisher Selim was growing impatient. It was Mahmut he was waiting for. He kept repeating to himself, 'I'll kill him. I must. He's a bloody murderer. The hand that strikes him will be blessed. He's a defiler of poor young girls, he's a monster, he must be killed. Whoever kills him will have earned his place in Paradise . . .'

His right leg swinging up and down frenziedly, his hand flying back and forth from the table to his mouth, he was lashing himself into a mad fury. In no time he had finished his breakfast. He ordered another tea, downed it at one go, then asked for another. Again and again the coffee-house keeper filled his glass. At last he rose, flung some money on the table and walked over to the Seagull Casino. Still no sign of Mahmut . . . He swerved back to the coffee-house, his anger mounting, then back to the Casino, up and down at a mad pace, oblivious of passing cars and trucks and of the screeching gulls swooping above him, until he heard Mahmut's laughter coming from the coffee-house. He rushed in and grabbed his arm. Mahmut was just starting to drink his tea. The hot tea spilled all over him.

'Get up!' Fisher Selim hissed. 'Quick, I've got something to tell you. Quick, quick, quick . . .' He was trembling all over. Alarmed, Mahmut followed him out and off they rushed, down the Florya road, past the presidential summer residence, until they reached the Yeşilköy highway.

'Listen,' Fisher Selim said, 'I've made a solemn vow. I'm going to kill that Halim Bey Veziroğlu. "Here's the money," I'll say, "give me my land," and if he doesn't I'll shoot him down, there and then, bang bang bang.' His mouth was awry and his eyes bulged. He was trembling.

Mahmut's hearty laughter startled him. 'You could never kill anyone, my good honest friend!'

'I will!' Fisher Selim howled, incensed. 'I'll kill him, I will!'
Round and round Mahmut he rushed, thrashing his arms,
stamping his feet, trying to make Mahmut believe him, while
the other only smiled calmly and repeated, 'You can't kill a
man, Selim, never.' Over and over Selim swore that he would
kill Halim Bey Veziroğlu, but Mahmut was unimpressed.
'Never, Selim, not you. You wouldn't even crush an ant.'

'So that's what you think?' Selim lunged at him, his hand
raised to strike. Mahmut was young, he ducked quickly and
dashed to the other side of the railway tracks.

'What do I care?' he shouted resentfully. 'Kill him, then. Let's
see you do it!'

The next few days and nights Fisher Selim spent making up a
whole lot of tales about Halim Bey Veziroğlu's crimes, strength-
ening his resolve to kill him. Then he approached Mahmut
again, a little diffidently this time. 'Listen, Mahmut,' he said,
looking him straight in the eye, 'I'm going to kill him.'

Mahmut met his gaze calmly. 'You can't kill a man, Fisher
Selim,' he stated and laughed.

Selim's life was nothing but one long torment now. He could
not sleep, he could not go fishing, he could not keep still.

That Halim Bey Veziroğlu, wasn't it he who, when threatened
with exposure by one of the girls he had defiled, a young beauty
only nineteen, had strangled her and thrown her body into the
sea like a dog's? Wasn't it he who had had Ibrahim the smuggler
shot in Beyoğlu because he had said he was sick of the business
and wanted nothing more to do with his dirty dealings? And,
what's more, when Halim Bey Veziroğlu himself was about to
be arrested, hadn't he had the police chief leading the investiga-
tion kicked out of his job and hounded from place to place?

And the shanties? When they were set up on that waste land,
did it belong to Halim Bey Veziroğlu then? He bought it later for
a song, a huge district with hundreds of dwellings, and had the
demolition squads sent up. And when the settlers refused to
leave, when they lay down in front of the bulldozers, the police
ordered the bulldozers to proceed and raze the houses to the
ground . . . Many children and old people were crushed to death
under the rubble. Thousands of settlers marched up to meet
the bulldozers, shouting, but the place had been encircled by
panzers which opened fire on the crowd, turning this squatters'
district into a battlefield, leaving many dead. And so Halim Bey

Veziroğlu came into possession of a vast tract of land. It is empty now, ringed in with barbed wire, waiting for the apartment blocks that are to be built on it. And the settlers have dispersed to different parts of Istanbul and are erecting new shanties, which the bulldozers will knock down again. They never tire of building, nor the others of demolishing.

Halim Bey Veziroğlu is steeped from head to foot in the blood of the poor.

'I must kill him! And I will! Just let him refuse me my land, just let him . . .'

'You kill a man? You couldn't even kill an insect . . .'

Fisher Selim had never been able to lay hands on Bald Dursun, yet even today if he should happen to meet him, that blood-thirsty murderer who had shot his family of dolphins, pumping black holes in their heads, he would fill his mouth with bullets. And who had brought those Italian ships here and made them drop anchor in front of Haydarpaşa, who indeed – this he had learnt much later – but one of Veziroğlu's associates, that hulking fellow who laughed not with his face but with his paunch. Skipper Bald Dursun had got all his boats and Mausers from him.

Many of the evils fermenting in Istanbul, throughout Turkey, stem from these men. Lift a stone – whether it be on the slaughter of dolphins, the destruction of the shanties, drugs, arms dealing – and you will find them underneath. And Halim Bey Veziroğlu is connected by his fingertips, as with an electric current, to them all.

How they sobbed, the dolphins, when the bullets hit them in the head, like babies, how they hurled themselves into the sky, writhing, bending, tracing arcs in the air, splashing back into the sea, staining the blue water with red blood, their white bellies upturned, floating on the waves . . . Hundreds of dolphins fleeing, pursued, shot the instant they showed their heads above the water . . . Not a single dolphin has ever been seen since, neither in the Marmara nor in the Black Sea. But in the old days . . . Ah, then . . . How they gambolled along beside passing ships, racing them in a whirlwind of joy, their blue backs flashing in the sun, while overhead followed thousands of seagulls, wing to wing, screeching gleefully . . .

He has severed the sea's life-giving artery, this Halim Bey Veziroğlu, drained it of its lifeblood.

Fisher Selim's long-pent-up rancour was flaring up again, spreading through his heart like poison. After so many years, he had discovered the source of all these evils. Halim Bey Veziroğlu. He must kill him, this man who had done him such a wrong, who had robbed him of his happiness. He would kill him, yes, and make good his escape to Uzunyayla. His mother must be very old now . . . As he entered the village, young girls and lads would come to greet him, playing the accordion, singing Caucasian songs, dancing the *lezginka*. That was the Circassian custom, whether here or back in the Caucasus. Guests of importance were welcomed with songs and dances and afterwards a big feast would be given in their honour. That's how it would be for Fisher Selim too. The young people would not know him . . . Uzunyayla is a long, flat, highland pasture, blanketed with fresh green grass as far as the eye can see, lovely as a calm sea . . . And from afar the green turns to sky blue . . . On this plateau the sun is serene in the sky, the springs are limpid, shining bright, filled with red-flecked fish. On the edge of the plateau are the snow-capped Binboga, the Thousand Bulls Mountains, and the winds that blow from there carry the scent of pine . . . Of pine and marjoram and thyme, of wild mint and flowering rowan. And when the rowan trees are in flower they are bent under the weight of the bees swarming over them. The people of Uzunyayla, whether Circassian, Kurdish or Turcoman, never give up anyone who asks for asylum. It was as well that things had turned out like this. Otherwise Fisher Selim would never to his dying day have returned to his homeland. His body, like a dog's, would have been thrown into a grave with none of the old ceremonial keening, the long, harrowing lamentations resounding from the village to the Binboga Mountains. In a sudden storm the vision rolled before his eyes. Halim Bey Veziroğlu steeped in blood, issuing orders to the police, to the soldiers, to everyone . . . Kill the shanty people . . . Bulldozers, tanks, panzers converging on the houses, people crushed, screaming, blood spreading over the blue sea, writhing blood-stained dolphins, water spurting blood-red, plane trees, houses, long yellow tresses, mossy bubbling springs, clear and bright, full of trout, herds of white horses flowing with tails held high over the green plateau . . . All in a jumble, the Marmara Sea, the fishnets, the blustering *lodos* wind, whirling, reeling in an angry dream . . .

He cornered Mahmut near the Municipal Beach. 'I *am* going to kill that Halim Bey Veziroğlu,' he stated jubilantly. 'His crimes have passed all bounds.'

Mahmut gave him one look and his eyes widened. 'Selim,' he pleaded, 'don't do it. Don't have that man's blood on your hands.' Taking his arm, he led him along the asphalt road to Yeşilköy and tried to bring him to his senses. 'They'll hang you.'

'So much the better; it'll be a relief for me.'

'Or, worse than death, you'll rot away in prison till the end of your days.'

'I don't care. I'll kill him and go to Uzunyayla ... And from there to Russia, to the high Caucasus, my homeland.'

'Veziroğlu's men won't let you take one step out of Istanbul, even if you manage to escape. They'll kill you.'

'Well, I'll have killed Veziroğlu himself, no?'

The more Mahmut talked, the stronger Selim's intent to kill seemed to grow. At last, Mahmut gave up. 'God damn you!' he cried. 'Go ahead then, and be damned.' And without another look at Selim he turned and walked away swiftly back to Menekşe.

Fisher Selim hailed a passing taxi and got off in front of the Greek Orthodox Church in Yeşilköy. Blind Mustafa had acquired a mansion hereabouts. Selim knew it well for he had often sold fish to its former owner, an Ottoman aristocrat. Blind Mustafa had bought the mansion from Nuri Pasha's gambler son, Hüsam Bey.

The mansion was set in the middle of a large garden with old plane trees, umbrella pines and cedars. An iron railing enclosed the garden, painted a crude green as was the wrought-iron gate. 'So this is where you live now, eh, Blind Mustafa?' Selim muttered. Here was another Halim Bey Veziroğlu. This one too had started off by smuggling arms and drugs, then gone on to buying and selling real estate, after which he had established factories and hotels. He owned partnerships in a great many businesses. His sons directed a factory each, while the youngest managed a notorious hotel, very convenient for the smuggling of whisky and cigarettes because it was on the seashore.

Fisher Selim hesitated as his hand went to the bell. A large sign read 'Beware of the Dog'. Then he laughed. Hey, Blind Mustafa, hey ... He pressed the bell and a tall white-coated manservant with a large Aleppo boil scar on his cheek came running up the garden path.

'What d'you want, agha?' he enquired.

'Is this Mustafa's house?' Selim asked, a little put out.

'Mustafa Bey,' the manservant quickly corrected him.

'I'm Selim the fisherman. I want to see him.'

'On what business?'

Selim thought this over. 'I'm an old friend of Mustafa Bey's,' he said at last. 'Just say it's Fisher Selim . . .'

'Wait here,' the tall manservant said. He went into the house and reappeared almost at once to open the gate.

At the door Selim paused, wiping his feet on the mat. He took off his cap and held it respectfully as he caught sight of Mustafa descending the stairs in a gold brocade dressing-gown. His hair had turned quite white, his squint was more pronounced, the left eye quite sunk in its socket, his dark-complexioned face deeply furrowed and his lower lip, so like a horse's, thicker and drooping now.

He was staring in amazement at Selim who still stood in the doorway. 'Fisher Selim!' he cried and hurried up to embrace him. 'Can it be? But come in, come in. Welcome, welcome . . . Woman, look who's come to our mansion. Look, look!'

'Who?' his wife called as she came down the stairs. 'Oh oh oh, but it's Fisher Selim!' She held out her hand. 'Welcome, Selim Bey, a hundred times welcome! We have never forgotten, Mustafa Bey and I, our good neighbour from Menekşe. We talk about you every day . . . Yes indeed.' While her husband took Fisher Selim's arm and led him up the stairs, she bustled off, saying, 'Let me make coffee for our good Fisher Selim like in the old days, with my own hands, yes, with my own hands . . .' She had grown very stout and lost all her former beauty, but she was as good-natured as ever.

The room Mustafa took him to was very large, and a blue-flowered silk carpet spread from wall to wall. The green velvet armchairs, emblazoned with real gold, were stuffed with down so soft that one sank into them up to the waist. Dotted around, on consoles and gilt tables large and small, sparkled a whole array of cut-crystal objects, ashtrays, sugar bowls, candlesticks and many others. In a display cabinet of rosewood embossed with large roses were gold sheaths for cups and glasses, filigreed like the finest lace by a master goldsmith. From the ceiling of this enormous room hung a chandelier with hundreds of sparkling crystal pendants.

'Sit down,' Mustafa Bey urged Selim, indicating the most imposing armchair in the room. 'That is my very own special armchair. The down was brought over from Japan, the framework is of Indian rosewood and the velvet comes from far-off China. Sit down, my dear Fisher Selim, make yourself comfortable.'

Fisher Selim was not comfortable at all. With his cap in one hand and both hands on his knees he perched stiffly on the edge of the armchair. It's only Blind Mustafa after all, he tried to remind himself, Blind Mustafa the smuggler, what if he does own this palace now? But the more he told himself this, the stiffer he became, his knees pressed tight together, his lips frozen in a bitter smile.

'Now, now!' Mustafa remonstrated genially. 'Don't sit like that. Make yourself comfortable. This is your house, the house of your old friend, Blind Mustafa, the arms-smuggler, miserable Blind Mustafa . . .' He smiled, a broad smile from ear to ear, and rising he pushed Fisher Selim deep into the armchair.

He sat down again and began talking about himself, how he had bought this mansion dirt-cheap, only a few millions, from that gambler son of Nuri Pasha, how he had come to Istanbul from his native country with five bullets in his body, acquired on a smuggling expedition across the frontier . . .

'D'you remember, dear Fisher Selim, how you helped us when we were building that shanty of ours? You gave us water and food too, you brought us your choicest fish. If it hadn't been for you we'd have starved that winter. Like now, you didn't talk much then. D'you remember when the police arrived to pull down our shanty and you gave them one look and they packed off without another word? You remember my eldest son, the one who was born in our native country, the handsomest? It was only with the children you talked and laughed. He's a very important man now, the biggest industrialist in Istanbul. When he comes here he always asks after you, after his Uncle Selim who gave not a damn for the whole world. If I could only see him again, he says, and kiss his hand, but I'm grown now, would he talk to me? Remember, Fisher Selim, remember? And at the time of the dolphin slaughter, d'you remember, my friend, how I gave you a brand-new German rifle without asking any money in return? Remember?'

Sunk deep in the armchair, very small, very distant, as though beyond the seas, Selim only smiled. Mustafa's wife appeared with the coffee, steaming, aromatic, in three large gold-sheathed cups on a silver tray.

'Welcome, Selim Bey, dear friend. How good of you to have remembered us,' she said as she held out the tray.

Fisher Selim suddenly felt more at ease. He raised the cup to his lips and took a small sip. She gave her husband his coffee, then set the tray on a table, took her own cup, buried herself in an armchair, crossed her legs, and began to speak with the same eagerness as her husband and in almost the same words.

Husband and wife talked on for a long time about themselves, about the high society they lived in, of how they were sick and tired of these worthless, incompetent idiots who knew nothing of real life, of the people who came to their house, poets, so addicted to drink, film stars, millionaires of whom it was impossible to understand how they had amassed such fortunes since they could hardly do up their own trousers, of television programmes and horse races and a whole lot of other things about which Fisher Selim was completely ignorant. It never seemed to occur to them that Selim might have come for some special reason. Once or twice he stirred in his armchair, but Mustafa Bey immediately protested.

'Please, dear friend! You've only just arrived . . .'

'You've only just come, dear Selim Bey,' his wife chimed in with a coquettish expression. 'It's not as if we were strangers. And, you know, it's so dreary, this huge mansion, we get bored to death. We long for our old shanty in Menekşe, Mustafa and I. The children are all busy industrialists, with no time for us, the dears. Mustafa always says, "If only it was the old days, in our small house . . ." Sit down, stay a little longer . . .'

She rose, collected the cups and, swinging her hips like a young girl, hurried off to the kitchen to make some more coffee.

Mustafa Bey had grown very fat and his mouth was twisted to one side.

'Our relatives from our home town don't come to visit us any more either. I never did anything but good to them, helped them with their needs when they were here, even telephoned the doctors for them. But they drifted away from us all the same. Why, back in our Menekşe shanty we were overwhelmed with visitors . . .' Bitterly he picked apart his relatives and then went on to do the same with his neighbours and acquaintances. 'It's a changed world, Fisher Selim, my dear old friend. There's no expecting the right hand even to help the left. Yesterday's friend is a stranger today. Why, I hardly know my sons, my daughter, my grandchildren, my own flesh and blood. With every passing day people and things are growing further and further away from me, strange . . . I feel cut off, bewildered. Those days long ago when I used to smuggle opium over the Syrian border under a hail of bullets, braving minefields, the days of my youth, penniless, miserable, Menekşe, how good they seem to me now! My sons . . . Strangers, different, high society, they are. They hate me, every one of them. Don't let her hear this, but they'd soon do away with me if they got the chance . . .'

To think how much blood he had shed, how many homes he had destroyed, to raise his sons to this status . . . He did not say so openly, but it was implied in all his words.

He sighed. 'So here you see me, Fisher Selim, alone, like the hoopoe bird, like a stone at the bottom of a well. Death would be better than this, idle, rootless, estranged . . . What price all the riches in the world . . . ? Ah, death . . .'

His wife came with fresh cups of coffee. 'Again?' she cried when she saw her husband's miserable face. 'The minute you get hold of somebody you go on and on with your old grievances. Why, even a bird teaches its young to fly and never sees them again. Even a bird . . .'

'But I'm not a bird!' Mustafa Bey moaned. 'A human being's different.' He was almost in tears. Quickly, he took his coffee and sipped it noisily, while to cheer him up his wife began to praise their sons, to extol their successes, their cars and yachts, all worth millions, but in the end she too reverted to the subject of their loneliness, and two tears ran down her cheeks.

'Sometimes we've a mind to leave Istanbul, this house, the children, and return to our village for good.'

'Even if it is too hot there,' Mustafa said.

'The heat never killed a man,' she said.

'Certainly not,' Mustafa said. 'I've got an old grandmother back there who's over a hundred and cutting her milk teeth! She's stronger than all my sons.'

Fisher Selim had finished his coffee and was preparing to leave when Mustafa Bey asked shyly, as if it had just occurred to him, 'Is there something you wanted of me, my friend?'

Flustered, Fisher Selim took a few steps towards the stairs without answering. Mustafa Bey clutched his arm.

'I won't let you go until you tell me what it is,' he said. 'You're the only friend I have left in this world. D'you think that, whatever happens, I would ever forget all you did for us? Come on, tell me.' His eyes were fixed on Selim with something of their old keen gaze, even the sunken left one bright now.

Fisher Selim squirmed, then suddenly blurted out: 'A gun . . . A gun . . .' His mouth went dry.

Mustafa Bey roared with laughter. 'I left off doing that kind of business years ago,' he said. 'I wish I hadn't. I wish I'd got killed in one of these encounters with the gendarmes, doing what I've always done, and not lived on to be a sport for dogs, despised even by my own children . . . No, I don't do that any more, but I'll give you my very own Nagant revolver. It came with me from the old country and I've always looked after it as the apple of my eye. Not a week's gone by without my oiling it. Wife, bring me my revolver.'

She had trotted off even before he had finished speaking and was soon back with the revolver in a brand-new leather case and some cartridge belts.

Mustafa Bey strapped it quickly to Selim's waist. 'Good! How glad I am that you should have it!' He exclaimed and taking Selim's arm he went down the stairs with him, breathing in with relish the smell of fish that emanated from his guest.

Fisher Selim left the mansion, his ears humming, his head swimming, strangely saddened. He hardly knew how he got home. Without eating or drinking he threw himself on to his bed and fell asleep.

He rose at dawn and went down to the wharf. Till sunrise he cleaned his boat and the engine and repaired his nets. He felt as light as a bird. Every now and again he took a fond look at the revolver attached at his waist. As he got up a small wave rocked the boat. Selim was well used to keeping his balance on choppy seas. He jumped on to the wooden pier with the agility of a young man and made his way to the railway station. He did not have long to wait for the train.

At the door of Halim Bey Veziroğlu's office were three heavyweight bodyguards carrying guns. Fisher Selim was a familiar face to them and they showed him in at once.

Halim Bey Veziroğlu was bent over his desk, working. He

lifted his head very slowly and came face to face with Selim. His eyes widened in a horrified stare and his face turned ashen. Resting his hands on the table, he pushed himself back in his chair. 'Welcome, Fisher Selim,' he stammered, trying fruitlessly to smile. 'Sit down, my friend. Please don't stay standing there.' His eyes flashed in sudden fury, but only for an instant. He looked to right and left, then at Selim again, his eyes shifting fearfully. Then somehow he took a hold on himself. 'I understand,' he said. 'You've put together the necessary sum, haven't you? But even if you haven't, the land's yours for whatever you can give me. Forgive me, my friend, if I've given you a little trouble. That land is yours. You planted seven olive trees on it. Have you got the money with you?'

'No . . .'

'Well, you can bring it tomorrow, whatever you've got, and I'll give you the title deeds. I've thought it over. As you know, land prices are going up with every passing day. At this rate you'll never be able to buy that land. As for me, I've got such a lot of land . . . This bit, I said to myself, shall go to Selim Bey. I hope you will be happy on it. May it bring you luck. May you live in peace and comfort in the house you build there, my good Fisher Selim Bey . . .'

Slumped in the armchair, his face purple, his eyes blinking in amazement, Fisher Selim could not speak. Beads of sweat stood out on his brow and his only thought was how to escape from the room. After a while he staggered to his feet. 'Thank you, Bey,' he blurted out, his voice choking. 'How shall I ever be able to repay this?'

Did they shake hands, did he say anything else? He never knew. Swaying, he lurched out of the room.

It was to Mahmut he went, straight afterwards.

'Have you killed him?' Mahmut asked, alarmed at Selim's flustered expression.

'No.'

'Then what happened?'

'Nothing. He's given me the land. Veziroğlu . . .'

'Well! Aren't you pleased?'

'But I don't want that land any longer. What business have I got in Çengelköy? I can't leave this place, it's my home. This is the sea I'm used to. I'm going to buy that plot of Zeki Bey's. The plane trees are taller there and I've got the whole of the Marmara

Sea at my feet. But what am I to say to that Veziroğlu now?'

Mahmut laughed. 'Did you give him the money?'

'No.'

'Then you won't go back there and that's the end of it.'

'Won't he expect me?'

'Of course not. He'll be only too glad . . .'

19

——◆——

The *lodos* wind was blustering away at its strongest. White foaming waves, high as minarets, pounded at the shores of the city and cascaded on to the coastal roads. It was raining and the leaden domes of the mosques shone dully. Not a single boat was to be seen on the storm-tossed sea.

Zeynel and Dursun Kemal were drenched to the skin. Last night, they had somehow found their way into a ship anchored in the port and had slept a fitful sleep there at the foot of one of its warm funnels. For the stray children of Sirkeci, boats were an ideal place to spend the night. Not only were they warm there, but also safe from the nightwatchmen, and as for the sailors, they were indulgent and did not throw them out in the middle of the night.

This morning Zeynel was feeling better and his mind was clearer. He stretched his limbs and rubbed his eyes, slowly shaking off a pleasant drowsiness. Then suddenly he started to his feet and dashed to the stairway. It was a very dangerous thing they had done, spending the night here . . . These long-distance ships were always full of police. How, when, had they got on board? He did not know. Dimly he recalled being surrounded on all sides by some twenty policemen, and Hüseyin Huri with a gun in his hand, ready to shoot, but he could not remember how they managed to escape. He had lost sight of Dursun Kemal. How had the boy found him again? He recollected a confusion of dreams in his broken sleep, curled up tightly against the warm funnel, one side of him wet, icy cold under the rain . . . Lame Hasan down to his waist in the water in front of the Ahirkapi lighthouse, struggling with a red mullet he had caught, huge, bigger than himself, the fish dragging him far out into the Marmara Sea . . . Burning seagulls . . . Swarms of policemen . . . And himself whirling in the darkness, a dense, solid, pitch-black darkness, and pouring over him tiny bullets like grains of sand, aflame . . .

He ran down the stairs, out on to the wharf and on towards the iron gates facing Tophane Fountain. It was still very early and there was nobody about in the streets. He had to find a taxi and get to Lame Hasan. He would be safe then. The nylon bags were held tightly in his hand. Not once had he let go of them, even sleeping with them under his head as a pillow. He glanced back, and there was Dursun Kemal, gazing at him adoringly, with shining eyes . . . A wave of affection swept over Zeynel, quickly replaced by pity. Poor Dursun Kemal, he thought, poor child, his mother killed, and by his own father, sixty gashes in her body, her breasts, her . . . Who knows how heartsick he is, what tears of blood he must be shedding inside . . . ? He went up to him and gently stroked his head. Tears filled Zeynel's eyes, his throat tightened and suddenly he saw himself dead, his twisted body riddled with bullets, frozen in blood. His wide panic-stricken eyes darted to right and left and lighted on a taxi near the fountain. He rushed up to it, followed by Dursun Kemal.

'To Kumkapi,' he said. 'No, no, to Ahirkapi.'

At Ahirkapi they walked over to the seashore and sat down on the rocks.

'The rain's stopped,' Zeynel said. 'The sun'll be up soon. It'll dry us.'

'Will Lame Hasan come now?' Dursun Kemal asked.

'Sure,' Zeynel said confidently. 'He's been doing this for sixty years, after every *lodos* wind, raking the length of the shore from here to Menekşe. Even at his age his eyes are like a hawk's.'

Lame Hasan, Yellow Hidayet, Cemal from Topkapi and Hüsnü from Kasimpaşa, these were veteran southwinders. The days after the *lodos* has turned the sea upside down, casting on to the shore a world of things that lie in its depths, are boon days for the southwinders. At first light when the bottom of the sea is clear and bright, brighter by far than in the daylight, then the keen eyes of the southwinder find it even easier to detect objects below the surface.

Southwinding is an old occupation in Istanbul, dating back to the days of Byzantium. Lame Hasan was a good fisherman, one of the best, but his real vocation was beachcombing. On such mornings the southwinder rises joyfully from his bed even before the sea has paled. He says his prayers and sets out for the shore, great hopes in his heart. What wonders has this sea not given to Istanbul's southwinders after every *lodos*! The so-called Spoonmaker's Diamond, the famous *Kaşikçi*, for instance, there's not another stone like it in the whole world, so large, so sumptuous, glittering with a thousand and one colours. ... Well, that very stone was discovered one day at crack of dawn by an Istanbul southwinder among the pebbles on the shore beneath the old city walls and he exchanged it for a wooden spoon! What does it matter if he only got a wooden spoon, the southwinder, he was the one to find that marvellous diamond, wasn't he? Ever since then, Istanbul southwinders have been fired with the hope of finding another such stone, an even larger one, and – why not? – they may still do so ... The sea is infinite, generous, bountiful.

And so the Istanbul southwinders are always there at dawn on after-*lodos* days, knee-deep in the biting cold water, their eagle eyes on the watch for the tiniest glint at the bottom of the sea. Gold coins they have found on these shores, Byzantine, Ottoman, Russian coins, gold ingots, emeralds, rubies, diamonds, pearls ... Bracelets, necklaces, brooches, rings ... Every kind of object is washed up from the Marmara Sea.

Nowadays, the southwinders have moved with the times. They all wear knee-high rubber boots and no longer freeze in the icy water. Only Lame Hasan has never got used to this devil's invention and still walks into the sea with his legs bare, his trousers rolled up. Everyone knows how Lame Hasan bought his beautiful house. He makes no secret of it. On the contrary, he is always proud to tell anyone he comes across.

'The sea was clear and bright, the sun just about to come up. All the brightness of the sun before it rises is gathered in the sea and every single object at the bottom – pebbles, coins, diamonds, fish, pearls, rubies, corals – seems much larger in this light. So there I was that day, and suddenly I saw ahead of me, only a little way off, a red blinking flame. Oh my God, I said, glory be! What on earth can shine as red as this at the bottom of the sea, shooting rays like shining arrows, zigzagging in the water, flaming red like a piece of iron in a forge? I ran, I swam, I flew, and dived on to the red glow. I picked it up and, oh my God, all praise to you, it was a ruby, a huge ruby large as my thumb! At that time there was a certain Master Hayk, an antique-dealer in the Covered Bazaar, a good honest man whom we southwinders all trusted. I went straight to him, just as I was, my trousers still rolled up, with that stone like a burning ember in my hand. "Why, Hasan," Master Hayk said, "but it's a fortune you've got there," and he opened his safe and began to count out money, so much I thought it would never end. "Here," he said, "take this money and buy yourself a house the first thing you do. A house of one's own is a must for everyone . . ." I did as he said and bought this very house you see here. God be praised for this generous bountiful sea . . .'

Lame Hasan had also found a lot of gold and rings and pearls. And once he came upon a statue, a precious antique, but by that time Master Hayk was dead and some other Covered Bazaar dealer bought it from him for nothing near its real value.

At one time, Zeynel had developed a yen for southwinding, but his thin body could not stand the freezing water. Once he was dragged out of the sea, half-fainting, his body blue, and for fifteen days he lay between life and death. His acquaintance with Lame Hasan dated from that time. It was from him he learnt what patience meant, how to persevere and never lose hope. Whenever the *lodos* wind had blown itself out, Lame Hasan would always be up with the dawn, making for the seashore in a whirlwind of joy, radiant with hope, not even limping any more, with the trembling premonition that a bright red ruby or a diamond twice as large as the *Kaşikçi* Diamond was there waiting for him. And even when he found nothing and in the evening went into Yanaki's tavern his legs blue with cold, empty-handed, he would still not have lost anything of his faith and good cheer. 'Here's a toast to Master Hayk,' he would start off, 'though he's dead and gone . . . Let's drink another one to all the good red mullet of the sea, to the sea's diamonds and rubies and gold. Come on, one more . . .' And his last glass would be lifted to Istanbul. 'Here's to our own Istanbul and its bountiful sea . . .'

It was not long before they saw Lame Hasan coming down the stone steps to the shore. He removed his shoes and trousers, tied the legs of the trousers together, putting one shoe inside each, then hung them round his neck, and, with a long smooth stick in his hand, started off westward. Zeynel and Dursun Kemal followed him. On and on Lame Hasan waded along the shore, never once looking up, thoroughly absorbed, tasting to the full the beauty of the mist-swathed sea in the half-light, the brightness welling up from below, the pure thrill of the search.

Thus, they reached Kumkapi. Once in while, Lame Hasan's

face would flash with joy. He would pick something out of the water and gaze at it in ecstasy.

... A very large oil tanker was on fire way up on the Bosphorus off Anadolukavagi. It had burst into flames without warning. All but five of the crew had escaped by jumping overboard. The others had perished. In an instant, the tanker was a mountain of flames, shedding a red glare over the shores of the Bosphorus, the houses, trees, fishnets, anchored ships, landing-stages, the many-coloured Laz fishing scows. The swift currents of the Bosphorus flowed like rivers of fire and the tanker, out of control, eddied down the strait as though caught in a vortex, tall flames high as minarets spurting from the blazing mass and flaring up into the night.

Istanbul was in the grip of fear. Villas and apartment buildings on the shores of the Bosphorus had been evacuated, for who knew where this mountain of burning oil would strike and explode? Perhaps the whole city would be set ablaze. Slowly floating down the strait, the tanker was nearing Çubuklu. The danger here was great because of the huge petroleum reservoirs on the shore. If the tanker came too near and the fire jumped to the reservoirs, then the whole of the Asiatic side of Istanbul would go up in flames. But just as it was about to enter Çubuklu Bay the tanker was caught up in another current and began to drift away towards Yeniköy on the opposite shore. The threat was now to the ancient, historic residences, each one a small palace, and to the lofty age-old plane trees that graced Yeniköy. The quay in front of Iskender's ice-cream shop was thronged with onlookers, all agog and secretly rather excited by the spectacle of the incandescent ship. The sky glowed bright red, and huge shadows and fiery lights filled the streets and squares of the city. Giant people, giant trees, giant boats hurtled through Istanbul in wild confusion.

In mid-course the tanker stopped, its flames higher, more furious than ever, while before it the dark waters of the Bosphorus flowed swiftly on in waves of fire towards the Marmara Sea.

All of Istanbul was astir and making for the Bosphorus in cars, buses, lorries, running as if to an unexpected diversion, and the streets, plazas and piers were packed to overflowing. The people of Menekşe too, at the news that not only a tanker but the sea itself was on fire, hastily rented a lorry and were in time to get to the burning ship on the second night. Lame Hasan had taken Zeynel along and never let go of his hand when the lorry stopped at Beşiktaş where they had a good view of the tanker. It was a wild dance of shadows, intertwirling, bending and twisting with the flames of the burning ship. Zeynel, his hand tight in Lame Hasan's warm hand, had huddled into a small ball between the press of legs in the lorry. Flames tearing from the churning mountain of fire were streaming over them. Zeynel dared not lift his head to have another look, but the fiery mountain took on different shapes in his mind. The tanker drifted on, shooting out flames like great birds over sea and sky, making the night as bright as day, and came to a standstill in the middle of the Marmara, spinning on itself at lightning speed like a sparkling top, its flames boring into the sky, until it burnt itself out. This was not only Zeynel's fancy. Lame Hasan and the other fishermen too told how the flaming ship spiralled itself up into the sky . . .

Lame Hasan stopped short. The surface of the sea was quite white, as though covered with snow. A few seagulls hovered immediately above him, motionless, their wings outstretched against the light breeze. Suddenly, Lame Hasan darted down, clothes and all, and emerged holding something. He glanced about him covertly and quickly dropped the object into his bag. Then he took off his shirt and undershirt, wrung them out and, throwing them over his arm, proceeded towards Yedikule almost naked, every now and then extracting the object from his bag and gazing at it with a broad smile.

Dursun Kemal nudged Zeynel. 'Look, Abi,' he whispered, pointing to a blue police van on the opposite side of the highway.

'Sit down,' Zeynel said, and crept away to crouch among the rocks under the embankment.

In the distance, near Büyükada Island, a short brilliant radiance flashed and was gone. Zeynel shivered.

. . . That head sticking out of the porthole in the burning ship, eyes bulging, mouth twisted in a horrible grimace . . . And Zeynel, terror-struck, running helplessly this way and that . . .

Zeynel and a few other vagrant boys were just settling down for the night under the funnel of a ship which had newly put into port when the fire broke out. It had not been easy to get on to the ship. They had waited, hidden among some large crates under the winch that was hoisting off cattle, horses and donkeys, double-strapped under their bellies, and hundreds of cackling poultry in large cages. Sheep and goats had been unloaded first and were now being herded among the crates by the shepherds. The boys had slipped in unnoticed in the wake of an elderly man carrying a huge register, and had quickly made for the funnel in joyful anticipation of a peaceful night.

Suddenly, a tall flame shot out of the hold. There was a deafening explosion and flames spread over the ship. In an instant the deck was an incredible turmoil of howling men, bellowing cattle, neighing horses and braying donkeys. All the ships in the harbour started sounding their sirens. Zeynel and his companions rushed madly about the burning deck and a little dog ran along with them. Finally, they managed to find the stairway. The little dog was left behind, engulfed by the flames, squealing . . . On the wharf some hundred buffaloes, thirty to forty cows and oxen, a hundred and fifty horses and donkeys, driven crazy by the tumult, the blast, the flames, stampeded out of the port, pell-mell, trampling over each other, and dispersed into the night. Frantic buffaloes careered through the streets of the city, lunging at people, particularly the dummies in shop windows. With a resounding crash the windows smashed, and the buffaloes, wounded, bleeding, whipped into a frenzy by the din of shattering glass, charged at every shadow, every light, at every window or door in their path. All hell broke loose throughout the city. Beyoğlu Avenue was a seething mass of men, buffaloes, horses and bulls, dashing wildly hither and thither. Then police and soldiers reached the scene. Shot after shot rang out, as in a battle, echoing and re-echoing through the whole city. The bulls and buffaloes hurtled to the ground, bellowing, their blood spurting through the broken windows of shops and banks, the horses sank down, neighing one last bitter whinny. When day broke and people ventured out of their houses, Beyoğlu Avenue was strewn with dead buffaloes, oxen, horses, and the streets were running with blood down to Tünel, Yüksekkaldirim and Şişhane. Beyoğlu was like a bombed city. Zeynel was crushed between two dead buffaloes, frozen stiff . . .

. . . In the Küçükçekmece slaughterhouse, under the bridge on the outskirts of the little town, a large, powerful buffalo had been stretched out on the ground and the butcher was cutting its throat. The knife had reached the bone when with unbelievable force the buffalo suddenly broke its bonds, shook off the butcher and the other men, flinging them right and left, and sprinted away, galloping like a horse, in the direction of Menekşe, blood gushing from its neck, its head hanging to one side. The men sitting in Menekşe coffee-house sprang up at the monstrous sight of the gory buffalo and dispersed like a covey of partridges. A couple of trucks and some cars were blocking the buffalo's way. The beast wheeled round and round, spurting blood all over the open place by the beach. Then it plunged into the sea and began to swim away, a red stain of blood spreading around it. The butchers arrived in hot pursuit with knives in their hands. They got into a motorboat and caught up with the fleeing buffalo. Tying a rope to its horns they towed it back to the shore, but as soon as its feet touched ground the buffalo wrenched itself free and began to gallop round and round in front of the coffee-house. Just then the gangster Ihsan appeared. He drew out his gun and fired three times. The buffalo crashed to the ground. As Ihsan replaced the smoking gun at his waist, a scream rose from the little bridge leading to the beach and Zeynel was seen to sink down against the railing, his whole body clamped fast in a rigid ball. They rubbed him with ointments, made him inhale all kinds of herbal infusions, but it was not until evening prayer that they could loosen his limbs . . .

The sun rose, its rays struck the water and rings of light preceded the little waves that came to break on the rocky shore. Little white clouds cast long shadows over the bright pebbly seabed. Lame Hasan's feet in the water lengthened and broke away from him as he plodded on. After a while he turned inshore and slumped on to a flat rock. Spreading his clothes around him, he opened his bag and began to examine his finds, smiling with pleasure. Zeynel and Dursun Kemal approached and crouched down in front of him. The hair on Lame Hasan's chest was quite white, his arms were emaciated and his ribs stuck out. His breathing was laboured. Harsh wheezing sounds issued from his throat. He was shivering. Zeynel felt a wave of pity for him. He coughed and Lame Hasan lifted his head.

'Is that you, Zeynel my child?' he said. He did not seem at all surprised to see him there. 'It's a good thing you didn't come back to me after that day. The house is surrounded by police. Even here in Kumkapi, they don't let a bird fly past. A whole lot of Zeynels they've arrested so far . . .'

'They're going to kill me, Uncle Hasan,' Zeynel moaned.

'They'll shoot a hundred bullets into my head. They'll blow my brains out. It's at my head they'll fire . . .' He leaped up and clasped Lame Hasan's hands. 'Don't let me be killed, Uncle Hasan, please!'

'Why, my poor child, what can your Uncle Hasan do?'

Zeynel was trembling. 'Don't let me be killed. Hide me from the police,' was all he could say.

Lame Hasan, his face sombre, his head bent, seemed not to be listening to him any more. Then, after a while, he looked up. 'Listen, Zeynel,' he said, 'go to Fisher Selim tonight. If anyone can save you, he will.'

'But he'll give me up to the police, that one, he'll kill me,' Zeynel cried in dismay.

'Now, listen to me, my child,' Lame Hasan said very gently. 'Tonight you go to Menekşe, but be very very careful, don't let anyone see you. Go straight to Fisher Selim. Tell him I sent you and that he's to take you in his boat to Limnos Island, to our Vasili. He's a fisherman from Samatya, but he had to get out of the country. Tell Fisher Selim I want this of him. If he refuses, then come back to me. If he won't . . .'

'He won't, he won't! He'll denounce me to the police. He'll kill me. He's got a gun. He'll fire a hundred bullets into my eyes. He'll . . .'

'Shut up!' Lame Hasan remonstrated. 'Selim wouldn't kill anyone. Tell him . . . Vasili . . . Why, I remember how we used to go fishing with Vasili way over to Limnos Island! Such red seabream we caught there! Each one weighed three okas. Red, so red . . . Yes, you go straight to Selim and he'll take you to Vasili. Vasili, don't forget the name. Vasili, the fisherman from Samatya. He was my friend, better than a brother to me . . .'

'They're going to kill me! Save me! Fisher Selim too . . .'

'Shut up, you dog, shut up!' Lame Hasan thundered. 'What kind of way is that to talk about Fisher Selim? Shut up, you dog . . .'

20

—◆—

All the cars of Istanbul had switched on their headlamps and
were packed close in a wide circle. Lined up too were some
panzers and in front of them policemen, their guns held ready,
were advancing, wary, angry, deliberate. The city-line ferries all
trained their searchlights over the square. Boat sirens, car horns
were blaring away. The circle was closing in on Zeynel. More
than anything his heart bled for Dursun Kemal. The poor child
would be killed with him. Try as he might, Zeynel had not been
able to shake him off.

Red, yellow, green, purple, the neon lights rain down on the
square, on Zeynel. Dazzled, shielding his eyes, he wheels this
way and that, but everywhere, barring his way, are the police,
the cars, a dense wall of light. Frantic, his tongue hanging out,
trying to find some dark hole to creep into, a crowd to get lost in,
the glaring searchlights on him, whirling in a flood of light, a
blind man, arms outstretched, groping, running, foundering.

'Come, Dursun Kemal,' Zeynel says. 'Through here.' And
stealthily they emerge on to the trading-wharves. The ground is
strewn with leaves of cabbages, leeks, cauliflowers, with orange
peel and rotten tangerines. Fruit-cases stacked high like a
parapet, shops, old-fashioned steelyards, platform scales,
mounds and mounds of vegetables and fruit . . . A pile of apples
high as a poplar, and the *hamals* in their dirty neckerchiefs,
scrambling to the top, emptying their loads, the apples rolling
down the sides of the pile . . . The pervasive smell of apples, of
fresh celery, of pungent myrtle fruit . . .

Dursun Kemal was asleep under the electric bulb, peaceful,
innocent, his lips pouting . . .

Zeynel took stock of the warehouse. All the *hamals* were
asleep, leaning against their packsaddles, smelling strongly of
sweat. Even in their sleep they were sweating, these *hamals*
who all day long carried loads weighing tons. The splash of oars
came from the darkness of the Golden Horn.

Zeynel knelt down beside Dursun Kemal and gazed at him. The vague thought flitted through his mind that this boy was the only human being he loved and a warm sensation, beyond love, beyond friendship, beyond affection, pleasant, different, deeper, swept over him. Dursun Kemal's thin, wistful face seemed longer in the crude electric light. He had no one left in the whole wide world but Zeynel, and Zeynel had no one but him. For days he had stuck by Zeynel, braving death and the police. Perhaps Zeynel did not exactly think all this as he knelt there gazing at Dursun Kemal's beautiful sunburnt face, fear-ridden even in sleep, perhaps he did not think at all, perhaps, moved by a deep warm tenderness he had never felt before, he only sensed it.

Tentatively he reached out to stroke Dursun Kemal's hair. 'Your father has killed your mother,' he murmured. 'He'd kill you too. Don't go back to him. You won't, I know. That father of yours is a monster . . .'

The colour photograph in that tabloid of Zühre Paşali lying stark naked rose before his eyes, her lacerated breasts red with blood, her belly, her whole body mangled, her shapely hips still beautiful. The heady remembered odour of her came to his nostrils, shaking him to the core.

He sighed, still gently caressing the boy's hair. Here he was, forced to go, to leave him. What would become of the child? Opening one of his bags, he took some wads of money and tucked them into Dursun Kemal's pocket. He's a smart chap, he thought, he'll pull through. Bending down he kissed Dursun Kemal on the forehead and pressed his warm hand. His heart aching, he turned away and walked out of the warehouse. At the fruit-trading wharf he stopped, unable to take another step. How could he leave Dursun Kemal behind? But wouldn't Fisher Selim say, 'Haven't I got enough on my hands without you bringing me this little bastard too? To hell with you both . . .'? And how would Dursun Kemal fare in those foreign lands? A terrible dread took hold of Zeynel. He could not do without Dursun Kemal, just as he was sure that the boy couldn't do without him. They had depended on each other all this time, each a comfort to the other. He ran back. Dursun Kemal was still asleep. 'Dursun Kemal,' he whispered, then stopped. No, it was no good, Fisher Selim would never take him anywhere with this boy. Quickly he ran out, but stopped again on the wharf, fear engulfing him like a rising flood. His shadow fell over the darkly gleaming waters of the Golden Horn. Seagulls were fluttering in the night sky, swooping up and down over the water, and suddenly behind them Zeynel saw the shadows of three men. They were coming towards him, walking, running, their shadows lengthening and shortening, bending and straightening, bumping into the swarming gulls and cleaving through them. They came to a stop at Zeynel's side and surrounded him and the seagulls enveloped them all in a smothering mass. Then the pressure lifted. Zeynel was alone. There was no sound in the night but the flapping of gulls' wings. Only for a moment, then once more the shadowy forms of men and birds were upon him, thrusting him against a hard wall of light. Again and again they disappeared and returned to hedge him in. He was struggling desperately to free himself when the shrill siren of a boat sounded from Galata Bridge.

'There he is, there! Zeynel Çelik, the gangster!' came a cry from the boat. 'Catch him, catch him! It's him, the gangster, the bloodthirsty murderer, the bank robber . . .' All the passengers in the boat were screaming at him. With one leap Zeynel broke through the barrier of seagulls, scattered the shadows of the men and dashed away. At Unkapani he found a taxi. The driver was asleep. He woke him up.

'To Menekşe,' he said.

He stopped the car near Florya railway station and went under the bridge to the Menekşe road. The throb of an engine came from the sea. Shivering, he walked through the dark and found his way to Fisher Selim's house, but as soon as he entered the tiny garden a great fear gripped him. He wanted to turn and run. Stealthily, like a cat, he circled the house, then stopped in front of the door, unable to make up his mind what to do. Seagulls were darting in and out of the lighted lamps of the railway station. He heard the humming of the night and the pat-a-pat of passing motorboats. One after another low-flying aeroplanes, their lights casting long beams over the sea, roared down to Yeşilköy Airport. Confused dream-like forms flashed through his mind. All the cars of the city, headlamps glaring, were bearing down upon him. Seagulls dashed in and out of bright-coloured neon lights. Long shadows holding machine-guns were pursuing him, at their head Hüseyin Huri and Dursun Kemal, their bodies stretching high as poplars. They were pressing him against a wall, throwing oily lassoes to catch him. Trains, ships, aeroplanes were hooting. Fierce gory buffaloes, smashing all the shop windows of Beyoğlu with their huge branched horns, were lunging at him. The crash of breaking glass resounded in the night. Splinters of glass rained over Taksim Square and policemen were shooting down galloping buffaloes in flames.

He sank on to the threshold of the house beside the climbing morning glory and fell fast asleep against the door.

When the door opened he fell to one side, then straightened up against the wall and went on sleeping. Fisher Selim ran back inside and switched on the light. At the sight of Zeynel huddled there and of the three large bags filled to bursting, he stopped short, utterly nonplussed. There was nothing he could do. He could not turn him over to the police, still less hide him in his house. The Menekşe folk would make short work of him when they heard of it. Fearfully he turned off the light and bent over Zeynel.

'Zeynel, my child,' he whispered. There was only a slight grunt from Zeynel. Suddenly, Fisher Selim recalled how Zeynel had set fire to his house. 'Get up, damn you,' he hissed and dealt him a sound kick. 'Get up, you dog!'

Zeynel, clinging to the wall, got to his feet, then slumped down again, as though bereft of life.

Fisher Selim's heart melted. How could he have kicked this poor boy . . . ? He knelt down beside him. But what if one of the neighbours had noticed? Then, the police would be here any minute. They would kill the boy on the spot. It would not suit the police, or the newspapers either, to have him caught alive. Why, if Zeynel were to go to the Security Department to give himself up, they would still shoot him and throw his body on to some empty plot and then pretend to have killed him after a long gun battle. Newspapermen would be summoned to the scene in the morning and would write fanciful accounts of how this fabulous gangster had been liquidated at last.

'Zeynel, Zeynel,' he whispered, shaking him. 'Look, the police are coming, lots of police . . .' He shook him more strongly. 'Have you gone mad, son? Wake up.'

Zeynel stirred. 'Police?' he murmured.

'Yes, yes,' Fisher Selim urged him. 'The coffee-house is full of them. What are you doing here, in Menekşe? Get up, go away.'

'They . . . Kill me . . . ,' Zeynel mumbled and dropped off

again.

'Damn it,' Fisher Selim cursed. Yet he shrank from shaking Zeynel too roughly. He was really sorry for him now. Was it this poor devil who had committed all those murders, robbed so many banks? He simply could not believe it, and if he had not seen with his own eyes Zeynel shooting Ihsan dead he wouldn't have believed that either.

He took fright again. If Zeynel was killed here, in his house, Fisher Selim would be the talk of Menekşe for years. He would be forever pointed at as the one who had informed against a slip of a boy. The very thought was enough to throw him into a dither.

He seized Zeynel and heaved him up. 'Wake up, child, the police . . . are all over the place . . .'

'The police?' At this, Zeynel grabbed his bags and bolted for the railway station, only to stop dead under the streetlamp, blinking at the station as though trying to identify it. Suddenly, he raced back to Selim's house, barging in through the open door. There was a loud crash inside and he shot out, whirled round and round Selim, then rushed in again. Selim quickly barred his way out.

'Stop, Zeynel,' he said. 'Stop!'

'Let me go,' Zeynel shouted. 'They're going to kill me. The police have found me. They're killing me!'

'Shh!' Fisher Selim held him in his strong grip and pushed him in. 'They'll hear you.' He switched on the light. Zeynel's eyes were starting from their sockets, his face tense, his lips purple.

Fisher Selim forced a smile and spoke gently to calm him down. 'Sit down, Zeynel, my child. You've only just woken up. Let me make you some tea. You'll feel better. Don't worry about the police for the moment.'

He made Zeynel sit at the table and, lighting his stove, quickly brewed some lime tea for him. Zeynel drank it up, his eyes still rolling with fear. Slowly he began to relax and, after he had drunk a few more glasses of the tea, Selim ventured to speak again.

'Well, Zeynel Çelik, tell me now, how are things with you?'

As though activated by a spring, Zeynel flung himself at Selim and clasped his hands. 'Save me!' he cried. 'They're everywhere. . . . The police . . . Killing me. Save me.' He was kissing Selim's hands again and again. 'Uncle Hasan said . . . He said you were the only one who could save me. He said you must take me to Vasili. Vasili from Samatya . . . Look, I've got a lot of money. Three bags full . . . They'll kill me. Shoot to kill. The police . . . Uncle Hasan . . .'

'Stop,' Selim said. 'Wait a minute. Lame Hasan's as crazy as you are. What do we know of Vasili these days? How long is it since I last saw him? Perhaps fifteen years. Who knows, he may be dead now . . .'

'He's alive!' Zeynel shouted. 'And with all this money . . .'

'I can't do it,' Selim said. 'How can I take you to the Greek Islands? Why, if nowhere else, you'd be caught as soon as we started to cross Çanakkale Strait.'

'We can sail by night.'

'It's even more dangerous then.'

'Vasili . . .'

Zeynel would not be put off. Fisher Selim lost his temper, he swore and shouted, then quietened down and pleaded, saying his boat was too old, it would never weather the rough waters of the Aegean, he had enemies in Greece, they would have him arrested . . . He talked himself hoarse, but the other was not even listening. 'Save me, they're killing me,' he kept repeating. 'Save me . . .'

Seeing it would soon be daylight, Selim gave up. He jumped to his feet. 'Look here, Zeynel that's enough! I'm going fishing. There's nothing I can do for you. The police are after me too, because of you.' He dragged Zeynel out and locked the door. 'You mustn't stay here another minute. This house is being watched. Don't you set foot here again, nor in Menekşe either.'

Swiftly, he walked away down to the shore, stepped into his boat, started up the motor and set off at full speed, not stopping until he reached Hayirsiz Island. He had fled from Zeynel as from a savage beast, but now he began to feel pity again. He's cornered, the lad, he thought. It's all up with him. Who knows, he may even now be lying there, killed . . . And what about those bags he never lets go of? They must be full of looted money.

He had cast his line into the water, but he did not at all feel like fishing today. A notion had taken hold of his mind, something he was ashamed even to admit to himself, yet was unable to escape, a pleasant happy thought that made his head whirl.

A large white passenger liner, all its lights ablaze, was gliding past like a great seagull, shedding its brightness over the pale dawn sea. Radiant pink clouds floated over the islands, silver-edged on one side, blueing on the other.

Selim caught a few fish, but they were not good enough for him and he threw them to the gulls. At every fish, the flock of gulls swooped down over the sea all in a ball and this diverted Selim. He went on with this game. All the fish, big or small, that he caught now were for the gulls. Sometimes, one of the birds, swifter than the others, would snatch up the fish in the air and dart away, arrow-like, towards the islands. More and more gulls came swarming down over the boat and Selim kept casting his paternoster line, pulling up as many as half a dozen scad at one go, which he tossed as high as he could into the air and then stood watching while the gulls, in a flurry of wings, scuffled ravenously over a single fish.

Selim remained until sunset in the midst of a throng of gulls so thick that Hayirsiz Island was hidden from view. As the lights went on in Istanbul and on the Islands, Fisher Selim started the motor and, cleaving through the wall of gulls, set out through the night, accompanied by a great flurry of wings.

He did not want to go back. There was an ache in his heart, a gloomy foreboding. What if he found that they had killed the poor lad? Then he smiled to himself. Zeynel Çelik, the gangster . . .

It was midnight when he sailed into Menekşe River. The lights in the coffee-house were still burning. Everything seemed quite calm and there was no one about. He moored his boat to the jetty and went straight to the coffee-house. There were several people there and in a corner the three policemen were playing cards. There was no sign of anything out of the ordinary. A wave of relief swept over Fisher Selim. He ran up the slope and into his small garden where some of the trees had been left half-blackened by the fire. Then he stopped dead, his relief giving place to rage at the sight of the huddled shadow on the threshold.

'Are you still here? Go away! At once! Or I'll turn you over to the police this minute.' Selim was jabbering with fury. 'How dare you . . . You burn down my house. You come to kill me. And now . . . Go away, get out! Now, this minute!'

'They'll kill me,' Zeynel moaned.

'Indeed they will! So you'd better scram.'

'I can't. They're looking for me everywhere. All over Istanbul.

Vasili . . .'

'Vasili, Vasili!' Waving his arms, Selim rushed away. But at the railway station he stopped and came back. 'Look here, Zeynel, tell your fucking Lame Hasan that Vasili's dead. Dead! I know it for sure, understand?'

There was no reaction at all from Zeynel.

All through the night, Fisher Selim, sweating from all his pores, shuttled back and forth between his house and Menekşe Station, pleading and threatening, all to no avail. Zeynel remained huddled up there on the threshold, mute and motionless as a stone.

The night was beginning to pale. 'I'm going,' Selim said, in a towering rage now. 'And I won't be coming back here. So, do as you like.'

He went down to the pier, sick and aching all over, boarded his boat and put out to sea. Refuelling at Yeşilköy, he steered for the Bosphorus. He was going to Rumelikavak, to see his old friend Skipper Tiny Hasan, and stay with him a few days. It was a long time since he'd seen him and it would be good to sit under the age-old plane trees of Rumelikavak again with the mussel-sellers busily prising open mounds of mussel shells, their hands all cut and running with blood.

Tiny Hasan welcomed him with delight, feasting him on *raki*, the very best fish and special Black Sea dishes, hardly knowing how to show his pleasure, but Selim's gloomy expression never relaxed. Every morning, he pounced on the newspapers, and as he read them the wild look in his eyes slowly faded and after a while, feeling a little calmer, he went out to the square under the plane trees and walked up and down, deep in thought.

On the evening of the fourth day, an uncontrollable panic took hold of him. He rushed to his boat without even taking leave of Skipper Hasan, and started off full speed for Menekşe.

As he went under the station bridge and up the slope he thought his heart would stop beating. Dawn was about to break, the sea just paling, shedding its reflection over the land. Then he saw Zeynel's shadow on the doorstep, gathered in a ball just as he had left him. An infinite joy spread through his body, a tingling radiance.

'Zeynel!' His voice was tender, full of love. 'It's me, your Uncle Selim.' With trembling hands, he inserted the key into the lock and opened the door. 'Come in,' he said. 'We're going to Vasili, to Limnos Island, to Greece . . .'

21

—— <•> ——

Dursun Kemal woke up with a start and leapt to his feet. Still half-asleep, rubbing his eyes, he made for the edge of the wharf and peed lengthily into the water. He was doing up his fly when his fingers suddenly tangled with the buttons. 'Zeynel Abi,' he cried, 'Zeynel Abi!' Quickly he darted through the stacks of apples, oranges, tangerines, cauliflowers, cabbages, leeks and radishes, knocking into empty crates and people. 'Zeynel Abi, where are you? Where have you gone?' Shouting madly, he rushed round the market several times, then stopped, his arms falling helplessly to his sides, his mind quite blank. Swarthy *hamals* with long black moustaches, bent double under tall piles of crates, the veins in their neck swollen, their eyes bulging, kept shoving him aside. 'Make way, make way!' Dursun Kemal gazed searchingly at everyone who went by. Finally he approached a tall man with a long wrinkled neck, crumpled trousers and a drooping black coat, and stared at him intently. The man gave a start, then smiled.

'D'you want something, my child?'

'Have you seen my Zeynel Abi? My brother Zeynel . . . He was here only a minute ago. With three bags . . .'

Surprised, but still smiling, the man bent over Dursun Kemal, his neck stretching longer than ever. 'I don't know such a person,' he said.

Dursun Kemal left him at once and intercepted another man. 'Zeynel Abi . . . he passed this way? He was holding three large bags . . .'

'Never heard of him . . .'

He questioned a shopkeeper, a woman, a municipal officer, a beautiful girl, some *hamals*. 'Zeynel Abi, my brother . . . While I was asleep . . . Three bags . . . Huge, full to the brim . . . Has he gone this way?'

The crowd in the market was growing denser. Undeterred, Dursun Kemal kept buttonholing every pleasant-faced person he encountered. By noon, it was becoming clear to him that no one had seen Zeynel. He stopped, irresolute. The high-roofed building, larger than any hangar, boomed and reverberated from the noise of the crowd, of people bargaining, arguing, swearing, complaining, laughing, buying and selling, hurrying to and fro.

Suddenly, he spotted a gaunt, hollow-cheeked man with a greying unshaven beard, a drooping white moustache stained with tobacco, and wearing a torn coat and trousers like stovepipes. His three-cornered eyes were sad, tiny, the whites invisible. Squatting against a stack of empty crates, he was gazing absently at the Golden Horn and drawing on a half-smoked cigarette with deep puffs that made his sunken cheeks still hollower.

Dursun Kemal went to him at once.

'You,' he addressed the man, 'do you know my brother Zeynel? Last night we slept here, the two of us. He would never leave me. What can have happened to him, where can he have gone to? I've been looking for him all morning. He had three bags with him, large as sacks, all chock-full . . . Have you seen him? Could the police have come in the night and I didn't hear them? Did they shoot him, kill him? I looked and looked, but there was no trace of blood anywhere. You work as a *hamal* here, tell me did they catch him in the night, did they handcuff him, was Hüseyin Huri with the police? Did you see anything?'

The man took another drag on his cigarette and looked up. 'Who is this Zeynel?' he asked curiously.

Dursun Kemal was thrown into confusion. 'My brother Zeynel? Why . . . He's a fisherman . . . There isn't another one like him for catching fish on this bridge nor on the other one. Only a few days ago . . . On that other bridge, the Galata Bridge, he caught thirty bonitos in just three hours.'

'Well, that's something!' the *hamal* marvelled. 'He must be a really good fisherman, that Zeynel of yours.'

'The best!' Dursun Kemal cried fervently. 'You know him, you've seen him, haven't you?'

'Well, no, I haven't.'

'But last night . . . Right there, see? We slept, the two of us, between those empty crates, on the linoleum . . . He'll come soon, won't he?'

'He will,' the *hamal* said with conviction.

'Of course he will!' Dursun Kemal cried joyfully. He rose and went on with his search until a sharp-faced, thin-moustached lottery-man, who was drawing lots for black-market cigarettes, waylaid him. The lottery-man pushed him into a corner and slapped his face.

'You're going to work for me.'

'I'm busy, Abi.'

'What business can you have, you whelp?' The lottery-man seized his ear. 'Want me to tear your ear off? You'll keep watch here at this door and warn me when the police come. I'll give you fifteen lira.'

'I've got something to do, Abi.'

'What've you got to do, you little bastard?'

'I'm looking for my Zeynel Abi . . .'

'Fuck your mother and your Zeynel Abi's too . . .'

The lottery-man was lifting his hand to hit him again, but Dursun Kemal ducked and shot away. 'Just you wait and see what you'll get when my Zeynel Abi comes! He'll pump you full of lead, he will. D'you know who he is, my Zeynel Abi, you blockhead? He's the gangster Zeynel Çelik!'

The lottery-man stopped short, a little shaken, while Dursun Kemal made himself scarce between the bright-coloured trucks that crowded the pavements and the street outside. He regretted having mentioned Zeynel, but, my God, how frightened the lottery-man had been!

Wending his way to the Spice Bazaar, Dursun Kemal had recovered some of his old confidence. No one could kill the gangster Zeynel Çelik. Wasn't he cunning as a fox, didn't the newspapers say just that about him? How he slipped fish-like through the tightest police net in the twinkling of an eye, how he vaulted from roof to roof, from wall to wall, so fast that the best marksmen could not hit him? No, no one would ever catch him!

With the firm conviction that he would come upon Zeynel at any moment, Dursun Kemal straggled through the crowds of shoppers, looking eagerly at people's faces, and emerged into the Flower Market. He was just stroking the nose of a rabbit in a cage when he became conscious of the bulge in his trouser pocket. He thrust his hand in and felt the wads of banknotes. At once he made his way through the covered market to the old *han* where the cloth-printer had his workshop. He knew of an empty room there. Stealthily, he opened the door and slipped in. He drew a stool under the light that came from a little window, then fearfully turned back and bolted the door. Now he was safe. He began to count the banknotes. What a lot of money it was! What could he not buy with all this money . . . ? And there was also the money Zeynel had given him before. He rolled up the banknotes, fixed them securely under his shirt and went out.

He longed for his old master, the warm voice, the gentle eyes, the shimmering white beard, the beautiful clever hands . . . Had he read in the papers about his mother's murder? If only he could talk to him, tell him how it had all taken place in front of his eyes . . . How, as his father was thrusting that dagger into his mother, he had closed his eyes and screamed, how his father had then lunged at him and would have killed him too, had he not fled, how his father had pursued him right up to Yildiz Park . . . Then, when he had come back home, he had found the house full of police, his mother lying lifeless in her own blood . . . 'Did you bring Zeynel to this house?' the police chief had asked him. He had been so afraid that he admitted it and the neighbours had borne witness. 'It's that ill-fated boy introduced the gangster into this house. He's the cause of his beautiful mother's death.' They had all said the same thing, every one, and had even seen Zeynel stabbing his mother . . . Dursun Kemal had tried to intervene. 'Mr Police Chief,' he had said, 'Zeynel didn't kill my mother. It was my father. I saw it with my own eyes. He was going to kill me too, but I escaped and hid in Yildiz Park. Zeynel didn't kill her. Why should he?' At this, the police chief had boxed his ears, and so hard that he'd been knocked down, his nose bleeding. And the neighbours had fallen upon him too, crying 'Liar, wretch, murderer!' They would have killed him if the police had not wrested him from their hands. As he fled, he could still hear them, 'Dirty vicious wretch, his mother's pimp . . .'

What if he went to the Security Department now and told them the truth? Who would believe him? No one, and he would be soundly beaten up for his pains. It was strange, but the police, the neighbours, everyone wanted to believe Zeynel was the murderer.

As he was brooding over all this, his feet had taken him back to the place where they had slept the night before. The newspapers, the old linoleum on which they had lain were still there. Suddenly, the roar of the huge closed market made his head whirl. He flung himself outside. On the wharf he caught sight of the policemen who had been there the other day, one of them scratching his bottom as always, the other spitting into the sea and their companions arguing and waving their arms. Dursun Kemal hesitated, then bravely walked up to them.

'Police Uncles,' he said in a trembling voice, 'have you seen my brother Zeynel? The fisherman Zeynel . . .' And then very quickly: 'It wasn't Zeynel killed my mother, it was my father.' Before the policemen had time to gather their wits, he took to his heels and disappeared among the crowd on Galata Bridge.

For a while he wandered in and out of boats, still searching, then made for the Sirkeci train terminal. There he caught sight of Hüseyin Huri deep in a game of craps with some other boys. Swiftly he turned away and rambled on, still with that feeling of being on the point of finding something he had lost. A bicycle caught his eye in a shop window. It was just like the one Oktay, the son of the bank manager at Beşiktaş, owned. How he flew on that bicycle! Oktay said he would soon win the Balkan bicycle championship. The girls were all crazy about Oktay, and about his sweat suit too . . . He went into the shop and caressed the bicycle.

'How much is this?' he asked.

The sales assistant look at him suspiciously. 'It's very expensive,' he said. 'It's not for you.'

'I've got a lot of money,' Dursun Kemal said, caught off his guard.

'Who gave it to you?' the clerk said, assuming a benign air.

Dursun Kemal saw that he was lost if he hesitated. 'Who do you think?' he laughed. 'My father, of course. My father's a sailor.'

The man still looked doubtful, but he mentioned a price.

'Good,' said Dursun Kemal. He inspected the bicycle in minute detail. 'Very good. Now I'll go home and get the money. Can't you make it a little cheaper?'

'We'll do something,' the assistant said, laughing up his sleeve.

On leaving the shop, Dursun Kemal felt a great emptiness inside. What was he to do, where was he to find Zeynel? He wandered up and down the bridge and went back to the Vegetable Market and to the place where they had slept. There was no trace of Zeynel. Where could he have gone to? He would never have left him of his own accord, this Dursun Kemal knew, but he had been so strange the last days, dazed, hardly knowing where he was going . . . Maybe he had got up in the night just to pee and then walked off, forgetting Dursun Kemal for a while. Maybe he was even now looking high and low for him, gazing eagerly into people's faces, or perhaps in fear, his eyes rolling like a chaffinch's . . .

He saw a barrow of bananas for sale and suddenly felt a gnawing hunger.

'One kilo,' he said to the man and, having paid for it, he went to sit on an old sailing boat moored alongside. Swinging his legs over the edge of the boat, he peeled his bananas and slowly ate them all up. He was scared now. His heart ached. He did not want to think of his father, nor of his mother, nor even of Zeynel . . . But what if Zeynel were to pop his head out of the hold this minute? He sprang up eagerly and lifted the hatch of the hold with eager hands. It was dark inside and smelled of tar, pine and rotting seaweed.

'Zeynel Abi, Zeynel Abi, it's me, Dursun Kemal. Are you there?'

Several times he called out into the darkness of the hold, but there was no sign of life. Despondently, he got to his feet and drifted back to the Spice Bazaar. At the back of the market he came upon a shop window full of marbles of every size and colour. In the middle, the marbles were heaped in a great pile, flashing brilliantly in the sunlight, shedding a wavering rainbow radiance on the wall opposite and tinging even the faces of passers-by with a riot of colour.

'I want a hundred and fifty marbles,' Dursun Kemal said to the shopkeeper with a regal air. 'These ones. And these . . . Ten of those . . .' He pointed out the colours and sizes and the man counted the glass marbles into a nylon bag. Dursun Kemal handed over the money and stepped out into the Spice Bazaar again, a carefree whistle on his lips. Here he bought some *pastirma* and also a couple of *simits* from a stand at the entrance. Then he went to sit on the steps of the Valide Mosque. As he ate, he crumbled up pieces of *simit* and threw them to the pigeons.

Here he was, getting everything he had always wanted. He had wished for a bicycle like Oktay's and now he was going to buy it. *Pastirma* and *simit* were among the things he loved most and now he was eating them to his heart's content, sharing them with the pigeons too. And look at those marbles, gleaming with a hundred different colours, clinking gaily in the nylon bag! A pain like poison came to settle in his heart. He saw his mother, her mangled body, heard her screams, her pleading with his father as he stabbed her again and again. The food stuck in his throat. And Zeynel Abi too, how could he have gone and abandoned him like this? Leaving the rest of his food on the steps, he rose, turning helplessly this way and that, wanting to scream, to throw himself to the ground and weep. He ground his teeth, seething, tense to breaking. A tall, dark, leathery lottery-man was passing in front of him, kicking at the pigeons on the pavement. In a flash, Dursun Kemal was at his throat. The man, big and strong as he was, struggled desperately, unable to free himself. His eyes were starting from his head, his arms flapping feebly by the time some men came to his rescue.

'But I didn't do anything to him,' the man was saying dazedly, as he retrieved his scattered packets of American cigarettes. 'I didn't even look at him . . .'

Four men had grabbed hold of Dursun Kemal and were carrying him away, his legs kicking wildly in the air. At last, tired out, panting like a bellows, he sank down on the steps of the mosque. Some of his marbles had fallen out of the bag. He was just about to start picking them up when the young *simit*-seller he had bought his *simits* from came up to help him.

'Here you are, brother,' the *simit*-seller said, holding out the marbles in his apron. 'My, but you are a brave one! Why, you were going to finish him off, that huge man, if they hadn't come between you!' Together, they put the marbles back into the nylon bag, the *simit*-seller still looking admiringly at Dursun Kemal. 'Fancy! That huge man! And how he bolted without another word as soon as he'd got his cigarettes . . .'

Dursun Kemal smiled gratefully. 'He was kicking the pigeons, did you see?'

'I saw him, the beast . . .'

'And I was feeding them with some of my *simit* . . .'

'Yes, I saw that too.' The *simit*-seller patted Dursun Kemal's dishevelled head.

Emboldened, Dursun Kemal signalled to him to bend down and whispered in his ear: 'Tell me, have you seen my Zeynel Abi around here by any chance?'

The *simit*-seller straightened up. 'Who is this Zeynel?' he asked.

Dursun Kemal pulled him down again and stuck his mouth to his ear. 'He's the gangster Zeynel Çelik. But he didn't kill my mother. It was my father did it. I'm in Zeynel Çelik's gang . . .'

'That can't be true.'

'But it is! I've got two guns . . .'

The *simit*-seller burst out laughing. He patted Dursun Kemal's head again and, still grinning, went back to his round tray and started hawking his *simits*. '*Simits!* Fresh and crisp! Warm from our famous Hasanpaşa Bakery . . .'

Dursun Kemal stamped his foot. 'Fool,' he muttered. 'Just wait till you see my guns. And police guns too!'

He ran up the steps of the Eminönü overpass and came to the bridge, which was as usual a tangle of cars and people. Cleaving through the crowd, he descended to the waterside under the bridge and stopped in front of the man who sold fishing tackle.

Many people, young and old, were leaning over the parapet, their fishing lines dangling in the water and the fish they had caught swimming in coloured plastic basins beside them. All around them, groups of admiring children clustered with cries of delight at every catch. From two rowing-boats alongside came the strong smell of fried fish and the shouts of the men selling it. At the end of the bridge, fishmongers had displayed their fish in wide basins and were putting them, live and jumping, into nylon bags for their customers.

Dursun Kemal selected a fishhook from the seller and a long blue nylon line wound round a largish float. He promptly fixed the hook to the swivel and attached the swivel to the line with expert hands. Then he bought a can of bait and, having baited his hook, cast his line. In a moment a fish struck and he quickly drew it in, struggling at the end of the line. It was quite a large fish. As he was unhooking it he came face to face with a small boy who was watching him with awe.

'Shall I get a basin for you, Abi?' the boy asked eagerly.

'You hold this line,' Dursun Kemal said, 'and if a fish strikes pull it up quickly.'

He was soon back, still holding the bleeding, twitching fish in one hand and a brand-new pink basin in the other. 'Give me the line,' he said to the boy, 'and you fetch some water in that pail there.'

The boy ran to let the green pail down into the sea. When he emptied it into the basin, the fish gave a jerk, then floated tranquilly round and round. The little boy's limpid green eyes glowed as they went from the fish to Dursun Kemal. It was not long before Dursun Kemal's right arm shot up again. 'It's a very large one this time,' he laughed, and the little boy laughed with him, showing a set of white pearly teeth. And indeed a huge bonito was whisking this way and that at the end of the line. Dursun Kemal dropped it into the basin. 'Freshen up the water,' he ordered the boy, who hurried up to the pail, rinsed it carefully and then filled up the basin again.

He was a freckled-faced little thing of about ten with a mop of frizzy, bright-red hair. His faded, tattered trousers only came down to his knees. He wore a blue shirt and a belt as large as a bandolier, with a shiny bronze buckle. He had no shoes and his bare feet were coated with dirt.

'Abi!' he said. 'What a marvellous fisherman you are! There isn't another like you here.' He sidled up to Dursun Kemal until their arms touched. 'Ah, if only I could be like you . . . If only I had a line and could catch fish just like you . . .'

Dursun Kemal turned to him and patted his head with avuncular affection. 'What's your name?' he asked.

'I'm called Ahmet, Abi.'

'And I'm Dursun Kemal.'

Ahmet licked his lips. 'What a nice name!'

Dursun Kemal likened him to a little dog wagging its tail, wriggling at his feet, longing for human contact. Ahmet could not keep still. He kept frisking round Dursun Kemal. His joy was infectious. Dursun Kemal felt a growing brightness inside.

'Where are your parents?' he asked suddenly.

Ahmet scratched his nose. 'I don't know.'

'What d'you mean?'

'Well, Abi . . .' Ahmet hesitated, scratching his neck this time. 'They've gone away.'

'Gone?'

'Well, it's like this, Abi . . .' Ahmet spoke quickly, smiling with all his white teeth, as though what he was saying had nothing to do with him. 'My father drank all the time. He always came home swaying on his feet and beat my mother. Then, we had this neighbour, Tuncer Abi . . . He fell in love with my mother and my father beat my mother a lot and he wept a lot

236

too . . . Then mother and Tuncer Abi ran away. She kissed me and said, "Don't be afraid, my Ahmet, Tuncer will come and fetch you too." My father got very drunk and cried a lot more. Then he took a gun and a long long knife and went off to kill Tuncer Abi and Mother. I waited and waited at home and a neighbour, Aunt Zehra, gave me some bread while I waited. But Tuncer Abi never came, nor my father either, and in the end Aunt Zehra told me to go away. "I haven't enough to feed my own children," she said, "you must go somewhere else . . ." '

'Where do you sleep, then?'

'At the station, in empty wagons.'

'Good for you,' said Dursun Kemal and pulled out another fish.

Ahmet clapped his hands and danced with glee. 'Abi,' he cried, 'please let me unhook it.'

'All right,' Dursun Kemal said.

Ahmet pulled the fish free and looked to Dursun Kemal for approval.

'Good, very good,' Dursun Kemal said and cast the line again.

'I'm waiting here for my Tuncer Abi. He's sure to come if my father hasn't killed him. The fishermen round here give me fish and bread to eat and I help them sell their catch. Sometimes I even have soup . . .' He pointed to the little cookshop under the bridge. 'There's an old uncle there who gives me a bowl now and then, good warm soup . . . He'll come, my Tuncer Abi, won't he?' The boy looked hopefully into Dursun Kemal's eyes.

'He will,' Dursun Kemal assured him.

'Yes, he must,' Ahmet said. 'Because otherwise . . .'

The bridge shook under the heavy weight of the traffic above, but in the little coffee-house underneath the usual sprinkling of old pensioners sat on, lethargic, paunchy, smoking their nargilehs. Boats kept drawing alongside the bridge, disgorging hurrying crowds, and then departed again engulfing more crowds with belching black smoke from their funnels.

At every fish that Dursun Kemal caught, Ahmet uttered cries of delight and capered round him, but Dursun Kemal's face was growing longer and longer. Ahmet could make nothing of this and clowned even more to try to coax a smile from him. A mist was slowly settling over the Golden Horn and the crowd under the bridge was growing denser, squeezing the boys against the parapet. Dursun Kemal had now lost all interest in what he was doing. His eyes were glued on the stairway.

'He won't come,' he moaned at last, clenching his fists. His face was drawn beyond recognition, his lips quivering. 'It's no use, he'll never come . . .' The line slipped from his hands, the float dropped to the ground under people's feet.

'The line, Abi!' Ahmet cried. 'It's going . . .' He caught it just in time.

'I don't want it. It's yours.' Dursun Kemal was breaking down. 'My mother . . . She's dead. My father killed her. He stabbed her in front of my eyes. She begged him, she kissed his feet. Haven't you seen it in the newspapers? He was like a madman with that dagger. She was screaming, dying at every thrust of the dagger. Blood gushed out of her . . . Such a lot of blood . . . She flung herself from wall to wall and the walls streamed with blood. The bed, the room was full of blood . . . I ran away because my father was going to kill me too. Then he brought the police home and he wept and he said the gangster Zeynel Çelik killed my wife . . . But he didn't. You don't believe Zeynel Çelik killed my mother, do you, Ahmet?'

'No, no . . .'

'And now Zeynel Abi's gone. He's left me. I was so sure he'd come here . . .'

'He will, he will.'

'He won't! He'll never come back again.' Dursun Kemal burst into tears. 'Oh, my mother . . . My mother . . . My heart hurts, it hurts . . .' His head on the cold iron of the parapet, he was sobbing uncontrollably. Ahmet soon joined him, weeping bitterly in unison, forgetting even to draw up the line, which was heavy with fish. Nobody paid any attention to the two children sobbing their hearts out on the parapet of the bridge.

Dursun Kemal was the first to lift his head. Their swollen reddened eyes met and suddenly they fell into each other's arms. Dursun Kemal cradled Ahmet tightly and murmured to him as if singing a lullaby, 'Don't cry, Ahmet, please don't cry . . .'

'All right, Abi, I won't.' The little boy's tearful eyes were already smiling.

'Here, take this fishing line. It's yours.'

'Really?'

'Look, you can have those marbles too.' Ahmet stared as though a wizard was standing before him. 'I've got a lot of money.' Dursun Kemal thrust his hand into his pocket and, taking out a wad of money, selected a few hundred-lira notes. 'Here, you can have these.'

Ahmet just stood there transfixed, unable to say a word in the face of such a miracle.

'Hey,' Dursun Kemal shouted. 'Careful, your line's slipping.'

Ahmet pounced on the line and drew out a huge fish. Quickly, he unhooked it and placed it in the basin. His eyes met Dursun Kemal's and the two boys suddenly burst out laughing.

For a long time, the crowds of passers-by saw two little boys facing each other and splitting their sides on the edge of the water.

22

All through that night Zeynel lay awake, thinking of Vasili and the places he would go to, Greece, Germany . . . His future loomed before him like a dark impenetrable forest. Still, he had such a lot of money . . . He would make his way to Germany, find a job, marry perhaps and have children. And at the first amnesty he could always come back. He would buy a good fishing-boat, equipped with radar, broad-keeled, painted blue and orange. He would have eighteen deck-hands addressing him as Skipper Zeynel, rising respectfully to their feet when they saw him. He was saved. He wasn't going to die. In a little while they would be setting out. What a trump he had turned out to be, Fisher Selim . . . He might be miserly, he might be money-grubbing . . . And hadn't he killed his friend, Hristo, one day at sea, so as to get his boat? Everyone in Menekşe and Kumkapi knew this, though they never spoke of it openly. They were frightened of him, everyone except Fatma Woman . . . Anyway, Lame Hasan thought the world of him. Fisher Selim had been quite a daredevil in his youth and it was only after he had fallen in love that he became so taciturn and aloof. People spoke of how he would sit on the shore in the moonlight, waiting for his beloved, talking to himself, lost to the world. They said she was a fair-haired beauty and that through all these years he had saved and scrimped only for her. But others said it was a mermaid he had fallen in love with and when some fisherman had killed her he had gone crazy and not been seen in Kumkapi or Menekşe for many years. In the end, he had run down the fisherman who had killed her and skinned him alive, gouged his eyes out and proceeded with unabated fury to slice him up in little pieces. They said he'd had seven children with her, three boys and four girls. He had taken the boys to his family in Uzunyayla, and there they still were, pining for the sea. As for the girls, they had slipped back into the water, mermaids like their mother, and could still be seen combing their long streaming golden tresses . . .

Though Zeynel had never quite credited this story, he remembered how in his childhood, back in that craggy wooded Black Sea village, he had heard tell of mermaids and how they fell in love with human beings. Everyone here, even little children, spoke of Fisher Selim's passion for the mermaid. Besides, he had been seen making love to her. And there were some who had seen him killing Hristo too, off the coast of Yassiada, striking him on the head with an iron bar, laughing as he stuffed him into a sack with a huge stone to drag him down to the bottom of the sea. 'One infidel the less in this world,' he had said. Farewell, friend Hristo, you've had more than your share of gallivanting with those brown-legged Greek girls . . .'

Should he have brought Dursun Kemal with him? Perhaps Fisher Selim would have taken him on as a deck-hand. Or would he have let him go hungry, refused to give him his due, beaten him black and blue? What would the boy do now, motherless, all alone in Istanbul city? What if Hüseyin Huri recognized him and turned him over to the police? Would the boy remember about the police guns they had hidden in the Valide Mosque? What had he done on waking and finding Zeynel gone? Was he angry? Or was he searching high and low for him all over the city? Darting around the flaming port, among stampeding buffaloes and crashing shop-windows, under a shower of splintering glass? How that girl's hands had trembled at the cashier's desk in the bank! She had fainted away too. And the policemen, how frightened they'd been of him! He could have stripped them naked and paraded them all over Beyoğlu. Naked policemen blowing their whistles, bellowing buffaloes, whinnying horses hurtling through flames and breaking glass . . . And over them all, over the naked policemen wielding guns and truncheons, over black roaring buffaloes, red bulls, rearing horses, a rain of flaming slivers of glass . . . And over a ship ablaze in the Bosphorus a great eagle gliding with wide tensed wings from the ship to Haghia Sophia and back again, swooping in and out of the flames, hurled hither and thither by a mad northeaster, its wings flurrying and fanning out. And Ihsan brandishing a dagger, stabbing and stabbing, and the blood gushing out, blood, blood, blood . . .

He rose from his bed and went into the garden. The shadow of Fisher Selim's skiff was bobbing near the pier. Yesterday, he had filled up at the depot and stored an extra six cans of petrol under the stern. All was ready. They were going. He was saved. A soaring gladness enveloped him. He was leaving behind all the horror, the blood and death and shame.

He went into the house and out again, on tenterhooks, afraid to wake the sleeping Selim, yet chafing to be gone. As the first aeroplane roared down into Yeşilköy Airport, he could wait no longer. What if the police were to come now, what if they caught up with them just as they put out to sea? He saw shadows stirring in the darkness and rushed inside.

'Uncle Selim,' he cried, shaking him frantically. 'Uncle Selim, look it's day already. They're coming!'

Fisher Selim lifted his head. 'Who's coming?'

'The police . . .'

Fisher Selim sprang to the door. 'It's only some fishermen,' he said as he switched on the light. 'Anyway, we'd better be getting on too. Bring me that suitcase.' He had bought a large brown suitcase the day before in Beyoğlu. It had a double bottom. 'We'll put your money in here. You'll need it in those foreign lands.'

Zeynel pulled the bags out from under the bed and gave them to Selim, who took out the packets of banknotes and packed them neatly in the lower compartment. 'Is it really as much as the newspapers say?' he asked.

'I don't know,' Zeynel said. 'It's a lot of money.' His eyes were fixed on Selim's hands as though hypnotized. Then, as Selim was about to empty the third bag, he grabbed it and looked at Selim pleadingly. 'Uncle Selim,' he said, his face flaming, his voice trembling with shame, 'that money's quite enough for me. Anyway, I'll find a job in Germany. You take this.'

'But I don't want it,' Selim protested. 'I'm not doing this for money.'

'If you don't take it, then I won't go,' Zeynel said. 'I'll stay here and the police will find me and riddle me with bullets . . .'

'Listen,' Selim said, 'you must give this money to Vasili so he can send you to Germany. So he can get a passport for you . . . You'll see how expensive all that will be.'

'But I need money here too, for when I come back. When there's an amnesty . . .'

'Look here, it's getting late. It'll soon be day . . .' But however much Selim argued, he could not convince Zeynel. 'All right, then,' he said finally. 'Wait here until I put this away

242

somewhere.' He took the bag and went out. Half an hour passed and Zeynel, shuttling in and out of the house, anxiously scanning the empty road, the sea, the darkened railway station, was more dead than alive by the time he returned.

Selim closed the bottom compartment of the suitcase and then placed over it the new suit and underclothes he had bought for Zeynel, a pair of shoes and some socks. He had even bought three ties. He laid them out carefully and then locked the suitcase. 'Come on,' he said.

The sea was only just paling and a few fishermen were also putting out. Selim fired the engine and set the rudder for Silivri.

'Shall I lie down on the bottom?' Zeynel asked.

'No,' said Selim.

'But what if they see me?'

'They won't notice. You're my deck-hand now. Sit down here behind me near the rudder and don't be afraid.'

'I'm not afraid,' Zeynel said, his teeth chattering. 'But rev up the motor so we can get away from here quickly.'

Fisher Selim gunned the engine to top speed, while Zeynel clung to the gunwale, all his limbs trembling.

As they came level with Büyükçekmece, the sun rose. Fisher Selim eased down the motor and they sailed on evenly through the calm sea. He looked at Zeynel's face and felt a pang of pity. He was quite green and his eyes were starting from his head. Selim pretended not to notice.

'Let me brew you some tea now, Zeynel. We'll have a good breakfast, the two of us, and in a few days we'll have passed Çanakkale Strait. We'll sail by night too, close to the shore . . . And then I'll hand you over safe and sound to Vasili.'

He slowed down the motor, kindled some sticks of wood on a tin plate, filled a kettle with water from a plastic flask and set it on the fire. It was soon boiling and he dropped a pinch of tea into it with his long fingers. In a moment, the fragrant smell of tea rose from the bubbling kettle. He turned off the motor and the boat glided to a stop, swaying slightly. From the shore came the crowing of cocks and the barking of dogs. At this sound, Zeynel's spirits rose. 'We're saved,' he murmured.

'So we are,' Selim said reassuringly. From the forehold, he produced a nylon tablecloth printed with large pink roses. He spread it out on the after deck and put some bread, cheese and olives on it. Then he poured out the tea into two pink-handled mugs. 'Well, let's eat,' he said and, breaking a large chunk from the loaf, he swallowed it down with a swig from his mug. He found the tea not sweet enough and added a couple of sugar lumps. 'D'you want some more too?' he asked Zeynel.

'Yes.'

They finished their breakfast and set off again, the boat gathering way and the seagulls, which had followed them ever since Menekşe, flying overhead. Three large passenger ships, their lights still burning, sailed past, one after the other. Zeynel thought he saw a group of policemen in the last one, but it went swiftly by, leaving their little craft rocking in its wake.

Blue waters flowed past . . . Dark, reddish, flaming . . . Süleyman's eyes had grown enormous, his mouth gaped. Remzi and Özcan were swearing. Their engine had broken down and the boat was adrift in the dark rainy night, tossed like a nutshell on the rough sea. They clung to each other against the gunwale, freezing, helpless, utterly lost. The boat was leaking, sinking . . . They were up to their knees in water. Terrified, Zeynel kept muttering over and over again the *elham* prayer which his father had taught him, with the advice that he say it whenever he was in a tight spot.

And now, clinging tightly to the gunwale, Zeynel was again repeating that prayer. His lips twitched, his neck was tensed and all the blood had drained from his face. Why hadn't he wanted to take the money I gave him, this stingy Fisher Selim? he was thinking. Because he plans to do away with me. Now, as soon as the sun has set . . . Then he'll take all the money . . . Fisher Selim is the worst moneygrubber on earth. Did he not strike Hristo dead to take possession of this very boat? And what about Skipper Bald Dursun? Didn't he leap into the sea when Selim shot him, bellowing like an ox, staining the water red with his blood, and didn't Selim fish him out and fasten a thirty-kilo marble slab to his neck and weigh him down? It's all lies what they say, that he did it to avenge the death of the mermaid. He did it for Bald Dursun's money. A whole bagful of it, he had . . . Yes . . . And in those days people were fleeing from Russia over the Black Sea to Istanbul, men, women, children, with bagfuls of money too, and Selim would pick up the refugees from the Russian coast in his boat, telling them he was going to take them to Vasili, and when they were way out on the high seas he would shoot them all, one after the other, boring great holes in

244

their heads, and the refugees would leap screaming into the water, but nobody heard their cries. He would tie heavy stones round their necks too, Selim, and throw them to the bottom of the Black Sea and take all their money and then return to Odessa for more . . . And in the dark rain-driven night, as the quails come dropping on to the shore with wet weary wings, Selim is there again, shooting them down . . .

'Do you have your Mauser rifle, Uncle Selim, here in this boat?'

'What Mauser, Zeynel?'

'Well, the one . . . When Skipper Bald Dursun . . .'

'Oh, that was long ago . . . I sold it.'

Zeynel felt better. But Vasili . . .

'What kind of man is he, this Vasili, Uncle Selim?'

'Vasili? Well, he's a good man. He was born in the Samatya quarter of Istanbul, you know. He and Lame Hasan were the best fishers in Istanbul for red mullet. And good company he was too. We'd swig a drop together at Yanaki's when we got back from fishing, and when he got to the mellow stage he'd take his *buzuki* and play old Anatolian tunes he'd learnt from his grandfather. What a man he was! Then he fell for the daughter of a Greek notable, but the notable said, "I've no daughter to give to that Karamanli Greek, to that Anatolian gypsy . . ." Was that a thing to say to Vasili, to the hothead he was then? "So, I'm an Anatolian gypsy, am I? Then, I'll show you what an Anatolian gypsy can do!" And he set fire to the notable's house that very night. He was going to kill him too, with all his family, but we held him back. Vasili would die rather than refuse a friend anything. So he just carried the girl off to Lame Hasan's house. That night we all got into this boat, the girl, Vasili, Lame Hasan and I, the boat was brand-new then and Hristo still alive, and we set off and in no more than four days, perhaps only three, we came to the Greek island of Limnos. Vasili had many relatives there, all from Anatolia, a whole tribe, and all speaking Turkish. What a welcome they gave us, feasting us on honey and *böreks* and mastic-*raki*! We often used to go back there afterwards, when things got a bit hot for us here. Vasili became very rich. He bought six fishing vessels and built himself a grand house, a real palace. Nine children he has. He's like a king there. Limnos, all those islands are good places. How would he have turned out, Vasili, if he'd remained here – a pauper, just another down-and-out fisher like us . . . You're lucky to be going to him. Maybe he'll give you work in one of his boats. Besides, you've got so much money – there's more than a million there surely – you can buy a boat yourself. There are a lot of Turks on that island. You'll pull yourself together and get married too and have children. Maybe I'll come one day to visit you with Lame Hasan. The people of Limnos all come from Anatolia, Muslim or Christian. They're as hospitable as can be, ready to share their only loaf of bread with you . . . But you could also go to Germany if you wanted. Be careful about your money. Don't exchange it cheaply. Make friends with our workers there, they need Turkish currency to send back to their families here. You'll give them your Turkish lira in exchange for marks and, since you've got nobody to send your money to, you can put it in a bank . . .' Warming to his subject, Fisher Selim talked on and on, and the more he talked the stronger grew Zeynel's apprehensions.

Why is he talking so much? The two of them must have tricked Vasili into sailing off with them. Then, while Lame Hasan held him down, Fisher Selim fired his gun and with a great leap Vasili fell into the sea, a black hole in his head. The sea frothed with blood, and when they lifted him back into the boat the girl flung herself over his dead body. With difficulty they dragged her away from him, all wet and bloody, and fastening a thirty-kilo slab of marble round his neck they sent him down to the bottom of the sea. Then they turned to the girl, deaf to her entreaties. She was very beautiful, just like Zühre Paşali, her breasts so warm . . . They stripped her naked and raped her, taking it in turns. Then, when they had finished, Selim fired a bullet into her head, making a dark, very dark hole out of which the blood spurted, and she too fell into the sea, and the sea frothed blood-red, and they pulled her out, tied a thirty-kilo block of marble round her neck and cast her down to the bottom of the sea . . . After this, Fisher Selim and Lame Hasan could not look each other in the face. For many years they did not speak to each other. Why, it's only a couple of years ago that Ilya reconciled them in the Menekşe coffee-house! 'What's past is past,' they said as they embraced. Why should they say such a thing if they had not killed Vasili? Yes, Fisher Selim must have gone to Lame Hasan and said, 'Send that Zeynel to me, tell him I'm going to save him and then I'll take him out to sea, shoot a hole through his head, he'll leap into the sea, his blood gushing,

I'll tie a thirty-kilo marble block round his neck and send him to the bottom of the sea and we'll share his money between the two of us . . .'

The flutter of seagulls' wings rose above the chugging of the motor. Zeynel moved nearer Selim and looked searchingly into his eyes. No, he thought, no, he *is* taking me to Vasili . . . Yet he began to inspect every corner of the boat, lifting the hatches of holds, feeling about in the bilges, until Selim noticed him.

'What are you looking for, Zeynel?'

'Nothing . . . ,' Zeynel said, confused. 'I'm looking at the boat.'

'It's a good boat,' Fisher Selim said. 'They don't build them like this nowadays, not even in Ayvansaray. It hasn't leaked once in all these years.'

Hristo's boat, Zeynel thought . . . I've still got my gun. I can shoot him before he does anything.

'You've got a revolver, haven't you, Uncle Selim? A big one. You could kill anyone with it, couldn't you?'

'I had one, yes, but I took it back to its owner the other day, to Blind Mustafa. What do I need a revolver for? I've got my hands.' He raised his huge hands and Zeynel shivered.

If he grabs me with those hands, he could crush me . . . Once at my throat he'd strangle the life out of me, like he did to Bald Dursun. He squeezed and squeezed, and Bald Dursun's eyes bulged, his tongue hung out, he turned purple and dropped dead. And Vasili too, he killed him like that . . .

'What was he like, this Vasili, Uncle Selim? Was he big and strong like you?'

'He was a huge brawny man, with arms twice as big as mine. Like oars they were. He never used the motor, but always rowed, and he went faster than any motorboat. After setting fire to that Greek notable's house, he tried to strangle him and it was all I could do to loosen his grip. He was a brave man, Vasili, a good friend . . .'

So Vasili existed, was alive . . . A huge strong man, he would never have let himself be killed.

'Did Vasili have a revolver?'

'Of course! Would such a young daredevil ever go without! In fact, he always carried two. I don't like revolvers, I never carried one.'

So Vasili had a revolver! A wave of relief swept over Zeynel.

It was past noon. The boat was chugging along with perfect regularity, like clockwork. The seagulls were still fluttering overhead and white clouds flowed eastwards, their shadows dappling the smooth surface of the sea.

Fisher Selim stalled the motor. 'I'm hungry, little Zeynel,' he said. 'Let's have a bite. It's long past noon.' Quickly, he opened the forehold and took out the nylon cloth with its pink roses, spread it out and put some halva, cheese and olives on it. Then he filled the mugs with water. 'Here you are, my agha. Come on, let's eat.' Suddenly he caught sight of Zeynel's eyes and stopped in shocked surprise. 'What's the matter, Zeynel?' he said. 'Don't be afraid, there's no danger at all. You'll see how we'll slip through Çanakkale Strait, easy as butter. You leave that to me. Besides, who would recognize you? The newspapers all printed someone else's photo instead of yours. Nothing's going to happen, please God. Come, eat your meal and don't be afraid. I'll take you safe and sound to Vasili.'

Never taking his eyes off Fisher Selim, Zeynel fell to eating as though he was not aware of what his hands were doing. Wild thoughts rushed through his head and would not be swept aside.

I was going to kill him . . . I set fire to his house . . . How can he have forgotten? They've laid this trap for me, he and Lame Hasan, and I've gone and fallen into it, fool that I am! Idiot . . .

Blindly, he gulped down great draughts of water and swallowed the bread, olives, cheese and halva until nothing was left on the table. He never even noticed Selim shaking out the tablecloth over the side of the boat and folding it away in the hold. One single thought held his mind: how to escape from the trap.

Fisher Selim was at the tiller now and the boat on its way, seagulls hovering up and down overhead. Smiling, he turned to say something to Zeynel and the smile froze on his face. 'What's come over you, Zeynel?' he shouted.

Zeynel sprang to the suitcase and dragged it to Selim's feet. 'Take it, it's all yours,' he panted. 'Don't kill me, don't strangle me . . . like Vasili, like Skipper Dursun, like Hristo . . . Don't kill me, don't, don't, don't!' He clung to Selim's arm, trembling like a leaf.

Selim slowed down the motor and began to reason with Zeynel. Why should he kill him? If he'd wanted to, he could have done it the night he set fire to his house or even last night as

248

he slept. He could have trussed him up and turned him over to the police when he'd killed Ihsan . . . All right, he'd burnt down his house, but Selim understood how things were. So why should he kill Zeynel now? Right through the afternoon, Selim talked, while the boat drifted slowly on. 'You know how I like you. I always have . . . That's why I've taken the risk of smuggling you out of Turkey to the Greek Islands.'

'You mean you're not taking me out to sea to kill me?' Zeynel said at last.

'Are you mad? Why should I kill you, my child?'

Zeynel burst out laughing and threw himself on to the after deck. 'Hurray!' he cried. 'No one's going to kill me, not the police, not anyone! Step on the gas, Uncle Selim, step on it . . . I'll bring you back a Mercedes from Germany. Quick, let's get through the Çanakkale Strait as soon as possible. Quick . . .' And he broke into a merry Istanbul song. He followed this with a Laz shanty, then a Çorum dancing song. What a lovely voice he has, the little rascal, Selim thought. But how frightened he was only a moment ago . . . Crazed with fear. I must take care tonight. He's capable of throwing himself into the water or even of killing me . . .

And then, in the middle of the song, Zeynel broke off, his eyes riveted on Selim's hands. He could feel them round his neck. That's how it had been with Vasili, with such blandishments had they beguiled him, Lame Hasan and Fisher Selim, catching him unawares, strangling him and throwing his body into the sea, taking his money, and the Greek notable's daughter . . .

The silence was lasting too long for Selim's comfort. He had to make Zeynel talk to distract him.

'Zeynel,' he said, forcing a laugh. Zeynel gave a start. 'Tell me, it wasn't true, was it, that you killed that woman at Beşiktaş?'

Zeynel's terror knew no bounds now. He seized on this chance. 'I did, I did!' he said quickly. 'She was my mistress. I took her to an empty kiosk at Ihlamur Palace . . . I mean, we always met there. And then one day I caught her with someone else . . . "So you'd do this to me, to Zeynel Çelik," I said. First I slashed her breasts . . .' Word for word he repeated the story he had read in the newspapers.

Aghast, open-mouthed, Fisher Selim listened with mounting fear. I must take that gun away from him, he thought. But how to do it without driving the lad still crazier?

'What about the Bebek murder?'

'I followed them. I knew those people from Florya. Very rich they were. I waited in front of their villa. And then when their car arrived I ran to open the door. The man laughed and gave me a twenty-lira tip. As they were going into the house, I ran after them, closed the door and quickly drew my gun. He leapt at me, a man twice your size, with hands twice as large as yours, he knocked my gun out of my hand. So I went for his throat and squeezed and squeezed. His wife was running madly about the room, beating her knees with her fists. I squeezed and squeezed. Twice your size he was, young too, his hands huge, yours are like a child's beside them. And then he went limp. He was dead. I picked up my gun . . .' On and on he rattled, working himself up into a fever, adding tenfold to the stories he had read in the papers.

'And the policemen?'

Zeynel's head was whirling as he reeled off tales of the men he had strangled, all men with prodigious hands who had not even been able to lift them against him. 'Like vices they are, my hands, like vices,' he repeated, waving them in front of Selim's face.

'And the bank?'

'The bank? There was a guard posted there, twice as big as you, your hands are like a baby's beside his . . .' Zeynel no longer knew what he was saying. His mouth was dry, but he never thought to drink. A dark night was closing upon him, dynamite exploded in the mountains, shots rang out, bombs were thrown, red-winged eagles fluttered in the night sky, fat quails with fearful swivelling eyes were falling, endlessly falling in the pouring rain, his father and mother were lying there butchered, his brothers and sisters too, all steeped in blood. Water flowed like frothing blood, blue, red . . . Vasili was pleading, 'Don't kill me, don't, Selim . . .'

'I hid my money beneath the old walls, in a little vault near the big gate, in the graveyard, and there . . . A man, twice as big as you . . . I jumped at his throat. "What are you doing here, near my money?" His hands, huge . . .'

Huge hands wide open, seagulls, policemen, flames, buffaloes, eagles, a head stuck in a porthole, eyes bulging, the rest of the man burning in the ship, shattering windows, policemen firing away all over Taksim Square, strange beasts with huge hands, bellowing as they pitched over on the asphalt . . .

'The man seized my throat. And I . . . I . . . My gun . . .'

Fisher Selim was on his guard. He wheeled round throwing himself down at the same instant. The exploding bullet only just missed him. Swiftly, he grabbed Zeynel's wrist and twisted the gun out of his hand.

'Shame on you, foolish boy!' he laughed. 'You might have killed me.'

Shoving the gun into his inside pocket, he revved up the motor. He was very angry, but tried not to show it.

Zeynel remained sitting at the back of the boat, broken images darting through his mind, crumbs of memories, vague details, and inside him a strange urgent expectancy. His eyes were fixed on the setting sun. It was a fiery red. In a moment, it would take on a purple hue and the aeroplanes gliding out of purple clouds would glitter like drops of gold, leaving white shimmering trails in their wake. But Zeynel saw nothing, heard nothing.

The sun was nearly gone, half of it sunk beneath the sea, the other half streaked by a purple cloud. The shadows were lengthening over the darkening waters.

Suddenly, Zeynel threw himself at Selim and locked his hands around his throat. The tiller shot to the right and the boat began to pivot on itself. Overhead, seagulls dipped, screeching, and rose again. Selim, gasping for breath, grabbed Zeynel's arms and struggled to free himself, but found it impossible to shake off his grip. He pitched and plunged, dashing Zeynel this way and that; the boat rocked dangerously, but still Selim could not free himself. He was suffocating, dying, when his fingers closed round Zeynel's throat and tightened with all the strength of his powerful fisherman's hands. Still he could not shake off the throttling grip. Frantic, he squeezed and tossed, until he felt Zeynel's hand loosen, his body grow limp. Slowly he let go and Zeynel sank to the floor.

In a daze, Selim could only stand there in the wheeling boat, his arms dangling at his sides. After a while, recovering a little, he bent over and took Zeynel's wrist. Zeynel's body was already growing cold. He reached out to his eyes and closed them.

The sun had set, leaving a red-streaked purple glow over sea and sky.

23

Fisher Selim hardly ever went out of his house now. People wondered when and where he bought bread and food. In his boat, moored under the beach bridge, the nets, fishing lines and floats lay scattered in utter confusion and sparrows and seagulls kept pecking at the breadcrumbs strewn all over the deck. It was an unbelievable sight.

At last, one day, Fisher Selim was seen making down to the sea. Without lifting his head to look at anyone, he began to tidy his boat. All day long he pottered about, his face sombre, the wrinkles deeper, darker, his head held low, and as evening fell he crept back home, still with that air of being ashamed to show himself.

Always alone, he roamed along the Florya lanes and in and out of the ramshackle Red Crescent summer camping huts, jerry-built out of packing cases, chipboard and plywood, and painted a thousand and one gay colours, and if anyone so much as approached him he shrank away, averting his eyes.

Once or twice at that time, I came across him too. He hesitated on seeing me, then quickly walked off in the opposite direction. And once I ran into him in Beyoğlu, but he made himself scarce in the crowd. A couple of times, long after midnight, I saw him standing outside my house, looking intently at my window.

His eyes were like a timid, frightened child's now. He had grown thin and pale and his bushy moustache drooped limply. Sometimes he went for days on end without shaving, which he had never done before, and he always wore a red kerchief tied round his shrivelled neck.

He fought shy of any human touch, and even of bird and beast. Ever since that day he had not been able to look into a mirror. He had always liked his own face. It seemed to him that God had never created such a handsome, noble, lovable countenance. That was why people were jealous of him. If he hadn't been so handsome, they wouldn't have been so nasty to him, would they? But now he could not bear his face. His hands too were horrible to him and he would do all in his power to keep his eyes off them whatever he was doing, even when he was repairing his nets. He longed to get away from the people he knew, from everything, into some other world, free of pain and sorrow and shame. To forget . . . But he could not forget, nor could he live on with that memory. Every moment, morning, noon and night, it was constantly in his mind, that shameful act. A loathsome sensation had come to settle in his heart and would not leave him. As he was throttling Zeynel, a drop of blood had trickled on to his hand, warm, sickening. At the very thought of it his gorge rose. And then, surely people knew that he had killed Zeynel. They knew it, surely, or why all those shifty looks? They despised him, they thought he had done it just for a handful of money, and he despised himself more than anyone.

Then, one morning, he woke up feeling light and joyous as a bird. His boat, which he had approached with loathing all these days, was as beautiful as on the first day he had boarded it, its paint fresh and shining, its nets glistening wetly. He went into the coffee-house and saw only kind, friendly faces. A mad impulse seized him to embrace them all, one after another, breathing in to the full their familiar sweaty smell. His eyes, bright and laughing, darted eagerly from face to face and the joy in him grew apace. He went out and saw a little boy. Lifting him up, he tossed him playfully into the air, then set him down and put some money into his pocket. The men in the coffee-house had never seen him do such a thing before. Singing one of his old familiar Circassian songs, he walked off towards Florya and they heard his voice from way off along the beaches.

He went straight up to Beyoğlu and strolled along the avenue and the Flower Market, looking happily at the passers-by. He did not want to drink, afraid it would spoil the magic feeling in him, this joyous sunny euphoria. He trembled lest it should elude him. He was a man reborn and the thought of Zeynel never crossed his mind.

And so he drifted through Istanbul, Fisher Selim, seeing in a new flood of light the sun and the sea, the crowds and crowds of people, the elegantly arrayed dummies in the shop windows, the toys, the assortments of gleaming crystal glasses, the ancient plane trees bathed in brightness . . . Laughing, dancing the *lezginka*, singing, reeling in front of the hundreds of car head-lamps beamed at him, slipping in and out of the heavy traffic, his feet barely touching the ground . . .

There was nobody left in the streets. Taksim Square was strewn with heaps of garbage upon which hundreds of cats were carrying on their struggle for existence, fighting over every scrap of refuse, clawing at each other's eyes, leaping, slinking from heap to heap . . . Yellow, orange, black, white cats, tabbies . . . These were the only living creatures abroad now, the soul of Taksim Square.

Selim stood planted on the green lawn of the square, a solitary figure in the few lights leaking from the high-class hotel nearby. His elation was slowly draining away, like a pink balloon pricked by a needle. Terrified, defeated, he saw the magic receding, escaping him like an agonizing palpable thing, and a sensation of imminent death overcame him. It was his life that was slipping away. Panic-stricken he rushed this way and that, struggling to recapture that vanishing magic. His heart hammering at his chest, he jumped into a taxi, with the vague idea of getting to a doctor, a friend, any living creature, before the last remnants of gladness were extinguished, and for a moment the sense of loss was suspended. Only for a moment . . . 'To Menekşe,' he said.

He came home utterly spent, writhing with shame. He had seen his hands as he paid the driver. He had even seen his own face as he wandered about Beyoğlu, joyful, like a shameless flower in bloom. Shameless, odious . . . He threw himself on to his bed. Everything that had taken place was passing through his mind again, down to the smallest detail, every word as clear as though it was being spoken now, this very moment.

You killed him, it was you, a voice inside him was screaming. You wanted to. To get his money . . . You killed a man who sought refuge with you . . .

But it's not my fault, it's not as if I really wanted to, another voice protested. I didn't kill him. I didn't . . . And if I did, then what? It's one microbe less in this world. He killed Ihsan, didn't he? And that woman at Beşiktaş, and the Bebek couple, and the student at Unkapani . . . Who knows who else and who knows how many more he would have killed . . . ?

He clung to this argument with all the force of his will, attributing to Zeynel all the most dreadful murders perpetrated in Istanbul. Why, if he'd been fool enough to take him to Vasili, he would have murdered him too, together with his wife and children, and gone on to Germany to commit further outrages, to kill Turkish workers and rape their wives and daughters. He was a madman, a butcher, a vampire . . .

But the next moment he knew it was all false, that the only person Zeynel had killed was the gangster Ihsan, and he sank again into the blackness of shame.

All through the night he wandered wretchedly round and round his little garden, shrinking even from the moon-drenched sea crossed by brightly lit ships. He was not ashamed of having killed. Everyone killed. Millions of men had killed other millions in wars without turning a hair. And so could Fisher Selim, now, this instant. For instance, he could have killed Ihsan without a qualm and drunk *raki* on his grave and danced the *lezginka* too. But this boy, helpless, friendless, trembling like a leaf, who had come to him for asylum, who had trusted his life to him, who had no one else to turn to in the whole wide world. The shame of it . . . Nothing, no amount of reasoning, could relieve him of this shame, not Zeynel's monstrous crimes, not the people he had killed or was going to kill, nothing . . .

As day dawned, he rushed into the house and wrapped the red kerchief round his neck, instinctively moved to hide the purple welt even from the rising sun.

So it went on for days. He could not sleep, he could not even get into bed, he could not bear to show himself to other men. He could not even look at his boat moored under the bridge at the mouth of the little stream. His hands buried in his pockets, the red kerchief always round his neck, crushed with shame, sinking below the surface of the earth if he met anyone, creeping through unaccustomed country lanes, he went to Yeşilköy to buy some food from a dim-sighted little grocer whom he imagined would only discern him as a shadow, though the little he ate, a bit of bread, some olives, a slice of cheese, was only just enough to keep him alive. He never touched Zeynel's money.

There were days when the weight of guilt so overwhelmed him that he threw himself down between the cherry laurels in the little garden, writhing, moaning, biting his arms, tearing at his hair and moustache. But on other days he would get up a different man, as though waking from a long sleep, a nightmare. Full of joy, he would hurry out to Menekşe or Beyoğlu to be with other people, praying to God that it would last, straining every nerve not to fall again into that bottomless void.

It was on one of these happy mornings, when the world rippled fresh and bright, that Fisher Selim ran to find Leon, the master mason.

'Master Leon, Master Leon! Get up quick! We're starting to build my house. Hurry, my friend, it must be finished in less than three months.'

His enthusiasm was infectious. 'Wait a minute, Fisher Seliim,' said Master Leon, smiling as he got up from his bed. 'What's got into you so early in the morning? Wait.' He went out to a tap fixed to the trunk of a tree and washed his face and neck with plenty of soap and water, dried himself and turned to Selim, who was standing above him like a restive horse champing at the bit. 'What's this now, so early in the morning?' he repeated.

'We're going to start building my house at once, tomorrow. I'm going to Zeki Bey now to buy that land of his, the plot under the big plane trees.'

'You know I'm always ready for you,' Master Leon said. 'Just say the word and I'll leave whatever I'm doing and come. Trust me.'

Fisher Selim embraced him. 'Tomorrow, then,' he said. 'Before daybreak . . .' And off he rushed to the carpenter. He found him drinking his morning tea, and all in one breath told him about his project. The fisherman's excitement spread to the carpenter too. 'Tomorrow,' he assured him. 'I'll be there before daybreak.'

Fisher Selim flew to the other craftsmen, barging into their houses like a whirlwind, infecting everyone with his eagerness.

'Tomorrow, early, before daybreak.'

'Before daybreak,' they promised him, one and all.

Then he went to Zeki Bey.

This Zeki Bey had at one time fallen in love with a girl from these parts and he had bought this land for her. He was going to build a beautiful house on it, but after the girl ran away with Cemal, the fisherman, the land remained unused for many years, a long plot that sloped down to the railway, overgrown with weeds and brambles. The sea was only two hundred metres away. All around, the land was fringed with large terebinths, planted no one knew when, their thick trunks rotting and hollow, and in the middle were three plane trees, their intermingling branches full of birds' nests. This was one place where Fisher Selim had never planted anything, not a single tree, not even a rosebush. He regretted it now, but this was no time for regrets.

He found Zeki Bey at home, an old man with a white, frizzy mane of hair and a bushy moustache yellowed with tobacco.

Fisher Selim introduced himself.

'I know you very well, Fisher Selim,' said Zeki Bey.

'I thought you'd forgotten me, Bey . . .'

'How could I forget you, Fisher Selim? Even if you don't talk much, even if you keep away from people, you're a man that one will remember always . . .'

With anxious pride Selim stated his business. As he spoke Zeki Bey sighed a deep sigh. He was strangely stirred, this man who for many years had forgotten how to laugh and love. 'It's a deal, Fisher Selim,' he said. 'The land's yours. It didn't bring me luck. God willing, it will prove more fortunate for you . . .'

Fisher Selim produced a large packet of money from his inside pocket. 'Take this, Bey,' he said.

'Why, thank you,' Zeki Bey said. 'I'll send you the title-deeds in a few days through my lawyer.'

'That's all right, Bey.' Selim's hands were trembling. 'Tomorrow, we'll start building. Tomorrow, at break of day . . .'

'God willing . . . God willing, you'll be happy and prosperous in your new house.' Zeki Bey's eyes filled with tears.

Fisher Selim made his way into the overgrown garden, repeating to himself, 'Tomorrow, before daybreak, before daybreak.' He sat down under the large plane trees from where he could see clear out to the Princes Islands. They seemed to have drawn nearer today. A warm sea smell floated to his nostrils.

In the morning, Master Leon found him there, leaning against a tree trunk, fast asleep.

By noon, the place was teeming with masons and carpenters. The foundations were quickly laid. For years now, most of these workers knew every detail of Selim's dream-house by heart, where the various rooms were to be, the kitchen, the balcony . . . It was to be something like Selman Bey's house at Yeşilköy, that Selman Bey who, because he was too poor to marry the girl he loved, had disappeared from Yeşilköy to return years later, a rich man with cars, chauffeurs and servants galore, and had built his house. Everyone thought it was for the girl he had left behind, but instead he had brought to it as a bride an eighteen-year-old beauty, after a fabulous wedding at the Hilton Hotel, and his old love had taken herself off and never been heard of again.

The house was completed in five and a half months, paint, polish and all, and even the garden was planted with new trees and flowers. On the last day, Fisher Selim gave a great feast for the builders and other workers and invited all of Menekşe too. He and some other fishermen put out to sea in the early morning and returned with mountains of fish. On the shore at the mouth of the old weir, a fire was lit and soon a tall pile of embers glowed on the shingle. A long table was laid there by the sea and countless chairs placed around it. Everyone brought plates and knives and forks. Truckfuls of bread were heaped on to the table and, while the fish were being grilled on one side of the wide circle of glowing embers and lamb and other meat grilled on spits on the other, the guests began swigging the purple wine Selim had bought. The feast lasted well into the night, to everyone's delight, and as the guests made their way back they could talk of nothing else but Selim's new palatial house.

For some time after that, Fisher Selim seemed tired. His arms dangling by his sides, he would wander in and out of the empty rooms or sit under the plane tree, never taking his eyes off the house. Then he would get up, circle the garden and go inside again, inspecting every corner, running his fingers over the windows and doors, the chimneys, the polished boards, rejoicing, sorrowing, swelling with emotion and hope, a constant smile on his lips. So it went on, far into the night, and then, his head dropping with sleep, he would make for his bed in his old shanty-house. And the next morning, he could not wait until he was there again, avidly inserting the key into the lock and rushing in, his eyes dwelling caressingly on every nook and cranny. Then he would go out and sit under the plane tree, staring unblinkingly at the house, lost in wonder, never tiring of looking at this palace that was his.

'Why, he's fallen in love with a house at his age, bless the man!' his Menekşe neighbours marvelled.

'Sitting there all day long . . . Forgetting to eat and drink . . .'

'Just as he fell in love with the dolphin . . .'

'He must have a screw loose.'

'And where did he find all that money?'

'Well, remember how he scraped and saved all these years?'
'If only he'd sleep in it one night at least . . .'
'Before Zeynel Çelik comes and sets fire to it . . .'
'And that Zeynel's sure to do.'
'Yes, Zeynel Çelik will never rest until he burns his house down and him too.'
'Only yesterday he was seen prowling around here.'
'With his whole gang . . .'
'Fifteen men!'
'With bombs . . .'
'And machine-guns!'
'My, my, my! What a blaze it'll make, that new house!'
'Well, what business had he to slap the great gangster Zeynel Çelik?'
'A man who has all Istanbul trembling before him!'
'Would Zeynel Çelik ever forget such a thing?'
'Never!'

All this talk certainly reached Fisher Selim's ears, but he had long stopped paying attention to what went on outside his house. And now, too, he had the garden to dig and prune and plant. Soon it was blooming with roses, specially brought in from the Italian's famous nursery near the old walls, with dahlias, forget-me-nots, large poppies, mauve pansies, scarlet sage, and even wild climbing roses, yellow, pink, red, a garden of paradise stuck there on the slopes of Menekşe, gleaming in the light reflected from the sea. The trees too, well looked after now, flourished and grew even more beautiful. The old peaches and cherry trees along the garden wall would revive next spring, their fragrant double-petalled flowers would open more vigorously and swarms of bees would cluster over them, their humming to be heard from way down on the asphalt road below.

Then one day it struck him that the house was still quite empty, that there was not a stick of furniture in it. He rushed off to Istanbul and went from shop to shop, finally settling on a set of gilt-framed, mauve velvet armchairs and a console table for the drawing-room, a bedroom suite complete with dressing-table and a full-length mirror, some chandeliers and chairs, and several coffee tables inlaid with mother-of-pearl. When all this had been put in place, Selim realized that his house had begun to look very much like Blind Mustafa's. 'Well, let it,' he said to himself. 'He's a good man, Mustafa. It's better like this.'

His Menekşe neighbours kept pouring in to see all these new things and Fisher Selim welcomed them all humbly, showing them over the house, always smiling as they marvelled over the gilt armchairs, the pink silk coverlet spread on the mahogany double bed and the elegant dressing-table on which stood a whole array of expensive perfumes in filigreed bottles, all waiting for their woman . . .

The house was finished and furnished, the garden in order, everything complete, but the miracle of which Selim had been so sure never materialized. For days, he shuttled between his shanty-house and his new palace, restless, expectant, running down to the station at every incoming train, cold shivers of joy and hope tingling down his spine, starting at every car that stopped on the asphalt, at every white ship that glided past on the sea . . . Every day, morning and night, his whole body a statue of expectancy, he waited there, unseeing, unconscious, not even knowing what he was waiting for as he sat stone-like in front of the rose-twined garden gate.

Suddenly, he lost all interest in the house. Now he spent all his time walking between Florya and Yeşilköy, his eyes on the sea, taciturn, not speaking to anyone any longer.

And one day he woke up utterly drained, empty, without support, the world about him black, his body numb, insensible. Without knowing what he was doing, he ran down to the little stream under the beach bridge, cast off his boat, fired the motor and quickly put out to sea.

The sky over the Marmara was darkening. Black swelling clouds churned in from north and east and west, and soon streaks of lightning flashed through the clouds, reaching right down to the sea.

From the tip of Hayirsiz Island, the sound of a shot reached some fishermen. At first they paid no attention, but then, as they steered their skiff in that direction, they caught sight of Selim's boat drifting haphazardly six hundred metres off the point of the island. They approached quickly and discovered Selim lying steeped in blood, his right hand dangling in the water. The bullet had penetrated his chest, a little below the old wound, and emerged, tearing the muscles. They felt him and found he was still alive. Without wasting another second, they took him to Menekşe. Özkan's son-in-law, Emin Efendi, who worked as a dresser at Cerrahpaşa Hospital, called a taxi and conveyed him as quickly as he could to the hospital.

24

—— <•> ——

Dursun Kemal took Ahmet to Beyoğlu and the two boys bought shoes, clothes, shirts, underwear and even coats. They had such a lot of money . . . Dursun Kemal confided to Ahmet how he came to have all this cash. Even if they spent it all, Zeynel Abi would give them some more. True, Dursun Kemal had lost track of him for the time being, but he would soon find him again because he knew all Zeynel's haunts. The two boys also bought a racing bicycle each from the Armenian at Yüksekkaldirim who sold them cheap. And one night, with Ahmet at his heels, Dursun Kemal slunk ferret-like into his house. There was no sign of his father, and for several days now the boys had been sleeping with a roof over their heads. They crept in late at night, when nobody was about, and left again in the early morning. Yet the neighbours must have got wind of their coming and going, for often one or another would leave some food on the marble table in front of the door.

Ever since the murder, Dursun Kemal's father had not set foot in the house. This Dursun Kemal learnt from Gypsy Hüsam, whom he came across one night, drunk as a newt. Reeling, hollow-cheeked, the gypsy buttonholed him in the street and rattled on and on about Zühre Paşali. It was not Zeynel, but Dursun Kemal's father who had killed her. All the neighbours knew it, but they were godless wretches, every one of them, inhuman, lying in the face of God just because they had been jealous of Zühre, jealous of her beauty, her firm breasts, her voluptuous hips, of the photo of the pasha whose daughter she was . . . Zühre's father had not been one of your fake pashas, but a real genuine one with a kilo of gold epaulettes on each shoulder . . . Swaying dangerously under the lamplight, his arms flailing, pulling at his hair, the drunken gypsy would have gone on for ever if Dursun Kemal and Ahmet had not made good their escape.

So they went on living in the house, bolting the door securely and ready to escape through the back window should Dursun Kemal's father chance to turn up. Their bicycles were safe too, hidden at the back of the house among the bramble bushes.

One night, they retrieved the police guns and cartridge belts from the cache at the Valide Mosque. Dursun Kemal emptied the cartridges like peanuts into his pockets and threw away the belts as he had seen Zeynel do. Ahmet imitated him. Their coats were large and reached down to their ankles, so nobody could have detected the guns strapped to their shoulders. Though heavy and uncomfortable to carry around, these guns gave them a proud satisfaction. Every day, Dursun Kemal bought the papers and read about Zeynel Çelik's adventures. It was like watching a police movie. Ahmet was barely literate, so Dursun Kemal read everything out to him. Ahmet listened, looking at the pictures of the gangster with his gun, his huge bushy moustache, his eyes glaring as though ready to devour someone, and felt a mounting fear which he was careful to hide from Dursun Kemal. He heartily hoped they would never come across him and, on the sly, he did everything he could to discourage Dursun Kemal from his search. But nothing could shake Dursun Kemal's determination to find Zeynel.

So they scoured the city on their bicycles, sometimes taking a boat or a bus if the place they were going to was a distant one, and Dursun Kemal never lost hope. He was sure he would find Zeynel one day, since it was plain that the police had neither killed nor caught him.

They felt at an advantage over other people, an easy superior confidence.

'Have you heard of Zeynel Çelik?'

'I have, so what?'

'What d'you mean, so what! Zeynel Çelik's my big brother.'

'Ha, ha . . .'

'And when he hears how you've treated us . . .'

'He'll cut off your ears!'

That was their stance whenever they found themselves in a tight spot. People would rue the day they had ever tackled these two little urchins. If anyone resisted, the boys would hurl stones and abuse at them. Should they meet with a tough customer who was not to be intimidated by either stones or the name of Zeynel Çelik, they would take to their heels, their overcoats tangling about their legs.

Sometimes they went to fish on the bridge. They were careful with their money now, and when they caught a lot of fish they set aside a portion for their meal and sold the rest. Dursun Kemal would often worry about Ahmet, reproaching himself for dragging the boy along on this thankless quest all over Istanbul. Just let him once get hold of that Zeynel! He'd have a few words to say to him! And then he would give up this vagrant life. Why shouldn't he take Ahmet to his old master, the cloth-printer? Several times he had made Ahmet draw something in the sand, and once on paper with crayons, and found the child had quite a gift for it. It wasn't as if Dursun Kemal had only himself to fend for now. He had to take care of Ahmet as well. He could not abandon him like this on the streets . . .

But what if the Master had heard of his adventures with the gangster Zeynel Çelik? And surely he must have. It was uncanny how he saw and knew everything. He was Master Adem, the noted cloth-printer from Bursa! He would never say anything to Dursun Kemal, only look at him, his warm loving eyes a little hurt, and how could Dursun Kemal resist that gaze, as crushing as a hundred-ton press? Ah, but how he longed to see his master again, to kiss his hand, to introduce Ahmet to him, to say 'This is my brother Ahmet . . .'

The belle of Sariyer district had been found dead in the forest of Sultansuyu, shot through the neck. That murderous gangster, Zeynel Çelik, had tried to rape her and, when she resisted, he had shot her and, according to his custom, had slashed her breasts and genital organs. The post-mortem indicated that the brute had raped her afterwards . . . The newspapers printed a whole lot of new photos, of Zeynel Çelik's youth this time, as a child, as a young man, always with a large gun at his waist . . .

Zeynel Çelik's new murder . . . It was in Baglarbaşi, near Üsküdar, that this ferocious killer had struck this time. A widow, living all alone . . . He had killed her for her money, and raped her too . . .

His next field of action was the Bosphorus. There he set fire to the oldest historic mansion, that of Canfedazade Zülfü Pasha, and by the time the fire brigade got to the scene it was burnt to the ground, with a descendant of the old family, the Lady Gülfeza, in it, and also a great number of valuable pictures and furniture.

The whole of Istanbul was living in fear of being attacked by this fiend, this bloodthirsty gangster . . .

Menekşe itself was all in a dither, especially after Fisher Selim had been shot like that, in broad daylight at sea . . . Zeynel Çelik had sent word to the hospital. Whatever you do, even if you hide him in a serpent's nest, under a bird's wing, I shall run that Fisher Selim down and kill him. You can surround the hospital with a whole regiment of soldiers and police, I'll still get him in the end . . . It was said that a strong guard had been posted outside Fisher Selim's room at the hospital.

'Who'd have thought it of that humble lad?'

'He and his gang have got all of Beyoğlu paying protection money to them.'

'That Sariyer belle, she was a real beauty . . .'

'I was sorry for the crippled woman.'

'If only Zeynel had got her out before setting fire to the house . . .'

'Now, how could he have known where to find her in that enormous mansion?'

'Why not?'

'Have you ever been in one of those Bosphorus mansions?'

'You could put the whole of Menekşe into one and we'd still get lost, that's how huge they are!'

'Why should Zeynel want to burn that mansion, I wonder?'

'He was paid to do it.'

'But by whom?'

'The present owners, of course! "Zeynel," they said, "get rid of that house for us, together with the cripple in it . . ." Because the crippled woman had the greatest share in the property and refused to let it be sold.'

'So Zeynel poured some petrol and set a match to it . . .'

'And when the fire brigade arrived he blasted away at them with his machine-gun.'

'Who would have expected this of that dumb snivelling lad?'

'Hush, the walls have ears . . .'

According to information given out by the police, Zeynel Çelik's dossier at the Security Department is swelling rapidly. The gangster's favourite victims are millionaires and beautiful women. His latest is the rich ship-owner Osman Mozikoğlu, whom he shot down in his Mercedes in the middle of Karaköy Avenue. As the gangster was making his getaway, the police caught up with him near Tophane Fountain, but after a long exchange of shots he managed to give them the slip, leaving three wounded policemen behind him.

The police are hot on the trail of the gangster who, only the other day, for no reason at all, made a raid on the Beyoğlu police station, wounding the chief officer ... The Criminal Bureau detectives, having received information that Zeynel Çelik was staying in a flat in Karagümrük, swiftly moved in, but unexpectedly met with a shower of stones from the poor folk of the district. The policemen, wounded as they were by this rain of stones, streaming with blood, still managed to surround the gangster, but again he broke out of the circle and escaped. Two hundred and forty-seven persons were taken into custody and charged with assaulting the police with stones, sticks and even guns in order to help the killer. It is not known what this bloodthirsty cut-throat may do next, especially as he is being hidden and protected by the poorer sections of the populace. The entire police force has been put on a state of alert and the people of Istanbul are required to be on their guard against this ferociously dangerous killer, a sex maniac into the bargain. Attention, you may be face to face with death any moment! Yesterday too the body of a young girl was washed ashore on the rocks between Fenerbahçe and Kalamiş. The girl had been strangled and is believed to be yet another of Zeynel Çelik's victims.

Istanbul was living in dread. People talked of nothing but the homicidal gangster Zeynel Çelik and refrained from leaving their homes after dark except for the most urgent emergency, for it was especially at night that Zeynel Çelik rampaged through the city, dealing out ruin and destruction. It was believed that this cruel cut-throat not only enjoyed the support of the poorer sections of the populace, but also had the backing of a secret extreme leftist faction ...

Then one day a telephone call from the Security Department to the editors of the Istanbul newspapers imparted a very secret, very important piece of news. The police had definitely ascertained the gangster Zeynel Çelik's lair and were launching a large-scale operation that very day. Would they send their reporters and photographers to the scene? They need have no doubts. This time the gangster would not escape. Steel-vested police, equipped with long-range guns, would also use tear-gas and smoke bombs. This time, the police would take their revenge on this elusive criminal who had stripped their comrades naked, wounded them, killed them. Angry and vengeful, they were resolved to finish off the business once and for all. They would open fire with no forewarning, because it was in that split second the gangster had always made his getaway.

In the afternoon, laughing and joking, the police and the journalists set out in an impressive procession for Unkapani, to a new three-storeyed apartment building in a narrow street in front of the Cibali cigarette factory. The place, and indeed the whole neighbourhood, had been surrounded by an unlimited number of police and all the streets leading to it were being held under the closest surveillance. Not a bird was allowed to fly past. The journalists were installed on the top floor of a building across the little street. From there they would have a good view of the whole proceedings and take plenty of photographs too.

The small low-circulation afternoon papers had brought out an early edition and newsboys were rushing down the Cağaloğlu slope, waving the papers and shouting shrilly . . . News! Read the news! Read about the gangster Zeynel Çelik! Read about the battle just now starting between the police and the gangsters . . . Will Zeynel Çelik break out of the police cordon? Read about the special police force and their steel vests . . . News, fresh news about Zeynel Çelik!

Dursun Kemal and Ahmet snatched a paper from one of the newsboys and without losing a minute jumped into a *dolmuş* for Unkapani, burning with excitement.

'What's up with you boys?' the driver asked curiously.

'They've surrounded him,' Dursun Kemal panted.

'They've cornered him,' Ahmet gasped.

'Who's that?'

'Look, it's in the paper.' Dursun Kemal showed him the paper. 'Zeynel Çelik.'

'He's our big brother,' Ahmet chimed in.

'Please take us a little nearer to the Cibali cigarette factory.'

'What about the fare, then?'

'Don't worry about that,' Dursun Kemal said.

'We've got a lot of money,' Ahmet said. 'Our Zeynel Abi . . .' Dursun Kemal quickly closed his mouth.

They got out in front of the Cibali cigarette factory. A policeman was hurrying by, his hand on the revolver that bobbed on his buttocks. They fell in after him.

'Zeynel Abi'll be all right, won't he?' Ahmet whispered.

'Please God, he'll send them all packing,' Dursun Kemal assured him.

A wide-spreading plane tree stood on the right of the beleaguered apartment building. As they approached, the policeman threw himself down, drawing his revolver, and at that moment came a burst of fire from right and left. After a while, the crackle of firearms stopped and steel-vested police with automatics charged into the building. A fresh burst of fire inside, soon over, and then the street was aswarm with police and journalists.

Two steel-vested policemen emerged from the building, holding the gangster's body by the arms. He was bleeding profusely. They dragged him along, his head banging on the pavement, and threw him on to the weatherworn cobblestones under the plane tree.

'Stand back, stand back!' Policemen were hitting out at the crowd with their batons, while the journalists' flashlights went on and off. 'Stand back . . .'

Beside the long body of the gangster was a tiny 6.35 revolver. His head was shaved bare and his three-cornered eyes had remained open. His long yellow face seemed to be smiling under the clotted blood.

The two boys were crouching on the ground behind the policeman when they heard the word passed around: 'They've finished him off!' Bursting into tears, they crept off and sank down against a wall, while people surged around the body under the plane tree and the clamour grew to such proportions that it could be heard from way off on Unkapani Bridge.

'Aaah,' Dursun Kemal mourned, 'they've killed my Zeynel Abi! What shall I do now?'

'Aaah,' Ahmet cried sharing his grief wholeheartedly, 'what shall we do now?'

They sat there at the foot of the wall, clinging to each other, until the crowd began to thin out. They were quite numb and their eyes were red with tears when they rose at last and with timid steps approached the body under the plane tree.

Suddenly, Dursun Kemal's eyes widened. He bent over the body and stared, his face gradually clearing.

'But this isn't him!' he cried, turning to Ahmet. 'It isn't, I swear it isn't. This man isn't Zeynel Abi, it isn't even the other Zeynel, the one in the photographs. This man isn't anyone at all. Hurray!'

The two boys retreated to the front of a shop with closed shutters and burst out laughing. Clapping their hands, bending double, they rushed back and forth to the body, staring gleefully at it, holding their sides and shrieking with laughter. And the bystanders gazed in amazement at the sight of these two small boys shaken by gales of laughter beside the body of the dead gangster.

25
—— <•> ——

One rainy morning, Fisher Selim came stumbling back to
Menekşe. He was distraught, in a piteous state. Like a sleepwalker, he groped his way through the little square in front of
the coffee-house and went down to the edge of the sea, wending
his way in and out of the boats drawn up on the shore. His
wound was bleeding and the bandages were stained with blood.

The rain was gathering strength, denting the surface of the
sea. In front of the coffee-house a crowd had collected.

'He's bleeding,' Özkan said.

'He's really become strange, this man,' Ibo Efendi commented. 'He must be in some kind of trouble.'

'He's in a bad way,' Ilya said.

'Bleeding like an ox,' Muharrem said.

'Let's get him to drink some tea,' Skipper Nuri suggested.

'Let me see you make that madman sit down!' Laz Ekrem
exclaimed.

'Look at him going round and round in this rain!'

'He's gone crazy!'

'And look, folks, he's got his pyjamas on!'

'He must have escaped from the hospital . . .'

'He's not himself.'

'If only he could be made to drink some hot tea . . .'

'Fisher Selim! Come on in. Sit down and have some tea.'

'Piping hot . . .'

'Your wound's bleeding.'

'Look, it's raining . . .'

The wet pyjamas clung to his body, which was nothing but
skin and bones now. His feet were bare, his tangled hair stuck to
his neck and forehead, and his Adam's apple jutted out like a
fist.

The northeaster was blasting away, lashing at the sea and
tearing the leaves from the trees.

Then a car stopped in the square and Emin Efendi leaped out.

He rushed to Fisher Selim and grabbed his arm. 'Stop,' he cried, 'you'll die, you'll die!' But Fisher Selim pushed on, dragging him along. 'Stop, you'll die, you're losing blood . . .' There was no stopping him. 'Help me,' Emin Efendi called to the others. 'We've got to get him inside. He ran away from the hospital. Quick, or he'll bleed to death.' Some men ran up, but Selim shook them off and walked straight into the sea.

'Selim, come back! You'll die!'

Selim pressed on, the water now reaching his chest.

'What are you waiting for?' Emin Efendi shouted to the young men standing around. 'Get him out. His wound's getting wet. He'll never recover.'

'Maybe he wants to die,' said Ibo Efendi. 'Leave him alone.'

'Nonsense!' Emin Efendi yelled. 'He's not in his right mind, that's all.'

A few young men threw off their clothes and plunged into the sea after Fisher Selim. Seizing him by the arms, they hauled him to the shore. He was swaying on his feet. Emin Efendi took his arm and led him gently past the Seagull Casino, under the railway bridge and up to the shanty-house.

'Has anybody got the key to this house?' he called to the crowd that had accompanied them and was thronging outside the garden hedge, oblivious of the driving rain, completely bemused by what was taking place.

'I have,' Fatma Woman said. She came forward and unlocked the door. They went in, followed by a few others.

'You light a fire, Fatma Woman,' Emin Efendi said. 'Here, in the grate. Don't look this way. I'm going to undress this man and put him to bed.'

He stripped Selim naked and dried him with an old towel he found lying about. Then he dressed the still bleeding wound and made him get into some underclothes.

'I must get a doctor,' he said. 'Make him drink some tea, Fatma Woman, until I come back.' He was a thin, dried-up little man.

The crowd outside assailed him, consumed with curiosity.

'He was taken into the operating theatre as soon as we got there,' Emin Efendi explained. 'The bullet had torn through him and the operation lasted a very long time. Then the doctors came out and said, "Well, Emin, you've no need to worry, your patient's out of danger." And then in the morning, I heard a loud hubbub coming from Selim's ward. As I was going to see what was up, Selim came dashing down the corridor. I grabbed his arm. He gave me such an extraordinary look, a mad, wild, blazing look, and flung me against the wall. The orderlies gave chase. No one could stop him. He knocked them all down, rushed out into the garden, and jumped over the wall, just like that, at one go! He was bleeding so much . . . Nobody could tell me what had happened, nobody knew. Like a wild, wounded horse he bolted out of the hospital, Fisher Selim . . .'

'You go and get a doctor,' Fatma Woman called from the doorstep. 'And take a taxi. I'll pay for it.'

'I'm going, I'm going,' Emin Efendi said hastily.

The crowd had not yet dispersed when a taxi stopped before the shanty-house and Doctor Orhan Suna, a familiar figure to Menekşe folk, emerged holding his large bag, followed by Emin Efendi.

Fisher Selim's convalescence was long and difficult. And all through it Fatma Woman and indeed the whole of Menekşe nursed him with care and love. Strange how they had changed towards him, these people who, when he was in good health, had lost no chance to spread malicious gossip about him. Now, they all joined together to help him recover. The choicest fish, the earliest fruit and vegetables, the freshest yoghurt, the richest honey and cream were for him. Doctor Orhan Suna visited him every afternoon, cleaning and bandaging his wound with his own hands. And Fatma Woman heated up water and bathed and scrubbed him as though he were a little child.

When Fisher Selim got up from his bed at last, he was as thin as a rake. Not once did he even look at his villa on the hillside. It was the neighbours who now watched over it. Sülü Yürek, a gardener employed by the Parks Department of the Municipality, tended the garden, planting it with the loveliest flowers from the town parks, so that it became perhaps the most beautiful garden in Istanbul. It was as though the villa and the garden were no longer Selim's but the common property of all of Menekşe. People were very proud of it, though they would have been happier still if Fisher Selim had overcome his obstinacy and moved into it.

Silent, abstracted, he would drift into the coffee-house, then, without a word to anyone, wander off along the Florya beaches to Yeşilköy or Çekmece, returning to shut himself up in his shanty-house, not to be seen for days, until one morning he would reappear in the coffee-house, his eyes dull, downcast, his face pale and weary.

On rainy days he seemed to revive. He would walk along the shore in the rain, his face lifted to the sky like a bird, and when he entered the coffee-house, his clothes dripping, people could discern a vague smile on his lips.

The first sign of recovery was when he went down to his boat early one morning and busied himself with his nets. All through his illness, the other fishermen had taken good care of the boat, giving it a new coat of paint, polishing the sun-bleached boards and cleaning and oiling the engine.

Towards evening, as the sun was going down, he put out to sea. When he returned after having sailed a mile or so, his face was smiling.

The change in Fisher Selim after this was incredible. Suddenly, he was talking to people, visiting their homes, helping the needy, spending money like water. There were no bounds to his prodigality. And every evening he assembled some young people, fishermen, deck-hands, factory workers, labourers and took them all to Beyoğlu. There they drank and made merry, returning in the small hours of the morning to continue their carousing around a lighted fire on the shore. Sometimes their revels would take place out at sea. And so Menekşe began to relive those generous, bountiful times of long ago. Once again piles of embers glowed on the shore and the appetizing fumes of grilling fish filled the air. Once again the little children could sandwich a fish in a huge loaf and devour it with the grease running from the corners of their mouth. The whole of Menekşe from seven to seventy rejoiced with Fisher Selim. Every day was a festive occasion, a time for happiness, for laughing, for dancing the *lezginka* to the tune of the accordion-players Fisher Selim used to bring over from the Flower Market in Beyoğlu.

And that was not all. One day, Selim bought for Laz Mustafa, who had nine children and could never make ends meet, a brand-new boat seven metres long, and a three-hundred -fathom fishing net too. When Laz Mustafa heard this, he rushed to the seashore and there, whirling round and round, running this way and that, beside himself with joy, he finally knelt on the ground and began to kiss the sea and the earth in turn, again and again.

There was no end to Fisher Selim's bounty. He gave dowries

to young girls and wedding-money to young men. He presented Fatma Woman with a knitting machine. He had Kadir Agha's boat repainted and a new bunk put in, for Kadir Agha had not slept anywhere else in the past forty years. He had people's tumbledown shanties repaired. Menekşe had never seen such affluence before. Fisher Selim was making everyone's wish come true. And with such exuberance, such a store of love as they had not had from their closest kin.

'What a lot of money he's spending!'

'There's no end to it.'

'For years and years he scrimped and saved . . .'

'Never spending a mite . . .'

'And now he's meting it out.'

'And so generously too!'

'That big house of his, standing there . . .'

'Ever since he's come out of hospital, he's never looked at it once!'

'He's got something against that house.'

'That palace . . .'

'It's because of the mermaid.'

'The mermaid who left him for the seven seas . . .'

'But she'll come back . . .'

'Fisher Selim will take her from the sea, her golden hair streaming down her back, and bring her home. He'll lead her through the flowers and hand her the golden key. "Open the door, mermaid," he'll say . . .'

' "Open the door, mermaid! Mermaid, open the door . . ." '

'It's when she left him and vanished beyond the seven seas that he . . .'

'Emin Efendi knows what happened at the hospital, but he won't tell.'

'Close as a clam, he is.'

'Why did he run away from that hospital?'

'And in pouring rain too!'

'Bleeding . . .'

'Why did he run into the sea?'

'After whom?'

'Who shot him out at sea?'

'Why did he weep so much all through his illness?'

'Who was it he kept raving about?'

'Repeating, "It wasn't her, it wasn't her . . ." Who was he

talking about?'

'Who was she?'

'He was waiting for someone, Fisher Selim.'

'Forty years he waited.'

'He lived only for her.'

'She never came.'

'Forty years he waited, on tenterhooks every day, and she didn't come!'

'So, then . . .'

One day, maybe six months, maybe a year later, Fisher Selim's storm blew over as suddenly as it had begun. The feasts and revels by the sea came to an end, the endless merry-making, the shouting and laughter that had echoed through Menekşe day and night. It was as though such a man had never even passed through Menekşe. The place seemed empty, desolate. Autumn leaves drifted over the dusty asphalt road along the sea. Only a few battered old cars were to be seen now. The press of cars trying to get through on the jam-packed asphalt, the itinerant vendors, the stands of fruit and vegetables, the melons and water-melons piled high all over the place, the crowds of bathers swimming or sunning themselves on the beaches and roads – they had all gone, vanished together with Fisher Selim.

The shanty-house was deserted. Not once did anyone see its door opening or anyone going in. But at the big house the gardener, Sülü Yürek, continued to tend the garden. It was the apple of his eye, growing lovelier, more splendid as time went by, the flowers proliferating, blooming with a different colour, another fragrance, every day of the year. Sülü Yürek had given so much time to this garden that he quite forgot his other job, which he lost, and his old-age pension as well. But he did not care, he was so proud of what he was doing. All the gardeners in Istanbul were helping him. Whenever Sülü Yürek spotted a new flower in a park or a garden, the very next day it would be blooming in all its glory in Fisher Selim's garden. And the Menekşe folk would line up along the wall and gaze in wonder at this magical sight. It was like a miracle bestowed on them, a source of gladness. And the lovely villa too . . . Fisher Selim? Maybe such a man, the lover of the golden-haired mermaid, had passed through the place and gone no one knew where. Maybe such a man had never even come to Menekşe . . .

*

Months later, Fisher Selim reappeared in Menekşe. He was unsteady on his legs and even more gaunt than before. His sleeves were rolled up and the reddish hair on his arms had turned white. He hesitated on the threshold of the coffee-house, then went in and ordered some tea, as though he had never been away and had only just come in from the sea. So much so that everyone was surprised when Ibo Efendi struck his cane three times on the floor and said with a smile, 'Welcome back, Fisher Selim.'

He was like a man who has nothing more to do with this world. Withdrawn, wrapped in thought, he wandered along the sands, always alone, unseeing, sometimes even stepping into the water up to his knees, then with the same sluggish gait returning to the shore. He never once took a look at his new house, nor even at his boat, moored at the mouth of the little stream. When he entered his shanty-house, he would lie prostrate on the bed, motionless, his body numb, bereft of life, deaf to every outside sound, sunk in a whirling void, a dream . . .

A copper glow irradiated the sea deep deep down. The fish, crabs, lobsters had all taken on a copper hue. Coppery waves rippled over a blue sea. The sun, rose-purple, had stopped, suspended on the horizon. Rose-purple clouds floated about it, staining the water purple. And under the water a rose-purple orb hung over the sparkling, coppery seabed, yet still encompassed half the sky. Aeroplanes glided like golden bullets through the sun, flashing rose-purple in and out of the clouds . . .

The square in front of the University was awash with blood. A bomb exploded in the crowd and all hell broke loose. Dust and smoke swirled about the moil of shrieking people and shots rang out. A few policemen bestirred themselves. Ambulances rushed up. Aeroplanes swooped in and out of the pools of blood in a steely purplish glow. Steel-purple rays of sunlight struck the pools of blood and more bombs exploded. A young girl was spinning round and round, one eye hanging from its socket. Seven dead, many wounded . . . So many . . . In Ankara, a baby shot dead in its mother's arms . . . The woman running through the streets, steeped in her dead baby's blood, screaming, rushing through the crowds, then laying her child on the pavement, rocking to and fro, wailing her lament . . .

Emerging from his house as though sleepwalking he would wend his way to Çekmece and eat something in a restaurant

276

without even knowing he was eating. Then his feet would take him to the Florya plain, away from the coast, and from there he would gaze at the far-stretching Marmara Sea which seemed strange to him now, as did the trees, the birds, people, everything . . . His was a vegetable existence now. All his ties with the living were severed, all his senses deadened. Only one wondering thought linked him to the world. Those large concrete apartment buildings that were being erected among the yellow patches of thistles and the ancient hollow mastic trees, on this plain which since time immemorial had been the haunt of myriads of tiny migrant birds . . . What would happen to the birds, where would they land when they returned this autumn? With wide eyes, he stared at the workers in the half-finished buildings, crawling about like ants, then at the aeroplanes roaring overhead. Bewildered, he read the papers, not understanding anything, then stumbled into bed again, only half-awake, slipping into the night, groping a bottomless void.

From a Murat car, machine-guns were levelled, vomiting fire. People fell screaming around him, steeped in blood. A youth lunged at him, eyes bulging, quivering. His hands were at his throat like a vice, he was struggling, twisting, squirming, he could not shake himself free. Sweating, he dashed out into the night, down to the edge of the sea and into the water, then crouched under the green light of a street lamp, wet through, panting.

The whole city – its people, its trees and waters and fish, its cars and minarets and birds, everything – was rushing in confusion, trampling over each other, frantic, in search of some refuge, pouring over the filthy noisome asphalt between Florya and Menekşe, which always stinks of rotting refuse and seaweed and sewage, thronging Süleymaniye Mosque, overflowing into its courtyard, all waiting in one common trembling dread for the bombs that were to be thrown, the bullets raining fire . . . Buses went past, packed tight with people, their eyes wild. Deafening howls accompanied the crackle of gunfire, the blast of bombs. A whole city, running madly, the old and the young, in a desperate rush for safety. And emptiness suddenly. . . . Not a single human being about, no cars, no buses, no trains. . . . Only stray cats and dogs prowling around the dustbins . . . Dogs roving through the empty streets, with up-curled tails . . . Cats trembling on the walls and roofs, with arched backs and bristling fur . . . Empty, too, the seas and skies, not the smallest skiff to be seen, not one aeroplane, not even a bird in the sky . . . And without warning they appear, the black-clad men, holding automatic rifles, their faces callous, their hands bloody, their three-cornered eyes hard. They come, snarling through their long canine teeth. And more black-clad men troop into Eminönü Square, carrying heavy sacks which they empty in front of the Valide Mosque, piles and piles of books . . . They douse them with cans of petrol and set fire to them. Tall flames shoot up as high as the minarets of the mosque, and the black-clad men whirl in and out of the flames, uttering wild shouts, while the black, burnt pages of the books swirl through the air, over the sea, sticking to the empty walls and the sky. And the black-clad men, angry, foaming, start firing at the roving dogs, the stray cats. And soon the fire-blackened streets are strewn with dead cats and dogs, and shrivelled pages of books come drifting down into their streaming blood . . .

The black-clad men have moved away. And now, thousands of fishing lines hung down into the sea, sparkling with millions of tiny pinpoints of light. The purple sun sat there, at the bottom of the sea, in a coppery glow. All around the flashing fishing lines swarms of fish surged to and fro, hooked by the thousands, darting off, only to encounter fresh lines let down from above and to be hooked in their turn. Fisher Selim, at the bottom of the sea, broke out in a sweat. He lifted his head and came face to face with Halim Bey Veziroğlu. Blood-steeped dolphins and black-clad men shooting at them, punching black holes into their heads, blood spurting from the black holes . . . Some of the dolphins leaped high into the air with baby-like squeals and fell back into the water. Others spun round and round like mill-stones, arching, tracing wheeling circles in the red-foaming sea. And the black-clad men kept firing away at the dolphins and at the jam-packed buses along the streets. A rumbling tumult rose from the city, a loud clamour . . . Cries of children being butchered rang through the bottom of the sea.

The surface of the water was strewn with rinds of melons and water-melons, with dead dogs and cats, dead bodies, dead fish, battered cars, charred books, a putrefying mass no boat could force a passage through. And Fisher Selim was fleeing, panting. Rasping sounds issued from his strangled throat. The strong hand of his pursuer grabbed his arm.

'Stop, Fisher Selim! Stop!'

'Who are you?' Fisher Selim shouted.

The purple sun, spreading over sky and sea, rested on the sea-bottom and the millions of fish-hooks hung glittering, waiting for the fish huddled in a corner of the sea, mountains of fish piled on top of each other, eyes bulging with fear, millions of steel-purple fish eyes fixed on the blinding flash of the purple fish-hooks . . .

'Stop, Selim! Halim Bey Veziroğlu's been looking for you for days now. He needs you badly. And me too . . . And lots more fishermen, old experienced ones from the Bosphorus, from the Marmara, from the Black Sea . . . Stop, Selim, stop! "I'll give him anything he wants," Halim Bey Veziroğlu said. He's had fishing experts, skippers, brought over from Europe. "But it's Fisher Selim I need," he says. Stop, Fisher Selim, stop!'

'Who are you?'

'Don't you know me, Selim? I'm Mahmut . . . Stop! You should see the ship Halim Bey Veziroğlu's bought from Europe! Not just one . . . Five, ten . . . Not ships, each one a factory that swallows up the sea, dries up its marrow . . .'

All equipped with radar they are, these ships, like so many eyes raking the bottom of the sea . . . Stop, Fisher Selim, stop! Each radar is as powerful as a thousand human eyes, a million eyes, unerringly picking out the fish wherever they may be, in whatever sheltered nook, at whatever depth. Black clouds of fish are beating about the sea with millions of eyes upon them, green, razor-sharp . . . Stop, Fisher Selim, stop! They spread their vast nets and the fish are caught up in thousands, sucked into the ship on one side, pushed out in cans on the other, glossy coloured cans with the picture of a fish on each one. They are swallowing up all the fish in the sea, these ships, and vomiting mounds and mounds of tin cans on to the shore . . . And trucks and trains and boats stand by to carry the canned fish to the far corners of the world. Stop, Fisher Selim, stop! The seas are empty! Empty, drained, killed by the thousand-eyed cannery ships . . . Stop, Fisher Selim, stop!

'What d'you want, Mahmut?'

'Halim Bey Veziroğlu is looking for you. Only our own fishermen know the ins and outs of these seas, he said, where the fish nest and breed and congregate. And Fisher Selim better than anyone . . .'

Not for nothing has Halim Bey Veziroğlu acquired all these ships. Not for nothing has he bought all those palaces in France and Italy . . . Not for nothing do the moneybags of this earth, the arms magnates, the captains of industry, the drug-traffickers, come to visit him in their private aeroplanes . . . Halim Bey Veziroğlu, too, has a private plane. He boards it in the morning and one hour later he is with Onassis on Scorpion Island, that Onassis who comes from our own Manisa town, whose name is Aristoteles, a man so rich he could marry the wife of the President of the United States, and so he did. He loves backgammon, Onassis, and so the two of them play a couple of games and then sit down to whisky and business. The other plutocrats of the world also come to Scorpion Island. They watch the game of backgammon and talk about the affairs of mankind, sipping a glass of whisky. They are both of Anatolian stock, these two, Halim Bey Veziroğlu and Onassis. Both playing mischief with the world . . . Stop, Fisher Selim, stop! Stop and give it a thought. They can starve the peoples of this earth, those two, if they want, hoarding everything for themselves, or they can shower bounty on everyone. Two people rule this world, both born in Anatolia, poor and needy, broken on the wheel of fortune, starting from scratch, and now spreading their branches over the whole earth.

'Veziroğlu wants you.'

'I won't go.'

'Not go to Veziroğlu? Why, his men will find you and take you to him even if you were the dragon of the sea!'

'I won't go.'

'Not go! Why, the Shah of Iran, the King of Saudi Arabia, even the President of the United States come to his feet! Even our own Vehbi Koç does so. Let's see you not go!'

Stop, Fisher Selim, stop! A long boundless plain, stretching far and wide under the sea, the colour of copper . . . The sun has stopped in the west, half in the sky, half under the sea, drowning the water in its copper glow, and planes and ships and trains are floating through the rose-purple orb. And millions of fish are snatching up the green-glinting radar eyes and darting away in swift flashes of green, vanishing in the copper radiance. They are all swallowing the fish-hooks, the millions of fish-hooks that hang in the water . . . Green eyes, fishing lines, fish whirling on the boundless plain at the bottom of the copper sea, all in a coruscating mass . . . Halim Bey Veziroğlu is at the bottom of the sea, in the Hilton Hotel, with eight yellow-haired girls . . .

'It wasn't her! She wasn't the girl with the flaxen hair . . . I swear it, she wasn't the one.'

One of those yellow-haired girls . . . Is it possible . . .? Her yellow hair streaming down her back, all a-shimmer, there at the bottom of the sea . . . It's that fish, that one . . . That dolphin, that one . . . That dolphin is the girl with the flaxen hair. And Halim Bey Veziroğlu is playing backgammon with the fish, with the girl with the flaxen hair . . . And all around them the fish of the sea are weeping. Weeping also are the girls with flaxen hair.

The sea is cluttered with the dead bodies of men and dogs and cats and fish. Boats cannot force a passage. Forward, Veziroğlu, forward! He is at the head of them all, his men, the black-clad ones, there in Eminönü Square, and with machine-guns they strafe the sea, the buses, the minarets, the fish and dolphins, the cats and dogs. Eminönü Square is up in flames and the deafening crackle of machine-gun fire resounds all over Istanbul, from the mosques and bridges, from Leander's Tower, from Galata Tower. And Veziroğlu issues more orders to the black-clad ones and they open fire on men and women and children. Some leap high in the air with a long shriek and fall back bleeding on to the pavement, others drop down, their backs arched like a bow, spinning like millstones, their blood spurting over the steps of Valide Mosque . . .

First came the fish, all the fish that had swallowed the hooks and the radar eyes. They came and massed upon the shore, shedding a radiance over earth and sky. Then the cats and dogs, the dolphins and the people appeared, all streaming with blood, and formed a wide circle round the black-clad men. Narrower and narrower grew the circle and the black-clad men retreated, still firing their machine-guns, and huddled at the foot of Valide Mosque, their eyes bulging with fear, trembling, rattling . . . Stop, Fisher Seiim, stop! The crowd is closing in, trampling over the black-clad men, pressing them like grapes. Furiously, the people crush and pound. And suddenly they draw back and there is not a trace of the black-clad men. Only a few scattered, broken machine-guns . . .

'You must go, Fisher Selim,' the Menekşe fishermen insisted. 'We shall all have to work on Veziroğlu's cannery ships. Haven't you heard? We're being displaced. The Municipality's going to build a sewage plant here, on Çekmece Stream. If not tomorrow, then the day after, bulldozers will be sent in and will raze our houses to the ground. It's all decided.'

'If Veziroğlu takes us on, we can make a good living. But if we don't go, he'll get fishermen from Greece and Italy.'

'We have no choice but to work for Veziroğlu.'

'Come on, Fisher Selim . . .'

'Your eyes can fathom the depths of the sea even better than that radar.'

'That's what Veziroğlu says.'

' "I can't do without Fisher Selim," he says . . .'

'Come on, Fisher Selim. Today's the day. Pull yourself together.'

'Just do this one more thing for us.'

'There's no choice for us but to work for Veziroğlu.'

'And he pays well, too.'

'He's got all those commandos at his beck and call, the black-clad commandos.'

'We have no choice.'

'Don't let us down.'

'You'll be the foremost skipper on these seas.'

'Instead of wasting our lives on these ramshackle boats, catching hardly enough fish to keep us alive, we'll be working comfortably in those cannery ships.'

'All snug and warm . . . No freezing in the winter or burning in the summer . . .'

'Spick and span they are, those ships.'

'Each one a huge canning factory . . .'

'I saw one in Russia. There were even doctors in it for the fishermen who fell sick, and beautiful nurses with white blouses and yellow hair.'

'Stop, Fisher Selim, stop! It's me Mahmut. Where are you going?'

Bulldozers are rumbling into Menekşe along the little stream that flows from the lake into the sea, demolishing houses, raising clouds of dust and smoke. Women are weeping, their hands beating their breasts . . .

Blind Mustafa's wife met him at the gate with long agonizing screams. The two white-coated servants standing rigid in attendance had a sneer on their faces.

'Mustafa's dead, Fisher Selim! Dead, my Mustafa . . .' She

clutched at him, weeping.

The house was silent, desolate. Mustafa lay in a huge gold-plated bed spread with white cambric sheets, his hands folded over his chest, his wrinkled face elongated, dark yellow. His blind left eye had sunk into its socket, leaving a dark hole. The other eye was closed and bulging out like an apple.

'He's dead, my Mustafa, dead . . .'

A bright-red cravat was tied about his neck and a red handkerchief thrust into the breast pocket of his navy-blue suit.

'There he lies, alone, forsaken, my Mustafa,' she was keening. 'Far from his kith and kin, his people, his land . . .'

All in the splendour of this palatial house, the wealth, the gold, the crystal . . . All his factories, all his sons, their wives, his grandchildren, where were they? Friendless, alone . . . In a desert he lies, my Mustafa . . . Eagles and vultures screeching above . . . Back there in the old homeland, ah, that we were there! All the village would be mourning for my Mustafa. The keening women would crowd into the house with long wailing cries. Death is difficult in Istanbul. All alone . . .

'Not even his sons have come, not even his grandchildren. Three days I've been waiting here, Fisher Selim, alone. All alone with my dead Mustafa. This death is worse than death. If his people back home had heard, they'd have come all the way from the far end of Anatolia to my Mustafa's deathbed . . .'

There he lies, his signet ring still on his finger, his white hair falling over his brow, tired, his lips curled in anger, bitter against the world, against death, this lonely death. He gave his all to his sons. Three days his dead body has been waiting for them to come. Telegrams have been sent to Geneva. And still he is waiting. How can a corpse wait? It is already starting to smell. The smell rises above the scent of the cologne sprinkled over him, over the whole house.

'Let it wait, my dead Mustafa's corpse . . .'

In Geneva, that's where they are. That's where they spend the summer, Mustafa's sons, their wives, their children. And now their summer is spoilt. Was this a time to die, Mustafa? Let him wait. Let the corpse wait . . .

'This revolver, pure gold, he left it to you, Fisher Selim. I cannot even keen over him. I'm ashamed to, here in Istanbul. Without a single lament he is gone, my Mustafa . . . Would that we had never come here, would that we had died of hunger in our barren village, our home! Ah, Fisher Selim, my good friend . . .'

A red eagle was circling over Yeşilköy. Seagulls perched in a long white row on the garden wall of the villa.

In his well-pressed trousers, the many rings glinting on his fingers, the pouches under his eyes sagging, Halim Bey Veziroğlu paced up and down his brightly lit office with the morocco leather armchairs.

'Do you accept, then, Fisher Selim?' Sure of himself, used to giving orders . . . 'You fisher people are being thrown out of Menekşe. We're going to build a large tourist hotel there. Why, the place is a natural paradise! How could we possibly leave it to a handful of shabby fishermen? I'm offering work, good jobs. So you won't all die of hunger. Put Menekşe out of your mind.'

He laughs and his paunch bounces up and down. People come in and out of the office, young girls . . . All of them bending in obeisance . . .

'I always get what I want, Fisher Selim. You shall work in my ships. That land you wanted, it's still yours. You can pay me back little by little . . .'

His voice is echoing, echoing . . .

'Stop, Fisher Selim, stop! You can't do this! He's our benefactor. He's our livelihood now.' Clinging to Selim, Mahmut is pleading with him. 'Stop, Selim, stop! They wouldn't let you near him anyway. Veziroğlu's got a hundred armed men around him, all crack shots. Have you lost your wits? Stop!'

It was raining and ever since early morning Fisher Selim had been walking in the rain, his mind quite numb, his eyes on a tiny little bird that was darting up and down, twittering merrily in front of him, and when it alighted in the garden of his big house he followed it mechanically. Then his eyes widened. He opened the gate and went in, inspecting every flower and tree, passing on into the house. For a long time he remained there, gazing at every object as though to engrave it on his mind.

Seagulls had settled on the sea, under the rain, rocking up and down with the waves. Below, the bulldozers were at work, scooping up the shanties and levelling the ground. The people of Menekşe were lined up, watching the destruction of their homes, as if it were a show. Fisher Selim loaded the gold-plated revolver and thrust it into his waistband.

Two black-moustached mastodons were standing at the door,

both clad in black, both dour-faced, like people who had forgotten how to smile.

'I want to see Halim Bey Veziroğlu.'

'Who are you?'

'I'm a fisherman.'

The large garden gate of the mansion opened on to a road that led to a mosque. Wide-spreading branches of ancient pines, planes and lindens overhung the waters of the Bosphorus. A path paved with coloured cobblestones set in flowery designs and planted on both sides with flaming scarlet sage went up to the mansion, which was a rambling two-storeyed edifice, painted a purplish brown and occupying the whole of the little bay.

'It's only a fisherman wants to speak with the Bey . . .'

Halim Bey Veziroğlu had seen Fisher Selim from the window. He hesitated, then called out: 'Send him in.'

He was seated at a wide table on which was a large portrait in a gold frame.

'Stop, Fisher Selim, stop!'

Fisher Selim pulled out the revolver Blind Mustafa had bequeathed him and, coolly, without a quiver, pulled the trigger. There was no surprise on Halim Bey Veziroğlu's face when he saw the revolver, not even fear. It remained impassive. Three times Fisher Selim fired and Veziroğlu slipped silently from his chair to the floor.

As darkness fell, Fisher Selim was still crouched in the arched boathouse under the mansion, listening to the tumult above. It was long past midnight when he emerged from his hiding-place. The mansion was quiet now, there was nobody about, not even at the gate, and he walked out quite easily. The police must be scouring all Istanbul now, he thought, and smiled. But who knew the ins and outs of this city as he did? Towards morning, he was in Menekşe. Mahmut was sitting in his boat, waiting for him.

'Stop, Fisher Selim, stop!' he said. 'You've ruined us all, you've done for Menekşe. Look, the whole place is crawling with police, look!'

The sea had not yet paled. There was no sound on the shore. Fisher Selim started the engine.

'Get off,' he said to Mahmut. 'I'm going.'

'I won't,' said Mahmut. 'I'm coming with you. I can't let you go alone like this.'

285

'Get off,' Selim said again.

Mahmut did not move.

Selim drew his gun. 'Out,' he said. 'Get out! You've got a family to take care of. If you want to do something for me, put the police off my track.'

Mahmut rose and jumped ashore.

Fisher Selim revved up the motor.

As day was breaking, he reached Hayirsiz Island and stopped a mile off the rocky coast. The sea was smooth and calm, but black clouds were churning in the sky. Soon thunder was booming and flashes of lightning splitting through the clouds, one after another. A thunderbolt struck the rocks and split into four fragments that streaked round the coast, and for one brief instant the whole island rose into the sky, glistening darkly, and fell back into the sea.

Fisher Selim stood at the stern of his boat, gazing with yearning at the purpling sea, the blazing flashes of lightning, the churning clouds. A warm rain wind caressed his face. The world about him appeared as never before, clear in its smallest detail, the fish and weeds, the bees and insects. In his blood he felt the slow roll of the sea with its millions of tons of water, he saw the billions of tiny sparks held in its every drop. Drained of all emotion, he stood motionless, a great rush in his ears, slowly letting himself be engulfed in a bottomless void.

Suddenly, a miracle burst over the sea. Fisher Selim blinked, unable to believe what he saw. He rubbed his eyes and looked again. In the dawn light, in the brightness shed by the flashes of lightning, cleaving through the blueing, greening waves of the dawn sea and tracing sparkling blue circles as they leaped through the air, a school of dolphins was approaching his boat in a whirl of joy. It was years since Fisher Selim had seen dolphins in the Marmara Sea. His legs gave way and he knelt down where he was, on the after deck, trembling with emotion.

The sun had risen behind the clouds, a huge rose-purple sun stood there over the sea, under the black canopy of clouds. Fisher Selim smiled. The sea, the sky, the clouds, the flashing lightning glowed, radiantly bright. He cast a glance towards Menekşe. The whole coast of Istanbul, with its domes and minarets, was drowned in a shimmering haze.

'But what shall I do now, what?' he murmured. Then he leaped to his feet in a tempest of joy.

'It wasn't her!' he shouted. 'She wasn't the one . . . It couldn't be. She wasn't the one I'd been waiting for.'

Nearer and nearer they came, the dolphins, hurrying towards him, leaping, gambolling, tracing wide sparkling arcs through the air.

He looked about him and the world was clear and bright, the huge open sea blue, newly fresh, lit up from deep deep down by a soft light, blooming like a flower of joy.

GLOSSARY

Abi: big brother

Abla: big sister

Ayran: a drink made of watered yoghurt

Börek: a kind of pastry with various fillings

Buzuki: a Greek popular musical instrument

Cacik: a salad made of yoghurt, chopped cucumber and garlic

Dolmuş: a shared taxi

Döner kebap: meat roasted on a revolving vertical spit

Elham: a sura (chapter) of the Koran

Ezan: the call to prayer by a muezzin from a minaret

Hamal: (in the Middle East) a porter of heavy loads

Hamam: a Turkish bath

Han: a large commercial building

Kazaska: a Caucasian dance

Kokoreç: sheep's or lamb's tripe broiled on spits

Lahmacun: a kind of meat pizza

Laz: a people of the Black Sea coast

Lezginka: a Caucasian dance

Lodos: the name for a special south wind in Istanbul, derived from Notus, the ancient Greek south-wind deity

Menekşe: violet (the flower)

Merhaba: greetings!

Mimber: a pulpit in a mosque

Mount Kaf: a mythical mountain thought to encircle the world and to be the home of the Phoenix

Pastirma: meat pressed and dried with garlic and spices

Raki: an aniseed-flavoured alcoholic drink

Red Crescent: the equivalent organization to the Red Cross in Turkey

Simit: a ring-shaped special kind of bread

Usta: master craftsman

Vali: the governor of a province

Yazma: hand-printed cloth